# TOWER
# OF
# SILENCE

# BAEN BOOKS by LARRY CORREIA

## SAGA OF THE FORGOTTEN WARRIOR
*Son of the Black Sword*
*House of Assassins*
*Destroyer of Worlds*
*Tower of Silence*

## THE GRIMNOIR CHRONICLES
*Hard Magic*
*Spellbound*
*Warbound*

## MONSTER HUNTER INTERNATIONAL
*Monster Hunter International*
*Monster Hunter Vendetta*
*Monster Hunter Alpha*
*The Monster Hunters* (omnibus)
*Monster Hunter Legion*
*Monster Hunter Nemesis*
*Monster Hunter Siege*
*Monster Hunter Guardian* (with Sarah A. Hoyt)
*Monster Hunter Bloodlines*

## MONSTER HUNTER MEMOIRS
*The Monster Hunter Files* (anthology edited with Bryan Thomas Schmidt)
*Monster Hunter Memoirs: Grunge* (with John Ringo)
*Monster Hunter Memoirs: Sinners* (with John Ringo)
*Monster Hunter Memoirs: Saints* (with John Ringo)
*Monster Hunter Memoirs: Fever* (with Jason Cordova)

## THE NOIR ANTHOLOGIES (edited with Kacey Ezell)
*Noir Fatale*
*No Game for Knights*
*Down These Mean Streets*

## THE AGE OF RAVENS (with Steve Diamond)
*Servants of War*

## DEAD SIX (with Mike Kupari)
*Dead Six*
*Swords of Exodus*
*Alliance of Shadows*
*Invisible Wars: The Collected Dead Six* (omnibus)

*Gun Runner* (with John D. Brown)

## STORY COLLECTIONS
*Target Rich Environment*
*Target Rich Environment Volume 2*

To purchase any of these titles in e-book form,
please go to www.baen.com.

# TOWER OF SILENCE

LARRY CORREIA

Copyright © 2023 by Larry Correia

A Baen Books Original

Baen Publishing Enterprises
P.O. Box 1403
Riverdale, NY 10471
www.baen.com

ISBN: 978-1-9821-9320-1

Cover art by Kurt Miller
Map by Isaac Stewart

First printing, April 2023
First trade paperback printing, February 2024

Distributed by Simon & Schuster
1230 Avenue of the Americas
New York, NY 10020

Library of Congress Control Number: 2022057967

Printed in the United States of America

10  9  8  7  6  5  4  3  2  1

For Jim

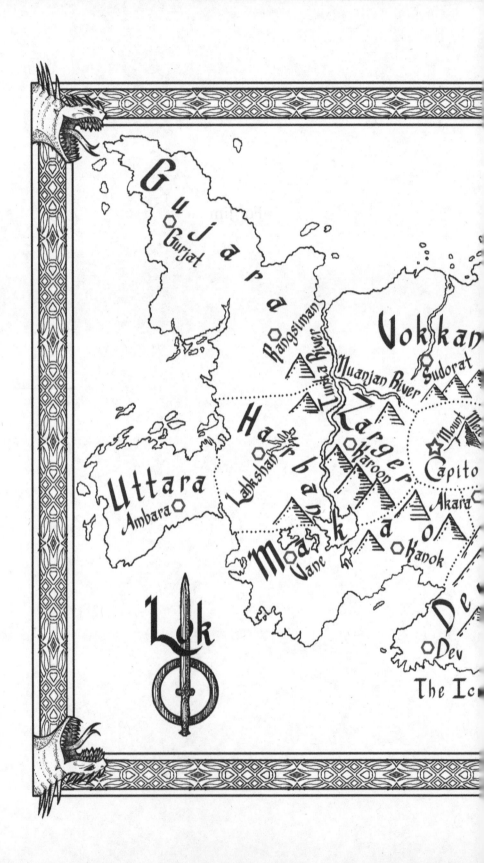

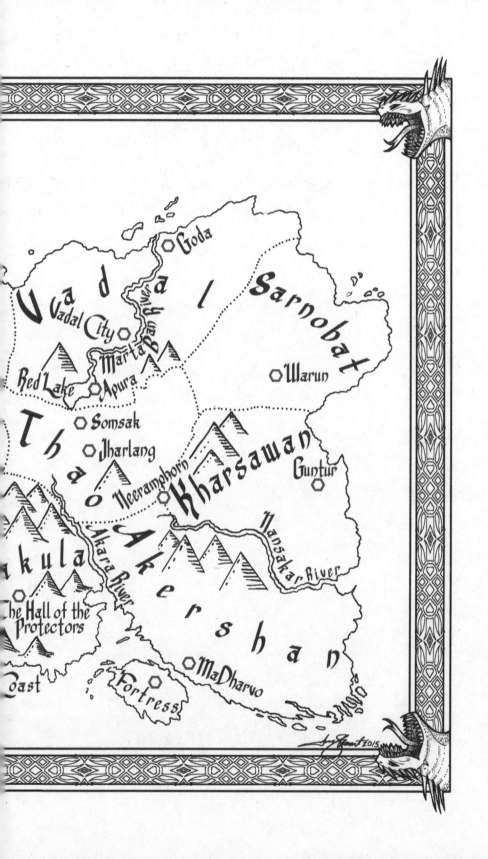

# Chapter 1

**30 Years Ago**

Omand watched in awe as the ocean consumed the land.

His mind could barely comprehend the size of the tidal wave. Mighty Vokkan oak trees, eighty feet tall, disappeared in the wave's shadow. It hit the beach, roaring with all the thunder in the world.

There was a casteless village there. Because of the never-ending threat of sea demons, only the non-people were expendable enough to live near the shore, only it wouldn't be demons who did these in, but the fury of hell itself.

The village was obliterated in an instant.

*Such power. Such destruction.* Omand had never been jealous of the sea before.

The water was still coming at them.

His fellow Inquisitors ran for their lives, but Omand remained watching. As always, he remained supremely rational, even as something so seemingly irrational unfolded before his eyes. The fear was there, but logically he knew their camp was a mile from shore, and atop the tallest hill in the area. Even as his senses screamed to flee, he knew there was no better place to go, at least none that he could reach in time. The wave would either sweep over their hill, or it would not. In the meantime, he would enjoy the show.

1

The wave toppled and spread. Churning white turned to roiling brown as the ground was torn to pieces and swept away. An entire forest was uprooted. Fields were buried. It carried massive boulders as if they were pebbles. The watery death covered that mile in a few heartbeats. There was another settlement in its path, worker caste, farmers by the looks of them, but then it too was smashed to bits. Houses were ripped from their foundations and bounced along atop the muddy mass, rolling until they shattered. Every resident who hadn't been instantly crushed would surely drown.

Thousands dead . . . just like that.

With astonishing speed, the ocean reached the Inquisitors' hill. Gigantic trees bounced off the rocks below. Plumes of mud shot up, drenching them in a rain of filth. Omand had avoided the sea for so long he had forgotten its odor of salt and decay. The churning mass of debris was shoved farther and farther up the hillside, but it was slowing, and with a calculating eye, he guessed it would not make it over the summit. So Omand watched, detached, as the dead and dying flashed by beneath him. Casteless or worker, it was hard to tell the difference when they were just bobbing corpses. Man, woman, child, even the livestock, pigs and cows, and wild animals, deer and birds—the ocean spared nothing.

If their leader had not insisted on setting up their camp for the night on this high ground, they would be among those dead. There had been a small earthquake before dawn. The shaking had barely roused Omand from his slumber, but he had thought nothing of it and gone back to sleep. A brief time later the Inquisitors had woken to the sounds of monkeys screaming and hooting in the forest, as if they were fleeing something in terror. Leave it to those clever animals to have more sense than man. Luckily, before the Inquisitors had broken their fast and moved out, they had seen the distant sea receding.

And now it had come rushing back with a vengeance.

Who would have guessed that the demons' home would be even more wrathful than its inhabitants? Thankfully, fear of sea-demon raids kept anyone of importance from settling too close to the shores, so none of these people would matter much. The Inquisitors had been sent to this province to root out a rumored gang of religious fanatics in the valley below. Those criminals were surely drowned now, so mission accomplished.

Despite the unimportance of the dead, a catastrophe of this magnitude would be a blow to his house. The water continued inland, turning small streams and canals into wide bolts of devastation. How far would it go? He did not know. Omand had heard of tidal waves like this happening before, but the last one of such magnificence here had been when his great-grandfather had been a child, and those tales spoke of a wave probably half the size of this.

For hours the Inquisitors' hill become an island, the only survivors above a sea of frothing mud and carnage. The others were terrified, but their witch hunter ordered them to remain wary. The ocean was always treacherous. There was no reason to expect it to behave any differently now that it was on land.

So Omand had sat upon a rock, smoked his pipe, and contemplated the fleeting nature of mortality as the bodies had accumulated below.

The next few days had been a hellish blur of labor and effort. As the water retreated, it left behind a ruined wasteland, stark and terrible beyond anything Omand had ever imagined.

Those born of the first caste did not normally get their hands dirty, but these were not normal circumstances, and the local arbiter had ordered all able-bodied men, regardless of caste, to help salvage whatever could be saved in the aftermath of the wave. Omand's duty was to capture criminals and torture confessions from them, so he was used to filth and stench and pain, but that work had a higher purpose, and was rewarding. Omand took joy in hurting people. He always had. In comparison to his noble obligation this sort of labor was degrading and beneath him, but he did as he was commanded and labored alongside those of lower birth.

It was exhausting to the point it became difficult to remember how much time had passed since the disaster—enough for some bits of ground to dry and the bodies atop it to bloat and begin to burst in the heat—when a casteless woman ran into the rescuers' camp, breathless and terrified, crying about some trapped horror. Most had paid no mind to the mad ramblings of the non-person, but Omand's superior was an experienced witch hunter—one of the Inquisition's elite—and often admonished his men that valuable intelligence could come from the most unlikely of sources, even a pathetic non-person.

The witch hunter had donned his golden mask before questioning the casteless, and when the hideous visage of the Law didn't frighten her as much as what she had claimed to see, they had known she was speaking the truth, for non-people normally avoided the Inquisition at all costs.

"Help! There be a demon! There be a demon in the woods!"

Though Omand had never personally dealt with any of the fearsome creatures, he had heard they were attracted by carnage, and there was certainly no shortage of that here. Though demons didn't usually stray far from water, today the water had come to them.

"Where did you see this beast?"

She pointed back the way she'd come from. "The bottoms. Or what's left of 'em."

Demons were living weapons. When they trespassed on land, they slaughtered man until their hunger was sated, and then they returned to the sea. Sometimes someone managed to kill a sea demon, but that usually required great effort and sacrificing many warriors in the process. Omand didn't know much about fighting demons, as that was out of the Inquisition's jurisdiction. That responsibility was left to their rivals, the Protectors. Except their witch hunter didn't seem to care that there were no Protectors here.

"Which way was it headed?"

"It weren't headed nowhere. It's stuck under rocks."

"Dead?" the witch hunter had asked, hope in his voice, because demon flesh was one of the only two sources of magic in the world, and thus an incredibly valuable resource. As one of the rare people born with the gift of wizardry, the Order of Inquisition had issued Omand a single demon tooth to fuel the one magical pattern he'd been officially taught. Even that one tiny fragment was incredibly valuable. An intact body would be worth a fortune.

"Not dead. Stuck. The wave left it here all broken and tore. If it could move it would've ate me."

The witch hunter paused, surely thinking about how handsomely the Grand Inquisitor would reward them for securing such a prize.

"Show me the way, casteless."

Omand had never seen a demon before. Even partially crushed beneath debris, it was still incredibly intimidating. Normally they were supposed to be sleek and black as night, but this one was crusted in drying mud. It had no discernable eyes, but it was clearly watching the Inquisitors, as its lump of a head turned directly toward them. As the group drew closer, its slit of a mouth opened, revealing rows of black razor teeth, exactly like the one in Omand's pocket. The creature made no sound, but the display made Omand think of a cat, hissing a warning.

It surely would have killed them all if it could, but the casteless had spoken true. From the look of things the wave had swept through these lowlands with a great deal of force, surely carrying the demon all the way from the sea, to be smashed between two rolling boulders. Its arms had been ripped off somewhere along the way, leaving behind jagged stumps. Demon blood was white as milk, and it had dried all over the rocks. The demon's lower half was still crushed flat beneath a giant log, and its white guts had squirted out. From the angle of its back its spine must have been broken. It was a testament to how incredibly resilient the things were that it still lived at all.

"We must kill it!" one of his brothers shouted. "Hurry, before it frees itself."

"Steady your nerves, Inquisitor. This is quite the momentous occasion. It is rare someone is able to look so closely upon a living demon and survive to talk about it. I wish to investigate further."

The witch hunter approached the demon cautiously as Omand and the others got ready to run for their lives. When the demon did nothing, their superior squatted down, just out of reach of the monster's jaws, to study it. Omand marveled at his courage, and after some time passed without the demon striking, Omand walked over and joined him. He may have been the youngest among the Inquisitors, but he was born of high status, and holding back would make him look like a coward. Omand was far too ambitious to be seen as a coward.

"You are braver than the others."

"Merely curious, sir."

"Tell me what you think, Novice Inquisitor."

Up close, the creature was even more alien than expected. It was shaped like a man, but only vaguely. The thing was terrifying, yet simultaneously piteous in its current situation. The mud around the demon had already dried into nothing but a few puddles. It had clearly been trapped here since the waters had receded.

"It's not going anywhere."

"I believe you are correct."

Even missing big pieces of its body, the demon still had to weigh at least four hundred pounds. Since it was still alive the magic would be exceedingly fresh—far better quality than the rotted demon parts that washed up on shore the Inquisition was usually able to procure. They would be able to harvest an incredible amount of magic from this flesh. Only it was then that Omand noticed the most curious thing. From the demon's stumps, it appeared new bones were growing, like weeds sprouting from the soil. Coated in the milky substance, tiny new claws could already be discerned sprouting from the end.

The senior had noted that as well. "It seems demons are like the lizards that can shed their tail and grow a new one."

Only these new limbs would be filled with potent magic. If a dead demon was worth a fortune to the Inquisition, what would a live one be?

"You are from these lands, Omand. Correct?"

"This is my house, but I am from Sudorat, south of here," Omand answered. "I was raised in the great house itself, of the first caste."

"Then your name will carry more weight with these people. We will require great secrecy. Gather the surviving workers. They will need to build a mighty cage."

The demon continued to watch them, fangs bared, as if it somehow understood its fate.

Years had passed since they had last met.

Omand had been promoted to witch hunter, traveled the entire continent, and learned much in the ways of magic. Being extremely effective at his obligation, he had risen in rank, status, and influence.

The stranded sea demon had not been so fortunate.

The Order of Inquisition had built a secret facility in Vokkan to hold their demonic prisoner, where it had lived in a state of endless torment. Each time the resilient creature was mostly healed—a process that took several weeks—it was harpooned and hauled from its tiny, filthy pond. Then Inquisitors would smash out its teeth with hammers, amputate the weak new limbs, slice off chunks of flesh and hide, then toss it back in the water. The harvested body parts were then sent back to the Inquisitor's Dome near the Capitol for distribution. The cruel process had netted the Inquisition a truly impressive amount of magic, so much so that those in the know had begun to refer to this place as *the farm*.

Among those Inquisitors, however, Omand alone had the foresight to realize that the prisoner could be valuable for more than just its flesh and bones. His illegal research into the forbidden works of the past had given him unique insights into the nature of demons, and he had formulated a theory about how to communicate with the beast. If the old tomes were correct, then demons were more than just nigh-indestructible killers, but beings capable of reasoning. Omand had requested a temporary assignment to the farm in order to test his theory.

The thing below him was a pathetic shell of the fearsome beast he'd seen left by the tidal wave. The demon seemed thin and sickly now, lying there, facedown in the mud. Milky white blood leaked from the strips that had been recently peeled from its back. Oddly shaped bones could be seen pressing through its black skin, like a victim of famine. He'd been told they kept it hungry on purpose. That slowed the healing, and thus the harvesting, but it also made the creature more manageable. Even starving, it remained incredibly dangerous.

The demon's home was little more than a big puddle, filled with saltwater hauled in from the Vokkan shore. Bits of rotting meat floated on the surface from its last meal—a fanatic who had been condemned to execution. The Inquisition was extremely pragmatic like that.

"Do not let its appearance fool you, Witch Hunter Omand," one of the local Inquisitors said. "Even freshly cut as it is now, it remains a quick and spiteful thing. We have lost seventeen men to it over the years, drowned or crushed mostly. We carve their names on the wall of the barracks as a warning so the rest of us never become complacent around the prisoner."

"I will be fine. Leave us."

"That's not a good idea, sir."

"If I am wrong, then you may feel great satisfaction as you put my name on your wall of warning...Begone."

The Inquisitors bowed and did as they were told. Omand was neither naïve nor prideful, but this experiment would require privacy, and if he was right, it would be worth the risk. For if the banned tomes were true, demons knew the secrets to unlocking powers beyond comprehension. He waited until the others had closed the gates of the enclosure before walking toward the muck.

In the ancient times, after the demons had fallen from the sky and torn the world apart, but before man had rallied and driven the invaders into the sea, wizards had formulated a way to communicate with demons, mind to mind. Their attempts at parley had failed, because the demons had been single-minded in their determination to destroy mankind. Only times had changed, and with this one, it was the Inquisition who held the advantage.

The demon stirred as Omand visualized the ancient magical pattern and called upon the fragment of black steel clutched in his fist to fuel it. He stopped just out of what he hoped was the creature's reach.

"Hear my words and understand, demon. I am Senior Witch Hunter Omand Vokkan, and I have come here to negotiate."

Bubbles floated to the surface. A sharp pain formed in Omand's skull as the demon answered. There were no words, only crashing images, and violence made thought. The effect staggered him, sending him to his knees. The demon's message was gone in an instant, but it left impressions behind, like footsteps in sand. Omand struggled to decipher them. *Confusion. Rage.* It despised being cut and burned by the Inquisitors. *A dark ocean.* The beast desired freedom.

It probably could have struggled up the bank and killed him right then, but the monster hesitated, as it was as curious as Omand about this strange communication.

Blood dripped between his fingers, because he had been squeezing the shard of black steel so tight it had sliced open his palm. Omand gritted his teeth, refocused the pattern, and tried again. "I can return you to the sea, but first you must submit to my will."

It was then that Omand the torturer discovered what real torment was, as his mind was assaulted with a thousand years of collected hate, for demons never forget a wrong. And worse, it seemed that each one was born retaining the knowledge of the demons that had come before it. It was the concentrated anger of a millennium. The agony would have felled a lesser man, but Omand did not relent. The pattern held.

Omand thought it was involuntary tears running from his

eye, but when he wiped them away he discovered it was blood. As the forbidden tome had said, communicating with demons was not for the faint of heart. "Calm yourself, demon, or I will have you cut and burned every single day for the rest of your miserable existence." Then to be sure, he tried to turn that threat into pictures in his mind, so the demon would understand the seriousness of Omand's commitment.

It worked, because when the demon spoke again, but rather than noise and pain, the impressions were soft, nothing more than a slithering whisper. The demon wanted to know what Omand wanted.

Witch hunter duties had taken him to the darkest corners of Lok and exposed him to secrets that had been kept since before the Age of Law, before the Age of Kings, from before the rain of demons had ruined the old world, from a time when their immortal wizard kings possessed magic granting the abilities great and terrible, ruling over life and death, creation and destruction, so mighty that to this day the religious fanatics still thought of them as gods. Only Omand knew the ancients had begun as men... It was their magic that had enabled them to bend reality to their will.

There was no reason why feats that had been achieved once, could not be achieved again.

"I know what brought your kind to this world, demon. I know why you made war upon us. Your old enemies have turned to dust. Their greatest treasure is beyond your reach now, but not mine. You will show me how to access the source. Only then will I throw you back into the sea."

The demon understood... but such knowledge would require far more than one demon's freedom. No amount of torture would make the demon reveal a secret so valuable. Then the slither grew to a scream. *No!* Their kind thirsted for something else. Their entire species held a desire for revenge the likes of which even cruel Omand could barely comprehend. Not just against the ancient hero who had thwarted them, but against every one of his mortal descendants. For Omand to be shown the location of the ancient source, an entire bloodline would have to be eradicated. Millions would have to perish.

"Your terms are acceptable."

✧　　✧　　✧

For the next two decades, Omand continued secretly working toward his goals, in the process becoming the most respected witch hunter in the Inquisition. He rooted out traitors and fanatics within the borders of every great house. Except each time, before he publicly destroyed their idols or burned their books, he privately studied them for himself, to see if there was any secret knowledge he could glean from them.

The demon was his only confidant. No one else understood his true mission. His network of allies and contacts grew. Those who stood in his way, both witting and unwitting, were removed through various methods, often framing them for a crime—slander, blackmail, and the occasional murder. When it came time for the judges to appoint a new Grand Inquisitor, Omand had made certain he was the only suitable candidate.

He enjoyed ruling over an entire order, but that was merely another step on his inevitable path toward ruling the entire world.

Having tired of making the long journey to Vokkan, Omand had commissioned the construction of a special chamber deep beneath the Inquisitor's Dome to hold their most important prisoner. Each time he communed with the demon, it offered tantalizing glimpses of the past but never the full picture, just enough for him to know that the legends were based in fact, and the power was real. Each time it denied him any new clues, Omand would have the demon harvested afterward as punishment for its stubborn insolence.

Today, Grand Inquisitor Omand stood before the thick glass of the demon's tank, triumphant, for thirty years of effort were finally bearing great fruit. The demon floated on the other side, barely visible through the murk.

"The assassination of the Chief Judge has forced the issue. The orders have gone out to every province in every great house. The casteless are to be destroyed. The blood of the children of Ramrowan has begun to water the land."

The Capitol moved with ponderous slowness in all things. Even having a casteless rebel strike down the Chief Judge with an illegal Fortress rod wasn't shocking enough to overcome the inertia of bureaucracy. The vote in favor of the Great Extermination had come swiftly afterward, but then it had become a manner of logistics and schedules, as petty members of the first caste squabbled over who would be responsible for what, and how it would all be paid for. Several months had passed, during which rumors had certainly spread to every casteless quarter in Lok of their impending doom. That delay gave the casteless time to flee or prepare to fight, but Omand didn't mind. Chaos benefitted his plans. The sooner the Law fell apart, the sooner he could install his puppet king to *save* it.

*Ramrowan blood suffer death*

Omand had taught the demon a few words, simply because it spared him the onslaught that was demon thought. He pressed one hand against the glass. "See that I speak the truth."

The demon drifted forward and pressed its blank lump of a head against the glass. It saw the images from Omand's mind and understood.

"Now show me where the source is."

*Remainder upon kill*

The answer was not unexpected. The demon was as determined as he was. Only they both knew it could potentially take years to eradicate all the casteless, and Omand was tired of waiting. "I do not think so. I have given you much, now I expect something in return. You will show me the location now, or I will call it off. I created the Great Extermination. I can end it."

The demon didn't believe him.

"There are many great houses that depend upon their casteless in one way or another. They will accept any excuse to avoid cutting their own throats. Regardless of what you do, my plans are nearly complete. Shortly, I will rule the Capitol from the shadows. Then I will continue to search for the source, with or without your help, only then I will be searching with all the resources of all the great houses at my fingertips. While you suffer the rest of your days knowing that you could have ended the bloodline of Ramrowan, but I snatched their lives from your claws." Omand made a fist and struck the glass. "Show me, demon!"

The demon relented.

The vision came upon him, as it had before, as if he was high above Lok, falling through the clouds. It was a memory from the rain of demons, so long ago. Only this time the vision didn't end as early as it had before, and the ground kept rushing up toward him. Closer and closer, until Omand was able to recognize terrain features—

And then it ended.

*Remainder upon kill all blood all*

Omand stepped away from the tank and wiped a red tear from his eye. "You play a risky game, demon. My patience wears thin. The Great Extermination will continue. Only now you've revealed enough information that I know where to send an expedition. My Order has already cataloged the ruins there. This time we will dig deeper. If I find the source without you, then I promise you will never see the ocean again." Omand turned and began walking away.

*Kill all Ramrowan blood*

Omand paused to smile, for he had put into motion a slaughter the likes of which had not been seen since this thing's ancestors had fallen from the sky and ripped the world apart. And nothing—demon, god, or man—would stand in his way.

"Enjoy today's harvest, old friend."

# Chapter 2

"Behold, the outsider who floated across the sea, to be found washed up on our shore as a frozen corpse. Except through some wizard's trickery it turns out he was not dead at all. This vile deceit was the first of his several crimes against the Workshop."

Only before that judge could list the rest of the allegations against him, another of the judges interrupted. "Is this the one the collectors claim to be the living avatar of Ramrowan?"

"I am Ashok Vadal." He stood below them at the bottom of a dimly lit pit, defiant, though he was in chains sufficient to bind an elephant. "I *claim* nothing. If I speak, it is true. Ramrowan reborn is a title I've neither held nor sought."

Seven men were seated on the wooden platform above him, each of them holding a candle. Ashok thought of them as judges, since their duties seemed to match that obligation in the Capitol, arguing over and ruling upon matters of Law. Except these were foreigners who had their own strange ways. They did not have *the Law*, but they still had laws, and Ashok had apparently broken a great many of them by coming to this damnable island.

"So you claim, *Ashok Vadal*." Though the islanders spoke the same language as in Lok, they possessed a curious accent that made it nearly as difficult for him to decipher as the garbage dialect used by the most isolated casteless. "Except all who dwell in blessed Xhonura know mainlanders are liars who cannot be trusted."

When applied to most of Lok, Ashok could not disagree with that assessment.

The Capitol and all the great houses were infested with untrustworthy liars. Ashok recognized that now. Except Lok was where he was needed, and he had already been imprisoned on the island of Fortress—or Xhonura as the locals seemed to call it—for far too long. It was difficult to tell the passing of the days, as he'd been kept chained in a dark, windowless cell, comatose at first, then starving and delirious, as he slowly recovered from the aftereffects of the magic that had somehow kept his body alive in the ice.

Surely weeks had passed since Devedas had cast him into the freezing sea. Long, terrible weeks, with barely any food or water, sustained only by magic and determination. This was the first time he had been out of that horrible cell. He did not intend to return.

"I intended no harm to this island. Let me free. I will depart and never return."

"How do you plan to get back to your wretched home, infidel? Our paths are secret and never shown to outsiders. Do you intend to swim with ravenous sea demons across miles of water cold enough to stop a man's heart?" Several of the men laughed.

"That is how I arrived. I assumed it was how I would depart."

The way he stated that so flatly left a few of the graybeards shaking their heads. "You will not convince us to spare you by claiming you intend to execute yourself. We are here to determine guilt and apply punishment. We do not gather at the Judgment Pit to waste our time listening to the ramblings of the insane."

"List the man's crimes," the one who appeared to be the eldest directed.

"The dead man awoke on the beach, striking fear into some of our collectors, and filling the heads of the others with infidel lies that he is Ramrowan returned. They say he is the Avatara, as prophesized. His mere existence has inspired rebelliousness."

Ashok couldn't help himself. He laughed. It was a grim laugh, but the first one that he'd had in a long time. It appeared that causing rebellion simply by existing was to be his fate in every land.

"What is so amusing, infidel?"

"I did not intend to cause rebellion... here."

"Yet you did. The Collectors Guild is in upheaval. Some among them have convinced the others that this man is Ramrowan born anew. The prisoner was put in the dungeons to be tested as per the instructions left by the master of the Workshop. By some manner of trickery he has not died yet. Word of his survival leaked to the collectors, and pleas have turned into demands, and even threats of a strike. That is the only reason this board has gathered early to hear this case."

Ashok scowled at that. He had been rotting in a dark cell, naked, chained to a wall, trapped, while his obligation, Thera, remained unprotected and in danger. He did not know how long he had slumbered after being placed here, but since he had woken up, there had been no opportunity to escape. His wrists, ankles, and neck had been shackled the entire time, so tightly that he could barely move, with steel links that even his hands were unable to bend. No guard ever got close enough to attack. His food, stinking chunks of fermented fish, was shoved at his mouth speared on the end of a long stick, and only came at rare, seemingly random intervals. Whenever the filth on and around his body became too thick, they would throw buckets of cold water down upon him. From the way that water had burned his eyes it had been treated in some alchemical manner, probably to stop an outbreak of plague in the prison. No one had spoken to him the entire time, despite having shouted himself hoarse demanding an audience with anyone in a position of authority.

There was no doubt that these terrible conditions were intended to kill. Any normal man would have succumbed by now. This wasn't imprisonment, it was a gradual, inexorable, murder. Ashok did not know what a collector was, but he owed them a great deal of thanks for forcing this audience. Because whatever these judges ruled today, Ashok was done dying slowly.

"In addition to his lies, the infidel injured several officers when they tried to capture him. He broke the limbs of three different men before the rest were able to ensnare him in ropes."

They had been lucky that Ashok had still been so cold he could barely move his arms, or he would have killed them all. Either the Heart of the Mountain or the shard of Angruvadal buried in his chest had somehow kept him alive as he had floated unconscious down the Akara River and across the southern sea, but that magical effect had left him extremely weak for a long time afterward. It turned out that even the legendary Ashok Vadal could not fight well with his blood turned to ice.

"I was frozen and still trying to understand what was happening when they laid hands upon me. Your servants are fortunate I was very tired."

"Plead your case and beg for mercy, cur."

"Beg?" Ashok did not understand what manner of man they usually sat in judgment over, but they clearly didn't understand who they were dealing with today. "I do not beg. I will not plead. I will speak clearly, and you will make a decision. Hopefully for your sake it will be a wise one. My arrival here was not intended in offense."

One of the judges extinguished his candle as Ashok spoke, while another angrily demanded, "You intended no offense? Yet you trespass on our shores, while claiming the title of our most sacred hero. At their guild house they chant the name *Avatara*."

"That was a mistake made by those who found me. I have held many titles, but Avatara is not among them."

Another candle was blown out. From their sneering manner, Ashok assumed that each dead light was a vote of condemnation, though he didn't know if his death required all of them to go out, or just a majority. Fortress justice left you to die in the dark, so perhaps the candles represented a small hope of seeing the sun again? It was a mystery. He had never dealt with a foreign law before.

"So the prisoner is not a common fraud but claims to be a man of importance. Tell us of these supposed titles you've held, mad fool."

Ashok bore the insults with calculated disdain. The judges were seated around the ledge a dozen feet above, surely thinking that they were secure. No malnourished, sickly prisoner could scale those sheer walls to reach them before being stopped. The heavy chains were still upon him, but they were dragging at his feet, not anchored to an immovable stone wall like before. Four men had escorted him into the pit and were waiting in the hall outside. There were an unknown number of guards stationed around the judges above. Each guard had been armed with a deadly Fortress rod—or gun as Ratul had called them—unlike any design Ashok had seen before. These seemed more refined than the simplistic weapons procured by the rebellion, and each had a knife mounted on the end to serve as a clumsy spear.

The instant the tension on those chains had been released, the future had been decided. The only question was whether Ashok's exit would be peaceful or bloody, because one way or the other, Ashok would not be returning to that cell ever again.

He could have protested his innocence. He could have made logical arguments, and then hoped for reason to prevail. Except these haughty foreigners had made him suffer in near unmoving misery, being slowly devoured by rats and fleas, and starving in his own filth, so that would not be the case. He no longer served the Law, but the same righteous anger he'd felt while burning the villages of lawbreakers or putting whole families to the sword was upon him once again.

"You demand to know my titles? Very well. The greatest among them was Protector of the Law, twenty-year senior, Ashok Vadal, bearer of mighty Angruvadal, the ancestor blade of Great House Vadal."

There was some muttering about that. "A bearer?" So even the island that had been cut off from the rest of the world for centuries knew about ancestor blades.

"There is no black steel in Xhonura! Where is your magic sword now, vagabond?"

"I was not finished. Those were my official titles. I am told Great House Vadal calls me Ashok Sword Breaker, for Angruvadal is destroyed. I have been called Black-Hearted Ashok, for the many terrible things I have done in service of the Law. The casteless named me Fall, and the rebellion declared me their general. Now you will call me *free*, or I will kill you all."

That last part took them by surprise. Apparently those being judged did not usually speak in such a manner. Ashok's faith in the Law had been destroyed, and he had devoted most of his life to serving it. He owed nothing to the false laws of a nation of separatist fanatics, especially respect for their judges.

"You dare threaten us?" Two more candles were hastily snuffed out.

"Were my words unclear? I have important duties I must attend to in Akershan. I have rotted in this foul place far too long." Ashok lifted one hand to display his shackles. The bands were so thick a demon would not have been able to break them, and there was in excess of fifty pounds of steel chain attached to each of his limbs. "Release me or I will do it myself."

After that only a single candle remained flickering above, and Ashok wasn't sure if that man was voting for mercy, or if he had been too startled by Ashok's nerve and had forgotten to blow it out.

"Jailers! Return this insolent barbarian to his cell."

Ashok didn't wait for the single door leading into the pit to open. Instead he called upon the Heart of the Mountain to give strength to his muscles. Gathering up the chains that weighed as much as his body, he leapt toward the wall. The sudden movement must have been far faster than anything the judges had been expecting because they fell from their chairs in surprise.

There was very little to hold onto, but Ashok clung to the smallest cracks of the stone by his fingers and toes and scrambled upward. The great swinging, clanking weight of chains threatened to drag him down, but driven by wrath and magic, Ashok continued.

The jailers rushed in below him, and he heard the metallic *clack* as the firing mechanism of a Fortress rod was cocked. Such illegal devices used to fill him with loathing, but he had grown accustomed to them in rebel hands. Seeing them used in battle from both sides had removed the mystery. They were simply a tool with strengths and weaknesses, like any other weapon.

Fortress rods took a moment to ready, and another to aim, so by the time the jailer fired Ashok had already pulled his body over the edge. The projectile slammed into the rock beneath him as thunder and smoke filled the Judgment Pit.

Even as inhumanly strong as he had once been, it still took Ashok time to lumber to his feet beneath the cumbersome chains. A guard rushed him, but Ashok struck the clumsy thrust aside, and used the man's momentum to launch him screaming into the pit. A second guard tried to ready his Fortress rod, but Ashok whipped him across the face with a chain. That one went down spitting teeth.

There were two more guards left on the upper platform. One of them even managed to trigger his Fortress rod, only it was a panicked, unaimed shot. Ashok reacted, lifting his hand purely by instinct, and the lead ball fragmented into pieces against one of his wrist shackles instead of hitting him in the chest. That had either been luck, or Angruvadal trying to keep him alive. Either was acceptable.

"He *is* Ramrowan!" one of the judges cried.

When Ashok picked up one of the chairs and hurled it at the last guards, they fled down a corridor, crying for help. Such cowardice disgusted him. Fortress must have relied too much upon their strange and terrible weapons to develop a proper warrior caste spirit, because no great house soldier would have broken so easily. He'd barely even killed anyone yet.

Unfortunately, even the projectile failed to destroy the shackle. All it had done was leave a lead smear across the steel. Fortress may have been populated by cruel fanatics, but their metalwork was superb.

Ashok stumbled, as atrophied muscles trembled. His plan had been to slaughter his way out, but he had underestimated just how weak his body had become. Starving and dehydrated, with cramping limbs, the only thing keeping him on his feet was the Heart of the Mountain.

The judges had been too surprised to flee, so Ashok grabbed the nearest by the neck and lifted him from the ground. "Who has the key?"

"I don't know!"

"Do any of you have the keys?" Ashok roared, but all the men did was cower. Of course, judges would not dirty their hands by touching filthy prisoners. One of the jailers would have to unlock him. His escape would require a different tactic. "Which of you is the highest status?" He shook the man he was holding. "Is it you?"

"No. I'm just—"

So Ashok tossed that one over the side into the pit. "Who is the most important among you?"

Their comrade landing with a leg-breaking thud and a squeal must have motivated the rest toward honesty, because they all pointed at the same man. That would do. Ashok grabbed him by the end of his beard and dragged a hundred pounds of judge and two hundred pounds of chain down the hall.

Ashok had no idea where he was going, except that the fleeing guards had gone this way, and it was going upward—and more importantly, away from that damnable cell. The whimpering old man was slowing him down, bouncing along the stone, so Ashok took him by the arm and pulled him to his feet.

"You will be killed for this."

"Dying by bullet or blade is preferable to that cell," he snarled in response. As they shuffled along, the judge continued his bleating. It was very undignified. So Ashok smacked him across the back of the head. "Silence."

There was light ahead. Real sunlight. As Ashok reached the end of the hall he felt actual wind on his face and breathed in clean air that didn't reek of mold and fish. It was fiercely cold. The light was scalding against his weakened eyes. Even if he were to die here and now, pierced by lead, that brief feeling of freedom would have been worth it.

They had entered a courtyard surrounded by walls. The guards who had fled were shouting at several of their surprised compatriots to gather their weapons, because the dead man had jumped out of the hole and was slaughtering everyone.

The cowards. This was no slaughter. He would be happy to show them slaughter.

Taking one of his arm chains, Ashok looped it around the judge's neck, and pulled the rings tight. "I am here."

Half a dozen Fortress rods were immediately swung his way, but he held the struggling, choking judge in the doorway between them. Thankfully they hesitated. It would have annoyed him to go through the effort of taking a hostage, only to have holes blown in him.

"Calm yourselves, warriors." He didn't know if that was their status on this strange island, but that respectful name would do. They wore an unfamiliar, plain-brown smock, but the uniform nature suggested they were some manner of soldier. Negotiation never came easy to a man who had simply taken whatever he had needed most of his life, but it was his best strategy in the moment. "Undo these chains, and I will spare your judge and leave. Or fight, and I will kill all who oppose me and then find the keys among your corpses."

The men hesitated, obviously unprepared for this situation. The Fortress rods pointed his way were shaking badly. This was clearly not a situation that they had been prepared for. Near skeletal men did not jump out of pits.

"Decide quickly," Ashok warned, because the judge's face was changing colors as he clawed desperately at the steel crushing his neck.

"Alright, alright," said one of the guards as he lifted his weapon skyward with one hand. That was apparently the highest ranking among these, not that Ashok understood any of the symbols sewn onto their clothing. "Don't hurt the guildsman and we'll let you go."

Ashok relaxed the chain a bit, and the *guildsman* gasped for breath. Whatever manner of office that was, a guildsman was clearly of enough status that these soldiers dared not risk his life.

There were eight guards in the courtyard, and probably more on the way. Any more and they might find their courage. "Undo these chains. Now."

With an angry gesture from their officer, one of the men was sent forward, reluctantly pulling a ring of keys from his belt. The man was clearly terrified of Ashok. Then he realized this was the one who had shot him.

"Forgive me, Avatara," the guard squeaked as he unlocked the damaged shackle on Ashok's wrist. "I didn't know it was really you!"

The steel had been tight for so long the flesh beneath was as white and fragile as the fish they'd occasionally fed him. Patches of skin stayed stuck to the metal, and the wound burned as it touched the air. He watched the guards carefully, ready to hurl the guildsman at the first to make a move, but they seemed too frightened to try. It was a mystery what being an avatar entailed, but he must have filled enough criteria that they were clearly terrified by his presence now. The soldiers' attitude was very different from those who had sat in condescending judgment over him. That was not too different from Lok, where the different castes often believed wildly divergent things.

As the other shackles were painfully removed, Ashok looked around for the fastest way out. The dungeon had been beneath a small fort. They were in what had to be the central courtyard, surrounded by mud-brick walls. Free of the damnable chains, he could climb over, but unfortunately he didn't know what was on the other side, and if one of these men found their spine before he made it to the top he would be an easy target. The only other option was a barred gate to the left.

"You." He jerked his head toward another guard. "Open that."

The soldier waited for his officer to nod that it was allowed, and then ran to do so. When the door swung open, it revealed a pebbled road, leading downhill.

The last ankle chain fell away, and Ashok had never wanted to scratch at his own flesh more than in that instant.

"Back up," he warned, and waited for the soldier who had unlocked him to move aside—that way he could keep the captive guildsman between him and all the rods. Walking his human shield toward the gate, Ashok hoped that path didn't lead somewhere even worse. It appeared the fort was on a cliffside. There seemed to be no immediate dangers waiting for him outside the gate, so this route would have to do.

"Your duty may require you to pursue me. If so, I understand. But know that my duty will require me to slay any who stands between me and my home."

Ashok shoved the guildsman at the guards and ran for the cliffs.

# Chapter 3

The date was unknown to him. It had become impossible to count the days in the dark, but Ashok believed it to be sometime in late summer or early fall. Except there were no trees to see if the leaves were changing. Or Fortress might always have such a miserable, cutting chill, since the island was on the very southern edge of the world.

From what he had seen so far, Fortress appeared to be a land of barren rock and black sand. The terrain here was unlike anything he'd known in Lok, consisting of boulder fields and jagged peaks. The only plant life seemed to be stunted grass and the occasional stubborn bush. He had not thought that a place could be harsher than the volcanic wastes of Devakula, but he had been mistaken.

He ran for hours, then slowed to a walk as the sun began to go down. It would have been far too easy to fall off a cliff in the dark, and in order to keep moving he needed the Heart of the Mountain to aid his body, not his eyes. When he stopped to listen carefully, he couldn't hear the shouting of trackers or the baying of hounds, which was fortunate. Following him would have been easy, considering how much blood his lacerated soles were leaving on the ground.

Naked except for a filthy loincloth the guards had tied around his waist before his trial, Ashok might have frozen to death that night if it hadn't been for the Heart sustaining him, much as it had during his imprisonment.

The worst part of being in that miserable dungeon hadn't been the endless hunger, or the pain of rotting skin and dying muscle, but the knowledge that by being there he was shirking his duty. Deprived of any opportunity to escape, that feeling had gnawed at him worse than the rats. It had given him time to think, though. To ponder on his many mistakes and failures, of friends who had lied to him, and of systems that had failed.

Once satisfied that he had evaded any pursuit, he had gone to sleep beneath a rock shelf.

He dreamed of Thera.

At dawn, Ashok awoke to the smell of cooking meat.

It could have been a trap to draw him out. They had to know he was starving—he had been fed so very little for so long—and he had seen absolutely nothing to forage during his escape. He had seen no signs of civilization other than the fort. That fire might have been started by warriors searching for him. If so, that was even more reason to investigate.

The scent was easy to follow. The smoke was coming from a narrow ravine below him. Ashok crept forward on his belly across the sharp rocks until he could see down inside. There was a lone figure sitting by a campfire. Still concerned it was an ambush, Ashok used the Heart to sharpen his senses—and the instant he did all the physical agony it had been pushing aside came flooding back—but there was no sign of others lying in wait, so he turned the Heart back to keeping his body alive.

Ashok stood and limped down into the ravine.

The man by the fire was old and wiry, dressed in bright orange robes, with his head shaved except for a single silver braid at the back. He wore an ornate sash that was clearly some symbol of office. As Ashok approached, the stranger studied him, seeming almost bemused. "When the collectors said they found a dead man on the beach who came back to life, I didn't know he would still look like death walking these many months later."

Though Ashok hadn't had an opportunity to see his reflection lately, the description was surely not an exaggeration. Thin as a famine-struck casteless, with hair grown long and matted with filth, and skin that was covered in sores and rat bites, Ashok probably appeared more corpse than man.

"So you know who I am."

"I only know what I've been told about you. Whether those tales are true or not, I've come to decide for myself. Please, sit, warm yourself. Eat." And when Ashok hesitated, trying to puzzle out the odd accent, the old man said, "You are a stranger here, unused to our customs. If I offer my hospitality it would be a terrible sin to betray you to your enemies or poison your food or drink."

The thought of poison as a trap had never even entered Ashok's mind, but that was because he was immune to most of those anyway. "Thus far I have not been that impressed by the hospitality of your people."

"Fair. The Guildsmen Council are cruel and pragmatic, yet simultaneously bound by custom to not slay anyone who claims to have the spirit of Ramrowan returned. However, that doesn't mean that they cannot imprison them in the hopes that nature will take its course and the nuisance will be removed. For it was written that Ramrowan required less sustenance than needed to keep a small child alive, for his body would be nourished by his righteousness."

"Your beliefs sound ridiculous. So my imprisonment was a trial to see how well I can starve?"

"It is more of a tradition now than anything. There have been so many frauds and false claims over the years that the guilds have dwindled in unbelief that Ramrowan will ever come back to us. Yet they must keep the masses appeased. After all, if mighty Ramrowan were to return as prophesized, what prison could hold him? If you are really him—"

"I am not."

"Then surely it would not have taken you nearly a year to escape."

"Impossible." A weakness had come upon him after coming out of the ice water, the likes of which he'd never felt before, and after being captured he had fallen into a great slumber. Only he couldn't have been asleep that long. "Do not lie to me."

"Don't believe me if you don't want to, but do I sound like I'm trying to lie to you?"

It did not. It appeared it was even harder to track the passing of time while alone in the dark than he had thought. "The month. It is the end of Bhadra, then?"

"We use a different calendar than you mainlanders so I don't know what you name the months."

"The last month of summer. Autumn begins in Asvina."

"My, you must have been in the water for many days even *before* getting here to not know *when* you are. It is still summer, but fall is upon us soon...Be at ease. I am of no guild. You are safe here. Rest, eat. Let us converse."

The elder had to be mistaken, as there was no way an entire year had passed. Even in his delirium it could have only been a month or two. For now he would attribute this misunderstanding to a difference of language. Ashok sat, and he had been so chilled for so long the nearness of the flames immediately made his flesh sting. An unidentified piece of meat was cooking on a spit. His stomach twisted with hunger pangs, while his mouth watered at the smell. The old man passed over a gourd that served as a water container. When Ashok drank deep, it was the best thing he had ever tasted.

"Who are you?"

"I am Guru Dondrub."

"Guru...I am familiar with that title." Ashok had once been sheltered by a decrepit forest casteless who had claimed that same honor. Keta had seemed to think it mattered, but Keta also fancied himself the high priest of a forgotten god. "I was told *guru* means you are supposed to be a wise man."

"Some fancy that I am wise. Others think me a fool. I have followed your trail all night because you are Ashok Vadal, an enemy from across the sea, whose stubborn refusal to die has created quite the commotion in Xhonura."

"I'm too busy to die." Ashok took the offered skewer of meat. "Why have you sought me out?"

"My people have waited centuries for Ramrowan to return to us. I have watched for sign of him my whole life. I'm checking to see if you are him. I have never been to the mainland, for I always believed Ramrowan would be reborn here, among his servants who remained faithful instead of the infidels who deny the gods he served, but I see no reason he couldn't be reincarnated among your people instead. I would hate to miss him just because his avatar got lost in our mountains."

Ashok took a tentative bite, then nearly gagged, because it had been so long since he had had any real meat, and this piece was mostly gristle and hot fat.

"Do you not enjoy seal?"

He had seen those odd creatures on the shores of Devakula,

flopping about and barking like dogs. He didn't like things that lived in water like fish or demons, but weren't either. It seemed duplicitous. Only Ashok was so hungry that casteless gruel would have been a delicacy right then. "I will honor your hospitality, then I must return to Lok."

"I'm sure you will, in time."

"There is no time." When he had been cast into the sea, the Capitol had been exterminating whole regions' worth of casteless, and Ashok was oath-bound to defend them. Who knew what had happened in his absence? "I have duties to attend to."

"What manner of duties?"

"There is a rebellion, led by a prophet. I am sworn to aid that prophet."

"And this entire rebellion will fail if you're not there?"

"The rebellion will more than likely fail even if I *am* there. It is mostly casteless fighting against the entire might of the Law and all the power of the Capitol and the great houses. However, it is my responsibility, so I must return."

"That sounds futile."

Ashok shrugged and took another bite of oily seal fat.

"Some would argue that life itself is futile, Ashok Vadal, though I do not ascribe to such pessimistic beliefs myself. However, you don't look healthy enough to fight a war right now. I marvel that you are alive at all, after the neglect of the guildsmen. The journey back to your homeland would be the end of you."

"I will recover."

"You sound certain."

"I am." Even though he was no longer a member of the Order, he would never tell this stranger about the Protectors' secrets. Ashok kept his vows, even to the institutions that were now actively trying to kill him. When it came to Protectors, it was either kill them fast, or not at all. His body would heal. It always did.

"Ah, to live a life with such certainty."

"Only about some things," Ashok muttered before going back to his meal, which was simultaneously sickening and a long-denied delicacy.

"I am envious. Even naked in the wilderness, starving, unarmed, alone in an unfamiliar hostile country, you think you have your path figured out."

"I have."

"Oh really? The guildsman I spoke with yesterday said you intended to leave the way you arrived. Sadly, even in the unlikely event that you were not devoured by demons, that is not how the currents work. Things from the mainland drift to Xhonura, but things from Xhonura are swept south, where there is nothing but icebergs. That does not sound like a very good plan to me."

Normally Ashok would have been annoyed at the stranger's prodding, but he had been alone for so long it was actually nice to talk to someone other than himself. "Fortress has remained unconquered because of the water between us. In rare years it is cold enough for the ocean to freeze solid enough to march across."

"And when it does, your warrior caste inevitably tries to invade us, only to be driven off by our guns." The Guru shook his head sadly. "It is most tragic to watch their bodies accumulate on the beach—until their blood attracts the demons, of course."

"I do not have the time to wait around hoping for a winter sufficient to walk home. I've seen firsthand that your Fortress magic—those *guns* you speak of—are sometimes smuggled to criminals on the mainland. The rebellion had some ourselves. Your people bring them in somehow. The Law never discovered your method, but it is clear there is another path your people use. I will return by this smugglers' route."

"And how would you find this most secret way?"

Ashok was unsure of the details. "I will make someone talk. They always do."

"A good plan. Direct, though it will be difficult since you know so little of our culture. One of the pitfalls of diplomacy, I suppose."

"There will be nothing diplomatic about it. I know enough about you to proceed. Your guilds sound like our great houses. Powerful factions making demands of one another. Nominal allies, yet sometimes foes. If this gun smuggling is approved by these guilds, then someone of high status among them will know the way. If the smuggling is against your laws, then your criminals will know. I will find out which, seek the suppliers out, and then force them to tell me how they get their weapons into Lok."

The Guru nodded along at his plan. "It is a well-kept secret. Those people will fight you. How many lives would you be willing to take in order to accomplish this goal?"

"I don't know. How many people live on this island?"

The old man chuckled, until it slowly dawned on him that

Ashok wasn't exaggerating. "You would be willing to commit such savagery in pursuit of your goals?"

"I do not enjoy it, but I am good at it."

Though elderly, it was clear his mind was keen, and he studied Ashok with calculating eyes. "You've taken a great many lives, haven't you, Ashok Vadal?"

He didn't need to answer. If Dondrub truly was a wise man, he would be able to read the truth from Ashok's countenance. Well over a thousand men had died directly by his hand, and who knew how many more had perished as a result of his actions. To most it would be a weight greater than the dungeon's chains, but to Ashok, killing had simply been his existence.

"Perhaps you are Ramrowan reincarnated, after all."

Ashok chewed more of the greasy seal meat in silence for a moment before saying, "Those are the beliefs of your people, not mine. I have spent my life believing there is no such thing as spirits. That there is no life after this. Yet... I think I met this Ramrowan once. If not a ghost, a memory of him that remained in the black steel of my sword. It spoke to me while I was at the edge of death."

"Ramrowan *spoke* to you?" Guru Dondrub scowled as he thought over the implications of that. "Hearing the words of the gods' champion is a bold claim, usually made by charlatans or mad men."

"Do I strike you as deluded or dishonest?"

The Guru shook his head *no*, or at least Ashok assumed the gesture meant the same thing in this strange land.

"Good." He went back to his meal, trying to eat slowly, so as to not make himself ill because his stomach had become so unaccustomed to real food. He would force it to stay down because his body required nourishment to heal. Magic could only do so much.

"I don't think they're allowed to talk about the Age of Kings in your lands, so do you even know what Ramrowan's mission in this world was?"

Keta had talked about it a lot. How the gods had sent a hero to give man magic, and drive the demons into the sea, and how Ramrowan's descendants, yesterday's kings, had become today's casteless, but Ashok didn't know what of that was real history and what was Keta's wishful thinking. "Not really."

"I could teach you about it."

"I already have one priest to preach at me. That is more than enough. I believe he makes his religion up as he goes along. I expect you would be no different. Only at least I know his intentions are honorable. Your intentions are a mystery. I am merely being open about my plans with you because if you are truly the wise man you claim to be, then you will see the wisdom in aiding me. The sooner I get off this island, the sooner your people will be safe from me."

"I will ponder on this."

The two of them sat in silence for a time, the Guru seemingly deep in thought as Ashok ate, comfortable by the fire. When the old man spoke again, his manner had become solemn, his voice barely a whisper.

"When you met Ramrowan, what did he tell you?"

Ashok had to think back to that moment, shortly after the molten chunk of Angruvadal had been buried in his chest, as he had waited on the edge between life and death. "He told me to finish what he started."

During their conversation, Guru Dondrub had told him there was a small settlement in the next valley where Ashok could rest and get supplies. Though it pained him to postpone his duties any further, the old man was right about him being in no condition to travel, so he had grudgingly accepted the invitation. He would recover his strength, then find a way off this island.

There was no reason for him to trust anyone on Fortress. All he knew for certain was that they had been enemies of the Law for centuries, the one place that did not bend its knee to the Capitol. The criminal alchemists of Fortress were despised and feared by all Law-abiding men.

Despite that, the Guru struck Ashok as a straightforward, genuinely curious type. The old man swore that their destination was outside the jurisdiction of those who had imprisoned him. Ashok doubted this was an ambush, but if it was, so be it. At least then he'd probably be able to loot a pair of shoes from the dead.

He had taken the Guru's offered blanket to use as a cloak. As they walked downhill, Ashok discovered that Fortress wasn't quite as unhospitable a land as originally thought. It was still biting cold, but on this side of the ridge there were a few trees and some grass, and in the foggy distance he saw herds of small hairy cattle. When Ashok remarked upon those, the Guru seemed surprised that he could see that far, but then he explained that they were an animal called a yak, which were the island's main source of milk, meat, and hair, and one of the few types of live-stock that could actually withstand the winters here.

"Do they not have yaks in your country, Ashok Vadal?"

"Maybe. I never had to concern myself about such things."

"Everybody should concern themselves with where their supper comes from. Keeping food in your people's bellies is the basic foundation of a society."

"I was of the first caste. Agriculture is the obligation of the worker caste, though much of the labor is performed by casteless."

"I thought you said that your leaders are killing off your casteless. Yet they are who grow your food? Your leaders must be rather stupid, then."

A few years ago such brazen talk about those of higher status would have caused Ashok to take offense. Every man having a mandated place had been one of the fundamental truths of his life. Except much of his old foundation had crumbled while consorting with rebels, and weeks in motionless solitary with nothing to do but ponder the Capitol's hypocrisy had eroded it even more.

"Many of them are fools, yes. A few are rather smart. Others are dumb, yet cunning. The Capitol is a place of treachery and lies." The words were bitter, as he thought about his battle with Lord Protector Devedas—who it turned out was just as much the criminal as Ashok was—or how Grand Inquisitor Omand had cruelly set Ashok down this path of rebellion to begin with. "It is vain men plotting against each other, with no cares who they destroy in the process of getting what they want."

"What are your leaders good for, then?"

"They make law. Law is necessary." It turned out that despite everything he had gone through, some answers were still reflex-ive. The wizard Kule had been thorough when he had rebuilt the broken mind of a casteless boy into a perfect servant of the Law. Ashok scowled as he reconsidered the issue for himself. Even Thera's rebels had required rules and order to keep them from destroying themselves. "*Some* law is necessary."

"You'd think foolish men would make foolish law."

In the old days, Ashok had never questioned the Law. He had simply done what was required of him, always. Good and evil hadn't mattered, only legal or illegal. There was no need for conscience when one had status sufficient to justify any act.

"Sometimes."

Guru Dondrub continued to pontificate as they made their way down a path so steep he had to use his walking staff to keep his balance. "It is my experience that there is a certain malady that powerful men often fall victim to, where they think their being clever about one subject makes them an expert on all the other many things in the world. They declare all their thoughts correct, merely by wishing them to be so. Then the masses must force false smiles onto their faces and cheer on their betters, even as those elites vomit up ignorance and proclaim it as truth."

"Are you sure you've never been to the Capitol?"

The Guru snorted. "If your rebellion triumphs, what manner of ruler would you be instead, Ashok Vadal?"

The question was unexpected. "I'm no ruler. I am bound to serve the prophet, so I will."

"Ah, but if you are Ramrowan reborn, then you are destined to rule. He was king once and it is said he will be king again. If it is a true prophet you serve, the old gods' commands shall come through them, but it will fall upon a mortal man to bring about their will in this world. The avatar of Ramrowan will be the one to rebuild his kingdom. It is said he will be a great leader."

"Then that is one more reason I am not the man you seek."

"Perhaps, but I'm still trying to decide." The old main pointed with one arthritic finger. "Our destination is atop that far hill."

As Ashok called upon the Heart to sharpen his vision, it momentarily stopped providing his body with strength, and the sudden impact of exhaustion and trauma nearly dropped him where he stood. The settlement consisted of one large building, surrounded by several small huts. Once he was certain there was no sign of soldiers waiting there to recapture him, he let his eyes return to normal, and waited for the light-headedness to pass. Ashok despised feeling feeble and hated using up the precious magic of the Heart like this, but he had no choice. He did his best to not let the Guru see his momentary weakness.

"What is that place?"

"It's a monastery. I suppose with religion being stamped out in your lands for so long you won't be familiar with the concept. It's a place where monks—priests of a sort—gather in study and contemplation."

More priests were the last thing Ashok wanted. He would have preferred the soldiers.

# Chapter 4

Keta, the Keeper of Names, high priest of the Forgotten, stood before the faithful, ready to give what would surely be the most important sermon of his life. The population of the Cove had increased so rapidly that he needed to use the largest room in the entire ancient structure to serve as their chapel, except even then the place was packed with people. Most were sitting on the floor, while more stood in crowds around the edges, with children on their parents' shoulders. The most nimble among them had even climbed up the exterior to watch through the round windows that ringed the room.

With many eyes upon him, Keta sweated. They were eager to hear what the latest revelation was, for rumors spread quickly in the Creator's Cove. By now all had heard that their prophet had once again spoken with the Voice of the Forgotten the night before, and it was the solemn duty of the Keeper to share the Voice's wisdom with the masses. Why else would he have summoned everyone who wasn't on a vital duty elsewhere?

No stranger to preaching, this was still by far the largest congregation Keta had ever stood before. As the rebellion had grown over the last year, a flood of refugees had been brought through the secret entrance into the Cove. There were thousands of them now. It was Keta's duty to keep them safe, sheltered, and enlightened as to the will of the gods. That was a heavy burden for one man to bear, and in that moment he was feeling it like never before.

Normally he enjoyed preaching to the faithful as much as they enjoyed listening, but today he would bring them great and terrible news from the outside world. Delivering this message would surely strike fear into their hearts. A dark cloud had hung over the Cove since Ashok had disappeared, and he worried that this new revelation would break even more spirits.

Except they deserved to know the truth.

It was odd. Keta hadn't been this nervous when he had struck the first blow of his first rebellion. You wouldn't think giving a speech would be harder than hitting a warrior with a meat cleaver, except it was. Now that he understood the real weight of leadership, he knew that his words had the power to lead men to destruction. His first rebellion had ended in failure, the slaughter of all the casteless involved, and the death of the last Keeper of Names, Ratul. He had to be better here, or else.

The faithful stared at him, excited, while Keta dreaded failing them. They were a disparate lot, having been born casteless, worker, or warrior, but all were free and equal in this wondrous place, brothers and sisters united outside the reach of the oppressive, tyrannical Law. How could he speak with so much at stake? It was hard to send someone to near certain death. How could he break up families, and turn mothers into widows and children into orphans?

Just as the crowd became restless, Keta began to speak, only his mouth was suddenly very dry, and he couldn't continue.

Some began to sense his hesitation and their faces displayed their worry. What would happen if they lost faith in him? Worse, what would happen if they lost faith in the Voice? The rebellion would crumble. Their many sacrifices would have been for nothing, the Law would triumph, and their gods would remain forgotten.

Javed must have sensed something was wrong, because he rose from where he had been sitting near Keta's feet and made sure the rest of the faithful could see that he was merely handing their Keeper some water.

Keta took the cup from him. Trusted Javed was the only other man who had been ordained to an office in their fledgling priesthood and he served as Keta's right hand. The former rice merchant had been a tireless servant, doing much good for the people of the Cove.

Javed leaned in close and whispered, "Do not fear. You're armed with the words of the all-seeing gods. Compared to that, what are the concerns of men?"

As usual, Javed was the reasonable one. *What would I do without him?* "Thank you, my friend." Keta gave his assistant a determined nod, then drank and handed the cup back. Javed returned to his place on the floor.

Having steeled himself, the Keeper of Names raised his voice so all could hear. Despite being small of stature, Keta had always had a great and commanding presence when speaking about what he believed in. It was why Ratul had first noticed him.

"Greetings, faithful. I have much to say today, for the rumors you have heard are true. Last night the Voice once again came upon our prophet, beloved Thera. For the first time since her miraculous curing of the plague that took so many of our brothers' and sisters' lives in this very Cove, the Forgotten has once again seen fit to bless us with his wisdom."

Most of the faithful smiled at that reminder. Some even cheered. The prophet had saved many of them from sickness. Others had been brought to this place by prophecy. They were probably expecting more good news. This would not be that. So Keta decided it would be best to ease them into the difficult part.

"First I must speak of the goings-on in the lands outside this valley. We have been blessed to live in these ancient halls, deep inside the mountains, safe from the eyes of the Law. Safe from those who would do us harm. It has been a year since the Sons of the Black Sword rode south to save the casteless of Garo…"

"Where we crushed the Protectors and drove them off like dogs!" shouted someone in the back of the room. The congregation laughed at the misfortune of their enemies.

Keta scowled until the laughter died, because this was not to be a sermon of celebration or frivolity. "And all that great victory cost us was the lives of many of our bravest men."

That grim reminder silenced them. *Good.* They needed to keep in mind the sacrifices of those who had gotten them this far, as he asked them to do the same for so many more.

"There have been grim tidings from the outside world. We thought that the crazed and senseless murder of our casteless brethren had been limited to just a few parts of Akershan, and it is that terror which brought most of you to the safety of this place. Only orders have come from the Capitol that this great evil is to be expanded to *every* house. The judges in the Capitol have ordered that *all* of the casteless, across all the land, are to be killed."

The congregation gasped.

Keta had not believed the news himself at first. It was madness. Even as vile as the Capitol was, he could barely conceive of such barbarity. There were millions of casteless spread throughout Lok. It was hard to even comprehend slaughter on such a massive scale. He'd had time to think through the ramifications. The congregation had only this moment. They were stunned. Then their emotions turned to terror, confusion, disbelief, or outrage.

"We have learned that sometime last year the Chief Judge in the Capitol was struck down by a Fortress rod, wielded by the hand of a casteless."

"Serves him right!"

"Perhaps, but in their rage, the rest of the first caste thirst for blood. Great and terrible will be their vengeance."

The order had gone out months ago, but word traveled slow at the edge of civilization. Keta had spoken with Thera and the other leaders for hours last night about what the Capitol's expanded extermination orders meant for them. They were all free men now, but they came from very different backgrounds. For those who had been casteless—like Keta—this was their loved ones being doomed. It was hard to see past that immediate threat. It was those among them born worker or warrior who could look with sufficient dispassion sufficient to see the bigger picture. They understood that in their haughtiness, the judges surely did not understand the chaos this would cause. It would disrupt every part of Lok, certainly leading to famine, and possibly to house wars. An attempted extermination of the casteless would be the greatest upending of the system since the Age of Law had begun.

And though the idea made Keta sick to his stomach, in such chaos lay opportunity. Or at least he hoped the gods thought so.

"We must fight!" someone shouted.

"Fight, we shall," Keta immediately responded. "For the Forgotten has declared that the time of our righteous war is at hand. Last night he commanded that many of us—many of you here today—will be sent forth in secret into every great house, where we will prepare our kindred to stand against the forces of the Law."

"But we're safe here. Out there we'll get killed like the rest!" That was said by a mother, as she protectively wrapped her arms around the shoulders of her child.

Keta knew he needed to give courage to the timid souls among them. "It is not all of us who must leave the safety of these mountains. Only those selected as worthy and capable by the prophet and the officers of the Sons of the Black Sword. Those brave heroes will travel in small groups into all the great houses, gathering the faithful and the casteless into armies, sufficient to stand against the Law, to do in other lands what we have done here. The rest of us will remain in the Cove, to tend the crops, and secure these halls as a sanctuary for all those in need."

As expected, far more people appeared confused and frightened than determined. They began to murmur to one another. The Sons had warned Keta it would be this way. The warrior caste was conditioned from birth to desire glory through violence. They'd be eager for the fight. Workers engaged in their own forms of conflict, but they saw war as something to be profited from when it was distant, and hidden from when it drew near. The casteless only knew how to run or beg for mercy, and those among them with the stomach for true rebellion—like Keta—were few and far between. The majority of the free people of the Cove had been casteless, followed by workers, with warriors being a distinct minority. Of course his congregation was terrified. Thus far their battles had been left to the brave, foolish, or bloodthirsty among them, while the rest had had been swept along as refugees.

He needed to remind them of what had been forgotten.

"*Enough!*" Keta roared, and thankfully the crowd obeyed. "The gods have spoken. With the gods on our side we will prevail. Do not forget what we have accomplished. Do not forget who we really are. Those born without caste have the blood of Ramrowan in our veins. The warrior sent by the gods, who gave magic to man, and who drove the demons from the land into the sea! The first king! The Law stole our birthright. The Law smashed our idols and erased our gods. For forty generations our persecution was so cruel that we forgot who we really are. And now the Law has come to finish the job, to kill us once and for all. Will you allow this?"

A few people shouted in the negative. But that was insufficient.

"Will you allow this?" Keta demanded again.

More of them shouted no.

*Better.*

"You may think we are no match for the Capitol, but the Capitol is no match for the gods," Keta assured them. "A few years ago our rebellion had nothing. Now we have an army. Fortress weapons! Allies! Money! And more magic than a great house." Sadly, Keta also knew they had no wizards to use all those valuable demon bits that had been looted from the House of Assassins, but there was no need to bring that up now.

"Ratul, the Keeper before me, taught of an ancient prophecy he discovered in a long-lost temple of the Forgotten. He saw six symbols there. Three would lead our people to freedom: the voice, the general, and the priest." He struck his fist against his chest as he said that last one. "These we have gathered. And Ratul saw the three symbols that would try to stop us: the crown, the mask, and the demon. What has become of those prophesied enemies? Our Sons of the Black Sword have defied the Law, killed many masked Inquisitors, and even defeated sea demons! We are as mighty as Ratul predicted."

"But how can we fight without our general?" someone demanded.

It was a good question. One that had kept Keta up many nights worrying. One problem with the Forgotten's prophecies was that they were usually very open to interpretation, and the Voice never said what to do if the man who was supposed to lead them to victory disappeared.

"Even death could not stop Ashok from doing his duty before." As Keta said that many of the faithful unconsciously touched the hook-shaped charms they had taken to wearing around their necks or wrists in remembrance of Ashok's miraculous return from the dead. Even though nobody here had actually seen Ashok come back to life and lift his impaled heart off a wizard's meat hook, they all believed the story. Keta didn't know if Ashok was alive or dead, and the Forgotten hadn't bothered to tell them either way, but the people *needed* to believe. So Keta would convince them.

"I know Ashok will come back to us, for there are prophecies of the Forgotten's warrior yet to be fulfilled. Until he does, the Sons of the Black Sword will continue what their founder started. They have won several victories over the forces of the

Law this season, sparing thousands of casteless from the sword, and driven back the forces of Great House Akershan who were sent to murder them."

That was an exaggeration. Thera had dispatched the Sons on a few raids over the summer to evacuate casteless back to the Cove. They had clashed with Akershani warriors, but both sides had avoided another large engagement. They had gotten lucky at Garo because the forces of the Law hadn't realized the rebels would be armed with so many Fortress rods. After that embarrassing defeat, neither the Protectors nor the army of Great House Akershan would blunder into such a trap a second time.

But that wasn't his problem. Keta was no tactician. His job was to inspire.

"Ashok will return. Until then the Voice has spoken. The gods have commanded that we must rise up and defend our brothers from evil! The time of our liberation is at hand!"

# Chapter 5

Thera listened to the first part of Keta's sermon from the back of the room in a borrowed hood and scarf, in the hopes that she wouldn't be spotted. If the faithful had known their prophet was among them, she would become a distraction. She needed them paying attention to Keta, because he was the one who was good at this sort of thing.

The warrior caste scattered among the crowd must have understood what Keta was trying to accomplish—they'd certainly heard plenty of commanders give motivational speeches before—and they began loudly shouting encouragement at every pause. Then the swamp folk caught on and added in their strange barking they used as a battle cry. Their enthusiasm gave the rest some hope.

Once she saw that Keta had successfully gotten the crowd swept up in rebellious fever, Thera snuck out.

Murugan Thao remained by her side the entire time. Her young bodyguard was also in disguise, because the people had learned to recognize him, and knew if he was near, so was Thera. Even though they were surrounded by faithful, he continually eyed the rest of the room with suspicion. Though he was a capable swordsman, Murugan kept a dagger palmed and hidden in his left hand because it would be faster to intercept an assassin that way, and easier to maneuver in a crowd.

Even though she was the most well-known person in the Cove, Thera was very good at not being noticed when she didn't want to be. It was one of the more valuable skills she'd picked up as a criminal. In order to keep up with her, Murugan had been forced to adopt her skulking ways. It had pained him to shave off the notable long mustache Thao warriors loved so much, but he took his duties very seriously. The warrior had never had the questionable benefit of living as a thief like she had, but he was a fast learner. The two of them made good time back to the garrison without being harassed by anyone wanting to touch the Voice. You'd think after Murugan had reflexively slashed a few hands that had suddenly grabbed for her, the rest would have caught on, but some of the faithful were slow learners.

She would have stabbed them herself if she'd been as fast as she used to be. Thera didn't like that she needed a bodyguard, and had taken great pride in her independence, but her once graceful hands had never fully recovered from the injuries she'd received in the graveyard of demons. Sure, she could still use a knife, but with only a fraction of the skill she'd had before. So in the off chance someone was in need of stabbing, Murugan would have to serve as her blade.

It was a long walk back from Keta's chapel. The Creator's Cove was a vast complex, carved all along the interior of a giant crater hidden in the mountains of Akershan. It had once been known as the Hall of the Marutas, which were supposedly some manner of vengeful storm creatures from before the Age of Kings who had hurled lightning bolts and roared like lions. Or so the old stories said. Now it served as the rebellion's foundation, a settlement away from the eyes of the Law. The faithful thought of the Cove as if the gods had built a perfectly good city, and then left it empty, clearly waiting for their chosen people to inhabit it.

Considering how blessed the place was with resources, fertile soil, and plentiful water, the faithful might have even been right. Not that Thera would admit that, because she hated giving the Forgotten credit for things he didn't deserve. Keta liked to tell his stories in a manner that made the gods sound caring. Based on her personal experience, Thera doubted that very much. Some of the gods might have been kind once, but the thing that spoke through her was anything but. The Voice was so pragmatic it was cruel. Its commands were callous yet vague. Its prophecies confusing riddles, lurking with pitfalls. Thera had come to believe the Voice had some ultimate purpose for them, but what that really was remained a mystery.

The forces of the Law still didn't know the Cove existed, or if they did, they hadn't laid siege to it yet. There was only one hidden entrance, and it was easily blocked by flooding. The mountains were too steep to climb over, and as long as their reservoir was left open to feed the lake in the valley below, no army could march inside. However there was nothing stopping powerful wizards from flying over the mountains and landing here. She had seen Lost House assassins transform into giant birds, and even been carried through the air in the talons of one. They had tried to teach her the pattern to create such a marvelous effect, but frankly, unless the Voice was personally guiding her, Thera wasn't worth fish when it came to working magic.

For once the main road that corkscrewed up the crater walls was mostly empty. Everyone who could was attending Keta's sermon. The place had become so crowded and noisy recently from new arrivals that the quiet seemed a little unnerving. It made her wonder what this place had been like, abandoned for so long, until Ratul had sought it out. The two of them walked toward the top terrace, near the entrance to the sluiceway and the tunnel that led to the outside world.

"Do you think Keta's words will work?" Murugan asked.

"Maybe." With everyone else she was forced to put on an optimistic face to keep them from losing faith. A bodyguard often saw their charge in their most human moments, so Murugan was one of the few she could be completely honest with. "It's vital the people believe we have a chance. If they lose hope, or worse, panic, we're doomed."

"There's no way we can save all the casteless."

"I know, but we can save some."

"We'll save none if we get killed in the process." Then Murugan sighed. "That's not how a warrior should talk. Forgive me, I must sound like a coward."

She knew Murugan was sensitive toward accusations of cowardice, even by the harsh standards of his caste, because he had been the only one who had broken and ran when the Sons had been confronted by the demon in the Bahdjangal. He had quickly returned to the fight, but his temporary failure had haunted him ever since. Some of the other warriors had even suggested to her that she deserved a bodyguard with a better reputation, but Thera disagreed. As her father had said, those who were most haunted by their old mistakes were the least likely to make new ones.

"There's nothing cowardly about being realistic, Murugan. Battles aren't won by good intentions. Though they do help— that is Keta's responsibility. Ours is to find a way to make the Capitol flinch."

Guards had been posted around this section of terrace since it had become the garrison for the Sons of the Black Sword. The Sons had expanded from the humble band that had rescued her from the House of Assassins into the rebellion's army, steadily growing in numbers since the days that Jagdish had first turned them into a coherent unit, and then even more as all the secretly faithful warriors in the adjoining houses had sought them out after their triumph at the battle of Garo.

*Where Ashok had gone missing...*

That stray thought twisted Thera's stomach with dread uncertainty, but she didn't have time to dwell on Ashok when there was work to do. She would do that later, alone, during the rare moments when nobody actively needed something from her.

As they approached the guards, Thera pulled down her scarf to reveal her face. Even though everyone here was free, supposedly equal and without caste, the warriors reflexively saluted her like she was the Thakoor of their former house. Old habits die hard.

She returned the salute as a proper, high-status woman of the warrior caste would. It had been a long time since she had held any real legal status, so it felt silly. Except her father, Andaman Vane, had been a great leader who had taught her that small gestures of respect from a superior made a great deal of difference to the men.

Though the Cove itself would be difficult to invade, that had not stopped the Sons from greatly fortifying this particular terrace. Risalder Eklavya was from Kharsawan, where the warrior caste took great pride in building fortifications. He had put together work crews. Trees had been cut and dragged down the mountain, and a palisade had been erected around a few of the ancient stone buildings. The tops of the logs had been carved down to points. Considering how little time Eklavya had been allowed on the project, it was rather impressive.

The other leaders were already assembled in the war room and debating their strategy. It was five desperate men trying to figure out how to stop the combined forces of the entire Law-abiding world using only their tiny army.

Just because it was impossible didn't mean they wouldn't try.

A map of Lok had been painted on one wall. The great houses that had representation among the Sons were very detailed, noting cities, fortifications, terrain and passes, rivers and crossings. The houses to the north and far west were not nearly so detailed, because if those places had warriors who were secretly religious fanatics too, the Forgotten had not seen fit to send any of them to join her yet.

Despite that, no house lands were entirely blank. Thera was from Makao, but her time as a smuggler had taken her north into Vokkan and Vadal, but mostly along the waterways preferred by smugglers because they were treated with disdain by the Law. Keta was from Uttara, the westernmost peninsula, but his knowledge was limited to casteless quarters. Remarkably, the majority of the map's roads and towns had been filled in by Javed because he was born of the caravan people, who never stopped moving. As a rice merchant he had visited every major city in Lok. The man's memory and knowledge of various house cultures and politics was remarkable. If Keta hadn't already drafted him as a priest, Thera would have found some other office for Javed among the Sons. He had proven himself invaluable.

The officers stopped talking as their prophet entered. These were her most trusted men, so at least she'd gotten them to dispense with the scraping and bowing. Oh, they had done that at first—as bad as the poorest of the casteless—only such deference had quickly become tiresome. It was one thing for them to worship the oddity that lived in her head, but it was another to put up with all their fawning adoration when there was a war to conduct.

To the masses, it was best to keep it simple. She was the Voice of the Forgotten. However, to these men, who she required wisdom from, it was vital that they understood that Thera Vane and the Voice were two distinct entities, for even the proudest warrior would hesitate to correct a god. Thera was fallible and vulnerable to pride and foolishness as much as anyone else. She needed counselors, not sycophants.

"I heard the water running, so the tunnel is being flooded again. I take that to mean the last of our spies have returned?"

"Yes, Prophet." Ongud, of the Khedekar vassal house of Akershan, struck Thera as something of an idealist—and taking a wife from among the faithful had made him even more committed—but he had the best mind for strategy of them. "We were just going over their report."

"And?"

"It matches what the other spies said. It's the same in Neeramphorn as MaDharvo and Dev, the extermination order has been given everywhere," Ongud said. "I pray the gods damn the Capitol for this, and its evil sinks beneath the sands."

"I'll put in a request, but I'm not expecting the gods to do our work for us. How has the Judge's madness been received?"

"Not well," Shekar answered. "No warriors are fool enough to openly defy the Capitol, but the orders are being followed slowly and half-heartedly."

Shekar may have looked like a savage, for Somsak raiders decorated their bodies with tattoos commemorating their greatest victories, and Shekar had many. The one for the battle of Garo—a purple field aflame—was still healing. He wore a demon from Bhadjangal, and even his face told the tale of burning villages, but she knew that despite appearances Shekar was extremely cunning. Dumb raiders died young.

"Explain."

"The Capitol's command arrived a while ago. The warriors of Kharsawan, Thao, and Dev have barely moved since. Akershan is only active because they started killing their non-people last year." Shekar paused as he remembered Thera had forbidden them calling the casteless that. "Sorry, Prophet."

Thera took no offense. The Somsak looked down on everyone, as was their violent nature. Casteless would be no different. "You think the warrior caste is delaying on purpose?"

"It doesn't take that long to mobilize if you're just riding down defenseless fish-eaters. I think us routing the Akershani at Garo put the fear in the rest of them. Why rush to kill casteless? There's no honor to be gained, but plenty to be lost. Especially when we Sons might be there waiting for them."

"We've mostly laid low since Garo, but all the nearby houses know we don't take kindly to those who harm innocent casteless."

Eklavya was an oddity, a man of secret illegal faith who somehow still remained a perfect example of the Kharsawan warrior caste's meticulous, orderly nature. "A defeat as great as Garo isn't soon forgotten."

That memory made Shekar smile and tap his tattoo of a burning field. "The warriors will stall until their phonthos tire of being screamed at by their first caste. But when they move, they'll move big."

"The larger the forces, the more supply trains necessary to keep them fed," Ongud mused. Though he led the Sons' cavalry now, his obligation in the army of Great House Akershan had been as a logistics clerk, a vital position that held no chance for glory. "The Sons of the Black Sword can't be everywhere at once, but fear of us can. That can be exploited."

"Most of the casteless can't stand and fight, but they can strike the Law where it is vulnerable and then disappear." Toramana was the oldest of her advisors and had been the chief of the swamp people. Hiding in the forsaken lands between the deadly House of Assassins and a sea full of demons, he knew a thing or two about hit-and-run tactics against superior forces.

"Most casteless can't fight, and when they do it's more riot than battle," Eklavya pointed out.

"We can teach them how to fight," Toramana insisted.

"I agree, Chief. I've managed to whip some of them into decent spearmen myself. Only it takes proper knowledgeable warriors to train passable fighters."

Thera shook her head. "We can't afford to split our army into pieces, but we can send out troublemakers. I was just listening to Keta putting a fire in their bellies. You'll have no shortage of volunteers."

"The Keeper of Names gives a fine sermon," Eklavya said.

Toramana nodded in agreement, but Shekar snorted and laughed. "Flowery words may inspire a fish-eater to fight, but it takes years to turn him into a raider!"

They may have been united by their faith in illegal gods, but that didn't mean they believed in them the same way. To Toramana the Forgotten was a wild god of the hunt, to Eklavya it was a god of wisdom and creation, while Ongud's god surely loved war and glory and riding a horse across the plains. Shekar would probably be delighted if the Forgotten demanded human sacrifice, but she'd never dared ask. Thera didn't really care what the gods were looking for in their worshippers, as she only cared about results, so she stopped them before the cultural bickering could begin anew.

"You don't have years. You have weeks. Shekar and Toramana have the most experience with irregular warfare, so they'll see to the training of the volunteers. I've got no delusions they'll be able to beat warriors in a real battle, but our saboteurs can still buy the casteless time. The longer this extermination takes, the costlier it becomes, the more likely the Capitol will relent."

Thera's last risalder hadn't spoken yet. Gupta had come from the worker caste, so he tended to remain quiet around those who had been raised warriors. That was normally a safe habit for a low status worker to keep. Warriors were prideful, quick to wrath, and the Law was very lenient when it came to them dueling over offense. Workers who were sufficiently wealthy were safe, but the rest minded their tongues. Gupta's obligation had been running a work crew in a small mining town. He'd barely had the notes to feed his family, let alone entertain the idea of hiring a proxy duelist. Even now, in a land without castes, after his paltan had slaughtered Protectors with the sixty deadly Fortress rods under his command, it was clear he was still hesitant to disagree with the warrior born.

"Something you want to say, Gupta?"

He took a deep breath, exhaled, and tried to not give offense. "You think too much about the wrong caste. The warriors aren't that important."

Ongud snorted. "What?"

"You're all forgetting the workers. I mean, it's good you're thinking about how to slow the warriors, and it's the will of the first caste we must break, but Lok is really run by the worker caste."

All of the warriors scoffed at that. Except Toramana, but he was an outsider who had spent his entire life in a swamp that had never been beneath the boot of the Law, so Thera suspected the chief didn't really understand the concept of castes at all. Among his people you either hunted well and ate good or were lazy or stupid and went hungry.

"Don't mock me." Gupta became flustered. "I'm warning you we're doing this wrong."

Murugan had placed himself near the door to alert her if

anyone else approached. "The Keeper of Names and his assistant are coming."

"You dig in the ground like a mole. What do you know of making war?" Shekar demanded.

"None in my paltan are warrior born, but that didn't stop us from stacking Akershani warrior corpses at Garo. Maybe your caste isn't as good as you think."

Those were fighting words, and Ongud and Shekar bristled. Eklavya was warrior born, but Kharsawan was slow to anger.

"Hold on." Thera held up one scarred hand as Keta and Javed entered. Javed seemed confused why the warriors were sneering at Gupta, and Keta was oblivious to that and still wearing a triumphant grin because of the successful sermon. Before the Keeper could tell them about how marvelously he had done, Thera said, "Let Gupta explain."

To his credit the stocky little miner straightened up and looked her in the eye. Thera imagined his version of the Forgotten appreciated fortitude.

"The first caste rules their houses, but only as long as their workers are agreeable. If we workers aren't happy, nothing gets done. Workers aren't that loyal to houses. Those of us from borderlands don't even know which house claimed us last until it comes time to pay our taxes. The higher-status men take us for granted. They assume whatever they want simply happens because they will it to be that way. We're angry when they don't listen to us, but we're used to it. We all know things really happen because they pay us to make it happen. But some things cost too much, even for the first caste to pay."

"What are you suggesting?"

"Workers depend on the casteless far more than we'd ever admit. All the horrible unclean responsibilities the Law has left to them are going to become worker obligations. You can't kill millions of laborers and expect the work to still get done. The judges can force men to work at the point of a sword, but it can't force us to work *well*. Everyone from my old caste knows this is foolish. There's no love of the casteless among my people, but none of us will want this."

"That does no good if your kind stands by and does nothing," Eklavya said. "Workers are useless if they don't rise up and fight."

"They don't need to. You're thinking like a warrior, Kharsawan. Fighting is your caste's obligation. Ours is to work."

"You say that, my friend, but I believe it was your paltan who took the most trophies in Garo." Toramana grinned as he reached over and smacked the far shorter man on the shoulder. "I'd say there's some fight in your kind."

Gupta shrugged. "The weapons of Ratul are complicated machines, but we can run machines."

"This is a war like we've never seen. Let us heed our brother, then argue, so together we can offer our prophet wise counsel," Toramana said to Shekar, Ongud, and Eklavya, and when his words seemed to sooth their warrior pride, it reminded Thera that Toramana had been a wise leader in his own right, long before his people had fallen in with her rebellion. "Noting the change of the wind doesn't stop it from blowing."

"I've read a lot of battle history, but gunners change everything," Ongud muttered.

"Some. If I had a thousand more Fortress rods at my disposal I'd march them against the Capitol to end this once and for all," Thera said. "But we've got sixty."

"Fifty-eight," Gupta reflexively corrected her. "Two have broken in a way that we lack the tools precise enough to repair them."

Thera sighed. That was the disadvantage of living in a crater too secret to engage in regular trade. "So what do you suggest we do with what we have?"

"I don't know, Prophet. All I can promise you is that there will be great discontent among the workers over this. If we can turn enough of them to our side even the first caste will have no choice but to spare the casteless and grant freedom to us faithful. Without us there's no crops. Let the first caste know what hunger feels like, and they will give in."

Thera looked to their merchant turned priest. Gupta knew how to keep men alive in a treacherous place, but mining was a different kind of danger from politics. "Do you think the workers could be swayed to help us, Javed?"

"It is possible, Prophet. Secret believers in the Forgotten are rare among the worker caste. My people are far more likely to worship profit than illegal gods. However, this extermination will be extremely unprofitable for some. We might be able to exploit this. Perhaps you should inquire of the Forgotten and see if he will give us his wisdom through you?"

It annoyed her when Javed asked for the Voice to come out,

but she had to remind herself that he was the only one here who hadn't seen the strange power manifest in person, had not heard the Forgotten's words for himself. That had to be difficult for a fanatic, so she tempered her response. "The Voice speaks when it feels like it."

"Alas, of course." Javed was clearly disappointed, but he placed his palms together in apology. "Then stalwart Gupta and I will ponder on this question together and see if we can come up with some suggestions to present to you. If we cannot turn the workers into allies, perhaps we can at least make one less enemy."

"Good. Anything else from the spies?" She was secretly hoping that there would be some new rumor about Ashok being seen somewhere, but she dared not say that aloud without seeming weak.

Ongud seemed uncomfortable sharing the next part. "Akerselem, the ancestor blade of my old house, has chosen a new bearer. A warrior named Bharatas, barely twenty years of age, so I'd never heard of him before, but... sadly... it appears that he's from Chakma."

"Oceans." Thera had seen Angruvadal slice apart an army of Somsak with her own eyes, so she knew just how deadly an ancestor blade really was. Now the nearest one was in the hands of someone from a town she'd once captured, which had suffered greatly because of her decisions. "I assume he holds a grudge."

"It's said that his hate burns with a righteous fire. Apparently the fool Pankaj executed Bharatas' entire family after we abandoned Chakma. His first public action as bearer was to swear a blood oath to destroy our rebellion and kill Ashok Vadal and every single man who ever aided him. While he wintered in MaDharvo he raised an army, and they're searching for us now. Word is he's a proper Akershani horse soldier, not some city boy who got rank by virtue of birth, so he'll be a dangerous foe."

That was dire news. Since Devedas and his protectors had left Akershan, the search for the rebellion had seemed half-hearted at best. After their defeat at Garo, it was almost as if the Akershani warrior caste had been hesitant to seek out a very dangerous enemy who seemed content to be left alone. Thera had only known one other bearer, and that had been the legendary Ashok. Except she couldn't imagine one of the most powerful weapons in the world would choose someone weak-willed to wield it. Ashok had supposedly been the most fearsome bearer of all, but if this Bharatas possessed even a fraction of Ashok's determination...

"With a black steel blade aimed right at our heart, maybe I shouldn't have been so optimistic in my sermon," Keta muttered.

"Even a bearer can only be in one place at a time, and the extermination isn't going to stop itself. This changes nothing. We proceed as planned. We will send saboteurs to every house, while the rest of you find me one valuable target for the Sons to strike. Your assignment is to think of the best way to hurt the Capitol, and make them question their path." Thera waited to judge her officers' reactions, but even menaced by a bearer they seemed as determined as ever. Say what you will about religious fanatics, but they certainly didn't lack commitment. "Soon we'll take the fight to the Law. Attend to your duties. I must speak with Keta alone."

The men filed out of the room. Murugan waited at the door, until she signaled that she meant for him to go too. Loyal Murugan nodded and left. She knew that her bodyguard would position himself down the hall, far enough to not eavesdrop, but close enough to rush to her aid if she called. Once they had the room to themselves, Thera was able to relax a bit. As she had spent so much time on the road with Keta, they were far beyond her needing to keep up a public face in front of him.

"I listened to part of your sermon. It seemed to go well."

"I think so. We've sure come a long way since it was just the two of us, hiding from Inquisitors, and you stealing our dinner while I preached in barns. Now we've got a multitude who have faith in us. I just hope that faith isn't misplaced."

The way he said that made her sad. "Usually you're the one trying to convince me that we're doing the right thing."

"We are." Keta then lowered his voice to a conspiratorial whisper. "I hate lying to the faithful, though."

"You did what you had to, just like the rest of us."

"I know, but—"

"The Voice hasn't spoken in a long time. We had no choice!" Thera swept one crippled hand toward the map painted on the wall. "How many thousands, no, millions of casteless are going to die before the gods get around to giving us another revelation? How many have died this season while we sat here, doing nothing?"

"I didn't say you were wrong." Keta stared at the painted lines, because the lives represented there weighed on him just as much as they did her.

The two of them were the only people who knew that there

had been no new revelation last night. That was a fabrication, created because her people needed *something*. "If they wanted a prophet who would sit meek and patient while people who look to her for help are slaughtered, the Forgotten shouldn't have picked a daughter of House Vane."

Thera despised the thing that had been living inside her head since she'd been a child. It was all-knowing, yet cruel. Demanding, then strangely absent for long periods of time. It had led her father to his doom and destroyed her family name, yet it had performed miracles and gotten them farther than any other rebellion before. It offered inspiration and guidance, then silence and pain. In the Cove it had healed, and in the graveyard of demons it had destroyed. The Voice had united her with Ashok, and now she cursed it daily for not even having the compassion to let her know if he was alive or dead.

"I know, Thera. The people will fight harder if they believe they are following the Forgotten's plans, rather than those cooked up by a mortal woman... even one they trust as much as you. Except it terrifies me to think, what if we're wrong?"

"Everything we've built will be destroyed, and everyone we love will die."

The Sons had become restless, hiding here during the season best suited for war. Once they'd heard about the Great Extermination, the people would have taken it as an affront to their gods. If Thera had done nothing, the people would lose faith, and everything would crumble. Sending out saboteurs to aid the casteless was a risk, but that alone would not be enough. The Sons needed to launch an offensive.

What if the gods had been keeping them isolated here for a reason?

*Then they should have spoken up when they had the chance.*

Life had been so much easier before she'd allowed herself to care what happened to anyone else. She had lost that shield when—infuriated by the sight of massacred women and children on the plains—she had ordered Ashok to go to war. As he had warned, there was no turning back after that.

"Then we will pray and work, Thera. I have faith we've not been led astray."

"You've got more faith in the Forgotten than I do."

Keta gave her a wry smile. "I wasn't talking about the Forgotten."

# Chapter 6

Javed had to wait until sundown to sneak out of the Cove. As the population had grown—along with his status among the faithful—it had become increasingly difficult for him to escape notice long enough to report back to his real master.

It was a long hike up the mountain to where he had hidden his tools. To keep the cache anywhere closer to his quarters would have risked discovery. Casteless had little to no concept of privacy and a tendency toward petty thievery. If his stash of poisons and magic had been discovered, it would raise questions that he could not afford to answer.

Besides, he didn't mind the walk. It gave him time to think.

Keeper Javed was known among the faithful as a merchant who had worshipped the Forgotten in secret, until he had been inspired to search out the rebellion and ended up saving a group of faithful from an evil wizard. Through his diligence and never-ending efforts he had become the right hand of Keta, the Keeper of Names, and been the second man appointed to the newly established priesthood of the Forgotten. In areas Keta lacked, Javed excelled. His gift for organization had enabled the Cove to thrive. His knowledge of farming and trade had helped bring about a bounteous harvest and secured vital supplies. Keeper Javed had become a beloved leader of the faithful, and an important member of the prophet's war council.

It was truly his finest performance yet.

Inquisition Witch Hunter, sixteen-year senior, Javed Zarger was known among his peers as one of the finest spies and assassins in all of Lok, but since he had very few peers, his reputation was barely known at all. He belonged to the most secretive branch of the Capitol's most dangerous order. Grand Inquisitor Omand had handpicked him for this assignment, and Javed knew that he had performed beyond expectations. Once the rebellion was no longer useful for Omand's schemes, then Javed would return to the Capitol for his reward...Not that he was in it for the status or riches, though such luxuries were nice.

Life required great challenge, or what was the point?

Ah, and what a challenge this assignment had been! The Grand Inquisitor had wanted him to ingratiate himself with the leadership of the rebellion, in order to keep an eye on Ashok Vadal, to gently guide him in whatever direction best suited Omand's goals, and to assassinate him should Ashok stray too far from Omand's script. Omand needed Ashok to be a menace sufficient to make the judges nervous enough to become pliable. Only the Black Heart had gone off and gotten himself killed in a duel, which was quite the setback.

Rather than give up, as many lesser witch hunters would have, Javed had continued to work within the rebellion. The Grand Inquisitor had tasked him with providing a menace, so Javed would provide him one. So he had continued to help refine the rebels into a weapon that threatened to distress the Capitol and, more importantly, promoted the religious fanatics' idea that Ashok would return to them. After all, the man did not need to actually exist for his legend to strike fear into the hearts of the great houses or rile their casteless toward even greater acts of violent defiance. When the bloody work was through, the judges would be replaced by a government of Omand's construction... a government that would owe Javed a great many favors.

Once the rebellion was no longer of use, it would be destroyed, and every fanatic put to the sword. Javed had no personal animosity toward these people. On the contrary, you couldn't work this hard to help someone make something of themselves and not take some measure of pride in their achievements. It was a simple fact their survival was predicated on their usefulness to the Grand Inquisitor's plots, and after the coup, order would need to be restored. They would have to die.

Strangely enough that thought made him...sad? Javed shook his head and cursed himself for the momentary weakness. A spy played a part, and he needed to live it so convincingly that the lie and the truth became indistinguishable. At sunrise he had pronounced blessings on newborn children in the name of the rebels' false god, and at sundown he was corresponding with the architect of their doom. He had worked so hard to help these people thrive that it was hard not to feel pity for what would inevitably happen to them.

For example, Keta the Butcher was a fanatic, through and through, and after swallowing the mad ramblings of Ratul, he had spread that illegal nonsense to other desperate fools ever since. Despite all that, Javed had developed a fondness for Keta. Though as fraught with pettiness, jealousy, and doubt as anyone who came from such low birth, Keta's sense of purpose enabled him to overcome his personal weaknesses. He was far too intelligent to be a mere casteless, as non-people were rarely bright, so Javed suspected Keta had been secretly fathered by a lustful man of a higher caste who'd had his way with a casteless woman, despite what Keta's precious genealogy declared. It wasn't often that Inquisitors were able to associate with someone so earnest and straightforward in their beliefs, and Keta truly was a decent sort, with grand dreams of creating a future for his people.

They were stupid, impossible dreams, but honest dreams nonetheless. There was a certain dignity to that.

Witch hunters had few friendships, Javed fewer than most. So when the order arrived for him to murder Keta, he would be sure to do it as quickly and painlessly as possible. The Keeper of Names deserved that much.

His cache was undisturbed. The forest was quiet. Certain that he hadn't been followed, Javed dug up the demon bones. These were the last of what had been issued to him by the Inquisition at the beginning of his mission, but he would have no problem replacing them, since the rebellion had in its possession a fantastic amount of magic looted from the House of Assassins. However, these bits were from the same demon prisoner beneath the dome, which made the communication spell far easier to create. None of them were humming with magic so no messages had been sent to him since the last time he had checked. He clenched one bone in his fist, concentrated on the required magical pattern, and gave his report.

"My cover remains secure. I have become the indispensable priest. The rebels are dispatching small groups to every great house to arm and train casteless. The main army is being held back for an undecided mission, though the Sons grow restless for a fight. Morale is high despite Ashok missing. They actually believe he's coming back. I've yet to hear the so-called Voice manifest, though many here truly believe they have. I'm still convinced it's some manner of trick and Thera is a charlatan. She would've made a fine witch hunter, as she's got her inner circle utterly convinced. She's asked me how best to sow dissension between the worker caste and the Law. Advise how to proceed."

Javed made sure the message was embedded into the bone, then sent it on its way. Now he had to wait for a response, which was unfortunate, because there was a great deal of work that needed to be done back at the Cove. There were work crews to organize, new refugees to house, and—

"Hello, Keeper Javed."

Surprised, he turned to see two youths standing on the ridge just above him. Dirty and barefoot, both had bows, and one of them was holding a dead rabbit by the ears. They'd not made a sound as they had approached, but then he recognized them as some of the swamp folk. They had grown up in an unforgiving wilderness hiding from demons and wizards—of course they were good at moving quietly in the woods.

*Saltwater. What had they overheard?* Javed smiled as he palmed the demon bone and tried not to look guilty.

"Hello, freemen. What are you doing on this slope? There's not supposed to be any hunting parties on this side today." He knew because he was the one who made the assignments, and he never posted anyone this direction on a day when he needed to access his secret cache.

"We were sent to the south but had no luck. Father always says hunters have got to follow the animals, not a schedule." The younger one—it took Javed a moment to remember his name was Rawal, and that he was one of Chief Toramana's many sons—held up his meager catch. "See?"

"Well done, hunters."

Unfortunately, the older of the two—his name was Parth—was too curious for his own good. "Who were you talking to?"

"I was saying a prayer to the Forgotten." Javed hoped to solve this dilemma the easy way. Rawal could not have been more than thirteen, Parth was maybe fourteen or fifteen, both of them still too small to join the Sons of the Black Sword. Killing them would complicate things, so Javed spread his hands apologetically. "Sometimes the Cove is too loud, and I go into the woods for some peace."

"Father says you are a very busy man, but we're lucky to have you," Rawal said. "Come on, Parth. We should leave him to his prayers."

*Listen to your little friend*, Javed thought. *For your own good, walk away.*

Except Parth pointed at the dug-up cache and sealed their fate. "Why do you bury demon bones?"

A lie would do him no good. The swamp people knew dead demon when they saw it. No matter how he explained it away, all it would take was for them to mention it to one of the more suspicious Sons, and it would bring scrutiny he could not bear.

"Where's the rest of your hunting party?"

Enough of his true nature must have shown through in that moment, because Parth took a nervous step back, fingers tightening around his bow. "Why?"

Except poor oblivious Rawal answered, "It's just us. The rest of them are wasting their time on the other slope."

Javed still held the bone in his hand, and it had enough magic left in it to fuel a transformation. He formed the pattern in his mind, drew upon the demonic energy, and willed his body into a new form.

The tiger leapt.

# Chapter 7

*≈≈≈≈≈≈≈≈*

"Forgive the interruption, Grand Inquisitor."

"What is it, Taraba? Can you not see that I am meeting with an extremely important man?" Omand Vokkan gestured across the map table toward where Devedas was standing.

"Apologies, Lord Protector." The masked Inquisitor gave a very obsequious bow toward Devedas, then turned back to his master and held out a fragment of demon bone. "It is one of the high-priority messages you've been waiting for, sir."

The Grand Inquisitor's eyes were the only part of his face visible behind his golden mask, and as usual those eyes were devoid of emotion and difficult to read. Omand turned toward Devedas. "I am sorry. We defenders of the Law must be ever vigilant. Would you grant me a moment, Lord Protector?"

Devedas was under no illusions about Omand's conniving nature. If their secret meeting was being interrupted by an underling, it was because Omand had allowed for it in advance. The action was probably meant as a slight, or perhaps it was a subtle test to see if Devedas remembered which of them was really in charge of this conspiracy.

"See to your business, Omand." Devedas waved one hand dismissively. "I need time to study the map and see what the houses have been up to while I was busy hunting down the most dangerous criminal in the world."

"Thank you." Omand took the piece of demon. The other Inquisitor quickly exited the room and closed the heavy door behind him, leaving the two of them alone in the large room. "This should not take long. Sending a message via demon parts is very costly, so the messages are, by necessity, brief."

"I am no wizard, but I am familiar with the concept."

"Of course." Omand closed his fingers around the bone, placed his fist to his temple, and closed his eyes to concentrate. The words imprinted on the thing were too quiet for Devedas to hear them all the way across the table, even if he called upon the Heart to aid his ears. Of course, that was assuming there was any message at all, and Omand wasn't just toying with him for some inscrutable reason. When dealing with the great spider at the center of the Capitol's web it was best to assume that every action was done with cold calculation.

Devedas did need time to go over the map anyway. Much had happened while he had been away searching for Ashok. Since he had been recovering from wounds in body and pride, he had sent his Protectors back to their regular duties, and then spent the long winter in Akershan. After the late snows melted, it had been a long journey back to the Capitol, and most of his time since then had been filled with political distractions.

The Chief Judge's map table was truly one of the greatest artistic achievements in the world. It was one of the few things Devedas actually found aesthetically pleasing in this city of opulence and corruption. Fifty feet across from east to west, the map itself was almost certainly the most accurate representation of the continent in existence, contoured to show terrain, with sculpted cities and towns, with every piece carefully painted by the finest artisans. There were hundreds of flags, varying in size, color, and symbology, representing the various armies of the warrior caste placed at what was believed to be their current locations. The only people allowed upon the map to move the markers about were specially trained servants, graceful young women who wore delicate slippers and silken gloves that would not mar the incredible work of art.

The table that held the map was so gigantic a horde of judges could sit around it comfortably, and the room was big enough to hold the multitude of staff and bodyguards such great men demanded. Today the vast room held but two. However, one of them was the master of all conspiracy, while the other was the future king of everything displayed on the map, so two was all that was necessary to change the world.

Devedas stood at the south side of the table, fitting for a man from that desolate frozen end of the world. The flags representing the armies of Akershan were spread out, fighting the spreading fires of casteless rebellion. There was a single purple flag, showing where a vassal house had declared independence from its Akershani overlords. Those were Devedas' new allies in Garo. Across the Akara River, white flags bearing a black mountainside were massing. Clearly, Dev was preparing to reclaim the lands they had lost a generation ago, after their bearer and Thakoor had committed suicide.

Devedas didn't like to think about his father.

It was not just Dev that was capitalizing on Akershan's current weakness. Thao and Kharsawan forces were converging on Neeramphorn. For a very long time that valuable trade city had been shared at the border of three houses, but it appeared that two of them saw an opportunity to seize that rich prize for themselves.

In the west, Harban and Makao's traditional hatred was festering, with several raid markers on each side of the border. He knew from experience that many of those raids would actually have been conducted by hungry Zarger and blamed on one of their richer neighbors. The western situation always had the potential to explode into another full-blown house war. Devedas had helped put a stop to the last one there, and that had been such grisly work he could still smell the mighty funeral pyres all these years later, bodies stacked high, with so much fat and hair for fuel that they'd burned for days.

It takes a lot of carnage to make an impact on a Protector.

Gujara and Uttara were usually too poor to be territorially aggressive, but it was clear their neighbor's growing conflict had caused them to send more troops to reinforce their borders, rather than exterminate their casteless as ordered. The westernmost peninsulas were more dependent upon their casteless for survival than the rest of Lok. They were probably hoping for a house war between their neighbors, as that would give them justification to not spend the resources killing their non-people. It was necessary to avoid famine, but such disobedience could be construed as an act of rebellion against the Capitol...

Omand sat on the north side of the table, appropriately casting his shadow over the wealthy lands of Great House Vokkan. Of all the stronger houses only Vokkan's armies appeared to be following the Capitol's orders and focusing on their casteless problem, rather than using the chaos to seize land from their neighbors. Knowing what he knew of Vokkan politics, Devedas assumed all those flags were lies. It was widely said, *Never trust the house of the monkey.*

Where Vadal and Sarnobat met was the densest cluster of flags on the map. The entire border was covered in the blue-gray and bronze of Vadal armies facing off against the black wolf of Sarnobat. There were a few raid markers indicating incursions on both sides, but the massing of troops indicated this was clearly shaping up to be a full-scale house war—perhaps the largest Lok had seen in a century. Normally Vadal would be hesitant to fully commit against smaller Sarnobat, leaving their back open to conniving Vokkan.

Harta Vadal must either be desperate or insane. Considering Vadal had just lost their ancestor blade, possibly both.

Omand finished listening to the magical message, and when he opened his hand, the bone had crumbled into dust. He dusted his palms off and the powdered demon drifted across painted Vokkan like snow.

"It is done."

"Anything I need to be aware of, Omand?"

"One of my spies in the south says the rebellion is going on the offensive again, trying to sabotage my Great Extermination. The rebels believe Ashok is still alive."

"They're wrong."

"Are you sure of that, Devedas?"

It had been the hardest fight of his life. He'd slashed Ashok's throat, but Ashok had crushed his skull so badly that even aided by the Heart of the Mountain the headaches had barely begun to subside enough to be out in sunlight without debilitating pain.

"Ashok is dead."

"That's good. After all, your reputation depends upon it."

Devedas knew the limits of a Protector's power better than anyone. The Heart could only provide one type of aid at a time.

There was no way Ashok could have survived his injuries and being cast into the rushing river. His choices would have been drowning or bleeding to death. Devedas had sent men to scour the riverbank all the way to the ocean, hoping to find Ashok's corpse so they could bring his head back to the Capitol as a trophy. When there was no body, it could be safely assumed that his body had been eaten by demons. The southern coast was infested with them.

"I'm not concerned about my reputation, Inquisitor. The name of Devedas is known in every house, where it is spoken of far more fondly than yours."

Omand chuckled. "I have no need of their adoration when I can have their fear instead. That is why I require someone like you."

*Ah, there it is...* Someone like him, but not him necessarily. "You will have your king. The people know me and will unite around my name far better than any other member of the first caste you could scrounge up now."

"Forgive me. I am not used to my fellow conspirators being as capable as I am. It has made me careless in my words."

Devedas knew there was nothing *careless* about Omand, ever. "You have your motivations, I have mine. I see the rot in the Capitol. Our system is broken and must be replaced. Lok deserves righteous leadership, not the vapid whores who lord over us today. *That* is why I am here. *That* is why I agreed to be your king. So let us dispense with this dance of words and get to the point."

"Very well." Omand gave him a respectful nod, then gestured toward the map. "The Great Extermination has begun and, as expected, it is throwing most of the continent into chaos. It turns out even fish-eaters will fight to the death when cornered."

"Whoever could have predicted such a thing...?" Devedas had tried to warn the judges, only they'd been too prideful to listen to someone who actually understood the true nature of slaughter. Yet another example of why those fools needed to be replaced.

"The Capitol moves with ponderous slowness in all things. This is not unexpected. However, once something so vast is in motion, it is very difficult to stop. It's like a tidal wave." That seemed to amuse Omand for some reason. "The orders were given, only then it takes time for the various players to shift the unwanted burden onto their unfortunate subordinates. The places where the most action has been taken are where the casteless are traditionally despised, and the least has occurred where the casteless are not viewed as a cancer."

"There's not much time until winter, and the southern half of Lok doesn't make war once the snow starts to fall."

"Then that's when the casteless will be starved instead." Omand shrugged. "I don't care how they die. Only that they die."

Devedas had always believed that Omand's Great Extermination was simply a tool to bring about a crisis sufficient to cause the fall of the judges, but he suspected that there was more to it than that. The non-people must have done some wrong to Omand somehow, because this seemed *personal*. Of course Devedas had no evidence of this, and it was pointless to speculate about a spider.

"There's house war brewing in the north. It appears the west is on the verge as well."

"Oh, there will be multiple wars," Omand assured him. "This map does not even tell the entire story. Vadal is strong now, but their leadership knows losing Angruvadal was a mortal wound. They must seize another sword or wither away within a few generations. Vadal will invade Sarnobat and force a confrontation." Then he pointed at the western side of the map, "Over here, driven by their ancient hate, Harban and Makao will be killing each other in great numbers within the month. I speak of total war."

There had been no speculation about that from his Protectors stationed there. Their reports had stated the border raiding was being kept within acceptable legal limits. "The last time they did that my Order beat the hate right out of them ... You're certain?"

"I'm as certain of war in the west as you are that Ashok Vadal is dead."

Devedas scowled but didn't respond to that. "The great houses have been busy this spring. There are smaller wars brewing in the east and south, over Neeramphorn and Garo."

"That last one, thanks to you. They may be smaller wars for now. But these things have a way of spiraling out of control."

*Especially when someone keeps pushing them.* Except Devedas didn't say that aloud, for at this point he was as much the Law breaker as Omand. It was difficult to recognize the pacts he had entered into and not feel the hypocrite. All he could do was focus on the good he was trying to accomplish while ignoring the evil necessary to get there.

"The judges must be fools to not understand what they've blundered into," Devedas muttered. "They've set fire to their home yet can't smell the smoke."

"It is fortunate for us that the wisest among them have been removed or are distracted. With the Chief Judge assassinated—"

"A terrible crime, done by a lone casteless with a Fortress rod." Devedas stated that with great suspicion. When he'd heard the news of the assassination he had been stunned as any whole man, as it was hard to imagine such an act committed by one so low, against one so mighty, on the very steps of the Chamber of Argument, in the city of Law itself, with the most illegal weapon in the world. It fit the tale Omand had been spinning far too well to be happenstance.

"I was as appalled as the rest of the Capitol." Omand said that with such earnestness that he was possibly the greatest liar who had ever lived. "Though the timing was fortunate for my dark councils. One does not rise to stations as lofty as ours by not taking advantage of opportunities when they present themselves. His tragic murder struck fear into men who had forgotten what fear tastes like. The vote for the Great Extermination was unanimous the next day."

"Your precious extermination will bring blood and terror to every corner of this land."

"It is necessary. Great change is not brought about in times of comfort. Do you disagree?"

"No," Devedas lied. He thought all that needless killing was madness, but now was not the time to further weaken an already tenuous alliance. Once he was securely and publicly in charge, *then* he would deal with Omand's excesses. The best way to take care of a spider was to step on it. "We'll do what we must."

"The backlash against the extermination has already begun. Now we must proceed to the next step, growing your influence so that when the Law crumbles, you will be seen as the logical choice to restore order."

"How long will this take?"

"Do not be impatient, Devedas. If war does not topple them, then the famine afterward will. A year, perhaps two. Or much less, if more opportunities present themselves." Omand made a sweeping gesture over the map. "It is hard to predict the outcome with so many parts in motion. You are well positioned as a beloved figure. However, your Order will need to take up residence in the Capitol again so that I can lay the groundwork for your ascension."

"The only reason the Protectors left is because you forced us to."

Omand chuckled. "Yes, but that was before we came to an understanding. Now we are friends."

"A friend would not try to take my woman hostage to use her as leverage against me."

Remarkably, Omand didn't deny that charge. "That was a regrettable misunderstanding."

Devedas had not gotten word from Karno recently, so that had been speculation. Omand's response confirmed that he had tried to capture her. "I'm not one of your Capitol dogs you can keep on a chain. Should your actions bring any harm to Rada, I will kill you."

"You would try." Omand might have appeared to be far past his fighting prime, but they both knew he possessed incredible magical power. What he had been granted by the Law would make him one of the strongest wizards in the world, and nobody was fool enough to believe that Omand had not learned even more illegal magic for himself in secret. The two of them stared at each other across the table for a long moment, before Omand continued. "That simple, passionate directness is why the people will love you as their king. However...I do recognize that I have given offense. I was merely concerned for her safety, but it was wrong to try to take Radamantha into protective custody. It will not happen again."

"Good."

"You may not believe me, but I truly only had the best intentions. I did not want her to fall into the hands of one of our mutual enemies, like Harta Vadal."

"Why do you mention him?"

Omand spread his hands over the northern part of the map as if accentuating the obvious. "He is but the first example who comes to mind. Vadal is the richest great house under our current system. What do you think Harta would do to any who threatened that system? Vadal is mighty in the courts, and they would never willingly give their power over to a king. For us to succeed, the will of Vadal will have to be broken. If Harta knew of our plots, what terrible lengths would he go to to stop us?"

At moments like this, Devedas wished he could see the Inquistor's face, in the hopes he could spot the lie. "Have you heard something?"

"Only rumors. Should there be anything substantial, you will be the first I tell. You have my word."

The word of Omand was worth saltwater. "What rumors?"

"That a young woman of the first from Harban was being kept as a...let's call her an involuntary guest...within the walls of the great house in Vadal City. But surely that must be someone else, as you must know where your woman is."

The emotions came quick. A sudden, nauseous worry, followed by a terrible anger. Harta Vadal was one of the scum who had created the fraud that was Ashok Vadal and gotten away with it. The thought of Rada in the hands of such a vile criminal...

Except Omand was also a consummate manipulator, so this might just be another attempt to provoke him. When dealing with such a man it was best to negotiate from a position of strength, or at least mutual benefit. So Devedas took a deep breath, unclenched his fists, and spoke with calm authority.

"Enough of this. We both know none of your other conspirators are popular enough to win the hearts of the people. They're seen as weak, or too biased in favor of their own house. I am the hero, with no house." Surely, Omand had seen the great fanfare surrounding his return to the Capitol. Wherever he went, adoring crowds turned out to see the Protector who had finally defeated the terrible Ashok. He knew that Devedas was beloved by every caste, and that was not the sort of thing that could be bought easily. "Then I am your partner, not your puppet. So you will spare me from your lies and games."

"Of course. As I said, it was merely a rumor. The Inquisition is told many things that turn out to be untrue. You understand how it is. You have your own resources."

Which Devedas would put to work the instant he was done here. "On the topic of Rada, my decision has been made. Once I am no longer bound by my obligation to the Protector Order, and am crowned king, Rada will return to the Capitol to be my queen."

Omand shook his head. "She is of the first caste, but there are many others who would be better to forge strong alliances. She's a librarian. Who cares about satisfying the Capitol Library?

That Order is of no economic or military consequence. You would be better off waiting to see which house is the most troublesome and then marry one of their Thakoor's daughters. Keep this one you fancy as a concubine."

"That is illegal."

"You will be king. Do what you will. The old kings took many wives. They were so afraid of their bloodline dying out that each of them had a herd of children, each generation growing more bloated in numbers and insufferable tyranny until they were cast down so the Age of Law could begin." Omand violated one of the Capitol's rules by reaching down and picking up one of the thousands of red tokens that represented casteless havens, which spread across the map like a rash. "Which is why we're burdened with so damned many of their wretched descendants today."

"The one wife will do. I'm seen as a man of violence. Her family is well known as peaceful scholars. Our union will send the message that there is more to their new king than just his ability to make war and kill criminals."

Omand appeared to think that over a moment. "An interesting perspective. I see the logic of this . . . You should have her come back to the city."

"I will when the time is right."

"Ah, I understand. Things may become unpredictable and dangerous here for a while. Besides, your man, Karno Uttara, is a most capable bodyguard. I am sure he is keeping her somewhere safe."

"He is." In truth Devedas had no idea where they were hiding, and that worry hurt worse than his Ashok-inflicted migraines.

"Then you have persuaded me, your future highness. We are in agreement. Radamantha Nems dar Harban shall be the Queen of Lok."

# Chapter 8

"What do you mean, *raiders*?" Rada asked.

"Multiple paltans on horseback, at least two, moving fast," Karno warned.

Rada stood next to the giant Protector on the balcony, so they were sharing the same sweeping view of the Vadal countryside, except all she could see were farms and fields, not a hundred mounted soldiers. Though she knew Karno somehow had the eyes of a hawk and her vision was terrible, even if a witch hunter hadn't smashed her last pair of glasses, she should have been able to see a bunch of galloping horses.

"Where?"

Karno leaned his bulk against the rail and squinted into the distance. Even hunched over, the Protector still towered over her, like a great shaggy bear standing on its hind legs. It wasn't that Rada was short either, it was just that Karno was that imposing and in comparison made everyone look tiny.

He pointed. "There."

All she could make out was a bit of dust cloud, rising above a distant farming village. "How do you know that's not Jagdish and his men returning from their raid into Sarnobat?"

"The locals would be cheering. Not screaming..." It was eerie how good a Protector's hearing could be at times. Their ears were as unnatural as their eyes. "They're headed straight toward us."

Despite the impending border war, Jagdish's estate had been a peaceful place the entire time she had been hiding here. It took a moment for the dire news to become real. "We're under attack?"

"About to be." Karno turned and walked away, pausing only long enough to pick up the war hammer he'd taken from Jagdish's armory. "I will alert the guards. Warn the servants, then find a place to hide until I come get you."

"Oceans." Rada hurried after him. She had read about raids but had never dreamed she would be on the receiving end of one. Raids were common. Warriors of one house would strike out against the holdings of another, with results ranging from mild harassment, to looting, to hostage taking for ransom, to vicious bloodthirsty murder. The Law supposedly placed limits on how often such events could occur, and how violent they could be, but she had been warned that such prohibitions were often forgotten in the heat of the moment, or outright ignored. Such were the rough traditions of the warrior caste.

"Are we in danger?"

"Yes."

They didn't call him Blunt Karno without reason.

Despite Jagdish's estate being near the border with aggressive Sarnobat, it had been peaceful the entire time she had been staying here. There was a Vadal garrison nearby, and raiders liked to travel fast and hit softer targets than a phontho's walled estate. Only Jagdish and most of his troops were off, striking into Sarnobat territory again, at Harta's orders. They had left several days ago. Rada didn't know exactly how many men Jagdish had left guarding the estate, but if Karno's instincts were accurate—and they always seemed to be—her hosts would be drastically outnumbered.

Rada tried to remain calm and remember everything she had read on the subject of raids. Regulations had been set down by the judges pertaining to border skirmishes between the warrior caste of the great houses, specifically concerning what sorts of activities were allowed or disallowed. This was to prevent excess depravity or economic disruption. Except when she'd mentioned these *rules of raiding* over dinner one night in an attempt to spark conversation, the warriors had laughed at her naïveté, and Jagdish had told her that Sarnobat was a very long way from the Capitol.

She should have known better than to focus on the official documents of scholars rather than the firsthand accounts of the subject. There was a whole section in the Library chronicling raids between houses, and many of those accounts made for a rather shocking read. Raids were often bloody and violent. There was usually murder and looting. Sometimes arson and worse. Much worse.

"There are children here, Karno. What about little Pari?"

"They will not kill her."

"Oh good!"

"A phontho's child demands too great a ransom. They'll kidnap her and kill everyone else. Remain calm, Rada. We have weathered worse than this. Keep your head and you will survive."

The guest quarters were on the third floor but overlooked the central garden. She saw one of the maids walking along below, carrying a basket of laundry, and shouted at her. "Raiders are coming to slay us all! Hide the children! Take up your swords! What are you waiting for? *Run! Go!*"

The maid dropped the clothing and ran away screaming.

Karno sighed, then started down the stairs. "The raiders are riding horses, not the wind. We have time to prepare. Try not to panic the staff until then."

"Sorry." Very few people could be as unperturbable as Karno. Rada had seen more bloodshed over the last year than most members of her caste would see over their lifetime, but she couldn't imagine being as nonchalant about it as Karno. He engaged in battle as casually as most men ate breakfast. Then she remembered her other obligation: "The mirror!" And rushed back to her quarters to retrieve it.

The artifact that had been entrusted to her by Vikram Akershan of the Historians Order was locked in a heavy wooden chest that she had requested from Jagdish. If raiders made it inside the mansion, they'd surely assume a chest like that was filled with treasure and smash it open or carry it off, and then find themselves the luckiest raiders ever because black steel was the most valuable thing in the world.

She unlocked the chest with a key she kept on a chain around her neck. The leather satchel was right where she had left it. She never ever let the thing inside see the light of day. The last time the mirror had been freed it had *eaten* a witch hunter's arm. A fact that made her extremely nervous carrying it about, but she had made a vow to keep it from falling into evil hands, and a Senior Archivist would never shirk an obligation. So Rada picked it up and slung the satchel over one shoulder.

She didn't even know what the frightening thing was for, but a vow was a vow.

The only other item in the chest was a sheathed dagger, which Karno had taken from an Inquisitor who no longer needed it, on account of Karno having murdered him. Members of the first caste often carried decorative knives on their person for ceremonial purposes, but this was a real weapon, long, with a wicked point designed to pierce vital organs and an edge for flaying flesh and opening arteries.

Rada snatched the dagger up and took it with her. She was no warrior, but she had tried to defend herself with a blade before. Hopefully such behavior would not be necessary again today, because the last time she'd stabbed someone it had not gone well for her at all.

Thakoor Harta Vadal had kept her in his great house in Vadal City as something between guest and prisoner. She'd spent that time trying to ingratiate herself to Harta in the hopes that he wouldn't hand her off to the Inquisitors as soon as it benefitted him politically. After a witch hunter had broken in and tried to take her, the only place she could think of to hide in Vadal lands was the household of a noble warrior she'd once saved from Harta's wrath. Jagdish had proven himself an honorable man who took great joy in repaying his debts—and who had no qualms about concealing her existence from his Thakoor—so the estate had served as her recent, and hopefully temporary, home.

Except now it appeared Rada had merely traded politicians and witch hunters for raiders. "Just my rotten luck," she muttered as she ran for the door.

The phontho's suite took up the entirety of the fourth floor. Jagdish was currently off doing warrior business, but that was where his child and nursemaid would probably be. Sure enough, Raveena was inside playing with Pari. The little girl was so adorable that it indicated Jagdish's late wife must have been quite beautiful. Jagdish rarely spoke of his wife, and when he did he became rather morose about it, for he had not been widowed long.

"Good morning, Rada." Raveena was a plump and motherly

woman, and though she was only of the worker caste, the two of them had enjoyed many pleasant conversations since Rada had been a guest here. "You look flushed. What's wrong, child?"

"We've got to hide. Raiders are coming."

Raveena blinked a few times in surprise. "You're sure?"

"Karno is."

"Master Jagdish said if the large one says something is true, then it is true." Without hesitation, Raveena scooped up Pari and wrapped her in a blanket. She was clearly frightened but was so experienced and gentle that Pari never even stopped smiling and giggling. "He also said if raiders are spotted we are to go to the root cellar."

"Why there?"

"It is the hardest place to set on fire."

"Oh." Rada hadn't even thought about them burning the house down.

As they hurried downstairs, Raveena gave terse warnings to the other servants, and she managed to be more articulate about it than Rada had been. Raveena had several children of her own, but her last had been stillborn, so she had been obligated to be the nursemaid of the new phontho. "What of my family? They live outside the walls."

"I think the estate's their target."

"That is good."

Of course a mother would feel better about her own life being in danger as long as her children were safe, but that didn't make Rada feel any more fortunate.

By the time they reached the ground floor, the entire household was in turmoil from the alarm. Workers and house slaves were hurrying about, attending to various responsibilities, which mostly appeared to be filling and staging water buckets, and removing anything flammable away from the windows.

"What Jagdish said about harder to set on fire..."

"That is the Sarnobat way: what they can't take, they burn. They put my whole village to the torch when I was young."

Of course Raveena knew firsthand how this dreadful business worked. She was a low-status worker in a borderland. Her life had been spent in the shadow of the house of the wolf. None of this was new or unexpected to these people. Vicious raiders were simply a part of life. Rada had grown up in the Capitol, which none dared threaten, so it was perfectly sensible for her to be feeling overwhelmed right then. That logical conclusion didn't help make her any less sweaty or nauseous, however.

All the shouting and banging of buckets upset little Pari and she began to wail. Something about a baby's cry made the whole situation far more frightening.

Through one of the windows she saw that Karno had informed the warriors, because they were assembling in the yard in front of the barracks to quickly and efficiently help one another into their armor. Unfortunately she only saw about a dozen of them. There were always a few manning the walls and gate, but even accounting for those, the Vadal men would be drastically outnumbered.

The kitchen staff had been preparing breakfast when the alarm had been raised. Ovens blazed and pots simmered, forgotten. Raveena grabbed up handfuls of naan to take with her as they passed through the kitchen. "If we're to hide, might as well not do it hungry." Then she spied a bottle of wine and took it as well. "Or thirsty."

Just outside the kitchen door was the earthen mound that covered the estate's root cellar. Raveena started down the steps with Pari, but Rada hesitated at the top.

"What are you doing?"

Rada honestly didn't know. "I should be helping."

The nursemaid tried to speak over the baby who kept screaming at her, but in a comforting tone that designed to sooth Pari's nerves...and perhaps Rada's as well. "This isn't for you, Rada. The first caste doesn't soil their hands. Let Master Jagdish's warriors do their duty. You'll just be in the way. Come down here, and you can help me distract Pari until it is over."

Of course she knew Rada was born of high status. Though Jagdish had kept their identities secret, and merely told his servants that she and Karno were to be treated as honored guests, it would have been harder for an elephant to hide its trunk than for Rada to disguise her upbringing.

"Don't worry. I'll send someone to protect you and Pari."

"Don't do that! Having warriors guard a door just tells the raiders there is something valuable on the other side. Now come on if you don't want to get killed."

She couldn't explain it, but despite her fear, the idea of cowering in a dark hole in the ground because of these ruffians... *offended* her. "I'll join you later."

"My oldest is nearly your age. I can tell when she is lying about doing something foolish too. Try to be safe. We'll be fine."

Rada bent down and kissed little Pari on the forehead to say goodbye.

She ran through the courtyard toward where the warriors were preparing. It was a simple place by the standards she was accustomed to, but it was clean, and filled with fruit trees that provided plenty of shade. Normally a nice, calm place to read, the courtyard was now alive with nervous energy. Men were stringing bows and gathering arrows. A single officer was pacing back and forth, giving instructions and occasionally grabbing hold of a soldier's armor and shaking it to make sure everything was fastened correctly. A crew of workers were drawing water from the well and dumping it on the wooden roofs of the barracks and the stables. The dogs in the kennel had sensed the nervousness and begun barking.

A lookout atop the roof of the house finally confirmed what Karno had sensed long before and began shouting about the enemy's direction and numbers. "One hundred—no! Two hundred! Maybe more!"

Most of the warriors seemed terrified, but others seemed excited, almost eager. The officer started shouting about what an incredible chance this would be for glory. Rada's recent travels had introduced her to many warriors but she knew she would never truly understand the mindset of men who would look upon such impossible odds with joy.

As she walked through the courtyard, looking for an opportunity to help, Karno saw her and approached. From the stomp of his heavy feet she could tell he was angry. "I told you to hide."

"I'm going to help defend this place."

"It's too dangerous." Karno didn't even slow down. His meaty hand easily wrapped all the way around her upper arm as he began guiding her back toward the house. "I gave them early warning. It is up to them what happens next. We must leave before this place is surrounded."

"No." Obstinate, Rada planted her feet. He was going to have to drag her. Not that such a feat would be difficult for him, but she hoped Karno would spare her that indignity.

Karno stopped and looked around to make sure nobody else was close enough to overhear them. "This is no game, Senior Archivist. As far as I know this is a legal raid. A Protector should not interfere. My obligation is to keep you alive."

"And you've done a splendid job so far. Only Jagdish has given us his hospitality when we had nowhere else to turn. I will not honor that by running away while his home is burned and his servants slaughtered. I might not be a warrior, but I can carry a water bucket."

Karno's eyes narrowed, and for a moment Rada expected him to just toss her over one shoulder and carry her back to the root cellar, but then he let go of her arm. "You are certainly no longer the sheltered librarian I met in the Capitol."

"It has been a rather eventful year. Come on, Karno. You hate running away."

"If I fight in front of these witnesses, then they will know what I truly am. Harta Vadal will hear of a Protector here soon after. Either way, our time here is done."

"You're terrible at being dishonest anyway."

Karno's brow furrowed. To a Protector, the Law was everything, and that Law said this fight was not his affair to meddle in. However, Rada believed with all her heart that Karno was a man of honor, beyond just what the Law mandated.

"So what do we do now, Protector?"

To his credit Karno never took very long to make a decision. Once a path was set, there was no hesitation. He started walking toward the main gate. "During the battle do exactly as I say so I won't have to explain your death to the Lord Protector."

"I'm sure Devedas would understand."

"No. He would not."

Karno approached the lone officer, who was older than expected, bald of head and gray of beard. Rada recognized that the shiny new patch sewn on his faded blue uniform meant he was a risalder, a relatively low rank who would normally lead a paltan of approximately fifty men, even though there were fewer than half of that here.

The risalder looked over, and up, at Karno. "Sorry. I've got no time for the phontho's guests right now. Please return to the house and—"

"I am Protector of the Law, nineteen-year senior, Karno Uttara."

The risalder scowled. "Phontho Jagdish told us you two were

tax collectors." Rada hadn't been certain what Jagdish had told his men about his guests, but that explained why the soldiers had mostly avoided them. "Aren't Protectors supposed to be in shining silver armor, with a golden token of the Law, riding around on war elephants?"

"It's a long story," Rada said. "They don't actually use elephants, though—"

Karno held up one hand to stop Rada. "Believe or do not. I will demonstrate who I am when the enemy arrives."

The risalder squinted, suspicious, but he was no fool. "Well, the tax collectors I've seen previously have been more weasel, less bull, so I assumed you were some manner of warrior, but who was I to question the word of noble Jagdish? I am Havildar—" He caught himself and corrected the rank. "Risalder Kutty."

"Congratulations on your promotion."

"Thank you. I got it just in time for us to get massacred. Assuming you are who you claim to be, how can I be of assistance, Protector?"

"I will assist you." Karno nodded toward where the lookout was still shouting from the roof of the mansion. "If he sees two hundred horses, there will only be half that many riders."

"I agree. They probably crossed the border overnight. It's the only way so many wouldn't get spotted. If they've made it this far over the border since dawn, they've been changing mounts. They must have been waiting across the border and had spies tell them when our main force left. I don't know how they snuck past our scouts. Sarnobat normally don't strike this deep. They move fast and light, kill who they can, take what they can, set the rest ablaze, and then run before Vadal counters. Phontho Jagdish has been such a thorn in their side since he got here, burning his home would be quite the feat."

Karno shook his head. "There is more prestige in taking hostages than leaving ash."

"Our walls will hold them," Kutty replied, with forced confidence.

"Twelve feet of plastered brick will barely slow them. Sarnobat raids Kharsawan constantly, and in that house your wall wouldn't be considered a fence sufficient to pen in sheep. They will attack from multiple angles, distracting us with fire arrows, then use hooks and rope to scale the walls."

"Sounds like you've fought Sarnobat before."

"Only their criminals, but I have brothers who were obligated from the house of the wolf. I am familiar with their methods."

Rada felt useless just standing there while Karno and Kutty conspired, so when she saw a group of workers hauling heavy rocks up the ladders so the soldiers would have more projectiles to hurl down, she went to help them. A couple of years ago a few minutes of handling rough stone would have left her delicate hands bleeding, but that was before her journey of survival and evasion had forced her to toughen up. Dealing with horse ropes and camping in the desert had robbed her palms of their softness. Still, she was nearly useless compared to the hardy worker folk, who had calluses from laboring their entire lives, but Rada found doing something kept her mind off the impending danger.

A short time later, the howls began.

Books had taught her those sounds were how the raiders of Sarnobat gave orders, and they practiced from childhood so that they could be heard over the noise of battle and hoofbeats, but hearing it in person taught her it was so much worse than that. The noises seemed inhuman. The howl of Sarnobat wasn't just for them to communicate with one another, but to terrify their prey. They were only men, yet it was unnerving, causing a visceral feeling like she was being stalked by a pack of animals that wanted to tear her apart and eat her flesh. She dropped her last rock on the pile and then rushed to find Karno.

He was atop the wall, near the main gate, so she climbed up the nearest ladder and moved carefully down the narrow walkway toward him.

The raiders were clearly visible now, having slowed their mounts to a walk, spreading out as they crossed the grassy pasture toward the estate. Their armor was dark beneath the bright Vadal sun. Their cloaks were brown, better to hide them against the ground, and many of them wore pelts over their shoulders or helms.

There were so many of them. And as she looked down the wall, Vadal had so very few in comparison. Maybe she should have listened to Karno.

Karno had armed himself with a bow that was nearly as long as she was tall. A great pile of arrows had been set before him, as well as several javelins. The war hammer was resting at his feet. He was still dressed in the basic, unadorned attire of a worker. She assumed the warriors here had no armor that could fit a man of his bulk.

Unlike Rada, Karno seemed completely at ease. "This wall is no place for you, Rada."

"I wanted to see first." Because she had only ever seen him hit people and things with various hammers, she asked, "Do you know how to use a bow?"

"It is not my preferred method, but a Protector is trained to an expert level with every type of arm." Karno pulled back the string just a bit. "This one was sitting in their armory, unused, because none of these men here are strong enough to draw it. Kutty said it was taken from the Sarnobat on a raid. No one else in Lok uses bows like this."

About half the raiders were dismounting. The ones on horseback seemed content to wait, while the dismounts formed lines. It was difficult for Rada's poor eyesight to discern what they were doing from so far away, but a few of them appeared to be lighting torches.

One of the Vadal soldiers launched an arrow their way, but it fell far short of the Sarnobat archers. Risalder Kutty immediately began berating that man for wasting arrows, and to hold until they were in range.

"Go now," Karno warned. She moved back toward the ladder, but then Karno suddenly shouted, "Get down!"

Rada crouched behind the parapet as arrows began to fall from the sky. As the shafts hit the bricks she was stunned at how much force the impacts had, even at this range. Their lookout screamed and fell from the mansion's roof, tumbling and rolling, until he went over the edge and fell into the courtyard.

"Their range is greater than I assumed. It is too late to move now. Stay close to the wall and you will not be struck."

Karno smoothly drew back the bowstring. Wood creaked with building energy, and he let fly when his fingers reached his cheek. The arrow went whistling away. Rada risked looking over the bricks to see the results. He must have missed as no one fell or cried out in pain, but it must have landed close because some of the Sarnobat archers shouted with surprise as they learned someone among the Vadal was able to match them in range.

"I am out of practice," Karno muttered as he took up another arrow.

Next came the fire arrows. They made an eerie noise as they passed overhead, crackling and fluttering. Many flaming projectiles landed in the courtyard. Some hit wooden structures, but those were immediately set upon by workers and their buckets. Whatever the arrowheads were wrapped in didn't want to quit burning, even after behind doused. But even as the workers fought those, Rada could see that the Sarnobat were preparing another volley of the things. A man with a torch ran down the line of archers, and as he passed by arrows ignited behind him.

She realized that Karno was tracking the one with the torch, bow elevated, leading him just a bit. Then the borrowed weapon released with a mighty *twang*. It was impossible for Rada's eyes to follow the flight of the arrow, but suddenly the man lighting the enemy fire arrows flopped face-first into the grass.

"Better," Karno said as he picked up another arrow from his pile.

The raiders clearly didn't like being matched. A commander barked an order and a few more men dismounted. Other torches were struck. Someone howled, and he was answered by two more slightly different animal noises from among the riders. Suddenly horsemen broke from each side, riding hard toward different sections of the wall.

More fire arrows landed inside the estate. A stack of hay next to the stables was struck and immediately caught. Pockmarks of flame appeared on the mansion walls. A hunting dog in the kennel yelped. A worker was struck in the back, and before his friends could help him, his shirt was afire. She could only see so much of the courtyard through the trees, but warriors were bellowing in pain just out of view, as they were pierced or scorched.

Karno went to work, quickly and steadily working his way through his supply of arrows. She noted that they were different from those the Vadal soldiers had in their quivers—longer, and with red fletching instead of gray feathers. The pull of that mighty bow was probably greater than Rada's body weight, but Karno kept launching arrows with methodical efficiency. His right hand would move back to his cheek, release, and a moment later another archer would be swept off his feet, or a rider would die in his saddle.

"They see me now. Stay low. Climb down. Go."

Splinters dug into Rada's palms as she crawled away.

Now that the Sarnobat had located Karno, they concentrated on his position. Many flaming arrows hit the parapet near him, burning with an oily hiss. He let fly, then reached out and *caught* a fire arrow an instant before it would have hit his chest. Spinning it about in his fingers, he nocked it to his own bow and returned it to the Sarnobat. One of the raiders screamed as he caught on fire.

Despite the workers' efforts, several parts of the estate had erupted in flames. Obscuring smoke filled the air. Hot embers were flying. Rada yelped as one struck her on the neck. Some workers formed a bucket brigade to fight the fires that had erupted in the stables, as others hurried to free the horses. The upset animals only added to the chaos. The smoke made it difficult for the defenders to see and breathe. Any Vadal warrior who looked over the wall immediately had extremely accurate arrows launched his way. It was forcing them to keep their heads down as the Sarnobat on horseback closed the distance in order to scale the walls.

If it weren't so terrifying it would have been fascinating. If she lived she would have to write up an account of this for the Library.

Vadal warriors would stand and hurriedly send an arrow, before ducking back down. A mere ten feet away a warrior rose, searching for a target. She didn't even see the arrow that hit him, it was so fast. One moment he was fine, the next an arrow appeared in his neck. He sank to his knees and looked right at her—through her—surprised, seeming almost apologetic. He tried to say something, but she couldn't hear the words. If there even were words. Blood came out of his mouth.

Rada scrambled to the warrior. She pushed her hands against the red river gushing from his neck. She could feel each pulse. She had read the surgeons' books on anatomy, but this was not like the books. Not at all. All she could do was try to hold the blood inside. It came out anyway.

*Move now.*

She thought that warning came from Karno. So she immediately did as she was told, and scrambled past the dying warrior. A moment later a flaming arrow fell out of the sky to strike the plank where she'd been.

Except when she looked back toward Karno to shout her thanks, he was preoccupied, and hadn't even been looking her way.

There were hoofbeats right on the other side of the wall! She could feel the vibration through her hands and knees. There was a terrible *clang* next to her head, and she instinctively flinched away from the noise. The device that had made that sound consisted of four metal hooks, and was attached to a stout cord. Suddenly the cord was pulled tight, scraping the hooks along the walkway until they struck the parapet and caught.

All along this side of the estate, more hooks were flying over the wall.

The raiders were climbing. The Vadal warriors hacked at the ropes or threw the rocks she'd helped stack over the side, but there were far more hooks than defenders, and Sarnobat men began swarming over the top. Now that they were closer she realized that their faces and arms were painted all in dark colors, only each face was split by a bright red line marked across both eyes.

She'd let herself get distracted. Karno had told her to climb down, but now it was too late as a painted raider scrambled over the parapet only a few feet away. She tried to draw her dagger, but her hands were slippery with Vadal blood. She could barely breathe from the terror. The raider's movements were smooth, practiced, nearly effortless as he vaulted over the top. His boots struck the wood right in front of her, and he was already drawing his sword.

*Drop.*

It was the strangest thing: In that brief instant as the raider raised his blade to end her life, the word wasn't shouted in her ear, it was in her head, and it was accompanied by an image of her rolling over the edge.

She did as she was told.

There was just enough time for flailing terror before she hit the ground. Only rather than a bone-shattering thud, there was a splash. The water slowed her the tiniest bit before her body hit the bottom of the horse trough. Such luck! She'd not even known that was there.

Gasping, she broke the surface, and flopped gracelessly over the side into the dirt. She still hurt from the impact, but bruised was preferable to broken.

Above her, the raider was trying to wrench his sword tip from where he'd planted it in the wood where she had been lying, but before he got it free, Karno hurled a javelin *through* him.

"Are you alright?" Karno shouted.

"I'm fine." Then she shrieked as the raider who'd been pierced through the heart hit the ground next to the trough.

"Stay below me." Karno returned to the fight.

In the shadow of the wall, at least she would be safe from arrows. The stables had turned into a roaring inferno. Panicked horses were running through the orchard. The Vadal soldiers were fighting valiantly to hold their positions, but they were too outnumbered, and everywhere she looked more raiders were making it over the walls. They'd taken one of the gates!

Rada drew her dagger and clutched it near her chest with shaking hands, fervently wishing that she had listened to Raveena.

"Fall back to the house!" Risalder Kutty bellowed. "Move! Move!"

Karno leapt down. It was remarkable that a man so large could land so softly. He had the bow and several arrows in one hand, the hammer in the other. He held the fearsome war hammer out toward her. "Hold this."

Rada took the heavy thing and then flinched when she saw the end of it was covered in blood, hair, and other organic bits. Pity the unfortunate raider who had tried to scale the part of the wall guarded by Blunt Karno!

The Vadal warriors were running, but Karno walked, calm and with purpose, pausing occasionally to send another raider into the endless nothing with an arrow. Rada stayed right behind him. She had experienced violence before, but never anything like this. She'd been threatened, chased, and beaten, but real battle was so far beyond her understanding that it was difficult to comprehend what was going on here. There was so much noise and death. Courage and rage. The peaceful courtyard ran red with blood.

Somehow several raiders had gotten between them and the mansion. The two of them were cut off.

Karno extended one hand back toward her. "Hammer." She slapped it into his palm.

Then the Protector showed the men of Sarnobat what real terror looked like.

The first raider never saw the blow coming. His head simply ruptured like squeezing an overripe fruit. Each time Karno swung that hammer another man was crippled or killed. He blocked sword thrusts with the haft, dodged swings, and each time he repaid Sarnobat with splintered bones or split skulls.

Rada knew that Protectors were somehow more than human, and she had seen Karno fight before, but never like this. Against normal men, it seemed Karno only did enough to stop them, and did not delight in shedding their blood. Against witch hunters, Karno held back nothing because they had magic of their own. This was worse. This was the full fury of the Protector Order, only applied against regular mortal flesh.

Armored chest plates did nothing when struck by a hammer so hard that the ribs on the other side exploded. Karno sent bodies flying away. Men bounced off tree trunks. Within the span of a few heartbeats, several of Sarnobat's bravest were broken and dying, and they didn't even have time to realize *how*.

*Attack left.*

The mysterious words were accompanied by a flashing image of a spear being thrust into Karno's spine, and this time she understood that the warning was coming from inside the satchel hanging at her side.

Rada glanced over her shoulder to see a raider running toward Karno, spear leveled, just like the terrible vision, and she reacted without thought. Lashing out with her dagger, she slashed the spearman across the forearm. Snarling, he turned, and she didn't even see the back end of the spear whipping around. The dense wood smashed into her shoulder. Tiny in comparison to the warrior, the blow swatted her to ground. The side of her head hit a tree root, leaving her stunned.

Karno turned just in time to see her get hit. Normally he fought with an eerie calm, but for the first time a snarl split his face. The Sarnobat warrior looked up just in time to see death coming. Karno hit him so hard that it tore his head from his shoulders. It bounced off the wall and rolled a bit before the body remembered to topple.

The world was spinning and Rada was in so much pain that it was hard to tell what happened next. Karno's display must have broken the nearby Sarnobat's will, because those remaining between them and the mansion fled. Then Karno lifted her into his arms and carried her toward the mansion. Arrows streaked past. Some were embedded deep into the bark as Karno ran between the trees. The impact of an arrow into flesh made a far different noise from hitting bark, and Karno staggered.

They crashed through some berry bushes. He got them behind

cover before dropping her, then winced as he reached toward the shaft impaled deep in his side. "Ah." It was rare to see Karno show that he was capable of experiencing pain.

"Karno!"

None of the Protectors ever spoke about the strange powers their Order granted them, but Rada had reasoned out a few things for herself. They could recover from ghastly wounds that would kill a man, or they could see like eagles, or jump like tigers, or fight like legends... but she didn't think they could do more than one of those things at once. If he fought with the inhuman intensity he had before, he would surely bleed to death. If he used his magic to heal, then the Sarnobat would kill him anyway.

"Can you run?" Karno asked.

The blow had left her dizzy, but the spinning was getting slower. "Yes."

He peered back through the bushes, calculating. Raiders were approaching, cautiously, bows readied. "I'll draw their attention. Then get through the workers' gate to the south. They didn't attack that side. Hide in the fields until they leave."

"I can't abandon you again!" she cried.

"I cannot abandon my obligation."

Karno had already demonstrated he was willing to sacrifice his life to save hers. Truly, he was a righteous man. Rada grabbed hold of the satchel. "The mirror can help! It talked to me a moment ago."

He just stared at her, as if thinking she must have hit her head much harder than expected.

"Come on, Karno. We should try to get to the mansion. Together, we could make it."

"That is the fire Devedas sent me to protect. But no." Karno showed affection about as often as he showed pain, but he reached out and put one bloody hand to take hers. "Feel no shame for Red Lake. We all have our duty. Yours is to survive."

Suddenly, one of the raiders upon the wall let out one of their animal calls. Only this one sounded different from the others. From the panicked tone, it was a cry of alarm. Danger was coming.

One of the Vadal warriors who was upon the mansion's balcony pointed toward the east. "Jagdish returns!"

# Chapter 9

When Jagdish had seen the smoke rising from his estate, fear gripped had his heart. He had urged his mount up the nearest hill and used his spyglass to better see across the fields. When he saw raiders milling about his home, his fear turned into an anger the likes of which he'd never felt before. His daughter was in there.

"Attention!" Jagdish stood in his stirrups and made the hand signals for those too far back to hear his voice. Five hundred weary men rode behind him on exhausted horses, but every head turned his way when they heard his furious shouting. "Raiders ahead!"

"Orders, sir?" one of his risalders immediately called out.

In the seasons that Jagdish had served in the east, he had earned a reputation of being a master tactician who never spent his men's lives carelessly. His fierce warrior spirit was balanced by careful planning. Of course none of that applied when it was his family being threatened.

"Charge! Kill them all!"

Jagdish didn't need to wait to see if they would obey him. He knew these men would follow him into the sea to fight the kings of hell. At first he was all by himself, riding hard down the hill and into the fields, but a moment later his men reacted and there came a great thunder of hooves behind him. There was no other sound like it in the world.

It appeared they had already breached the walls. The raiders outside saw them coming. There was no way to miss so many furious horsemen. The Sarnobat outside the walls were drastically outnumbered, and immediately began fleeing, disorganized.

For one moment Jagdish was no longer a commander, but simply a father watching his house be set on fire with family in it. Except he was too much the soldier to lose control of the situation. The fury stayed the same, but it would be a calculated fury.

"Let none escape! Second paltan left. Third paltan right." He didn't know if his risalders heard him, caught sight of his hand signals, or if they'd just learned enough from serving him that they guessed his will, but the flanking paltans broke away to cut off the Sarnobat's escape. Their horses were already tired, but with their homes at stake, his men would ride them to death if necessary and then run the rest of the way on foot.

The distance closed rapidly. From what little he could see it appeared Sarnobat had taken the walls but failed to take the house. Soldiers in Vadal gray were still hurling arrows down from the upper balconies.

He heard their damnable howls and yipping cries, familiar now after several clashes against the warrior caste of the wolf house. The raiders who had been atop the walls were climbing back and whistling for their mounts. The main gate was thrown open and Sarnobat warriors ran through it, desperate to escape. That gave Jagdish some small measure of hope, because if there wasn't still an effective Vadal resistance inside the estate the raiders would have buttoned up and tried to negotiate their way out with the hostage's lives.

*Please let Pari be safe.* Jagdish had served with religious fanatics, but as a Law-abiding man he had no gods. Except in that desperate moment, he begged for aid. It seemed an instinctual thing to do.

Arrows streaked past him, narrowly missing, but he had no concern for his own life. Instead *Please let Pari be safe* repeated over and over in his mind, like a mantra, as he rode by himself into the fleeing raiders. His men would be there soon, but for a moment it would be Jagdish alone.

Jagdish drew his sword, and the battle was joined.

He rode down an archer, spun about, and slashed a rider from the saddle. Bones crunched beneath hooves. It was a haze of blood and fury as Jagdish laid about him. He parried a sword thrust without thinking, and then had to hang on as his steed reared back in pain as an arrow was embedded in her side. Jagdish crashed to the ground, armor clanking as he rolled through the dirt, but then he sprang immediately back to his feet, just in time to turn aside a descending axe. He pushed into that raider, and did a brutal draw cut through his midsection, spilling guts.

All phonthos had personal bodyguards. Jagdish was no different, though his unexpected one-man charge had left them scurrying to catch up. They arrived a few heartbeats later, and more raiders fell to spear thrusts and hammer blows. Havildar Mohan dismounted and rushed to Jagdish's side to protect him. The skilled warrior intercepted a raider along the way, bashing his brains out with a spiked mace. Zaheer and Joshi stayed mounted, placing their bodies and their mounts between their leader and the remaining archers.

He didn't want to be guarded. Now was the time to slaughter these Sarnobat scum in return for this trespass. Only Jagdish had to push his righteous anger aside long enough to be a proper commander. With no more living targets nearby, he surveyed the field, rapidly taking in everything he could. The raiders were outnumbered and running, with pursuit close on their heels. The last knot of resistance were those who had been caught near the main gate with no way out.

Jagdish started toward them. "First paltan on me. To the gate!"

There was nothing to do now but see it through, so he returned to the battle with his conscience free of responsibility.

No one had ever accused Sarnobat of breeding cowards. Trapped, they fought like the snarling wolf upon their flag. They rushed outward, in one last desperate attempt to get away. Only Vadal had far superior numbers, and since Jagdish had personally overseen the training of his men, they had the superior skill. The Vadal troops worked together, half dismounting and rushing forward on foot, while their mounted brothers used their elevation to fire arrows unimpeded into their foes. The last rush wasn't a haphazard one either, as the Vadal men took a moment to form into a line, then pushed forward as one. As soon as a Sarnobat man stumbled, multiple spears were thrust into him, and any body already lying on the ground wearing the wrong colors got stabbed for good measure.

It was clear who the enemy commander was. While the others only had splashes of red paint on them, this one's entire face was red, and the upper jaw of a wolf served as the visor for his helm. The Sarnobat officer knew all was lost and tried to take the honorable way out. He spied Jagdish, clearly marked by his bright phontho's sash and turban, and bellowed a challenge for the two of them to duel, leader against leader.

It was a demand respected by equals, only this dog had come into his *house*, and Jagdish wasn't feeling particularly honorable with his baby girl on the other side of that gate, so he pointed and ordered, "Kill that one."

Bows thrummed and spears were hurled. The Sarnobat leader collapsed in a bloody heap.

Jagdish strode through his gate while his men overwhelmed the remaining Sarnobat there. Some of them threw down their swords and tried to surrender, but Jagdish didn't pause long enough to see if his men granted them that mercy. That probably depended on if the particular warrior they were trying to surrender to had family inside the estate or not.

"I am Phontho Jagdish and this is my home!" he bellowed.

Inside the courtyard there were only a few Sarnobat left. When they saw the gray-clad line approaching, they put down their weapons and raised empty hands. They were quickly surrounded by Vadal warriors with bloody swords.

"What should we do with them, Phontho?" Mohan asked.

Jagdish looked around. His orchard was littered with bodies. His stables were burning down. The smoke stung his eyes. He almost ordered his men to slit the prisoners' throats right there, but, even furious, cruelty was not Jagdish's way. He took a deep breath before saying, "Bind them."

"Th-thank you, noble warrior," one of them stammered.

"Don't thank me yet, scum. If a single hair has been harmed on my daughter's head you'll regret my not killing you fast." Jagdish kept walking toward the mansion. His other bodyguards dismounted and rushed to stay near him. The mansion had been scorched, but not caught fire. It appeared one of the heavy doors had been repeatedly struck by an axe, but the enemy had not breached.

Stepping over bodies, he recognized each of the Vadal dead, warrior and worker both. They'd served him for these last few months, and unlike most masters, Jagdish had taken the time to speak to every single one of them, to learn their names, and to treat them with respect. Workers and house slaves came out from where they had been hiding as they saw him crossing the grounds. Some cheered, but others were still too shocked from the violence they'd just experienced to make a sound.

"Joshi, gather a crew to put out that fire. Zaheer, gather however many fresh horses escaped the stables and get them to the outriders to swap saddles, and then have them run down any stragglers." It was clear that his bodyguards didn't want to abandon him in a courtyard that still might be hiding hostiles, but they did as they were told. Jagdish called after them, "And take the hunting dogs from the kennel to track their scent. I don't want any of these Sarnobat bastards making it back across the border."

Mohan stuck with him, and Jagdish didn't try to give his final bodyguard another assignment, because that might cause a revolt.

The damaged door swung open and old Kutty rushed out, splattered with blood, a fresh bandage wrapped around one hand. "You've got the best timing in Lok, Master Jagdish! That little pocket clock of yours must be magic."

"Is Pari alright?"

"She is. Raveena's got her."

Jagdish had been so focused since seeing the smoke, that Kutty's calming words made his knees go wobbly. It was like a great weight lifted from his chest, and he could breathe again. He wanted nothing more than to see his daughter, but duty came first. "What's your status?"

As the seasoned warrior gave his report, Jagdish cringed when he heard the estimated numbers for the dead and wounded. As he looked over the ruin of his estate, his anger began to grow anew. "How could so many raiders make it all the way here without being spotted by the Mukesh Garrison? Phontho Gotama's men were supposed to be patrolling the border while I was away."

"How would I know? Gotama's a political appointment, so he's probably a dolt." Kutty had been promoted, disgraced and demoted, then promoted again, more times than ten regular warriors put together. Such men were usually too honest for their own good, which was why Jagdish had recruited him.

"Gotama will answer for his failure," Jagdish vowed.

"I sent a runner to Mukesh to get help as soon as your giant friend sensed the raiders coming. Good thing he was here, or we might not have held."

He'd not seen Karno or Rada among the dead. "Where are my guests?"

Kutty pointed toward the stables, where a group of workers had formed a bucket brigade. Jagdish was surprised to see that Rada was among the line, passing buckets of water along like the rest. The librarian was filthy, with leaves stuck in her hair, and her dress was torn and splattered with blood. That wasn't very firster of her. She was full of surprises.

"I'm afraid their secret is out, though, Jagdish. The big one had to announce what he was. Not that there'd be any doubt after we watched him best a squad of raiders by himself. I've always heard Protectors fight like demons. The tales weren't exaggerated."

"Ah..." Jagdish had been dreading the day that he'd have to explain to his Thakoor—who already despised him—why he was sheltering a woman who had fled from his control. "Tell whoever knows Karno's true status to keep it to themselves."

"I will, but you know the boys will talk. They always do."

"They can hold their tongues long enough for my guests to be well on their way before Harta Vadal finds out they were here." Jagdish paused as Mohan handed him a rag to wipe his sword on. He cleaned the blood, then sheathed the blade. "I must speak to them. Mohan, go to Raveena, and make sure my daughter doesn't come out until every single inch of this place has been searched for hostiles."

"If there are any Sarnobat still lurking about, you'd be the better target, Phontho."

"Let them try." But when Mohan hesitated, Jagdish sighed. His bodyguards were extremely loyal. It was because he had gathered men who had been on the outs with their caste and given them a chance to regain their honor as warriors, much like Jagdish had done for himself. Redemption was a rare opportunity among their kind, so it was treasured when offered. "Go. That's an order. The conversation I'm about to have is one that you don't want to hear. This way when the Thakoor's men or any Inquisitors ask what was said, you can swear you heard nothing."

Mohan bowed, then went to check on Pari. Kutty returned to helping with the injured.

Radamantha Nems dar Harban might have been a high-status

lady of the first caste, but she was working as hard to stop the fire as anyone else. Jagdish had served in the Personal Guard of Great House Vadal, surrounded by the most important people in the richest house in the world, and he could count on the fingers of one hand the number of times he'd seen a member of the first caste stoop to doing anything that could be vaguely described as manual labor.

The stables were a complete loss, but the fire needed to be controlled to keep it from spreading. Despite their desperate labors, and the fact many of their friends had just been hurt or even killed, the workers greeted Jagdish with joy, for their kind master had saved them. It would break their spirits if they realized that it was his actions that had made them a target. Jagdish had been commanded to provoke the Sarnobat toward war, and he had been so successful that his name had become infamous and despised within the house of the wolf. Of course they had struck at his home while he was away...

The intense heat of the fire matched his mood.

The librarian's clothing was damp. Her fine silks had been torn, and it looked like she had rolled in mud. There was a nasty, bleeding welt on her temple, and yet she kept on passing buckets, clearly struggling against the weight and tired arms, but trying hard not to spill any precious droplets that could be better used to quench the flames.

Karno, meanwhile, was sitting on a log, one hand pressed against his bloody side. There was an arrow next to him, and from the gory look of the thing, it had been recently plucked from his guts. Jagdish stopped next to him. "I would ask if you're going to live, but I've seen Ashok survive far worse."

"Being wounded provides me an excuse to shirk firefighting duty," Karno replied flatly.

"I'm told my household is in your gratitude. You saw them coming long before our lookouts would have, giving my men time to prepare, then stacked quite the pile of raider corpses yourself."

"I was doing my duty."

"Were you now? It seems what it means to uphold the Law isn't as clear as it used to be."

Karno's only response to that was a bemused grunt, because it wasn't every day that one of the ultimate enforcers of the Law was forced to hide from the Law's Inquisitors.

"I was already in Rada's debt. Now I'm in yours as well, Karno Uttara."

"There is no debt. You risked your status by sheltering us. Now it is time for us to leave."

"We must speak before you do. While I was away I've heard rumors from the south."

His warriors were rushing over and forming a second bucket line, so Jagdish, honored phontho, war leader, recipient of the highest award for valor in Vadal's warrior caste, and master of the estate, got in line to help.

# Chapter 10

~~~~~~~~~~

Pari was asleep atop a pile of blankets. Jagdish marveled that she was able to sleep so soundly even after a crisis. He smiled, as that trait must come from his side of the family, because all warriors developed the ability to take a nap on demand. Luckily, Pari took after her mother in appearance...snored like her too. And that thought made Jagdish chuckle...then grow sad.

He had never dreamed that with hundreds of warriors under his command, life would be so lonely.

Jagdish had once traveled across half of Lok to get back to Vadal, even though his only hope of survival was to be granted mercy by a merciless Thakoor, and he had been carrying enough wealth in demon flesh and bone to stop in any other house along the way and buy himself a judgeship. Yet he had returned to his homeland to try and restore his name anyway. By a miracle he had been rewarded with status and glory beyond his wildest hopes. So it was an odd thing, this bitterness he felt. He had achieved everything he had dreamed of, yet what did all that matter if he had lost what he truly loved along the way?

Jagdish stood before one of the many windows of his luxurious quarters, as the sun painted the courtyard below orange. From his pocket he took the tiny watch he had won in a wager at Cold Stream Prison and absently checked the time. It was an unnecessary act, but the feel of the tiny gears spinning in his palm comforted him. He'd only had time to get out of his armor, clean himself, and change into clothing that did not stink of sweat, soot, and death, and already there was much more to do.

There was a knock on the door. Jagdish put the watch away and said, "Come in."

It was one of his bodyguards, Zaheer. "Your guests have arrived, Phontho."

"See them in, and have the kitchen bring us some food."

"Anything in particular?"

"Whatever's easiest for them." The servants had been through enough today and he felt guilty for making them labor further, but he still had decisions to make and meetings to conduct, and he couldn't do that distracted with hunger. Such was the life of a high-status man.

Zaheer stepped out of the way so that Karno and Rada could enter. They had washed and been given new clothes. Karno was in the formal blue-gray and bronze uniform of a Vadal officer. It was the wrong house and station, but that particular shirt had been the only thing large enough any of the house slaves could find, and it was still far too tight.

Rada immediately bowed in the most proper northern custom. "Our presence as requested, Master Phontho."

"Enough of that, Rada. When you met me I was in rags, and today you fought to keep my house from burning down. If that doesn't make formality unnecessary, I don't know what does."

Rada sighed. "Karno was useful. I didn't accomplish much."

"As I tell my soldiers, it's more important to always do the right thing than a big thing. Most ladies of your status would have sat and watched the spectacle while complaining about the noise. How are you?"

"I've got a bump on the head, but honestly, I've never been so tired in all my life. I can barely keep my eyes open." She held out her trembling hands. "Yet, I can't stop shaking."

"That's normal after some excitement. You get used to it."

"I don't know how you warriors do this. I've never been through a raid before."

"That's life on a border. It happens all the time." That wasn't at all true, but no proud warrior would ever admit to feeling vulnerable and wronged to members of the higher caste. He gestured toward the pillows around a low table. "Sit and rest. It's been a hard day."

They did. Rada winced as she angered one of the many minor injuries on her body. Karno had received what would have been a mortal wound to any normal man only a few hours ago, yet he barely showed any discomfort now. Such was the nature of Protectors. As Ashok had taught him, it was kill them fast, or not at all.

"We will leave in the morning," Karno stated without preamble. He had never struck Jagdish as a man fond of excess conversation.

"That's wise. I'll see to it you have plenty of supplies and fine horses to carry it all, as many as you want." Jagdish held up a hand before Rada could claim she didn't deserve such generosity. "It's a gift. Besides, Karno could simply use the authority of his office to take whatever he needed if he wanted anyway."

"Karno wouldn't do that."

The Law said Protectors could requisition whatever they required, and the lower castes had to oblige them, regardless of how much harm taking that property caused. Rada didn't seem like the sort to enjoy that sort of officious bullying, though. She was truly an oddity among her caste. Karno simply gave him a polite nod of acknowledgment.

"It is as you say, then, Rada. I'm not going to argue with somebody who once swayed silver-tongued Harta Vadal into saving the life of a poor condemned soldier." Jagdish grinned. "I'd offer you a military escort all the way to whatever border you wish to cross as well, but I'd guess you'd rather I not know your next destination."

"That's probably for the best. I will miss this place. Despite a profound lack of reading material, it was rather nice...until recently."

"I'm sorry you had to reveal yourself, Karno. If the other warriors stationed nearby had been doing their damned jobs, and been guarding this place like they were supposed to, it wouldn't have been necessary."

Karno shrugged. "Mistakes happen in war."

So did getting challenged to a duel by another commander and having your head cut off as payment for your neglect, but Jagdish didn't say what he intended to do to Phontho Gotama aloud, as there was a lady present.

Rada noticed that little Pari had woken up and made a happy noise. "Oh, can I hold her?"

"Certainly." Jagdish was a proud man of the warrior caste. It wasn't like he knew much about raising children until they were old enough to hold a sword. This early part should have been Pakpa's responsibility. He truly loved his daughter, as a father should, yet she was a constant reminder of what he had lost...of what might have been had he accepted his place and not chased after Ashok Vadal in an outlandish attempt to restore his name.

Rada picked Pari up and held her close. "I will miss you, little flower."

"She adores you. You'll make a fine mother someday."

"Oh, thank you, Jagdish. I worry about you two. Raveena is a fine maid, but a little girl needs a mother. I knew too many girls in the Capitol who were raised by maids because their mothers were too busy, and they all turned out awful. Chatty, vapid, gossiping things who were barely literate. When is your house going to arrange a new marriage for you?"

"I've been rather busy trying to provoke a war." In truth, he was of high enough status he could request a wife today, and the Law would arrange for him one of the finest maidens of Vadal's warrior caste tomorrow. Any warrior family would be honored to marry one of their daughters off to a man who had earned the Param Vir Chakra, Great House Vadal's highest award for valor. Except, his last marriage had been arranged as an insult, to a woman of the worker caste, a lowly baker's daughter, in order to seal a contract concerning the supply of bread. Yet that had turned out to be the best thing that had ever happened to him. No...A soldier only got so much luck in one lifetime, and Jagdish had already used up more than his share. "Maybe someday."

"You're a good man, Jagdish. Don't deny yourself happiness."

"I won't. And may your situation resolve so you can get on with your life as well. I hope that the news I have helps you toward that."

Rada had kept the details of why she was in hiding secret at first, but she had slipped eventually. They had been gathered for a dinner, and one of his other guests had asked Jagdish about what it had been like, fighting alongside the infamous Ashok Vadal. He had begun to tell the now familiar story once more, when Rada had become surprisingly incensed, and declared that the brave and noble Lord Protector Devedas would surely catch that foul criminal. Jagdish had heard such things many times while telling stories about the Sons of the Black Sword, but Rada's feelings on the subject had seemed particularly intense and personal.

Afterward, Jagdish had asked her about the outburst, and she had told him the truth of her relationship with Devedas. Which had been yet another unexpected surprise about the curious young lady, but it certainly explained why she had such an important and capable bodyguard. Jagdish had been glad to give her his word that he would not speak of it again... mostly because it spared him from any further awkward conversations about how his illegal house guest's secret lover, the chief Law enforcer in the world, was on a mission to kill Jagdish's good friend, the most wanted criminal in the history of Lok.

"While we were in Sarnobat we intercepted one of their messengers on his way back from the Capitol. Lord Protector Devedas has returned from the south, triumphant."

It took a moment for understanding to set in, then Rada began to smile. "It is done? Has Ashok been brought to justice? Is the Black Heart dead?"

Jagdish nodded. "The messenger confirmed it. He'd seen the grand parade with his own eyes."

Karno looked toward the sunset, and just for a moment, the giant let a small bit of emotion show. Jagdish had seen that distant look many times on the face of soldiers who had just been told an old comrade was gone. Ashok might have betrayed their Order, but he and Karno had been brothers once.

As had Jagdish... "I was told they held a great celebration in Devedas' honor. He is the hero of the Capitol now."

"I can't believe it. This is wonderful!" Rada was ecstatic. When she laughed, Pari laughed too. "If he's there, then I can finally go home. No more running. No more being a hostage to bitter men! You have no idea how much I miss my library. I thought I was going to have to go from here to hiding on another goat farm, or once again sleeping in the sand and having to shake scorpions from my shoes! I can go *home*!" Then it slowly dawned on her who she was speaking with, and a sudden and profound shame crossed her face. "Oh, Jagdish, I'm so sorry. Ashok was your friend, and I'm carrying on like a fool."

"He was my friend, but I bear neither you nor your Lord

Protector any ill will. We all have to march a different road. When we parted Ashok understood where his road would certainly lead. You'll be told Ashok was a monster, and to some he was, but to me he was a man of honor, the likes of which the world has rarely seen."

"He was the best of us…" Karno muttered, then abruptly stood up. "Pardon me. I must prepare for tomorrow."

Jagdish understood. A warrior could show passion to the world, but never weakness.

"Are you alright?" Rada asked. "Leaving seems inappropriate."

"I'm your Protector, not your chaperone. Say your goodbyes. We have a long journey ahead of us tomorrow."

Jagdish stood and gave a very respectful bow. "Farewell, Karno Uttara. Should we ever meet again, may it be while we are on the same side of the Law."

Karno returned the gesture, then left.

After the door was closed, Jagdish returned to his cushions. "That's an honorable man there. You're in good hands, Rada."

"Why would you say that about being on the other side of the Law from a Protector, though? Karno is just, and would never harm anyone who didn't have it coming."

"The Protectors frown on illegal house wars, while my orders are to hound Sarnobat until a full war breaks out, hoping they'll send their bearer so we can kill him and take his sword. I've been told this bright, albeit illegal, strategy of Harta's was originally suggested to him by an advisor from the Capitol. An odd young lady who has allegedly memorized as many books as Ashok Vadal has killed men."

"Well, that last part is certainly an exaggeration. I don't know if there's that many books in all the Capitol." Rada bounced Pari on her knee. "But you should know Harta had already decided on this plan long before he asked me to speak to his phonthos about the history of black steel blades. He's a very calculating man."

"I've gathered that. Which is why I assume I'll be the one blamed for starting his illegal war."

"What do you mean?"

"Think about it. Harta rewarded me with this rank because he couldn't be seen punishing me, but to him I will always be the man who rode with Ashok, the fraud who caused his mother's death and broke his family's sword. Vadal will seize Sarnobat's ancestor blade—should they be foolish enough to send it to the front—but eventually the Capitol will send the Protectors to restore order. That usually means executing everyone responsible, and I've already personally led half a dozen border incursions since spring."

Rada was very smart, but not what Jagdish would consider worldly. Once she focused on a new idea, however, he could almost imagine her mind working like the complicated gears spinning in his clock. She was probably recalling some book about politics and finding historical examples that confirmed he was right properly damned.

"The judges can't abide house wars. Harta gets the credit for your successes, his house gets a new ancestor blade, then you take the blame for his ambitions. This makes political sense... But what will you do? Surely you can't just blunder on to your death."

Jagdish shrugged as politics was a new world to him. "I don't know yet. Except... maybe when the time comes for the Protectors to hang me, you could put in a word with your new husband that I was an excellent host."

"I would, but Protectors have to step down from that obligation before they can wed, so I don't know if Devedas would be able to sway them."

"I was joking, Rada. I'll figure it out. In the meantime, it's no longer safe here for noncombatants. I'll be sending Pari to live with her mother's family for a time." The idea of his flesh and blood being raised by bakers wounded his pride, but the front was no place for the innocent, and after today, there was no doubt he had succeeded in provoking a war. "Your idea—or Harta's as it may be—isn't a bad one. Vadal does need an ancestor blade, so this is our best chance to take one."

"You'd save your house, just so it could sacrifice you?"

"I'll do my duty, as we all must, no matter the difficulty or danger. Just like you or Karno did coming here, or your Devedas hunting Ashok, or even Ashok in his own manner, because there's no way that man turned criminal by his own free will."

Rada didn't seem to care for that comparison. "Ashok is different, though. His whole identity was based on a lie. Ashok was made into something he was not."

"Is that very different from what Harta did for me? Declaring me to be a hero rather than a criminal? I much prefer promotion to execution, but let's not pretend my attaining this station was particularly honorable."

"I meant no offense. I know something about obligations being twisted by lies. It's how I got involved in all this mess to begin with..." Then Rada hesitated, like those extremely fast gears were struggling with a particularly hard decision. The last time Jagdish had seen her like that, she'd been deciding whether to tell him about her affair with Devedas or not.

"Spit it out."

"You spent a lot of time around Angruvadal, that entire time Ashok was one of your prisoners and then more with him after the blade was broken. Did Ashok ever say anything about the black steel... *talking* to him? Or maybe it predicting the future?"

That was certainly a strange turn in the conversation. "I recall him talking about how it aided him. It retained the instincts of all who wielded it before, and I know that it would warn him of danger sometimes. Black steel is scary. I've seen wizards do incredible things with a tiny fragment, but an intact piece, who knows what that's capable of? I'm not sure how—"

There was some commotion in the courtyard below. Jagdish rose to see that several horsemen had just arrived, and they were flying a banner he recognized. "Phontho Gotama... About time you showed your face, you son of a fish-eating whore." So much for not being vulgar in front of a lady of the highest caste. "If you'd excuse me, Rada, I need to deal with this blight on my profession. Would you—"

"I've got Pari," Rada assured him. "You're not going to duel him, are you?"

"Of course not," Jagdish said as he picked up his sword belt. "He's too old. He'll surely have a bodyguard stand as his proxy."

She was aghast. "You warriors are maddening!"

Zaheer met him at the door. "Sir, Phontho Gotama is here." His bodyguard noted his commander was buckling on his sword belt. "I see you are aware."

"Oh, I'm aware."

Jagdish pushed past him and went down the stairs, past the house slave bringing up his dinner, through the main hall that was currently serving as a field hospital, and out into the courtyard. Rada and Zaheer followed him. Jagdish didn't even pause long enough to put on his shoes.

The delegation from the Mukesh Garrison was dismounting. Jagdish had briefly met Gotama once before but knew nothing about the man beyond his reputation of being smug, yet capable. Though equals in status, Gotama was twenty years Jagdish's elder, which was a normal age for a phontho. Jagdish was extremely young to have risen to such a prestigious rank. Was today's mistake actually some kind of attack against him? Had Gotama knowingly let raiders pass as some manner of payback against someone seen as an upstart, or a potential rival? It disgusted him that such behavior was even a possibility, and that any member of his caste could be so dishonorable as to risk the lives of fellow warriors, but the other possibility was incompetence, which was nearly as bad.

Jagdish walked with purpose across the courtyard. "Gotama!"

The other phontho was a tall, wiry man, with a shock of white hair, and many scars across his face. "Ah, Phontho Jagdish. It is good to see you are well and your house did not burn—"

"Are you a traitor or a fool?"

Jagdish's angry words drew the attention of the entire estate. Many of his men were watching, some of them wearing bandages from the day's conflict. The bodies had been carried outside for cremation, but the casteless were still washing off the blood. If anything, the assembled witnesses were just as displeased as Jagdish.

"I'm neither." Gotama didn't seem particularly surprised by this turn of events. "However, I see grave offense has been taken."

"Offense has been given!"

As soon as Jagdish said those words—the legal prerequisite for a duel—the mood in the courtyard changed, because when a proud warrior claimed offense, bloodshed was almost certain to follow. Gotama's bodyguards immediately moved protectively in front of their phontho.

Jagdish approached them, alone. If he were going to duel it would be here, beneath his fruit trees. He didn't know how good Gotama's chosen swordsman would be, but in the unlikely event he was better than Jagdish, let his last act be to water the grass.

Gotama's men moved their hands to the hilts of their swords.

"Easy, lads. He's right to be mad." Gotama had clearly expected this sort of reception as a possibility, as he continued addressing Jagdish, friendly, but firm. "I've heard tales of your skill and fury, Jagdish, demon killer, so I'd rather not have it aimed at me. Calm yourself long enough to hear my words and understand that this offense was *not* intended."

"It was your garrison's duty to guard the border while mine was striking into Sarnobat, taking treasure and hostages for the glory of Vadal. Except I came home to find *this*." Jagdish gestured at the ashen wreckage. "Explain yourself."

"I'm not accustomed to anyone making demands of me other than Harta Vadal himself, but I understand your anger is a moral one. The seventh and tenth paltans of the Mukesh Garrison were supposed to be on patrol at the time the Sarnobat raiding party must have passed through. When I heard what happened my first inclination was to bring you the heads of those risalders in a sack as an apology, but I'll have to spare their lives after I heard their explanation."

"Which is?"

Gotama snapped his fingers, and another warrior rushed forward to hand him a piece of paper. Then he pushed past his bodyguards. When they went to follow him, he waved them away, and approached Jagdish on his own. That took an impressive amount of bravery considering Jagdish's reputation as a duelist who had volunteered to spar against Black-Hearted Ashok every day. The older phontho held out the paper, and Jagdish snatched it from him.

The first thing he noticed was that the letter had been printed on a press, but there was a handwritten note at the bottom that had been personally signed and stamped by a senior judge of Great House Vadal and..."The Grand Inquisitor Omand Vokkan?"

"The golden mask himself. This letter was presented to my seventh and tenth, and they were immediately obligated to obey under penalty of Law and weren't even given time to wait for another unit to send replacements. I'm lucky one of my risalders was disobedient enough to sneak off a runner with this to inform me or I wouldn't have known at all. I'd have thought they were deserters."

"Who commandeered your men?"

"Inquisitors," Gotama said the word with so much sneering disgust that it must have taken all his will not to spit on the ground. Perhaps Jagdish had misjudged this man? "Several of them, a witch hunter among their number, arrived at the border checkpoint, told my men congratulations, we require all of you to escort us to our destination, so move out immediately, or face the wrath of the Law."

"Those masked bastards."

"Sarnobat must have been waiting on the other side, and when they saw their opportunity, they took it."

"I can't believe I came home to find the wolf at my door because of Inquisitors."

"If you want to become even angrier, read the whole letter and see what they expect the rest of us to do. You can read, right?"

Jagdish snorted. Many warriors couldn't, but everyone who served in the Personal Guard of House Vadal had to be literate, so he did. The hastily added note at the bottom said the bearers of this seal were authorized to claim whatever Vadal forces they wanted. It had been signed by a Vadal judge stationed in the Capitol, and it had likely come straight from there and had not gone through their Thakoor first. There was no way Harta—despite his many flaws—would remove defenses while trying to start a war.

Then there was the part that had been printed on a machine. That usually meant many copies had been made, so this message was intended for wide distribution. Jagdish's frown deepened as he read through madness. "Every warrior is supposed to stop whatever we're doing and go slaughter every single casteless we can find? What manner of idiotic nonsense is this? This isn't Akershan. There's no casteless rebellion in these lands. Is this what they took your soldiers away to do? Kill defenseless non-people?"

"No. They're to be used for guard duty for some secret Inquisition business to the northeast. I recognize your disgust, Jagdish, because I share it. This dereliction of duty brought violence to your house, and shame to my name." Then Gotama surprised him again, by giving Jagdish a respectful bow, exposing his neck to the sword. "My sincere apologies."

This was not at all what he had expected. Jagdish rubbed his face in his hands and said, "Stand up. Now I'm embarrassed for both of us."

Gotama rose and gave him a knowing smirk. "I suspected you would be a man of reason. Others say it must have taken a savage to hunt down swamp wizards, but I wagered anyone who could pull off such a feat and live had to be clever as well. I am glad I guessed correctly."

"Are you two still going to duel?" Rada asked hesitantly, from a safe distance away. "I'd rather not approach with a child in my arms if there's going to be swords swinging about."

"We're good." Jagdish raised his voice so the whole estate could hear. "Offense has been forgotten. All is well."

Many of his men looked disappointed, because they had seen how good Jagdish was with a blade. Gotama's bodyguards seemed very relieved. They must have heard the tales.

"It will be truly well when these disrespectful Inquisitors are forced to choke on this note." Gotama kept his voice low so only Jagdish would hear. "I thought you might like to come with me to reclaim my soldiers? The masks might be prideful enough to be discourteous to one phontho, but even they can't be dumb enough to disrespect two. They have a day's head start on us. We should be able to catch them and be back before Sarnobat gets up to anything new."

"I like this plan. Agreed."

Rada came over. "May I see that letter?" Jagdish gave it to her, only to have her squint and move it back and forth before her eyes. "Drat. I miss my glasses."

"Is this lovely young lady your wife, Jagdish?"

"My wife is dead. The child is mine. This woman is a guest of my house."

"Apologies again." Then Gotama cocked his head to the side. "A widower, eh? You know, I have an unmarried daughter."

"Not now," Jagdish told him, because Rada appeared to be under great distress.

"You spoke of the casteless, Jagdish? What did it say about them?"

The letter was so grisly and outlandish that it was difficult to summarize. "It says the Law requires the killing of all the non-people in Lok. Every last one. The workers are supposed to deprive them of food and water, while we warriors are supposed to put them to the sword, burn them, or drown them in the sea. It's to be called—"

"The Great Extermination," Rada whispered, horrified.

"You know of this?"

"It's all my fault."

# Chapter 11

~~~~~~~

True to Guru Dondrub's word, the monastery proved to be a quiet place for Ashok to heal. The monks' simple diet was a feast compared to the near nothing he had been subsisting on, and they seemed happy to share it. Ashok ate an astonishing amount of their food. A week of rest and exercise gave the Heart of the Mountain time to repair his battered body, but it was an impatient time, restless with thoughts of home, and interrupted constantly by the Guru's questions and inane tests.

Sometimes Dondrub asked about the cultures of Lok, or some aspect of the Law. Other times he tried to find out Ashok's philosophy on various topics, as if trying to ascertain if he would make a proper leader or not. When his answers didn't fit the Guru's preconceived notions of right and wrong, a lecture would inevitably begin. Except Ashok had no time for such foolishness. He was not some Capitol judge, sitting in the shade while slaves fanned him, leisurely pontificating about things he barely understood without repercussion. Ashok had work to do, and that required him to get off this damnable frozen island.

The monastery was a small building of mortared stone, and almost entirely lacking in comforts or ornamentation. It was high on a rocky hillside, and it reminded Ashok of the Hall

109

of Protectors and his time as an acolyte there—not in size, but rather in its stark utilitarian nature.

The monks slept in tiny alcoves on mats made of woven reeds. He had been assigned one of those and given some of their simple robes to wear after he had scrubbed the filth from his body in a freezing mountain stream. Since his hair and beard had been so matted and infested with lice, he had cut it all off. Even though he was taller and broader than the others, emaciated, robed, and shaved bald, Ashok could have passed for one of the monks. Except as far as he could tell, these men had devoted their lives to peaceful contemplation, which was where the semblance ended, as Ashok had walked a very different path.

The monks didn't talk much. He was told some of them even took vows of silence that lasted days, months, or whole seasons at a time. This was a marked improvement to the only other priest Ashok had previously been exposed to, as Keta rarely shut his mouth. However, when these monks did speak, they were difficult to understand. Their language was similar to his, but the people of Fortress had a dialect that was hard to understand, and they often used unfamiliar words. It required listening carefully to avoid confusion. The guru was the only one of them who seemed to speak in a manner close to what the Law mandated as the standard tongue across the great houses.

On the second day at the monastery, Ashok had found a stick of the proper length and weight to begin practicing his sword forms in the yard. Healing required exercise. Having been chained near unmoving for so long, fatigue was immediate, but Ashok continued working, clumsy at first, but skills so ingrained returned quickly. The monks seemed to pass their time tending their gardens, chanting to their strange idols, or reading old tomes, but Ashok's warlike practice always drew spectators.

The strange bald men sat upon stones and watched as Ashok ran through drills that had been taught to him by sword master Ratul. To him, the familiar actions were comforting. To the quiet monks, they must have seemed frightening.

Over the years the Heart of the Mountain had rapidly repaired many terrible wounds that had been inflicted upon his body. Except those had been localized—a broken bone, a laceration from a sword, or a puncture from a spear. It turned out that starvation caused a more generalized injury of the entire person, and thus took more time to recover. Unless there was something to the Guru's claim that he'd slept through most of a year, and he was now recovering from that mysterious hibernation, but Ashok still found that idea absurd.

Despite all that, soon he would be capable of returning to his duty, and that knowledge helped Ashok work through the pain.

"I'm told the outsider once again raises his imaginary sword against imaginary foes," Guru Dondrub said as he approached. "It is like watching a dancer dance, only without the music or beauty."

He knew the Guru was wrong about that. There was a certain beauty to be found in combat, but very few men were capable of truly appreciating it. Ashok finished the drill with a decapitating strike. "It is necessary to practice until effective movement happens without thought."

"Ah, but one would assume acting without thinking would lead to bad consequences."

"You think before you act, not during. There is not time to pause for reflection in combat. You may be considered wise, but you do not know much about war."

"That is true. I have been fortunate in that respect."

"I have not . . ." Ashok wiped the sweat from his brow with the back of his hand. "What do you want now?"

The old man leaned upon his staff. "I hoped to continue our conversation from yesterday. Where were we?"

"You were hoping I would say something to convince you I'm this ancient hero you seek. I remain not him."

"Good. Then we're all caught up." Dondrub looked toward the assembled audience of monks, and shouted, "Don't you all have work to do? I was just going through your collection of Vedas and noted your library is very dusty. Perhaps you should be spending more time studying and less time gawking."

As the chastised underlings scurried off, Ashok said, "I am thankful for your aid, and the hospitality they have shown me, but I must return to Lok soon."

"Is this more acting without thought? You're not yet strong enough to fight your way through an army of smugglers to discover your way home."

"Such a battle would not be necessary if you simply told me how your people get there."

Dondrub spread his hands apologetically. "I've already told you this is a secret I do not possess. That secret belongs to the guilds, and I'm not of any guild."

Ashok had learned that guilds were somewhat different from houses, as they were not divided by territory, but by skills. "Which ones know?"

"The Traders, the Collectors, perhaps the Weapons Guild. The first two are few in number now. The last is great, but I doubt more than a handful of their number have been shown the path."

"How do I find them?"

"I would tell you where to go, but our names for places have no meaning to you." As Ashok scowled at that, the Guru quickly added, "However, in the morning, I can take you into the nearest town. You have some allies among the guilds there. The collectors who found you on the beach believe you to be the Avatar of Ramrowan. I'm sure they will be glad to help you."

Ashok gave him a respectful nod. "Thank you."

"But first—"

"There it is."

"What?" Dondrub feigned innocence. "Will you not humor an old man on his lifelong quest to serve his gods?"

"Fine." Ashok put the stick back where he'd found it, since he wouldn't be needing it any longer. "Give me more of your riddles."

"They are not riddles, merely an attempt at better understanding. Tell me, Ashok Vadal, what do you know of magic?"

"My knowledge is limited."

"You were the bearer of one of the great and rare ancestor blades, relics forged by the hand of Ramrowan himself. So that is a lie."

Ashok was many things, but he was no liar. He would blame this insult on a difference of tongues. "Angruvadal chose me. I did my best to carry it with honor, but I failed. I am no wizard."

"But you know the different types of magic?"

"Legal and illegal," Ashok replied automatically.

"That is not what I meant. I mean the sources, not whether your Capitol controls them or not."

"Black steel or demon."

"And?"

Ashok hesitated, for what did this strange old man know of the third way? "Historically, there have been only two."

"If this prophet you serve has truly been called, then you know there is another. I speak of magic that comes not from the sea or the sword"—he pointed one arthritic finger upward—"but from the sky. It was said that when a new age was to begin a holy bolt would come down from the heavens, as a sign the gods had chosen a new mouthpiece for their will. The Voice would have access to all the knowledge of the gods, and power limited only by their willingness to use it. It is quite the gift."

Thera had performed feats the likes of which Ashok had never seen from any wizard, but it was no gift. It was a constant source of sorrow and danger, and it had made her a target of very evil men. Ashok had protected Thera's life, but it was a life cursed with trouble because of the Voice. Only he would speak of none of that before this stranger.

On the other hand, in his land all things pertaining to the gods had been erased by the Inquisition, while these foreigners seemed to retain much of that knowledge. Maybe he could learn something here that could help Thera? She had been eager to let Sikasso take the Voice from her, but even the House of Assassins' skilled wizards had never figured out how.

"Tell me what else you know of this Voice, Guru."

"Only what Ramrowan told his children before he left this world. It is easier to show you." He began tottering away on his staff. "Come. It's not far."

He followed. There was a seldom-used path that led down the hill, across a rocky shelf that looked out over the misty valley below, and then down into a narrow ravine filled with sharp rocks. Ashok was thankful for the sandals he had been given, because the soles of his feet still ached from the journey across this land of razors.

"This is the reason they built this monastery here. There are ruins in the valley, with carvings that date from just after the time of Ramrowan. The monks do their best to maintain them. You go ahead, it will take me a moment to make my way down."

Ashok took one look at the old man, using a staff to balance himself on the treacherously steep path, and shook his head. "I will assist you." Taking him by the arm, Ashok helped him down the slope. The rock around them soon took on a different character, from broken and sharp, to smooth, as if it had been worked by some unknown tool. It reminded him of the hidden chamber that held the Heart of the Mountain or the complex of buildings within the Creator's Cove. They were descending into what had clearly been a room once, except the roof had been torn away in some long-forgotten cataclysm.

"I take it you've seen the ancient's methods of construction before."

"I have."

"Then you know sometimes they liked to leave messages in stone."

"Those are rare in my land." What hadn't been erased by time was taken away by the Historians Order—unless the signs were deemed to be religious, then the Inquisition smashed them into dust. "I have seen a few."

"Tell me of those."

"The most noteworthy was a map. Not just of Lok, but the entire ancient world, and all the other continents. My sword master said those were once home to many nations, with different languages, different color skin, and even different laws. No one knows what happened to those after the demons came."

"It is said in those days man had filled the whole world! Such a map would be quite the sight to see, but this is not like that at all."

The back wall had a huge metal plaque affixed to it, covered in raised symbols, most of which meant nothing to Ashok. There were common letters upon it, but they were mixed with unfamiliar ones, put together to form words he couldn't decipher. "What is this?"

"It was meant to be a monument, to commemorate important events. This is just one part of the story, but there are many of these scattered across Xhonura, to chronicle important events. Together they tell a story. I imagine these were scattered across your mainland as well, but your Law probably had them melted down."

"Read it."

The old man squinted as he moved closer to the wall. "In the beginning, the gods took this barren world and made it fruitful for us. They made the air pure and covered the land in plants and animals for us to harvest. They placed man here, so that we might grow in number and wisdom, and for centuries we prospered. Some of the gods even walked among us, while most of them remained above, watching over the world from their castles in the sky, like Upagraha."

"The gods live on one of the moons?" That sounded bizarre to him. If the gods lived on one of the moons, why not Canda? It was the bigger and brighter moon, waxing and waning majestically, while Upagraha looked tiny in comparison, nothing but a fast-moving light across the sky every night. "You believe all this nonsense?"

"How could you not, bearer of Ramrowan's sword? It is time you hear his real account. Not the crippled version, pieced together by desperate blind men, after centuries of your Law trying to obscure the truth."

Though Ashok knew he had been wronged by the Law, it was hard to entirely forsake that which had made him. The idea of listening to religious fanaticism remained a distasteful one, but he was not doing this for himself. He was doing it for Thera. "I will listen and try not to disrespect you further."

"I would still preach the truth even if you mocked every word as I said it, because the truth is the truth. I share this in the hopes you can take it back with you, to share with your priests, in the hopes they will learn from our mistakes."

"Continue, then."

The Guru did, and it was obviously part reading, and part telling a familiar story. "It says while we are the children of the gods, the demons were the foul offspring of something else, a dark force that lived among the stars, jealous of our gods' accomplishments."

That part Ashok found plausible, because it sounded like what Thera described having faced in the graveyard of demons, and she was one of the few people in the world whose word he trusted.

"The gods had created black steel as the ultimate manifestation of their powers, a substance able to alter the world according to their whims. It was created in a forge that required heat great as the sun." Dondrub traced his fingers over the symbols reverently. "The evil tried to copy this miracle and gave life to demons instead. The demons hated the gods, for the gods rejected them. The demons made war on the gods, and all of mankind watched as the two sides filled the heavens above us with fire and thunder for many days. It was war the likes of which had never been seen before or since. Except as this war in the heavens raged, the gods could not protect their children below..."

"The rain of demons," Ashok said.

"Yes. Wherever the demons fell, they laid to waste. Our land of prosperity was torn asunder. Knowledge was lost. Rivers ran red with blood as our old world was destroyed. One by one the other castles were torn from the sky, including the forge of the gods, until only Upagraha remained. Many gods perished, yet ultimately the last of them prevailed. Once the evil was defeated, only then could they turn their eyes back to their creation and were horrified to find that our people were being massacred by the demons."

This part Keta had talked about many times. "So the gods sent one warrior riding down from the sky in a vessel made of black steel, to give that magic to the survivors, so we could drive the demons into the sea."

"It delights me that some small measure of truth has not been ruined by your blighted Law! Except you are only part right. Ramrowan was not ordered here. He begged the injured gods to let him go to us. For Ramrowan was more than just a mortal warrior. He had been bred to be a soldier of the gods. Improved in every way, with the very blood of the gods running through his veins." Dondrub's hand paused at one of the carvings. He tapped it twice. "He was a fusion of flesh and black steel magic, the first Protector."

Ashok scowled, because that symbol was familiar. It was one of the repetitive designs, usually inlaid in silver, traditionally marked upon Protector armor. "I know that one."

"I thought you might. Except in those days your kind were created to be Protectors of humanity, not Protectors of Law. That perversion came later. Using a special device that had been given to him by the gods, Ramrowan was able to make more Protectors like unto him, but they were pale imitations, as magic alone could not make them equal to his blood."

That device had to be the Heart of the Mountain. "What do you know of this process?"

"Very little."

"You should keep it that way."

Dondrub didn't seem to know how to respond to that, so he continued his tale. "These Protectors were mighty, but they were mere shadows of Ramrowan's power, for how can any man, even one augmented by black steel, approach the power of someone who is part god? It is said he could call down fire and lightning from the sky. Nothing could kill him, neither blade nor bullet, burning heat or icy cold. Yet even he needed help to defeat the demons, so from his ship Ramrowan created the weapons that would come to be known as ancestor blades and gave one to each surviving tribe in Lok. Once they were united together, they pushed the demons into the sea."

"The ocean is hell. Let the demons have it. Man will retain the land. Trespassers will be dealt with. Thus it has been. Thus it ever shall be."

"You don't get it, do you?" Dondrub asked. "I should not be surprised. You believe whatever your Law tells you, only your Law is deluded and has forgotten the old ways."

"You are fortunate I no longer take personal offense for slights against the Law, old man."

"The Law lies. There is no *truce* between man and demonkind. They *will* return. Not one or two at a time as they have in recent centuries, but an army of demons, to finish what they started."

"I've fought more demons than anyone." It wasn't bragging, rather a statement of fact. "I do not doubt their capacity for hate. Five at once might as well be an army, but there is no sign of an invasion."

"Do you have eyes that can see beneath the sea, Ashok Vadal? The gods know all that is and what may be. Mighty Ramrowan's final words declared that the demons would return in time, and we must be ready to stop them, or all would perish."

"When?"

"Only the gods know. Which is why we must remain vigilant. More importantly, Ramrowan warned that only someone with his sainted blood would be able to unlock the full might of the gods to repel the invaders when the time came. Without this chosen bloodline, we would be doomed. This was so vital that the sons of Ramrowan made sure that their bloodline could never be eradicated."

Keta had preached about this next part many times, so Ashok was curious to hear the old man's version. "What became of these sons?"

"They ruled as kings. They took many wives, to perpetuate their line, as did the generations after them, until their family was so great in number their bloodline could never die out."

"And?"

"And what?"

"Will you not speak of how these kings ruled as tyrants over the castes they had created to serve them, taking whatever they wanted—women, treasure, and land? Until the people they were supposed to save grew to hate them more than the demons they had started to forget. The castes decided this legend was a lie, an excuse for their kings to do evil, and rose up to slay their masters. Those who were spared were declared less than people and condemned to live in filth forever. The Age of Kings ended, and the Age of Law began."

The Guru nodded slowly. "I am surprised. Your Law has long forbidden speaking about the origins of your casteless. I'm surprised you know how they came to be."

"My rebellion's priest loves to tell stories."

"Then he was taught better than I expected. You encouraged me to speak, curious to see if, in my bias, I would leave out uncomfortable truths about our forebearers. This time you were testing me, and in my weakness I failed. Very clever. Then let us speak of the uncomfortable truths. The kings may have been descended from gods, but they had the appetites of men. Great was their hubris. It was surely worse than your priest knows. Imagine, being the only thing standing between your people and certain oblivion. Wouldn't that fill you with pride?"

"I have. It did not."

The Guru cocked his head at that. "Then you are an odd one, Ashok Vadal."

"And I think you are probably as deluded as my priest Keta. How are casteless supposed to defeat an army of demons?"

"Are you not yourself born of that line? Have you not beaten demons?"

Ashok scoffed, because he was hardly the average casteless. "What is this power of the gods they are supposedly able to claim?"

"That knowledge has been lost. It is said that it will be revealed again when the time is right."

"How convenient for you." Ashok grew weary of these religious types and their vague pronouncements. "I've seen demons tear through entire paltans of well-trained warriors, like a fox among chickens. Yet you would feed non-people into their hungry jaws in the hopes your god will answer their cries. Enough. You said there was something about the third way of magic. Where is it?"

"Over here."

Ashok followed the gesture to the bottom portion of the plaque, and tried to decipher the message to himself, but to no avail. "Read it to me."

"'In the final days before the demons come again, a messenger will be sent from Upagraha to choose a mortal conduit to be their Voice. Whoever shall receive this gift shall be blessed above all others, for the Voice will have direct access to whatever knowledge the gods see fit to grant them. Neither black steel nor demon is as mighty as the gods' will. The Voice will perform miraculous works in their name.'"

"How does one get rid of this Voice?"

"What?" Dondrub may have been a wise man, but he clearly had never thought of anyone asking *that*. "It's mightier than black steel...why would...I don't..."

"So it doesn't say." Ashok was disappointed, but unsurprised. If there was an easy way to escape that burden, Thera would have found it by now. She was a determined one. "You are almost at the end. Finish it."

Dondrub was still trying to grasp the idea of willingly giving up the power of the gods, but he just shook his head and went back to the message, disturbed enough he was simply reading now rather than spinning a familiar tale. "'The gods will choose priests to strengthen the Voice's people, and a mighty warrior— the spirit of Ramrowan upon him—to protect the Voice's life, a great king to rule over all the land.'"

Ashok snorted in derision.

"What?"

"This silly passage is why you keep testing me to see if I would be a good ruler?"

"It is. Why does this amuse you? These words were carved by priests who personally served Ramrowan!" Now it was the Guru's turn to take offense. "This is sacred. Don't mock these words."

"I do not mock them. I mock your comprehension of them. I might actually be the Forgotten's warrior. I've seen enough that I do not doubt the reality of the Voice, nor the fact that it is my duty to protect her."

"*Her?* The Voice is a *woman?*"

Ashok held up one hand to silence him. "However, your mistake is taking this to mean the protector and the king are the same man. I know the one who would be king. He's the reason I ended up in the ocean. His name is Devedas. Perhaps you should check if *he* is Ramrowan? Though don't be surprised when he runs you through with his sword for talking about illegal religion."

"That can't be . . ." The Guru turned back to the words that he had surely read hundreds of times before. "Impossible. There have been other wise men who have interpreted it that way, but that can't be right . . . And a woman? Are you sure the Voice is female?"

Of that fact, Ashok was extremely certain. "Yes. Her life matters to me more than the rest of you combined."

"Ah . . ."

"That's all?"

"Is this not enough?"

"No." Ashok pointed at the last section of text. "I may not know these letters, but I can count the words. Finish it."

Dondrub looked at Ashok, then the final symbols, then Ashok again. "Well, that is of no importance."

"I spent twenty years hunting criminals. I can tell when someone is hiding something from me. Continue."

The Guru tried to act as if he had not been caught. "It'll be sundown soon. I'm old and it's a climb. Perhaps we should—"

"Read it and I will know if you lie."

"Very well . . ." The Guru sighed. "It says despite the efforts of protector or priests, it is foretold the Voice must be sacrificed, as there is no other way to stop the demons forever."

Ashok's hands reflexively clenched into fists. Even if the threat against his charge was millennia old, it still remained a threat. "You are wrong."

"Not this time! That previous section has some archaic wording, but the last line is a straightforward declaration. There is nothing to misinterpret."

"Then your gods are wrong."

"Do not blaspheme in this holy—"

"We are done. I am leaving now. Take me to your smugglers."

"It's a long walk!" Dondrub protested. "The paths are treacherous in the dark. It will be freezing. We'll fall down a cliff."

Ashok grabbed a handful of robes and hauled the Guru toward him, lifting him to his toes so that they were face-to-face. Even recovering from starvation, Ashok was mighty in comparison to the frail elder. "I do not care if you show me the way, send a guide, or draw me a map, but I am going home *now*."

# Chapter 12

The Guru rode upon a cart pulled by a yak, led by a monk. Ashok walked. Five of the monks had accompanied them, each of whom was carrying a lantern on the end of a pole to keep their group from making a wrong turn in the dark. The path was narrow, with rock walls on one side and a steep drop on the other.

The night was very cold, so the Guru was wrapped in a pile of blankets. The rest of them made do with their too-thin robes. Ashok could survive nearly anything, but this chill was enough to make him pity the monks.

"It is said discomfort leads to enlightenment, Ashok Vadal. Do you believe this?"

Ashok just gave the Guru a noncommittal grunt. He was tired of foolish questions.

"I do not know if I agree, but it is said that deprivation is good for the soul. These monks forgo comforts in an attempt to master themselves. That is why you should be happy for them. They needed to take the cart to town to get supplies anyway. This way they can make the journey in the bitter cold and pitch black, in order to bring themselves closer to understanding the nature of the universe."

"Why don't you get up and walk, then?"

"I'm not seeking enlightenment. That's their path. My purpose is to seek out the avatar of Ramrowan. And since we will be parting ways soon, I was hoping you would indulge an old man's curiosity a bit longer."

Ashok's patience had worn thin. "If you ask me anything else about philosophy, I'll throw you off this cliff."

"I will stick to practical matters, then. You said this man who would be king...Devedas? That he is the reason you wound up in the sea. Tell me about him."

"I would rather not."

"If the vast but barbaric nation to our north is to have a new governor, it behooves the people of Xhonura to know about his nature. Consider this answer a repayment for the kind generosity of these monks. Surely a place to lay your head, several days of nutritious gruel, and some moth-eaten robes to wear are worth some conversation in return."

What could Ashok say to this stranger about his once brother? "Devedas is the Lord Protector, but a secret criminal, plotting to overthrow the judges. We were close, and he was the best man I've ever known. When last we met, we dueled to the death. It was the hardest fight of my life, but I prevailed."

"You killed him, then?"

"No. I was about to, but I was stopped."

"How?"

Ashok paused, because repaying hospitality only went so far, but part of him wanted to talk about what had happened, because he didn't really understand it himself.

"I was poised to crush his head, but Angruvadal told me to spare his life, because Devedas was still necessary."

"How could this be? You told me Angruvadal shattered long before you went into the ocean."

"It did." Ashok placed one hand on his chest to feel the ragged scar tissue there. "When it was destroyed, a molten shard of it was launched into my heart. It eventually cooled, yet I can still feel it there. I believe some measure of Angruvadal's magic remains, as it sometimes warns me of danger and possibilities in battle, like it did when it was whole."

When the Guru didn't respond, Ashok looked back over his shoulder. By the light of the lantern hanging over the cart, he could see that Dondrub was staring at him, mouth agape, eyes wide.

"Impossible! There's black steel . . . *inside* your body? Black steel destroys mortal flesh. It is toxic. How are you still alive?"

"Angruvadal was my oldest friend. It did not wish to kill me." Ashok returned his attention to the path. Even his reflexes could not stave off gravity, should he step blindly off a cliff.

"No man could withstand having the element of the gods embedded beneath his skin. The magic found in demon flesh is weaker, which is why it can bond with a human, yet even then it will eventually cause the host to turn into a horrific hybrid creature."

"I have fought those," Ashok stated. "They are foul things, more dangerous than either of the beings they're made from."

"Demon is nothing compared to the magic of the ancients. Wizards say a fragment of black steel the size of my fingernail contains more magical energy than the whole body of a sea demon. Black steel is pure magic, designed by the gods themselves. No man could withstand such perfection."

"Do you doubt my word?"

"I'm not saying you're lying. I'm just struggling to understand." A moment later, the Guru asked, "Then this ghost of Angruvadal commanded you to stay your hand, and you did?"

"No. I still tried to kill Devedas, only when I did not listen, Angruvadal stopped my heart."

"Like a heart attack?"

"I would assume." Ashok had not enjoyed being chastised by his former sword, but its purposes were inscrutable. "I was rendered helpless. Devedas survived, his allies arrived, and I ended up unconscious in the river." He believed that had also been Angruvadal's doing, to keep him from being pierced by a volley of Garo arrows. It might also have been how he had made it across the icy sea, placed into a state similar to the southern frogs or lizards that survived each winter encased in blocks of ice, only to return to life in the spring.

Despite his obstinance, apparently Angruvadal still had need of him.

The Guru whistled. "And you say Angruvadal is your friend. I would hate to see what it does to its enemies!"

Over a thousand times, Ashok had seen what Angruvadal did to its foes, severing limbs and exploding bones. By its mysterious and unforgiving standards, it had treated Ashok with great compassion in comparison. "It is unpleasant."

"If what you say is true, Ashok Vadal, then you would be a unique specimen among mankind. No one has attempted to claim such power for themselves and lived to tell the tale, since the days of Ramrowan himself at least, and he was molded by the gods to be their perfect soldier. What would it even mean to be a hybrid of flesh and black steel? How could such a thing exist without the guidance of divine architects? The implications of this are . . . troubling."

"That is the least of my worries."

Except the Guru was too lost in thought to hear Ashok's muttered response, and they continued walking for a time, with the only sounds coming from the creak of the wheels, and the endless cries of unfamiliar seabirds. Of the wise man's many questions, he had finally gotten an answer that had rendered him too preoccupied to speak. It made Ashok wish that he'd told that story sooner.

However, their conversation had brought another incident to mind. During his battle with the wizard Sikasso, he had pronounced Ashok a hybrid, the same as him. Was this true? He had been killed, hung from a meat hook, yet had come back to life. Whether that made him some kind of magical abomination or not, it didn't change the importance of Ashok's vows. It was his duty to protect Thera, and anyone who intended to sacrifice her, whether they be man, demon, or god, would have to go through Ashok first.

"How much farther to this town?"

One of the monks gestured to the northwest. "We get there near sunrise, Avatara."

"Do not call me that."

"As you wish."

# Chapter 13

〰〰〰

The island of Fortress had always been a mystery to Ashok. He knew what he had been allowed to know, nothing more. It was a land of criminals, isolated heretics who refused to submit to reason and order. Despite being kept apart by a narrow patch of sea, their dangerous, illegal weapons sometimes found their way into the Law-abiding world to stir up trouble. There had been many failed attempts to invade, but separated by the demon-infested sea, the island might as well have been on a different world. The warriors who didn't drown or get torn apart by demons ended up blasted to pieces while trying to scale the various fortifications along the northern coasts.

As a young Protector, Ashok had often dreamed of being tasked with bringing justice to this place, because in those days the idea of so many living outside the reach of the Law had offended him greatly. A pragmatic man, Ashok did not have an imaginative nature; however, as a young Protector he had often wondered what it would be like to bring justice to this place. The coast would be like a vast castle, with defenses beyond comprehension. Beyond that would be a land of dedicated fanatics, armed with illegal weapons, willing to fight to the death.

In person, it was not nearly so impressive. On their journey down the mountain they passed very few farms, and he saw almost no tillable ground. Unless they had discovered a way to digest rocks, the population of the island could not be very numerous. It was doubtful the parts he had not seen yet were any more fruitful, and he reasoned that it would only get colder and more unforgiving to the south.

The town took up the top of a large hilltop. Through the haze of coal smoke, he saw that the buildings were low and wide, similar to how they lived in Devakula, built into the ground to retain warmth and resist wind. The town was surrounded by a wall, but it was only ten feet tall and made of brick. Such defenses would barely slow a demon, and they were near enough to the sea that Ashok could occasionally smell the saltwater and decay on the wind. In Lok, only the lowest of the low would dwell in a place so terrible. Demon incursions must have been a continuous danger.

"Do your Fortress rods work against sea demons?" Ashok asked the Guru, since the sharpest spears wielded by the strongest men rarely managed to pierce their hide.

"I wouldn't know. I'm a man of peace. Not a man of war."

"Demons will eat either." Then Ashok noticed one of the monks looked like he wanted to say something. "Speak up."

"Before taking my vows, I was in the Weapons Guild. Regular bullets bounce off demons. Soft lead flattens against their skin. But there are special guns for demon. Big." He spread his arms wide. "With heavy bullets of solid copper, with points like needles."

"Those will fell a demon?"

"Sometimes. It still takes many many bullets."

"You built guns?"

The monk nodded. "Yes. To take lives. Now I am here, sorry for what I've done to the gods' children. Now I try to make lives better."

Ashok didn't care about this monk's feelings of guilt or his attempted repentance, but if he had been wasting time with a supposed wise man when one of the men he was staying with had known the way home all along, he would be very displeased. "How do you smuggle these weapons into Lok?"

"My old guild builds and uses them, but don't sell. Only the Traders Guild takes the under path all the way to the mainland to see the infidels there." He pointed toward the town. "There be a Collectors Guild here, though. They go to the down below too. But not to trade, to scrounge the dark. The collectors know how to get across."

"As I assured you they would, Ashok Vadal. I would not lead you astray," the Guru said from atop the rocking cart. "But it is good you are so distrusting, for there are vipers in this place. Once we are inside those walls, it would be best if you let me do the talking. You are a stranger here and do not know our ways. By your current appearance these people will think you merely another monk, unless you open your mouth, and needlessly complicate all our lives."

"Very well."

They approached the gate as the sun rose over the mountain peaks. There were guards atop the wall, dressed in sealskin and armed with long Fortress rods. It wasn't until they got closer that Ashok realized there were hundreds of pockmarks in the brick, probably created over the years by lead projectiles. These walls weren't only for keeping out demons...

"You war amongst yourselves."

"Of course." The Guru sounded incredulous. "The guilds are quarrelsome. Conflict is the natural state of man. Did you assume Xhonura was so different from your land?"

Oddly enough, Ashok had. As if all of Fortress would be organized like a single great house, only as a society of criminals united together against the Law. He should have known better.

When they reached the gate, it was clear the guards there recognized the monks, but from their sneering contempt didn't care for them. For a moment Ashok thought the guards would turn them away, but they were allowed to pass through without issue.

The streets were muddy. A fine grit of coal dust coated every structure. Even at dawn's light, men were already laboring, marching back and forth carrying sacks and tools. It reminded Ashok of the workers' district in Neeramphorn, except poorer. Filthy people, thinner even than Ashok's current pathetic state, were sleeping near the gate, huddled in improvised shelters made of ratty blankets held up by sticks. The few of them who were awake held out cups as the monks passed, begging. Ashok didn't know what passed for money in this land, but apparently the monks had none to give...or perhaps this place was so harsh that even its supposed holy men could not be bothered to care?

"I did not know you had casteless here," Ashok said softly, so his foreign accent wouldn't be overheard by the guards.

"There are no castes in Xhonura. These are merely the poor."

They looked like casteless to him. "What's the difference?"

The Guru shrugged. "They are free to stop being poor."

"Your law allows them to sleep in your streets?"

"Where else would they go?"

They were approached by one guard who Ashok assumed outranked the others, because he had more symbols embroidered on his arm with colored string.

The Guru crossed his forearms, high on his chest, which was apparently a gesture of respect here. "I am Guru Dondrub of the Nalanda sect. These monks wish to purchase provisions, and I seek the Collectors Guild."

"Go that way until you see the southern gate. Their guild house is on the right side." The guard gave the monks a disgusted look, then cleared his throat and spit on the ground. "And we'll have no trouble from your cult this time—or else."

The monks kept their eyes averted as they led the yak cart away. Ashok was not good at feigning meekness, and when he met the guard's gaze directly, the man scowled. "What are you looking at, scum?"

After that insult, Ashok thought about answering, *A dead man.* He may have been born casteless, but that didn't mean he was good at putting up with insolence. Except pride would not aid him now, so he lowered his head, said nothing, and followed the others.

Once there was nobody near them, the Guru said, "I should have warned you. There has been a schism. There are competing factions among the followers of great Ramrowan. Ours is not currently the most favored here."

"That was obvious. Will this conflict harm my mission?"

"It shouldn't. These collectors are not apostate. They still believe in the correct way."

Then Ashok didn't care. This whole island could sink into the ocean after he was gone, and all would be well with him.

There were signs on many of the larger buildings, but the letters were different enough that he couldn't read them. That was a strange feeling, for in Lok, even the most distant houses used the same alphabet, as the Capitol mandated. From Sarnobat to Uttara, words were the same.

The townsfolk watched the monks and their clattering cart pass by, but very few of them paid the new arrivals any mind. The way Keta had spoken about the ancient priests of Ramrowan, they were supposed to have been mighty influences upon the people. This was not disrespect, like the guards had shown them, but it was at minimum indifference. Either Keta's history was wishful thinking, or the mighty had fallen a very long way.

"They dwindle in unbelief," the Guru said, almost as if he could read Ashok's thoughts. "We are seen as a nuisance now. For too long my kind kept demanding obedience, while promising them that the end was near. Stay faithful because our glorious reunification with the gods is at hand. Stay faithful because the spirit of Ramrowan will return soon, and you must be ready. Obey or else! People can only hear that so many times before they quit caring."

That made Ashok curious, because it was nothing at all like how Keta conducted himself as a priest, working himself ragged trying to serve and better his people. "What did you do for them?"

"A good question. To my predecessors' great shame, we took their tithes and gave them nothing in return but empty promises. We were aloof. Distant guardians of ancient wisdom, parading about in our fine raiment. It's no wonder over the years the guilds grew in influence while the priests became increasingly irrelevant. Even if you were who I hoped you were, I don't know if the people would believe."

Many times Ashok had seen Keta sacrifice his own comfort and safety to help his people. He never puffed himself up or made himself out to be greater than his followers. He asked for nothing extra, even though the faithful in the Cove would have been happy to give it to him. His only desire was to serve.

"My priest is better at this job than you are."

The Guru sighed. "I pray he is. The other sects, their temples are wealthy, while ours has forsaken riches as we try to regain our humility. I do not know if it will be enough in time... There is the guild house."

The building looked like all the others, an oddly triangular style—probably to keep too much snow from collecting and collapsing the roof—that would have been at home in frozen Devakula. The words painted on the wall were as meaningless as any other sign in this place to him, but their symbol was a pair of scissors—which brought back the memory of the clothing being cut off his frozen body on the beach—a pick, and a lantern.

"What do they collect?"

"Whatever they can. They are a small guild, yet important for traditional reasons," Guru Dondrub said as one of the monks helped him down from the cart. "Their jurisdiction is resources that neither grow, nor are dug from a mine. They prowl the ruins beneath, sending expeditions to search for anything the ancients might have left behind. When they aren't doing that, they patrol the shores, as the currents bring many interesting treasures from the mainland to our shores."

Only the most wretched of Lok's residents lived by the ocean, and he could only imagine what they would throw in the water. "They are collectors of trash."

"They found *you*."

That amused Ashok because most of the Law-abiding world would say that proved it.

"By now you must have realized this land is lacking certain resources. Nothing goes to waste in Xhonura." One of the monks handed the Guru his walking staff, and he started tottering toward the guild house.

Something was amiss. Ashok sensed the danger approaching long before the others. A group of five men had begun following them, and from their manner, he could tell they were exciting themselves toward violence. In Lok, he would have assumed they were worker caste, practitioners of some hardy physical trade, but in this strange land, who knew? However, the young man who was clearly their master was dressed in robes similar to the monks'. Only his were bright yellow and appeared to be much higher in quality.

"Someone is following us," Ashok warned.

Dondrub glanced that way, saw who it was, said, "Oh bother," and began hobbling faster toward the guild house. "Pay them no mind and hopefully they will leave us be."

Ashok realized the monks around him had become afraid. Nervous glances were made toward the yellow monk, and then quickly hidden.

"Who are they?" Ashok asked.

"Followers of Ram Sahib," replied the monk who had once built weapons. "Last time we came here they beat a few of us and left us lying in the road."

"Their leader's teachings are very different from mine. Our sect avoids conflict. Theirs embraces it. Ignore them and go about our business."

Except the man in yellow shouted, "Stop right there, Dondrub!"

The Guru sighed but did as he was told. "Whatever they do to us, brothers, you must hold your tongues and your tempers. You especially, Ashok Vadal, please, please do nothing. They will have their fun, and then move on."

"Ram Sahib is a man of status here?" Ashok asked.

"He is the Ram and high priest of Xhonura, who controls the workshop in Ramrowan's name. All the guilds pay homage in exchange for his blessing."

Coming from a land where religion was banned by Law, the whole thing seemed nonsensical to Ashok. Here the religion seemed to be its own kind of law. "I'm not allowed to kill them, then?"

"No!" the Guru hissed. "Revealing yourself as an outsider would have far worse repercussions for us than any petty barbarity these children could inflict upon us today."

The yellow monk and his gang approached. They wore long dark coats and carried a mishmash of weapons. All of them seemed to have knives worn on the front of their belts, but two of them held Fortress rods—long, awkward things much bigger than the ones Ratul had procured for the rebellion—and one man even had what appeared to be a proper sword, though he was wearing it slung over his back, like a fool. It would be difficult to draw with any speed that way, so it was more than likely worn for show.

"Hurry, brothers, to your knees, before they take offense." The monks quickly lowered themselves into the muddy street. Ashok scowled, but then followed their example, soaking the scratchy fabric around his legs in a puddle. "Avert your eyes. Do not provoke them."

The locals had stopped whatever they were doing to watch the two groups collide. Their cultures may have been very different, but even Ashok—who struggled to understand the feelings of regular people—could tell many of them were bothered by what was happening. Dondrub's monks might not be popular, but they weren't despised enough for the villagers to want to see them harmed. Ram Sahib might be an important man, but his followers' actions did not make him a beloved one. Mothers took hold of their young children and rushed them away, trying to shield them from what was bound to be a violent spectacle. It seemed mothers were the same that way regardless of nation.

"Well, if it isn't the mad hermit, Dondrub. You've got some nerve, showing your ugly face here," the young man crowed. "Ram Sahib has declared that no other paths are to be preached among his holy followers, especially not from the likes of you heretics."

"Apologies. We're only here to buy food, Honored Reverend Kumara," Dondrub begged the yellow monk, who was probably less than a third his age. "Then we will go back up the mountain to our monastery and trouble you no more."

One of the two thugs armed with Fortress rods circled around the kneeling monks. Ashok noted that though the weapons were in their hands, the actions had not been readied to fire yet. They were prepared to intimidate, not to kill. The one with the sword was laughing at them.

He recognized their kind. Once having held great authority, the former Protector had no respect for those who abused whatever petty authority they had been delegated. It was a sickness caused by arrogance, and any Protector acolyte who had showed tendencies toward being a bully had that quickly beaten out of them. Their power was to be used serving the Law, never themselves. Though Ashok had parted ways with the Law, his disgust for such weak behavior remained.

A thug examined the monks' cart. "This is sturdy. I bet it could haul a lot of potatoes." He patted the yak's furry head. "The animal's in good health too. We could use a rig like this."

"Please," a monk said. "We need that to haul our goods home."

"Too bad. It's ours now," the *honored reverend* proclaimed. "Your sect is supposed to enjoy suffering. I'm happy to help you do so."

"Our Guru is elderly!" the same monk cried. "You can't expect him to walk all the way up the mountain on foot!"

The yellow monk gave a small nod toward one of his men, who immediately swung the steel-clad stock of his Fortress rod at the protesting monk's head.

That blow might have been enough to crack a skull, but they never found out, because fast as a striking cobra, Ashok caught it first. The wooden stock hit his palm with a *whump*, and the gunman blinked in surprise at the hand that had seemingly come out of nowhere.

Ashok waited there, still on one knee, arm stretched wide to intercept the attack, gauging their reaction. It was clear they hadn't expected much resistance, as the reflexive grasping for their weapons was clumsy. Only Ashok had already calculated how best to murder his way through the lot of them by the time the fastest among them had realized they might be in for a fight.

"Please! There is no need for confrontation," Dondrub urged.

When the gunman tugged on his weapon to try and get it back, Ashok maintained his iron grip, and the man's best efforts couldn't budge it at all.

It was the swordsman who stepped forward first, and it was a miracle he managed to draw a blade that was as long as his arm from over his back without slashing his own neck or removing his ear in the process. Ashok could have crippled him in five different ways by the time that weapon was ready to swing, but he just fixed his indifferent gaze upon the swordsman, and Ashok's expression alone was enough to make him hesitate. It wasn't anger, so much as indifference.

When the unwitting gunner pulled one more time, Ashok let go of the Fortress rod, and the man promptly fell on his ass in the mud. Ashok stood, drew himself to his full height, and surveyed his potential enemies. He stared through the yellow monk, not saying a word, until the young man took a nervous step back. Doubtless it was understood that Ashok would end his life with as much nonchalance as swatting an annoying bug.

"We should be going now!" The Guru was not trying to protect his monks from these men. He was trying to protect these men from Ashok. "Please take our cart and our yak as gifts and give Ram Sahib our thanks for this lesson in humility. I'm so sorry we disturbed your morning."

The obsequious display annoyed him, yet Ashok said nothing. He would bear any indignity as long as it put him one step closer to Thera.

Dondrub took Ashok by the arm and guided him toward the guild house. "Forgive his insolence, Honored Reverend. This one is not right in the head." Then he whispered to Ashok, "Stay your hand, please, I beg of you."

Luckily for the Guru, the predators had been too surprised by Ashok's sudden resistance to continue harrying their prey, and their new prize gave them something to gloat over. Most of them were unaware of how close they'd come to the edge. Only their leader continued watching them, suspicious, as Dondrub and his monks retreated.

Once they were far enough away to speak freely, Dondrub said, "Go to the market, brothers. Buy your provisions quickly, cause no disturbance, and then we must go." As the others obediently parted, he turned to Ashok, "It's alright. One skinny yak and a worn-out cart is a small sacrifice to keep the peace."

It was impossible to keep the disgust from his voice. "Peace? You talk so eagerly about how my starving casteless should battle an army of sea demons, while you can't even stand against scum like that? Complain all you want about the evils of my land, yet everything I've seen about yours shows it to be just as petty and cruel. Enough of your lies, Guru."

"How have I lied?"

"You said you did not have castes here, but you do. You merely give them different names."

The Guru seemed shamed by that. "It is a perversion. Ram Sahib is a dangerous man. He claims to be the tenth reincarnation of Ramrowan, and enough of the guilds support that to make him very powerful here."

And Ashok had thought that the doctrines Keta fabricated seemed foolish. "Then you've already found your avatar, ten times over, and you can leave me be."

"Obviously Ram Sahib is not the one! He's a despot."

"I don't care." Ashok reached the collectors' door and thumped it with his fist repeatedly.

It opened a minute later—during which Ashok never stopped knocking—and a stocky, disheveled man with a vast mustache and bald head stood before them, smelling of strong drink, clearly angry at whoever had interrupted his nap. "What do you want?" Then an odd look came over his face as he recognized Ashok, and gasped. "The dead man lives!"

"Of course I know the way to the land of the infidels, Avatara," Moyo of the Collectors Guild said. "But I can't take you there now! That's impossible. We'd be killed."

Ashok sat near the fire, eating. Moyo had been quick to offer them bowls of soup made from fermented fish, and it was a testament to how hungry Ashok had been that even that disgusting casteless fare was a welcome feast.

"You found me on that beach before the demons did. That is enough."

"I appreciate that, but to be honest I just thought you were another floating corpse. I tried to stop the guildsmen from taking you away after you woke up, but I've got no sway over their kind. I spit on them."

Ashok felt the same way about the mock judges. "I will not ask you to die on a stranger's behalf. If you will not guide me, then tell me how and I will do it myself."

"I could, I suppose, but I'd be sending you to your doom. It takes years of learning to read the signs right. I've been doing it since I was a boy and it's still dangerous. We collectors only go part of the way down, and never this time of year. Only the traders go all the way across to exchange goods with the infidels, but they only go in winter, while the dangerous things sleep more. It's still bad this season. In another month, maybe; two or three would be better, as there's things that hunt in the dark. Bad things."

"I've dealt with demons before."

"Worse," Moyo said, wide-eyed. "There are worse things than demons down there."

Ashok doubted that. He had once fought a demon big as an elephant and lacked the vision to think of anything more terrible than that. "This path runs *beneath* the ocean?"

Moyo looked nervously toward where Dondrub was slurping his soup. "I can't speak guild secrets before a priest. No disrespect, wise man. It is commanded that there must be secrets between church and workshop."

"Ram Sahib does not agree."

"Well, he's not in my guild house now, is he?"

The Guru smiled. "You are the last of the righteous, Moyo Kapoor. If the other guilds were as devoted as you collectors, Xhonura would be in far better shape. I understand and shall leave you to your plans."

"The Guru knows your secrets already," Ashok stated.

Moyo laughed nervously. "No. What? Impossible. They are well kept!"

Except the Guru gave Ashok a very sly look. "What do you mean?"

"You are of no guild, *now*. But not always. You've been to Lok. You're the only one on this island who does not completely mangle proper language while speaking to me."

"You retain the suspicious nature of the Law enforcer you

once were, yet you are wrong. I did not go to Lok. Lok came to me. Ratul Memon dar Sarnobat and I spent weeks discussing the ways of your people, before I agreed to help him procure a great many guns for his rebellion."

Ashok shouldn't have been surprised. "The traitor Ratul was a well-traveled man."

"Your old sword master also had a very high opinion of his greatest student. Nonetheless, I have kept my word and brought you to someone who knows the path. So I will be on my way." The Guru sighed as he put down his empty bowl and reached for his staff. "The joints creak. Help me up, please." Moyo seemed honored to do so, rushing over to offer the old man his arm.

"Did you get the answers you wanted, wise man?"

"I did, Ashok Vadal, but if that is a good thing or not, I don't yet know yet. Godspeed on your journey."

As Moyo escorted Dondrub toward the door, Ashok finished his meal and analyzed his surroundings. The guild house was humble and nearly as utilitarian as the monks' quarters. Though it seemed Moyo was the only one present today, there were ten bunks, and a great deal of equipment—ropes, picks, shovels, packs, and harnesses—organized into orderly rows on shelves. What he didn't see, however, was any proper weapons, which told him something about the nature of these collectors. It was not good to make assumptions in this strange land, but it appeared they were worker-caste equivalents, and not the kind who were permitted to be armed.

Moyo returned. "Now we may speak freely, Avatara."

"I am Ashok. That priest spent the last week trying to decide if I was your reborn king or not. The fact he left so eagerly should tell you what he decided."

"Eh...Dondrub is a wise man, not a know-everything man. I saw what I saw. I don't need priestly learning. Only Ramrowan can't die. You can't die. Simple."

Ashok had to shake his head at that. "I have certain gifts. I doubt I am immortal. My enemies simply have not tried hard enough to kill me."

"I convinced the other collectors about who you are too. That's why they've gone home. We declared there'd be no collecting done until the Avatara was given a trial and released. I'm happy our threats got the guildsmen to come around!"

He seemed so proud of the prospects that his strike had worked that Ashok was tempted to let him believe that, but dishonesty was not his way. "There was a trial. It did not go well. So I escaped instead."

"Oh..."

The truth was always best, but Ashok didn't want to crush his spirits. "However, I would not have been given the opportunity to escape if it had not been for the demands of your people. For that, you have my gratitude."

"Well then..." That seemed to cheer him. "Did you kill many guildsmen on the way out?"

"One maybe." Normally Ashok would have been meticulous about remembering every blow struck in battle, but that day hunger and weakness had made it so that he was not as exacting in his record as usual.

"Excellent!" Moyo clapped his hands with glee. "Good riddance. They're very bossy."

"I have one question for you, Collector, for I don't believe what the Guru told me. How long has it been since you found me on the shore?"

That got him a curious look. "About a year now, why?"

Ashok just closed his eyes and exhaled, for everything he was striving to get back to might already be destroyed. "It doesn't matter."

"Let's get you kitted up and then we can go. I will take you as far as I can into the down below and teach you to follow the signs the rest of the way."

"You said it was too dangerous this season?"

"Oh, it's mad dangerous, Avatara! So is hiding a fugitive in my guild house, but not as much. Only a lunatic or a collector would have the guts to go down below now. You're part god, so you'll live, but I'll probably die. Promise after I'm killed and eaten and some beast has shit out my bones you'll be sure to tell the gods that it was Moyo who found you on that beach, Moyo who helped you escape prison, and Moyo who was brave enough to lead you through the broken kingdom."

Ashok wasn't convinced that the gods paid that much attention, but he could do that.

# Chapter 14

~~~~~~~~~~~

Guru Dondrub watched through the spyglass as Ashok Vadal and Collector Moyo walked out of the town. From so far away it was difficult to keep track of them. Even lying on his belly and steadying his elbows against the rocks, the trembling of his bony hands caused the glass to bounce about wildly. It was worse than trying to peer through a hollow reed. The pair had not dallied long after Dondrub had left town. Not a surprise there. Despite still having not fully recovered from his ordeal, Ashok did not strike him as a man overflowing with patience.

"So what did you think of him?"

As usual, she had appeared so suddenly that he hadn't even heard her approach, and now she was standing only a few feet behind him on the mountain path. It was as if she was carried about on the wind. Her sudden arrivals and departures no longer startled him. Such was the nature of heavenly beings.

"Ashok Vadal is as you described, though not quite what I expected."

"How so?"

"I've been told about his nature at his mightiest—the relentless killer, the fearless combatant, the merciless Protector—only I got to see Ashok at his weakest, with his ribs poking through his

139

skin, face gaunt, having been a feast for vermin. You can learn much about a great man when he is brought low."

"And?"

Before Dondrub could answer, he noticed that the pair was being followed. Honored Reverend Kumara and his lackeys were following Ashok and Moyo. It didn't take the gift of prophecy to expect that might happen. From the look of things Kumara had gathered a couple more friends and his reinforcements were armed with blades and clubs. The boldness of the peculiar monk must have upset Kumara, and given time to stew, of course he had decided to take his revenge. Tyrants could never abide a defiant man. A lesson was about to be taught, or so they assumed.

"One moment. It appears Ram Sahib's men are about to try our guest. Would you like to watch?" He offered her the spyglass and saw that today the heavenly messenger had appeared in the form of a young maiden of the Herders Guild. "Here. It was found in the down below and magnifies things ten times over."

"I don't need that to see."

"Lucky you. My eyes weren't particularly blessed by the gods even before they grew old." Dondrub turned back to the show. It took him a moment to find them again through the narrow field of view. Ashok and Moyo were burdened beneath extremely large packs. They could have dropped them and run away, but Dondrub knew Moyo. He would never willingly abandon his guild's equipment. And Ashok . . .

"Is that a pickaxe he's unstrapping from that pack?"

"I believe it is," she answered.

Barely a week ago Ashok had been starved near to death. Now he was badly outnumbered, and two of Ram Sahib's men had flintlocks. Except it was clear from his decisive manner that none of that made any difference to Ashok. He must have ordered Moyo to hide, because the shorter man ran away and crouched behind some boulders. Then Ashok waited, pick in hand, as his enemies approached.

There was no way to hear the words said from such a great distance, but Dondrub could imagine them. Like most authoritarians, Kumara was not a man of great imagination or variety. He would be shouting a challenge, demanding compliance, expecting meekness, that sort of thing.

Ashok must have responded in an unexpected manner, because the overzealous band went from proud and haughty to hunched and nervous. It would not take much, with that strange alien accent from the mainland. He had probably met Kumara's challenge by announcing himself an infidel and a fugitive. Ashok did not seem the sort to delay the inevitable.

What happened next was so sudden that it was difficult to track. Damn his shaky hands upon this magnifying tube! Ashok hurled the pick. A gunner fell. A moment later the sound of the weapon discharging reached the Guru's hillside. The second gunner fired as well, only Ashok had already rolled out of the way. He lost view of Ashok for a moment, but that was enough time to leave another man prone, and Ashok yanking the pick from the dead gunner's head.

As the remaining gunner reloaded, Ashok methodically worked his way through the others. Piercing skulls and punching holes in chests. They didn't even have time to understand doom was upon them. Dondrub cursed, because whenever he lost his view, by the time he found it again, another man had already died.

"You have a foul tongue for a holy man."

The gunner must have been Weapons Guild once, because his reload was very quick. Only Ashok hooked Kumara through the ribs with the pickaxe, steered him around as a shield, and the next bullet hit the honored reverend instead. Ashok ripped the pick out in a vast shower of blood, and then sent it hurtling end over end into the fleeing gunner's back.

Then the sound of the shot reached them.

"He *is* Ramrowan reborn."

"Perhaps," Mother Dawn answered. "Or something like that. Your understanding is close enough. Inheritance is a complex thing."

"That's what they deserve for stealing that yak."

"Karma," she agreed, but then admonished him. "Your sect preaches pacifism. You shouldn't be enjoying this so much."

Dondrub turned back to face the thing that looked like an innocent girl. "Bad intent brings bad results. When presented a choice, the followers of Ram Sahib chose the villainous path. The universe has been slightly corrected. Ashok went through them as if they were nothing."

"By Ashok's standards, they *were* nothing. Your island relies on firearms for defense, and because of that you have neglected the more archaic martial skills. Understandable, as your firearms are a far more practical way to make war. Except Ashok hails from a land of sharpened steel, where prideful men are constantly testing themselves against one another, the smallest mistake means crippling wounds or painful death, and he was one of the few required by their Law to accept every challenge. Even in a place like that, he was considered the best of the best. You should have seen him when Angruvadal was whole and in his hand, rather than broken and buried in his heart. Before that I once saw him slice through over a hundred fearsome Somsak in a single morning."

"What's a Somsak?"

"Terrible neighbors."

Dondrub was incredulous, for even when dealing with angels some things sounded too far-fetched to be true. "What he said about having black steel in him is true, then?"

"It is. And I believe his time in the guildsmen's dungeon has given that shard time to do its work. All that remains of Angruvadal is one with Ashok now. What will become of the two of them, I do not know...But what were you saying about Ashok's character while he was weak?"

Dondrub turned the spyglass back toward the distant road, where Ashok had picked up the sword of one of the fallen. The possible avatar spun it a few times, testing the balance.

"I misspoke. There is no *weak* there. Perhaps of body, temporarily, but there is no stop to the man. He may fail. He may die. Except he will do so as unrelentingly as he lives. I hesitate to call him proud, as that is not accurate. Pride implies an emotional capability I doubt he has. Ashok Vadal simply is what he is and will do what he does."

"I agree with your assessment. As a creature of Law, he was predictable. Now that he creates his own way, the outcome becomes a mystery. I struggle to predict what he will do, even though I've spoken to him more times than he knows."

"Is he always this unpleasant?"

Mother Dawn giggled. Though the sound was appropriate for her current form, it seemed odd coming from a being of her divine nature. "Sometimes. Just remember, joy is rare and fleeting in this cruel world for most. Imagine being him. Considering the things he has done on behalf of his old Law, it's a miracle he possesses any decency at all. Hopefully, the code he is creating for himself will be enough, or the descendants of Ramrowan will simply trade one form of tyranny for another. He is almost ready, though I don't envy the next task before him."

The new sword must have been acceptable to Ashok, because he relieved the former owner of the scabbard, and took the weapon with him. Moyo had come out to loot the bodies of their valuables. He was a collector, so that was in his nature. When he was finished the two of them slung their heavy packs and set out once again toward the nearest entrance to the underworld.

Dondrub suspected they were far enough out of town that no one else had seen the fight. His monks had already been seen departing in the opposite direction, so hopefully his sect would not be blamed. Ram Sahib would probably assume his men had been murdered by one of the bandit gangs that infested this area. At least Ashok had done him the favor of not leaving any witnesses.

"This is it, then," the Guru muttered. "This age ends, and a new one begins."

"Will it be another age for man, or a time of demons? That will be for the inheritor to decide. As was written on his workshop walls, by passing his tests, Ramrowan's servants would know him. He could not freeze. He could not drown. He could not starve. Only one test remains—the most dangerous test of all."

"Ashok doesn't know what he tempts by going down there. Neither the collectors nor traders guilds understand what the land below really is. It pained me not to warn them."

Mother Dawn didn't seem to share his concern, or more likely, she did, but was better at hiding it. After all, she had been meddling in the affairs of man for a *very* long time. "You did what was necessary, Dondrub. Ashok had to go unknowing into the lair of the Dvarapala. Angruvadal has made its choice. We will honor it."

Yet doubt nagged at him. "I know that was the commandment, but what good does it do to help a man heal, only to let him walk blindly into the reach of a fallen god who has been simmering in its hate for a thousand years?"

"I have no comforting words for you, Guru. His fate is out of your hands. If Ashok is the one, he will prevail. If he's not, he will die. The question for you is, will the people of Xhonura rise to the occasion? Will the workshop be ready to serve the

Forgotten's Warrior when he calls for aid, or will you fail your master once again?"

"You don't need to remind me of our failures, Mother Dawn. I know them well. I taste their bitter ashes every day. This time we will be ready."

# Chapter 15

━━━◆◇◆◇◆━━━

When at first the boys had not returned from the hunt, Toramana had not been concerned. Parth and Rawal were young, but they had been raised in the Bahdjangal, where it wasn't odd for the hunters of their tribe to spend many days away from the village, foraging to survive, and only returning home after they had gotten a proper kill. That had been in an unforgiving swamp, trapped between the House of Assassins and the sea. In comparison, the forests above the Creator's Cove were a relative paradise. There were no crocodiles, venomous snakes, or roaming demons here, just plentiful game and solid ground.

It was on the second day that Toramana grew worried, but not enough to ask for help. His tribe had a reputation to maintain. If two of his young hunters had gotten lost in terrain as tame as this, it would bring shame to the People of the Woods. They were unique among the faithful, nearly as poor as the casteless, only they had never lived in the Law-abiding world. Their ways were their own. Toramana had earned Ashok's respect and been named one of the Sons' officers because his people were superior archers, trackers, and scouts. He couldn't afford to lose face before the so-called civilized men by having it known his own flesh and blood had gotten lost in the woods.

Worse...if the others helped search, what if Rawal was found by a *city man*? Such indignity would never be lived down.

Instead Toramana had sent several of his loyal hunters to track the boys and discreetly bring them home. Yet, after two days of failure, Toramana had been forced to swallow his pride and bring dishonor to the swamp people by asking for help.

Keta—as always—had been eager to help. His assistant, Javed, had gathered volunteers to send up the slopes to look for them.

None of these illustrious leaders had thought to trouble Thera about such a mundane matter as two missing boys. She hadn't found out until a day later, when she had asked one of Toramana's tribe where everyone had gone and been told of the swamp chief's prideful hesitancy to ask for help. She was the Voice of the Forgotten, busy running a settlement and planning a war. Everyone just assumed she would be above such petty concerns, which frankly annoyed her to no end. She wasn't some aloof Thakoor, lording over her people from her opulent estate, and she hated it when the men defaulted to old habits and treated her like their prior first-caste masters.

Thera was warrior caste at heart, and happy to have the excuse to put on her boots and walk up a mountainside. Besides, she'd been feeling overwhelmed trying to come up with a plan of attack against the Law that would offer any chance of success and could use the fresh air. A search party was a fine excuse to stop banging her head against the wall for a time.

Of course, it would do no good for her to simply walk up the slope and present herself to Javed for assignment as if she was any other mundane member of the Cove. The faithful would surely fawn over her, and then she'd end up more of a distraction than a help. Normally she would have commanded some of the Sons to accompany her, but most of them were busy training the next group of saboteurs who were to be sent out shortly. She'd need more eyes than just hers and Murugan's so she turned to the only other people staying at the Sons' terrace who weren't occupied with something important...

The slaves she had freed from the House of Assassins had nothing better to do. Their brains might be mush, but they had eyeballs and sense enough to point.

During her time in the Lost House, she had been stunned by the wizards' ruthless callousness. Every one of them had been recognized as a child because of their magical gifts, kidnapped from their real families, and taken to Lost House Charsadda to be raised as an assassin. Those who were vicious enough to adapt to their cutthroat ways and pass the trial in the Graveyard of Demons became full members of the house. The stolen children who were deemed unworthy to face the trial for whatever reason had their minds magically broken, leaving them as docile slaves to their haughty brethren.

Many of those slaves had been killed when the demons attacked the Lost House, but twelve had survived. Thera couldn't just leave them in a cursed swamp to fend for themselves, so she had brought them along. And oddly enough, they had obeyed her, probably because technically she had passed the trial in the Graveyard of Demons, which would make her a member of the Lost House, and thus their rightful master. The thought made her sick, but they'd been so simple they needed somebody to guide them, or they probably would have just died in the swamp.

Though the slaves had been relatively helpless at first— emotionless simpletons, only acting when directed—the spell had seemed to weaken over the ensuing seasons. Most of them remained mute or inarticulate, but the effect was clearly fading, and some of them were beginning to show signs of real personality again. Thera had seen moments of genuine emotion, and even curiosity, from a few of them.

They were still only trusted with simple, repetitive tasks, but Thera reasoned there was nothing simpler than walking through the forest in a line until you tripped over a body. So she had gathered the girl cutting vegetables in the kitchen, and the three boys who had been mucking out the horse pen, and commanded all of them to accompany her.

It wasn't a pleasant march up the side of the crater. Rain had been falling sporadically for the last few days, a fact that had surely hindered Toramana's trackers. They met another group of faithful on their way down, and once they got over their excitement at being addressed by their prophet, they pointed her toward where they had left off. When she saw how organized the searchers were, with all the woods around the top of the Cove having been divided up, and they were concentrating on the area where the boys had been last seen hunting, Thera guessed correctly that the search must have been organized by Javed. Their second priest was very meticulous like that.

Unfortunately, there had been no luck yet. That was a grim sign, because if the boys were still alive, surely they would have heard all these people shouting their names. Some had begun to fear that the boys had foolishly tried to scale the rugged mountains above the forest. Ashok had told her that such a climb would have been difficult even for him. If a pair of unskilled boys tried that they would have surely tumbled to their doom.

After the other group left, Murugan told her, "They are looking where they are expected to be and finding nothing. I have an idea."

"What's that?"

"In Thao lands, we pride ourselves on climbing rocks. Warrior and worker both, except we know which ones to learn on. You practice on the ones that won't kill you, *then* move on to a real challenge."

Thera had grown up in a land of misty hills. The most interesting thing to climb near House Vane was a tree. "Why would you do that?"

"It's exhilarating." Murugan grinned. "It must sound odd to a flatlander, but the higher you go, the braver you must be."

She refrained from asking her bodyguard how high he'd ever climbed, as Murugan was sensitive about anything that might be seen as questioning his courage. "The swamp people come from a mud bar that's only a few feet above the sea. You think their children might have overestimated what they could do?"

"Possibly. Sometimes a climb will look reasonable from the bottom, but then once you're a ways up it, things change, luck runs out, and it's hard to make your way back down. Your arms get tired, fingers bleed and slip, your legs cramp, miss a toe hold, and next thing you know..." Murugan made a whistling noise. "Thud. A not uncommon way for young warriors to die where I'm from."

"Then it makes sense we'd find them at the bottom. If you were an adventurous child, which one of these would you try to climb?"

Without hesitation, Murugan pointed at a jutting peak to the northwest. "That one."

It looked like every other rock to her, though it was the tallest point around the Cove. "Why?"

"Because I've been tempted to tackle it myself. Just look at that thing... It would be a challenge, and at the end you'd be treated to a view the likes of which only the gods usually get to see."

It was a good thing she kept her bodyguard so busy, otherwise he'd go off and break his neck. Yet Murugan's logic was sound. The swamp folk were daring. They weren't warrior caste, but their pride in their physical accomplishments was equal to warriors'. That would be quite the feat to brag on. It was as good a place to look as anywhere else.

As the six of them walked toward the peak, she could hear other searchers shouting the boys' names through the trees. *Parth. Rawal.* Thera had met both. They had been among those who had followed her around the swampers' village all winter. They seemed like good boys. She hoped for the best but feared for the worst.

Unfortunately, two-thirds of Thera's group couldn't talk, so there would not be as much shouting of names. "Spread out and watch the ground. We'll keep a few yards between us."

"If they see something you expect them to speak up?" Murugan asked pointedly.

Thera sighed as she looked over her magically damaged crew. "Just... get my attention somehow. Alright?" They stared blankly back at her. When they'd done that in the House of Assassins she'd found it unnerving. Now that she knew their story, their witless nature just made her sad. "Got that?"

Two of them managed to nod. It would have to do. They spread out and did as they were told.

"They seem to be improving," Thera said.

"Oh, in leaps and bounds, Prophet."

"Don't mock me, kid. They're still in there. They'll snap out of it eventually. When Dattu saw his brother Kabir murdered, it shook him from the spell long enough for him to light the spark that destroyed the House of Assassins."

"I wasn't mocking. I vowed to serve whomever the gods chose. I give thanks every day they picked someone who believes in mercy."

Thera grudgingly accepted that compliment.

The rain had made the ground soft, and the pine-needle cover was slick. They were quickly drenched and chilled. They spent an hour walking between the trees, as she and Murugan shouted themselves hoarse to make up for the silent remainder.

They were nearing the tempting peak when Thera heard someone whisper, "*Stop.*"

At first she'd thought that had been her bodyguard, but then she realized that it had been a woman's voice. In disbelief she turned toward the only other female in the group. The slave was plain, short, and probably only a couple of years older than the boys they were looking for. She was so quiet and unobtrusive that it was easy to forget she was there at all. Having no way of knowing her real name, Thera had named her Laxmi.

The slave was staring at Thera, wide-eyed.

"You talked!"

"Stop," Laxmi repeated, this time with more urgency. She was shaking, only it wasn't from the cold.

Thera realized that the poor girl was terrified. "Everybody hold up!"

"What is it?" Murugan moved his hand to his sheathed sword.

"I don't know." Thera walked slowly toward Laxmi, and tried not to sound too excitable. No reason to agitate the poor thing anymore than she already was. "Can you tell me what's wrong?"

Laxmi looked ahead of her, where there was a relatively dry patch, clear of needles and protected from the brunt of the rain by a thick knot of branches.

"Tiger."

By the time Murugan drew his sword, Thera already had a knife in each hand.

Thera squinted at the dirt patch, thinking the poor girl had to be imagining things, because tigers were rare in this part of Lok, and there'd been no sign of such a dangerous predator inside the Cove—until she saw the massive paw print for herself. "Oceans!" Then she instinctively looked up as her father had taught her, to make sure the beast wasn't crouched in the trees directly overhead, waiting to leap down on its prey.

Murugan rushed over until he could see the track as well. "That's a *big* cat."

"Tiger... Not tiger," Laxmi whispered. "No. Worse."

"She's gone from silent to babbling. What's she going on about?"

"I don't know," Thera told him. The poor girl hadn't spoken for who knew how long, but something about the track had shaken her from her stupor. "This sure changes the search, though."

"It might have carried the boys off. They'll do that, you

know—hide their kill in a tree trunk or something." Murugan looked around nervously. Even a skilled warrior was wary when it came to a silent hunter that could remain unseen until the instant it sank its fangs into your neck.

Thera commanded those who were too oblivious to realize there was danger near. "No more spreading out. Everyone draw near." Then she moved to Laxmi's side; she was staring off deeper into the forest. Thera squinted in that direction but couldn't see anything except for trees. "What is it?"

"Omkar," she squeaked, clearly terrified out of her wits.

That name stirred bad memories, for he had been Thera's appointed teacher in the House of Assassins. "Omkar's dead."

"An evil, evil man."

"I know...Was he your teacher too?"

Laxmi turned toward Thera and nodded vigorously.

Though Thera had been considered special enough to be spared his wrath, Kabir had warned her about Omkar's vile nature. The fat man had delighted in sadistic murder, malicious even by the assassins' standards. It was rumored he was as cruel to his students as his targets.

Thera sheathed one of her knives so she could put a comforting hand on Laxmi's shoulder. "Omkar's dead. He can't hurt you anymore. Understand?"

"I know it's not him," she squeaked. "But like him."

The girl had spotted the track, but Thera had no idea why that reminded her of the fat old killer from the House of Assassins. It was a curious bit of nonsense, but the tiger was a bad enough omen on its own for now.

"Come on. We need to warn the others there's a predator in the Cove."

Hours later, the bodies had been found. Thera knew even before the messenger reached her, because Toramana's cry of rage and grief had echoed off the mountains. She was told the boys had been mauled and then stuffed into a tiny cave, only a quarter mile from where Laxmi had found the track.

As tragic as that was, something else had begun to gnaw at Thera's mind, but she hesitated to speak of it in the woods where there might be unseen listeners. Instead she cautioned Murugan to tell no one else about the slave waking up, and then they had walked back down to the Sons' terrace. The whole time Thera kept an eye on the girl, but if Laxmi wanted to speak more, she hid it well.

Once safely home, Thera had taken Laxmi to her quarters, wrapped her in blankets to get her warm, and fetched some of the stew that the girl had been preparing earlier. Thera had left Murugan outside to guard the door, with instructions to turn away anybody unless it was Ashok miraculously returned or the Forgotten himself.

Thera sat across from the slave and gave her a chance to eat before prodding her.

"This is good," she told her. "You're a fine cook."

As usual the girl wouldn't make eye contact, she just kept staring into her bowl, seeming small and forlorn.

So Thera tried to talk to make her feel at ease. "I'm a terrible cook. Warrior wives are supposed to know how to feed our husbands, but I never learned that well. Probably one reason he didn't like me! Among many. Of course the casteless here are even worse, as they've never been given spices in their lives so they're afraid of them. A casteless would eat an old shoe and be thankful. We've got terraces where spices grow like weeds and hardly anyone here who can do a damn thing with them, but not you. This is the best stew I've had. We're lucky to have you."

Surprisingly, Laxmi said, "Thank you."

Thera grinned, as even that little interaction suggested the assassins' magic was crumbling. "I've been calling you Laxmi for the last little while, but I don't know what your real name is."

"Laxmi is better. I'd like to keep that one."

"Sure. Whatever you want." The spell really was broken for her. That meant there was hope for the others as well. Thera breathed a sigh of relief. "We've talked before. Well, *I've* talked. But I feel like I should introduce myself. I'm Thera."

"I know. You're the one who saved us."

"It was a group effort, Ashok and the Sons of the Black Sword and me."

"You were the one who wouldn't leave us behind, even though your hands were hurt."

That was true, but Thera liked to imagine that she had merely done what any decent, honorable sort would do in the same circumstances, burned hands or not. "Do you know where you are?"

"The Creator's Cove, home of the faithful."

"You must listen to the Keeper of Names' sermons?"

Laxmi nodded, like she was embarrassed to say yes.

Thera tried to lighten the mood. "Of course you have. Keta talks enough for all of us! He's got a sermon for everything."

Laxmi actually smiled a little. "I like them. My parents said religion was illegal. Master Omkar laughed at it. But I like it when the Keeper talks about the gods and us."

Good. In a life so miserable, it was good that she could find happiness in that. "How much do you remember about... where you were before?" Thera was hesitant to call the House of Assassins by its name, because she wasn't sure what that reminder would do to the poor girl.

"All of it."

"Oh..." Thera could only imagine what that entailed. "Where were you from before that?"

"Gujara."

"The northern jungles. I hear there's a lot of tigers there. Is that how you recognized the track?"

Laxmi shook her head. "Yes but no."

"The track was hard to see. How'd you know it was there?"

"The magic lingered. I could feel it before I could see it."

Thera went cold. The delicious stew formed a nauseous lump in the pit of her stomach. This was what she'd been afraid of. "You can sense magic?"

Laxmi nodded vigorously.

"That's a rare talent. I've only known a few people like that. One of them was Ratul, a brave man who protected me. Another you probably met, a worker named Gutch. He was the big, jolly one who wintered in the swamp with us. You're very special to have such a gift."

"I'm not that good at it. I have to be very close."

"I want to ask, in the woods, you spoke of Master Omkar..."

"He taught me several patterns."

Impressive, if true. The Lost House wizards usually knew two or three different spells by the time they attempted their raid on the Graveyard of Demons. "He tried to teach me some, only I wasn't very good at magic, though."

"I was." Surprisingly, Laxmi actually looked at Thera as she spoke, revealing there were tears in her eyes. "I was very talented with the patterns. That's not why he declared me unworthy to take the trial. They...they..."

"It's alright now. That foul place has been destroyed."

"Good."

Thera let Laxmi collect herself before asking, "The patterns Omkar showed you—one of them was the tiger pattern, wasn't it?"

Laxmi sniffed and nodded, confirming Thera's worst fears.

*The Cove has been infiltrated by a shape-shifting wizard.*

Was it Sikasso's men, come for revenge? Or was it the Inquisition, preparing to destroy the rebellion once and for all? If the Law knew about their hideout, the rebellion was doomed. She would have to alert her officers, but subtly, so as to not alert the tiger.

It was a challenge to keep her voice calm while her blood ran cold. "Listen, Laxmi, for now, speak of this to no one else."

"That will not be hard for me."

It took a moment for her to realize the poor girl had actually been making a joke, and then Thera snorted and laughed so violently she spilled some stew. "I guess talking too much hasn't been an issue for you lately! Welcome back."

There were actual real human expressions on Laxmi's face, a sort of emotional, weary joy. "It's still foggy, but it's nice to think again. Or some thinking at least, but it's like I can start a thought but it's hard to get to the end. But it's better than before. The pattern puts you in a dream where you can't help but do what you're told. Master Sikasso called it *quieting the mind.*"

"You were taught that one?"

"I was. I was very far along in my training before I disappointed Master Omkar for the last time. He said I was good at magic, but weak."

"Meaning you didn't want to murder innocents."

"Master Omkar said that was how the house earned its way. He thought I was soft, so he ordered me to kill a slave. I hesitated, so he did it for me. The next time when I hesitated, I became the slave. You understand?"

"All too well. If it's any consolation, Javed cut Omkar's disgusting head off and gave it to Keta as a present." Then a thought struck her. "You know how to do this quieting of the mind, but do you know how to make minds...unquiet?"

"I think so. Maybe? The patterns were set on them, but they

start to fray. I might be able to pick apart the threads." Then Laxmi beamed as she successfully completed that train of thought. "Yes! I can help the others! I know how."

Thera had rescued twelve people with the extremely rare ability to use magic, who all had at least some training from the most dangerous wizards in the world, *and* her rebellion currently possessed more demon than most great houses to fuel them.

That could change *everything*...

If they survived that long.

# Chapter 16

～～～

The casteless village had been destroyed. Every last one of the non-people had been put to death. Man, woman, and child. As the Law required.

Bharatas didn't give a damn about the Law. To the ocean with the Law. For him, these casteless had died because they were in league with Black-Hearted Ashok, his vile prophetess, and their false god. That was all the reason he required. He'd used mighty Akerselem to cut down the non-people just as cruelly as Ashok's rebellion had murdered his mother, his father, his brothers, his sisters, and all the other innocent victims in Chakma. He'd shown these casteless as much mercy as Ashok had showed his paltan at the battle of Dhakhantar, where the Black Heart had killed all his comrades and then left Bharatas for dead on the plains.

The mighty ancestor blade Akersalem had taken many lives today, but they weren't really people, so they didn't count. Those brave enough to fight had never had a chance. No mortal could stand against an ancestor blade. This hadn't been battle, but a slaughter.

And the process would continue, day after day, until Great House Akershan ran out of casteless blood to spill or Ashok Vadal revealed himself.

The flea-ridden yurts had been set on fire. The bodies would

157

be left where they fell, to feed the buzzards and make the grass grow tall next season.

Some of his men approached, and they were dragging a prisoner between them. They hurled the man into the dirt at Bharatas' feet, so they could give their house's bearer a proper salute. Bharatas returned the gesture. He was far younger than most of his veteran soldiers, but they'd learned to show him great respect, for Bharatas fought with an intensity and cunning that few other warriors could match, and that had been before he had been picked by one of the mightiest weapons in the world to be its bearer.

Bharatas studied the man, lying on his side, stripped of his clothing, with his hands tied behind his back. "What's this?"

"A rebel, found hidden among the fish-eaters, but he's a whole man. Worker caste. It appears he was teaching them how to fight."

"Ah. But what does a worker know about fighting?" Bharatas asked.

"More than you, cowards," the prisoner spat. "Massacring the helpless."

One of his warriors promptly kicked the man in the ribs, but then Bharatas reached out and grabbed him by the armor before he could give him the other boot. "Hold. He's not wrong."

"But, sir—"

"Stand away. I want to talk with him."

The warriors did as they were told, and they left their bearer in the middle of the burning village with the rebel. Bharatas lowered himself and sat cross-legged in the dirt, waiting for the man to quit coughing. The air was filled with rising smoke, so it was good to sink below it. Bits of trapped moisture turned to steam and popped inside the burning homes.

When it seemed like the prisoner could breathe again, Bharatas said, "Your description of what we're doing here is accurate. This *is* cowardly. This isn't a proper war. It's a waste. It brings dishonor on my house, and shame to my caste."

"Then stop," the rebel gasped. "I beg you, leave the casteless alone."

"I wish I could, but I can't," Bharatas said truthfully. "I don't want to fight helpless fish-eaters. I want to face Ashok Vadal and the Sons of the Black Sword. That is my purpose. These are just the best things available. He vowed to protect the non-people. So I slay them and await his response."

"Ashok is dead."

"A lie."

"It's true," the captive wheezed. "Ashok died at Garo, killed by Devedas and thrown into the sea."

Bharatas just chuckled. "Do you know how I know you're lying? I was one of the best duelists in Akershan." He undid the tie beneath his chin, removed his helmet, and placed it on the ground next to him, then ran one hand through his sweat-soaked hair to display the gigantic scar where his scalp had been peeled from his skull. "Despite that, Ashok Vadal gave me this. And we were even on horseback, and no Vadal man should be able to match an Akershani on horseback."

"I'm from Dev."

"I don't care. As I was saying, Ashok did that to me. He bested me, after he'd already killed many of my brothers, and they didn't even wear him down. Afterward I thought that he must have been using his black steel blade, but it wasn't until I took up Akerselem and saw what it could do to the human body that I understood Ashok hadn't even bothered. He used a normal sword. If he'd struck me with Angruvadal that hard, it would've split my head in half, right through my helm, and considering how strong he's supposed to be probably through my entire body and not stopped until Angruvadal was embedded in my horse."

"I wish he had."

"Heh, you haven't met that horse. Kurdan is a good girl. Losing her would've been a shame." Bharatas waited, but the worker was too frightened to react. "Oh come now, that was amusing. What I'm saying is that I know Ashok's not dead." He touched the grisly scar again. "Because I'd feel it here if he was. Bearer to bearer. I think vowing to take Ashok's life is why my sword chose me. It approved of my greater purpose... Relax, worker. I don't want to kill you."

"Liar."

"No offense is taken. I understand why you'd think that, but I'm not a liar. I need to know where the rebellion is. Tell me how to find them, and you can go. Walk back to Dev. Akershan forgives you. Oceans, I'll give you a strong horse and enough rations to get home. I don't care about you at all. I want Ashok Vadal, or his prophet bitch will do."

That sparked a fresh rage in the prisoner. "Don't speak of Thera like that. She's the Voice of the Forgotten!"

And she was responsible for the death of everyone Bharatas had ever loved. That false prophet's ambitions had ruined him. Once a happy warrior, seeing what had become of Chakma had killed the Bharatas who had been and left a hollow thing behind. He'd filled that husk with anger. Even after being chosen by an ancestor blade, the greatest honor a warrior could imagine, instead of triumph all he could feel was an ashen emptiness and a desire for revenge.

"So you're a true believer, then, in the old gods?"

"I am," the worker professed with far more dignity than a naked, beaten and bound man should muster. "We remember what the rest of you have forgotten."

"Your prophet, this Thera, she sent you here to help these casteless, didn't she?"

He said nothing. That was answer enough.

"I was told the fanatics in Chakma did terrible things to my sister, before they cut her throat and threw her body over the wall. They hung my little brother in the street, like some kind of...example. To warn against what, I don't know. He was only ten years old." Bharatas paused to wipe the sudden moisture from his eyes. "But I don't blame you for that."

The worker seemed surprised by Bharatas' raw honesty. "I give you my word, warrior. Those atrocities were the work of Pankaj, a false prophet, who denied the commands of the true prophet. She commanded there was to be no abuse against any who didn't raise a sword against us. No raping. No looting. No arson. She's benevolent and kind."

"She sounds pleasant. Show me where she hides and you may go free."

"Never!"

"Why are you worried? If your gods are real, surely they'll protect her from the likes of me. I have a thousand riders with me, but what's an army to a god? Show me the way, or I will have no choice but to have you tortured until you talk." Bharatas looked him in the eyes, so that the worker could see this was no trick. There was no sophistry, just a statement of things that would come to pass. "I plead with you, worker, don't make me do that. There's no honor it. It's an awful process. The constant screaming in camp is bad for morale, and it scares the horses. It's pointless suffering, because all men break eventually, no matter how strong they think they are. You will talk. Everyone does."

The worker was silent for a long time, pondering his fate. "Ashok Vadal wouldn't break."

Bharatas thought it over, then nodded. "That is likely true. There is an exception to every rule."

"I did lie to you," the fanatic admitted. "Ashok surely lives, because he can't die. He died once before, hung by a hook through the heart by the half-demon wizard Sikasso, and he came back to life anyway. The Forgotten's Warrior will return and punish everyone who has ever harmed the faithful, for his word is stronger than death!" With a roar, the worker surged to his feet and tried to rush, headlong, into the nearest fire.

Bharatas had been expecting a suicidal move like that and caught him by the ankle. The worker fell, and with his hands tied behind him, went face-first into the hard-packed ground. The warriors came running.

"Keep him alive and tightly bound, no matter what," Bharatas ordered, as they restrained their prize. "Any harm he manages to inflict on himself, I will do double to you."

"It'll be done, bearer," the senior said as they hauled the worker to his feet.

"He knows where their prophet hides." Bharatas picked up his helmet and stood. "I will send for torturers."

"There's no need for that!"

It was the lone Inquisitor who was obligated to accompany his army, and he appeared between the fires, walking with smug purpose. "I was told you had captured a prisoner. Questioning rebels is the responsibility of my Order."

Simply seeing that mask with the snarling visage of the Law filled Bharatas with disgust. He had more respect for the religious fanatics than the Inquisition. For an Order that specialized in secrets and conspiracies, their inability to find the heart of the rebellion in Akershan had been *too consistent*. There had been far too many complaints from other shrewd warriors about how any captives they took who might know the rebellion's location had a tendency to die beneath the Inquisitor's knives before they could give up their secrets.

So Bharatas simply killed him.

Akerselem was a black blur as it effortlessly sheared through the top half of the Inquisitor's skull. Since blood never stuck to a black steel blade, Bharatas had returned his sword to the sheath before the body toppled and all its brains spilled out.

The worker screamed. Even his men were shocked by the suddenness of it.

That had been very illegal, but his ancestor blade didn't seem to find the act dishonorable, and Bharatas had more important things to concern himself with. The morals of ancestor blades were supposed to be inscrutable to the mortal mind, but he had told the sword his vow. It wanted him to find Ashok, of that he was sure. So anything he did to further that goal would be considered acceptable.

"Never speak of this to anyone. I'll send a letter telling our Thakoor that our Inquisition escort died bravely in battle against rebels, and to send us a new Inquisitor at his earliest convenience." He waited for his surprised soldiers to nod their understanding. "I suppose I will find time to write that letter in the next month or so."

Then he went to the fanatic and put his hand against his cheek, forcing them face to terrified face. "You are a brave fool, worker, but you are right about Ashok Vadal. I am certain he's still alive because I am the one who is destined to kill him."

"A-Ashok wouldn't break," he stammered as he was dragged away. *"Ashok would never break!"*

Bharatas just shook his head sadly. "You are no Ashok."

# Chapter 17

A land beneath hell. It was unthinkable. Ashok had never dreamed that such a thing could exist as a place lower than the sea.

Their trek had begun simply enough, as Moyo had led him up the north coast of Fortress. That part of the island seemed to be covered in ancient structures, including the massive stone walls that gave the island its name in Lok. The walls seemed to be the only things that were manned. It put into perspective how difficult it would be for any warriors who managed to march across the ocean in one of the rare years it had turned to solid ice, as they would have to dash their bodies against those imposing walls, the lowest of which was still easily thirty feet tall, all while being picked apart by Fortress rods. Ashok saw many gunners—or weapons guildsmen as they were known here—stationed along the way. Their lookouts paid no mind to Moyo and Ashok, since collectors and monks were a common sight here.

It took several days to reach the entrance, and though Moyo had tried to explain it to him, either he lacked the words, or Ashok lacked the imagination to grasp the true nature of their journey.

The entrance was an unnatural square, wide enough to fit five wagons side by side, cut into a cliff face less than a mile inside the ocean wall. In shape and style it reminded him of the structures carved into the crater of the Creator's Cove. Every sharp line had been eroded by time, yet somehow the great constructions of the ancients never completely crumbled into dust.

Just inside the opening was a vast room, its original purpose long forgotten. The floor had been broken by an earthquake so long ago that—protected from the wind—a great tree had grown from the crack. It seemed odd that such a generous space, safe from the elements, wasn't utilized by the locals, but Moyo had said this place was haunted by the ghosts of their ancestors, and best avoided by any who lacked his guild's wisdom and the blessing of the church of Ramrowan.

Though none would live here, they must have thought it was a fine place to store their dead, as there were piles and piles of human bones stacked along every wall, thousands of them. Mostly bleached white, but many were coated with green moss.

"Collector dead, trader dead, and the occasional guildsman who demanded the honor," Moyo had explained with reverence. "Centuries' worth. These are all our ancestors who braved the down below. Even those of us fortunate enough to die elsewhere get returned here out of respect. If you toil in the underworld, you've earned the right. There's a great many more bones scattered along the way of those who didn't make it back."

"An ossuary," Ashok said, thinking of those who died within the Inquisitor's Dome. Unlike the malicious intimidation of that foul tower, there was an eerie peace to this place. It seemed dignified. "We have one of these in the Capitol."

"For your honored dead?"

"The opposite."

That had only been the beginning of their journey. It had gotten stranger from there.

The tunnel continued for a long ways. The downward slope was so gradual and consistent, it was difficult to notice. The part that was being used for a tomb ended abruptly, and it was almost as if the air they were breathing was different and charged with a nervous energy. At the abrupt line where the bones ended, Ashok had somehow known they were now beneath the sea.

The ocean was hell. What could possibly be *under* hell?

Ashok couldn't feel fear like a normal man, but even he had hesitated a moment before continuing downward.

With lanterns held high, they had gone down what seemed to be an endless tunnel. It was spacious, far bigger than the drainage shaft the rebellion used to enter the Cove. There was a trench down the center, ten feet wide, but of unknown depth, because it was filled with murky water. Moyo told him that it was of consistent depth, about three feet deep, and despite Ashok's concern, nobody had ever seen a demon in here.

As the day went on he began to see strange frogs swimming in the trench, and he was cautioned that no matter how hungry he might become, eating them inevitably caused an unbearable agony in the stomach followed by death. Ashok hadn't been tempted, but that was still good to know.

Moyo was a wealth of knowledge like that. He passed the time explaining how his guild and the Traders Guild left supply caches all along the way, of food, water, and most importantly, lantern oil. Even their weighty packs would only get them a fraction of the distance necessary. These caches were so well disguised that only someone trained in looking for guild sign—coded symbols chiseled into the rock—would be able to find them. Anyone else who tried to cross the down below was doomed to be lost in the dark forever.

There were occasionally doors cut in the tunnel, or mysterious shafts that dropped straight down into unknown regions below, or sections where the walls had crumbled, revealing open spaces on the other side. Each of those areas was marked with guild sign, and Moyo used them to teach Ashok the written language of his kind.

"Through this gap there was treasure," Moyo said, tracing the lines with his fingertip. He had cautioned Ashok to always use touch, and feel the sign, as your eyes alone were not to be trusted in the flickering lantern light. "But see that slash? That means it's depleted now."

"What manner of treasure?"

"From that square, tile. The ancients made fine tile, smooth, nearly indestructible. Perfect for a collector to fill a bag and bring back to the workshop. And this twisty line? Wire. The ancients' wire doesn't rust. But it is all gone now. Anything near the entrance was picked clean long ago, by expeditions sent in my grandfather's grandfather's grandfather's day. Every year my guild sends one expedition just a little bit farther, a little bit lower, to see what we can still find." Moyo moved from that spot to another and placed his hand over a symbol next to a doorway that opened into seeming nothingness. "And this one? That number means a hundred-foot length of rope will get you to the bottom with some to spare, but the air has poison in it, so you will not return. We are not desperate enough to collect down there!"

Ashok felt each of those symbols for himself, memorizing the cuts with his fingertips, because if something happened to Moyo, it would be the only way he would be able to get home. Ashok didn't like counting on anyone other than himself.

Moyo talked a lot, pontificating on all manner of subjects Ashok had no familiarity with, and when he wasn't talking, he hummed a tune. When asked why he did so, Moyo said it was best to make a constant noise, so that the things in the underworld knew there was man about, and to skulk away. They were blind so wouldn't see their lights, but noise made it so they could avoid each other. Surprise meetings led to conflict.

When Ashok asked, "Conflict with what?" Moyo had simply shrugged. He didn't know. He'd never seen any of the things himself, but this was hard-earned collector knowledge, passed down through the generations.

It was more than likely superstition. Ashok suspected the real reason the scavengers taught themselves to make noise was because the unnatural quiet would eat at a man's sanity. Beyond the echo of footstep and the crackle of flame, there was *nothing*. Never before had Ashok experienced such stillness. In the times they stopped to sleep, it was so quiet that he could hear his own heartbeat. Slow and steady.

Without sun or moon to guide them, they slept when they were tired, and walked when they woke up. At each hidden cache they replenished their supplies, and Ashok was especially careful to learn those markings, because running out of oil was a terrible prospect. It would be too much like being back in that foul Fortress prison, only without the chains. The Heart of the Mountain could sharpen his vison at night, but this place was so pitch black that even Protector gifts weren't able to help his eyes much.

Moyo was a strange man, even for a foreigner, and it didn't help that he didn't have the Guru's knowledge of proper language, so Ashok was often confused by what he was trying to convey.

"Soon, will be to the clear. We'll use no fire for a time."

"Why?"

"So demons don't try to break in. Simple. Can they break in?" He shrugged. "They have not yet, but collectors never tempt them! It is said that once a collector taunted a demon through the clear, and it remembered, came on land a year later, went straight to his home, and killed him in his bed! Don't worry. If it is day, there is just enough light to walk through the clear, but also just enough to see the demons watching us from outside."

"How?"

Moyo said a word that Ashok didn't know, then thought it over, scowling. "Like glass." He rapped his knuckles on his lantern. "Or crystal maybe. If it is night, we will stop and rest till dawn. If it's day, we'll tie ropes to each other. Keep your left hand on the wall and your right on my pack. That way if there's a new hole and I fall in, you will catch me."

As Moyo had said, there was light, though it was extremely dim, and it was coming from the tunnel ahead. They extinguished their lanterns and walked toward a strangeness that Ashok would never comprehend. The clear—as the collector called it—turned out to be a construction the likes of which Ashok had never before seen, as there was nothing in Lok like this.

The top half of the tunnel had turned to glass. On the other side was water.

Endless water.

Even a man without fear had limits, and Ashok had to stop to compose himself.

There was ocean above and all around. It was a view into the depths of hell. There were fish. Swarms of tiny ones, and strangely shaped leviathans floating in the distance. Yet there were no demons, thankfully.

"Ah, we are in luck. It is a bright sun above the world today, Avatara."

If this was bright, he did not wish to experience what Moyo would consider dim, for very little sunlight made it to the bottom of hell. No wonder demons had no eyes. They would be nearly useless in their home.

"How far does the water extend above us?" Ashok demanded.

"Beats me. I think this is still shallow. It goes much deeper. There's other lower tunnels and other clears, only they're so very deep where there's never no sunlight at all. Or used to be, before those tunnels broke and flooded and were lost to us. I suppose demons live in them now. There's tunnels like this under your mainland too. Legend is the ancients dug them beneath the whole entire world."

Hell had a floor. Ashok had never thought of hell having a floor before, but here they were, walking upon it. The ground outside was made of silt and strange chaotic rocks, and monstrous plants in lurid colors that swayed about in some sick parody of a breeze.

"The clear is one thing we can't collect. Not that we would, because if there was a hole we'd all die in the flood and never be able to collect down here again. But even if we wanted to, tools can't so much as scratch it."

Hesitantly, Ashok touched the glass... only it wasn't glass at all. There was an energy to it, and even without testing, he knew it would be as hard as diamond, for this was a similar creation to that which the Forgotten had placed around Thera to protect her in the graveyard of demons. This invisible substance was the only thing holding back the entire weight of hell.

"Are you alright, Avatara? You're breathing kind of funny."

"We are in the home of evil itself."

"Oh no," Moyo laughed. "That's still ahead a ways!"

Thankfully, the clear didn't extend very far—it felt like a mile at most—before they were safely back beneath rock. Even though the sea was still above them, Ashok felt better when it was out of view.

They had seen no demons in the water. He was glad of that. The Law had taught him that the land belonged to man and hell belonged to demons, but who owned this strange world in between? Who would be the trespasser here? Judges enjoyed debating such questions of legal minutiae. If Ashok had come across a demon, the two of them would have solved the issue in a much more direct manner.

# Chapter 18

〰〰〰〰〰

Jagdish, Gotama, and their small cadre of bodyguards had ridden southwest in pursuit of the seventh and tenth paltans of Gotama's Mukesh Garrison, and the Inquisitors who had obligated them.

Strangely enough, Rada followed them.

Karno had been very displeased by this. The two phonthos were going to confront *Inquisitors*. It made no sense for them to go someplace sure to be crawling with the very Order they'd been hiding from. Rada couldn't even make a compelling logical argument for this tactic because following them hadn't even been her idea. How could she explain to the Protector that she was hearing a voice inside her head that was incessantly demanding that they needed to accompany Jagdish or else terrible things would happen?

She couldn't even dismiss it as some sort of hysteria or trauma related to her adventures, because that same whispering had saved her life during the raider attack, and she was almost certain it was coming from the terribly frightening black steel artifact she was carrying in the satchel slung about her body.

It would do no good to beg and plead with a man of absolute integrity such as Karno. It wasn't like he could be swayed once he had decided what was right, and his orders were to keep Rada safe from harm. Going out of their way to find a witch hunter was the opposite of safe. And it wasn't like Karno could be lied to either. It was almost as if Karno's complete honesty rendered him immune to deception. Either that, or Rada was simply a terrible liar and no match for someone whose profession required him to constantly deal with dishonest criminals who were far better liars than a librarian could ever hope to be.

Thus Rada had no choice but tell him the truth, regardless of how deranged it made her sound.

"The Asura's Mirror . . . talks to you?"

"I hesitate to call it *talking*, Karno. It's more like it forms extremely strong impressions in the mind, which one would then approximately translate into language in order to convey the meaning."

The giant Protector stared at her blankly.

"Basically, yes. The artifact is talking to me, and it is adamant that we must go with Jagdish or else."

Karno had paused in the act of saddling one of the horses Jagdish had so generously given them. "Or else what?"

Rada had made her plea near the charred remains of the stables, where it was just the two of them, and there had been no one else close enough to listen to their private conversation. It was bad enough this household knew who they were now; she didn't want them to think of her as crazy too.

"I'm not sure what *or else*. It's just giving me a general sense of unease that bad things will occur if I'm not there." It was far stronger than that, but Rada hesitated to describe it as profound dread, because that might make Karno even less inclined to let her go. "Please, believe me. I don't know why my presence is required, but it will be."

Jagdish and Gotama had already left earlier that morning, but recently enough that the two of them would be able to catch up. She had already hesitated to speak to Karno for too long as it was.

"Black steel told you that?"

"As I explained, not in so many words, no, but you know I'm not inclined toward exaggeration. This isn't some mere flight of fancy. The artifact is giving us a warning. We'd be fools not to heed it."

Karno simply grunted an acknowledgment and went back to cinching up the saddle, as infuriatingly untalkative as usual. She was really hoping that he wouldn't tell her that her impressions were wrong, a result of getting bumped on the head, or worse, she was simply tormenting herself for her part in the terrible bloodshed that was about to engulf all the land and trying to find some way to salve her conscience.

"You've dealt with such black steel material before, Karno, at least by proximity. I've read every book in the Capitol Library on the subject. We both know how incredibly powerful intact ancient black steel devices can be. Who is to say what this thing can or cannot do, or what its ultimate purpose may be? Vikram might have known more than he told me, and oh what a fool I was to ever accept his obligation, but it's too late for regrets now. I gave my word, so I think it might be like an ancestor blade, and now the mirror considers me its bearer. What kind of bearer would ignore their artifact's council?"

"But do you trust it?"

"What?"

Karno looked up from the buckles to stare her square in the eye. "Do you *trust* it?"

It was a fair question, for the last time Karno had seen the mirror out in the open it had eaten a man's arm. "Uh...Well..."

"Thought so. Saddle your animal."

She sullenly did so as, first caste or not, Karno didn't trust servants to do such important labors for him or his charge. As he had taught her, nobody else would care about the little things that were vital for her safety as much as she would. While she worked—on both the straps and her disappointment—Karno checked on the extra animals and supplies Jagdish had left them.

Her Protector had saved her life more times than she could count now, but this had to be done. Rada was determined that if he wouldn't accompany her on this mission, then she would go by herself, and he would have no choice but to follow...Or more likely, he would simply stuff her in a sack and carry her to the Capitol on the back of a pack horse, as Karno was the sort who took his orders very seriously.

He returned to her side just as she was finishing her work. "I will tell you of an event I have never before spoken of with anyone, and I trust it will remain in your confidence."

That made her curious as Karno was not one for stories. "Of course."

"What you ask me is foolishness, potentially drawing the

attention of Inquisitors…only I do know something about the whisperings of black steel. I was an acolyte of the Protector Order at the same time as Ashok Vadal. His sword was kept from him while he trained. Angruvadal remained stored in our vault during those years."

"Devedas told me about that. He said your acolytes must learn to only count on their own strength, and the strength of their brothers, and never be allowed an advantage like a magic sword."

"Except Devedas was the greatest among us, not a clumsy child from distant Uttara, too large for his age, who had not yet learned how to not trip over his own big feet. So Devedas was never assigned the ignoble duty of night watch over a mostly empty vault, the only thing inside of which could defend itself from thieves far better than any mortal guard. Yet guard Angruvadal I did. Night after night, many of which I was tempted to try and draw that sword."

Rada had read the horrible stories about what ancestor blades did to anyone they found unworthy when they tried to wield them. Not that anyone could understand what black steel was thinking, but if the sword didn't approve of you it would cut you. If it really disapproved it would remove limbs.

"Angruvadal already had a bearer, Karno! Why would you risk such a thing?"

"I was a poor boy from a poor house striving against the sons of Thakoors, phonthos, and judges. I longed to prove myself to my brothers. There is no higher honor than to be chosen by an ancestor blade. I thought if I could simply draw that blade, there would be no more need to train anymore. It is hard to explain to an outsider how harsh the life of a Protector acolyte is. Cold. Exhausting. Unforgiving. I would guard that vault, so tired I could barely keep my eyes open, but knowing that if I were caught sleeping the beating I'd receive would be merciless. The shame worse. All while that sword was there, tempting me. Not with what it really was, but what it symbolized. Like all youth, I was unwise. Impatient."

Blunt Karno was such the opposite of frivolity that Rada had a hard time imagining him as anything less than a rock of duty. Frankly, she had a hard time picturing the giant as a child at all.

"My pride ate at me, until one night, I decided to draw Angruvadal. If it killed or maimed me, so be it. I would be great or nothing…" Karno lifted one mighty hand, as if carefully placing his calloused fingers near an imaginary grip. He waited there like that, fingers slowly closing, trembling, as if he was reliving the memory…for so long that Rada became nervous, until Karno suddenly snatched his hand away.

"Then I didn't."

"Why?"

"Angruvadal warned me not to." Karno turned back to his horse. "Mount up. We must hurry if you expect to catch up with Jagdish."

She couldn't believe it. Rada had succeeded in swaying Karno Uttara! Surely that was an achievement very few others could claim. And that was also probably the most words she'd ever gotten him to speak in a single day! Hurrying before he changed his mind, Rada had leapt upon her horse and then ridden from the estate as if her life depended on it.

Despite that relative triumph, part of her was disappointed she'd succeeded in convincing him, for her heart desired nothing more than to go home. She had never longed for the life of an adventurous vagabond. With Devedas back, she could return to the comforts of the Capitol. She missed him as greatly as only separated lovers could, but more, she pined for her old, simple life: the Library and her important work there. She missed her family, even her spoiled little sister.

Her journey had taken her from the squalor of a goat farm to the opulence of Great House Vadal, as prisoner and pawn, and now that she finally had a chance to go home, here she was, chasing after some warriors because a black steel artifact had told her to do that instead. An artifact that never should have been her responsibility to begin with! The Asura's Mirror belonged to the Historians Order, not the Archivists. She was eager to give it back to them, and to never think about the frightening thing again. The few times she'd peered into it, she could have sworn *something* on the other side had been looking back. Now that something was communicating with her, which was even worse.

Despite pinning her disappointment on the mirror, there was one other reason Rada was hesitant to go home, though it was buried so deep that it was hard to articulate how or why she felt the way she did. The Capitol was where a grave injustice had begun. An injustice that her cowardice had helped perpetuate.

She knew her part in the matter was near inconsequential. If she'd not been intimidated into writing a false report about the history of the casteless, then somebody else would have. If she'd been brave enough to speak up in the Chamber of Argument, the plotters simply would have had her killed.

Rada had done the best thing she could think of, by seeking out Devedas and telling him of the conspiracy. Only now she knew that had turned out to be insufficient as well, and all the casteless in the world were to be murdered. Logically Rada knew that wasn't on her head, because if the fearsome Lord Protector Devedas couldn't stop the judges from voting for such madness, what difference could one librarian make?

Only when her logic and guilt clashed, guilt triumphed.

Thinking about the contents of the Inquisitor's letter had kept her up all through the night, and whenever she did manage to nod off to sleep, the damnable mirror would wake her up with feelings of unease. To return to the Capitol would be to return to the scene of her failure, and she was not ready for that yet.

So with the mirror prompting her that she needed to go and prevent some unknown harm, what choice was there? It probably wasn't related to the great evil her cowardice had aided, but it was something, and doing it would have to be enough to ease her conscience. She was powerless to stop the Capitol from murdering millions of casteless, but she could do *this*. Whatever *this* happened to be remained to be seen, but it would have to do. Then she could get on with her life.

An hour later they had caught up with Jagdish's band. Ten warriors had stopped their horses in the middle of the road to see who was pursuing them. Jagdish was clearly annoyed by their presence. Even the most gracious of hosts didn't want to bring the fugitives he had been harboring to a potential confrontation with Inquisitors. Rada had no good argument for that and didn't relish the idea of telling a bunch of Vadal warriors that she was carrying around a priceless ancient artifact that was bossing her around, but luckily Karno stepped in and simply declared that as a Protector of the Law, he wished to travel with them for a time.

Which settled the matter, as nobody argued with a Protector. Not even stubborn Jagdish.

Once Karno had declared it a matter of Law, Gotama asked, "So the big one actually is a Protector?"

"He is," Jagdish admitted.

"Does that mean we shouldn't pick a fight with the Inquisitors, then?"

"As long as any duels you provoke meet the legal require-
ments, Phontho, then your actions are of no concern to me or
the Protector Order."

"I'd advise against it, though," Rada interjected. "Inquisitors
really hold a grudge. I'm so sorry to trouble you again, Jagdish,
but we need to tag along. I promise to stay out of sight when
you meet with them."

"Aye . . . *meet* with them." Gotama snorted. "I'll not repeat
the kind words Phontho Jagdish was saying about the masks all
morning, or his detailed imaginings of what he was going to do
to the men who left his house open to the wolf."

The assembled soldiers all grinned at that, and since Rada had
heard Jagdish go off on a tirade before, she could only imagine
it was because his threats had been so elaborate and colorful. If
he'd been born a judge instead of a soldier, he would have made
a fine orator.

Jagdish just scowled until his men stopped smiling. "I'm
still angry, but I'm not a fool. Gotama wants his troops back,
and I'll settle for an apology and some proper groveling. I'm
sure our illustrious Thakoor wouldn't approve of us causing a
stir, but we can't fight a war with the Inquisition stealing whole
paltans." Then Jagdish looked toward the other phontho and his
bodyguards, and nodded politely, as if excusing himself, before
riding closer to Rada and Karno, as half these warriors clearly
didn't know about her particular circumstances. "Are you sure
you want to be there? I thought you wanted to get back to your
precious library. We're going in the wrong direction for that."

"Trust me, Jagdish, I'll stay out of the way and pretend to
be a servant or something. I'm practically a master of disguise."

"She brought a scarf," Karno stated flatly.

"Did she bring enough fabric we could convince them you're
a tent?"

Rada hadn't thought of that. A man of Karno's considerable
stature certainly stood out in a crowd, and after his last encounter
with Inquisitors had resulted in so many of them dying, he was
surely feared in their circles now.

"We will remain out of sight while you speak to them. If

there are any repercussions due to our presence, that will be between my Order and theirs. Vadal will bear no responsibility."

"Good to hear, Protector. Onward, then."

The group they were following had a considerable head start, and the Inquisitors must have been pushing them hard for so many to be traveling so fast. Fortunately their numbers made them easy to track. At first the paltans had stuck to the trade road, but then they had taken a less-used path through the rich Vadal farmland toward the northern Goda forest.

Vadal was truly a beautiful place, the most bounteous of all the great houses, with the nicest weather, and this was one of the rare times Rada got to actually ride and take in the sights rather than fretting because she was being pursued by someone. Though she was a lady of the first caste, Rada found that she enjoyed the company of these raucous warriors, which was remarkable, since Rada barely tolerated people at all. She'd been raised to think of warriors as dumb muscled brutes, but there was an honesty to their kind. Especially once they forgot she was of higher station, which was easy for them to do, since Rada lacked the haughty attitude common to most of her caste. Any first-caste arrogance she may have once possessed had been purged from her over the last year. It was hard to feel superior to others while running for your life or hiding.

Also they had all heard about how she had joined in the defense of the estate, which seemed to earn their respect. Her many visible scrapes and bruises were certainly a good reminder of her efforts.

Her mother had always warned her about the barbaric inclinations of young warriors. Perhaps they would have been ruder to a woman if given the opportunity, but if any of these had been so inclined to depravity, none would dare with Karno and Jagdish present. The threat of violent dismemberment ensured respectful behavior. The Capitol would probably be a nicer place if more high-caste youths had to worry about getting their hands cut off if they failed to keep them to themselves.

When night fell they built a fire and camped in a field of yellow wildflowers. As Rada lay beneath the stars, listening to the warriors jokingly insult one another, she wondered at how she'd ended up here, so far from her sheltered upbringing and her beloved books. Because the answer was her complicity in a terrible crime, she tried to force the guilt from her mind and ponder happier things instead. It made her feel flighty and girlish to think of handsome Devedas, but that was better than mulling over impending genocide.

The two phonthos sat by the fire, sharing a wineskin. They were keeping their voices low, but Rada could still hear them. She'd discovered that most warriors were a little deaf and unwittingly talked louder because of it. That was probably the result of all the constant yelling and getting bashed over the helmet.

"It's easy to ignore a letter from a distant arbiter, but what will you do when Harta gives us the official order?" Gotama asked.

"Vadal will be too busy making war on Sarnobat by then to worry about rounding up our non-people," Jagdish answered. "Warrior versus warrior. Sarnobat's hard as nails. A proper fight, as it should be."

"For now. Will the war last longer than the Capitol's insistence, though?"

"That depends on how good we are and how dumb our enemies are."

"May they be very dumb indeed." Gotama took a drink, then passed the skin over. "I've been soldiering longer than you have, so trust me, Jagdish, those orders will come. The worst ideas outlast the best. Bad ideas are survivors. They're going to make us go kill casteless."

"I know, but I meant what I told you earlier. This is one order that I'll never obey. Nor will any man under my command so long as I live and breathe. This extermination is wrong."

"You'd risk your rank? Oceans! You'd risk your life! For stinking fish-eaters?"

"I'd not massacre innocents from any caste or none at all. I'm a warrior, not a butcher, Gotama. There's no honor in that. Besides, I've known some casteless who were brave and smart and even noble as any whole man."

Gotama looked around suspiciously, as if was about to say something subversive. "Do you speak of the Black Heart?"

"I wasn't even thinking of him, honestly." Jagdish took a long drink, as if he knew he'd need the wine to help him sleep. "I got to really know a few casteless rebels in my travels. Fanatics and heroes yearning for dangerous freedom, but most of them just wanted to be left alone. They love and laugh, and fight and hope, just like us."

"I didn't know Harta had promoted a poet. You're an odd man, Jagdish Demon Killer."

"Still want to try and marry your daughter off to me?"

"Maybe I should wait and see if you get disgraced and executed first."

"A wise plan. See you in the morning, Phontho Gotama."

As Rada fell asleep, she wondered how many more lives her cowardly silence would ruin beyond the poor casteless themselves.

The next morning they came across angry merchants who'd had their livestock feed confiscated by the Inquisitors. Warriors couldn't just take whatever they wanted from the worker caste. They were required to pay for it. Even in times of crisis any property that was seized, the warriors would have to settle up afterward. However, the Inquisition was a Capitol Order, not bound by such conventions. Like the Protector Order, the Law said they could take whatever they required to complete their duties, and the workers had no choice but to comply. It was striking to Rada how much animosity this created toward the Capitol. It seemed a very ill-conceived policy.

Meanwhile, she noted that each time they needed supplies, Jagdish would debate with the worker over the price, and then pay slightly more bank notes than the agreed-upon amount. When she inquired about why he did that, he told her that workers were proud in their own way, so haggling was customary. The small bonus was a sign of respect, so they'd be eager to do business with his kind again in the future. She had found that a surprising insight from a warrior into the mind of a different caste, but Jagdish had just shrugged it off and said he knew how workers thought because he had been married to one.

The farmers they passed on the road had seen the big group of warriors pass by the day before. Jagdish noted though there were supposed to be many casteless who lived in this region, they'd not seen a single one all day. An overseer even complained to them and begged Jagdish to keep an eye out for his disobedient non-people who had not turned up to do their assigned farm labor. The casteless quarters of the small villages they passed appeared to be entirely deserted.

All the non-people had gone into hiding. The fact that they had somehow gotten word of their extermination before the warriors who were supposed to carry it out gave Rada some small measure of hope. But only for a little while, because then she reasoned, how long could they all hide?

Two of Jagdish's bodyguards, Joshi and Mohan, had grown up in this province, so they'd been taking turns serving as lead rider. At one point in the afternoon Mohan quickly rode back to the rest of them, shouting that the paltans had changed direction. Rada barely knew the man, but from the look on his face he seemed very confused by this.

"What is it?" Jagdish asked as he signaled for the rest of them to halt and take a break.

"They turned off this road onto an odd path. I've never been down it myself, but I know of this one. It's a dead end. From the tracks they've been riding with haste, but we should catch them later today."

Jagdish was clearly pleased by this. "Good. This errand has distracted me from my duties long enough. What's their destination?"

"That's the part that baffles me, Phontho. Nobody lives out there. It's a long, bad trail just to get to a valley of nothing. There're no workers settled there as far as I know. It's too isolated and the road too bad to make it worth cutting the timber. There might be hunting camps along the way, but that's it."

"Maybe this is where all the local casteless have gone, then," Rada suggested. "If the Inquisition knew they were hiding there, that's why they needed to take so many of your soldiers to kill them all."

"Doubtful," Gotama said. "Witch hunters wouldn't travel so far across house borders for something so mundane as non-people. Their kind is reserved for serious affairs. Besides, how would they even know? From the complaining workers it sounds like their casteless fled over the last couple of days, long after these Inquisitors would have left Sarnobat. If they got special orders to come all the way out here, it's got to be something bigger—like religious fanatics or illegal wizardry or a wandering demon."

"A demon?" Rada asked nervously.

Karno chuckled at that, which was probably the first sound he'd made all day. "Inquisitors can't handle demons. They'd send a Protector for that."

"Fair. We're too far from the ocean or the Martaban anyway." Gotama thought it over. The old man seemed to enjoy puzzles.

"My bet is illegal witches hiding in these woods! Probably stealing virgins to sacrifice to their false gods. But don't fear, my lady, as we've all been told Jagdish knows a thing or two about massacring gangs of illegal wizards. Right, Jagdish?"

Except Jagdish was silently scanning the dark woods, suspicious. "Nayak Joshi. Come over here."

That was the youngest of the bodyguards, and Rada thought of him as barely more than a boy, unable to even grow a beard yet. Except if Jagdish had picked him for bodyguard duty, Joshi must have had some measure of skill.

Joshi rode closer. "Yes, Phontho?"

"This area would have been under your father's protection. Do you know of any rumors about the valley at the end of this trail?"

"Ah . . ." The boy hesitated a bit too long. "Nothing proper Law-abiding people would ever speak of, no, sir."

Jagdish gave Joshi a wry look, then glanced at Gotama. "Phontho, I'm sure you've heard that when I was given this station, it was so sudden that there was no army for me to command, so I searched for warriors from across Vadal who had no other obligations, then I recruited the best of them."

"That's well known. We all expected your army to be a mess. Usually there's a good reason a man doesn't have an assignment." Jagdish's other men immediately bristled at that, but then Gotama quickly added, "But as it's been made clear by your many successful raids with them, that isn't the case with the ones you got."

"I knew how to pick them because I've been them. A good soldier can get disgraced and shunned for events beyond his control. Men like us just need an opportunity to show our worth, which everyone here has done. Which means Nayak Joshi will be able to speak freely before you now, without any loss of face. Agreed?"

"Well now I'm curious, Jagdish." Gotama's saddle creaked as he leaned forward to listen. "Spit it out, Nayak."

"In that case, sir, my father warned us to stay away from this trail. Workers used to cut timber here. Only they avoid it now because it's said to be cursed. They say that part of the forest is haunted. Of course, the Law says there's no such thing as ghosts, but you know workers. Right?"

"They found something, didn't they?"

"Ruins. Very old, but not very impressive. The Inquisitors in Mukesh were notified, and they came and scoured the place for anything religious. Then the Historians carried off anything they found interesting back to the Capitol."

"Historians do that," Rada said. "Like obnoxious little rats scurrying. That Order is the worst."

The warriors gave her a quizzical look, but of course they could never understand the bitter rivalry between Archivists and Historians. If there had been anything written here, the operation would have been obligated to the Library instead, rather than those illiterates from the Museum.

"And what did the illegal looters find?" Jagdish asked pointedly.

"Nothing of real value. All the treasure hunters complained about a bad feeling to the ruins, like they were always being watched, but they could never say by what. They poked around some but never found any black steel or forbidden trinkets worth selling, so they gave up."

"How's a junior nayak know how successful the local criminals were?" Gotama asked.

"My father was accused of taking bribes from magic smugglers to have his warriors look the other way."

"Was he guilty?"

"Guilty as the ocean!" Joshi laughed. "Sorry. I'm still bitter about him ruining our name. There's very few commanders who want a warrior serving in their paltans whose father was hung as a criminal."

Gotama laughed. "I'm starting to see why your men work so hard for you, Jagdish."

"Vadal has gone without a real war for so long that men of our rank have grown squeamish, worried more what the pampered ignorant first caste will say about how pretty our armies look, as opposed to how good they can fight." Jagdish looked toward Rada. "No offense intended."

"None taken!" Rada was the last member of her caste who would ever defend the vapid, shallow, useless nature of most of her peers. "I know them better than you do, and I don't particularly care for most of them either."

"Alright, then. Something in those ruins suddenly interests the Inquisition enough that they think it needs guarding more than our border. Let's go disabuse these fools of that silly notion."

They rode into the shadowed forest. Rada carefully placed one hand onto her leather satchel but the mirror inside remained silent.

# Chapter 19

Overthrowing the government required a great deal of work and an impeccable attention to detail, so it had been another very busy day for Grand Inquisitor Omand. There had been judges to threaten, bankers to bribe, and high-status warriors to frame for terrible crimes. He had fanned the fires of war in the west by ordering the assassination of an important Makao arbiter, while leaving evidence that the murder had been ordered by the Thakoor of Harban. Reprisals were sure to follow. Plus word had just arrived that heavy fighting had broken out between Thao and Kharsawan inside the city of Neeramphorn, which was pleasant news since Omand had barely needed to spend any resources at all to exacerbate that simmering conflict.

Best of all, across the land casteless were dying by the thousands. If things remained on schedule, soon that would be by the millions. Omand had no personal vendetta against the non-people. They had never done him wrong. He was so far above them, how could they? It was the demon's animosity that required their demise. Their sin was existing. Omand simply needed them to die so that he could live forever.

"Is there anything else, Taraba?"

His loyal assistant checked the briefing he had prepared—which would surely be burned the instant this meeting was over—and said, "We're still waiting for a report from the expedition you sent into Vadal lands. Our nearest agent was a low-status Inquisitor, so he obligated some local workers and started excavating the area as per your instructions. The witch hunter you dispatched to oversee the operation should arrive soon if he hasn't already. The last message said they had crossed the border and obligated two paltans of local warriors to guard the site."

"Good, good." Omand and the prisoner floating in a fetid water tank in the dungeons below were the only ones who knew the true purpose of that particular mission. "Speaking of Vadal..."

"It appears everything there is proceeding as you predicted. We have arranged for Lord Protector Devedas to find out that his woman was being held by Harta Vadal."

"Did you decide to plant rumors, Taraba, or something more direct?" Omand had no issue delegating assignments to properly skilled underlings. How else would they learn? He cared not how the work was done, as long as it was effective.

"Direct, sir. Anonymous letters, which will appear to have been penned in the halls of the great house itself have been sent, informing the Protectors that they are very concerned the Law has been violated in Harta's court, because a Capitol Archivist is being held there against her will. I believe Lord Protector Devedas will be suitably outraged."

However that issue sorted itself out, Omand would benefit. If Devedas killed Harta, his greatest political foe would be removed, and then Omand could simply go about painting Harta as a villain, slain by Lok's greatest hero, just as he had slain Ashok the Black Heart before that. If Harta killed Devedas, then the narrative became a tragic tale, of how a champion of the people had been murdered by a foul and treacherous Thakoor who was seeking to overthrow the Law. That would require Omand to find himself a new figurehead, but the *idea* of Devedas would serve either way.

"Excellent. Then I believe I will relax for a time and enjoy my pipe. You may go."

"Of course, sir."

Omand turned his chair toward the fine glass window. The Grand Inquisitor's office offered a magnificent view of the Capitol. The Inquisitor's Dome was perched high upon the slopes of Mount Metoro, and his office was near the top of that lofty tower. He did not mind the stairs, because they kept him fit in his graying years.

The climb was worth it, for beyond his window was the best view of the greatest city in the world. From up here it was like looking down upon the tiny cities on the Chief Judge's map table. Omand enjoyed watching the highest-status men alive scurry about, small as fleas, so far beneath him.

The only place that offered an arguably better view of the Capitol than the Grand Inquisitor's office was atop the dome itself, but there were so many condemned prisoners chained up there right now—being slowly cooked to death by the sun—that it was too crowded to enjoy it. Plus, the smell of the recently dead was unbearable, and it would remain that way until the vultures were done with them.

"Taraba, do you know what this building was before the Inquisition claimed it as our own?"

His assistant had been walking away, and paused, hand upon the door latch. "I believe it was some manner of church until the first witch hunter seized it."

"Something like that. It predates the construction of the Capitol by a long time, but the ancients knew how to build incredibly durable structures. It belonged to one of the multitude of different religions the tribes believed in back in those days. This peculiar bunch was a minority even among those. They didn't believe in burying or burning their dead. Death could not pollute fire or soil." Omand had to laugh at that foolish superstition, for he understood that death went wherever it felt like. "Instead they'd left the corpses on the roof for the birds to eat, and once the bones were picked clean, they'd sweep them into a hole, where they would tumble through a central shaft to their final resting place, a great cavern of bones, which now lies beneath our dungeons."

"What was once a fanatic's ceremony has become an effective tool of punishment and notable deterrent to Law breakers," Taraba said. "Marvelous."

"Indeed." The occasional whiff of rot upon the wind alone was enough to remind the Capitol who watched over them. Omand took off his mask so that he could place his pipe stem in his mouth. Taraba was one of the few who he could let down his mask before... the physical mask at least. "The first time I was obligated to serve in this tower, I served as a torturer, and my quarters were next to that shaft. I could hear the bones rattling as they fell. I was certainly deterred."

Taraba laughed, because that was the thing reliable underlings did when they assumed their master was trying to be humorous. Only Omand was not. That sound of clattering bones still haunted his dreams on occasion. Taraba abruptly stopped laughing when Omand stared at him blankly with his true face.

"Do you know what they called this place back then?"

"My apologies, Grand Inquisitor. I do not."

"No need to apologize. Your instructors probably deemed it forbidden religious knowledge, if they even knew the name themselves. It was called the Tower of Silence."

"An ominous name."

"Not to the original users, I suspect, but for our use, I find it strangely appropriate. Ominous, even. We loom over them, quietly watching. Silently vigilant against any who would break the Law. Acting only when their crimes and shortcomings force us to." Omand prepared his pipe, filling it with fine Vadal tobacco. "There is no gravitas to the title, *Inquisitor's Dome*. That is a simple description of our ownership and architecture, nothing more. I prefer the ancient name. I think we should return to it."

"The religious connotations are lost so I doubt any of the judges will take offense at an official name change." Taraba was not the sort to be bound by tradition. Which was unsurprising for a man who had once disguised himself as a filthy fish-eater and used a Fortress rod to assassinate the Chief Judge on the steps of the Chamber of Argument.

"To them it is just a change of name. To our allies it will be a bold symbol that a new age is upon us."

"Tower of Silence is a fine name for the home of the Inquisition, sir."

"I shall make an official announcement in the morning, then." Omand drew a match, but before he could strike it, there was a commotion on the other side of the door. Booted feet, moving swiftly. Omand had put down his pipe down and returned his ceremonial mask to his face by the time the runner knocked. Properly adorned, Omand nodded for Taraba to open the door.

The Inquisitor who rushed inside was one of the few trusted enough to serve as a monitor among the racks of demon bones that were waiting to receive messages from the other bones they'd been paired with, carried by witch hunters across the land. He hurriedly bowed, indicating his news was more important than propriety. "Grand Inquisitor, there is an urgent message from Witch Hunter Shiladitya."

Shiladitya was the reliable man who Omand had put in charge of the expedition into Vadal lands to search for the prize the demon had shown him. "I have been expecting this message, Inquisitor Varman. What about it causes you to interrupt my meeting?"

"It was a damaged partial, sir. The pattern fragmented during sending. That normally only happens when—"

"The sender is violently interrupted." Omand held out his hand. "Bring it to me." Varman rushed past Taraba to present their master with a single knuckle of demon bone. The adjoining joint would be in distant Vadal, in the capable hands of one of his best witch hunters. Inquisitor Varman scurried away as Omand held the bone to his temple and visualized the complex pattern necessary to free the information imprinted inside.

It wasn't a report. It was a warning. Omand listened, and it was a good thing he had put his mask back on, so that his subordinates would be spared seeing that their leader could still experience disappointment and anger, the same as any regular man. As Shiladitya's message disintegrated into incoherent screaming, the knuckle turned to dust.

Omand abruptly stood and started toward the stairs, grinding the ash between his fingers as he clenched them into a fist. Varman fled, while Taraba unquestioningly followed, but trailing a respectful distance, perceptive enough to recognize the fury in the Grand Inquisitor's walk, and wise enough to not to ask any questions.

With every step he took toward the dungeons, Omand's anger grew. It wasn't just being betrayed. Betrayal was always to be expected. It was that he had walked into this one. He had allowed his eagerness to overcome his suspicions. Normally, he was the master of the great game, but even a master can slip.

Omand had been played by a demon.

When he reached the dungeons, he passed the saluting torturers as if they weren't even there. Taraba realized where they were going and grabbed a torch from the wall to light their way.

As they neared their destination Omand snapped at Taraba, "Wait here."

The young Inquisitor was clearly nervous, because in all the years he had served the Grand Inquisitor, he had never before seen Omand Vokkan this upset. Very few had ever seen this level of emotion from him, and fewer still had lived to tell of it.

Omand barked at the guards, "Begone!" and they immediately fled.

The prisoner was floating in the filthy tank, its lump of a head already at the glass port, as if it was waiting for him. *Gloating.* Grasping a piece of bone from a pouch inside his sash, Omand pressed his other hand against the glass, and called to mind the complex pattern that would allow him to converse with the creature.

"You deceived me. I sent my men into a trap. What have you unleashed?"

*Doom*

"You promised me the source!"

*Remainder upon kill Ramrowan blood*

And then it showed him the terrible things Witch Hunter Shiladitya had seen as he had died. The entire expedition had been brutally massacred by what they had unwittingly freed. This particular demon magic was different, unlike anything he had encountered in his extensive travels. Even jaded Omand was temporarily taken aback by the savagery of his Inquisitors' deaths in the vision.

*Punish*

Along with that grim word, Omand was granted some understanding as to the nature of the thing that had just slaughtered the expedition. It was a living weapon, a terrible ancient thing, designed to gradually spread for hundreds of miles, killing untold numbers before its lifespan was through. Even after the scourge subsided, that entire region of Great House Vadal would remain poisoned and uninhabitable for generations.

That was unfortunate...for Harta Vadal.

The demon had led Omand astray, fooling him into believing it had inadvertently shown him where the source was hidden, while that vision had been a decoy all along. Instead of securing a priceless treasure, his men had disturbed a terror forgotten since the great war between man and demonkind.

Only how had the prisoner seen and been able to share Shiladitya's and the others' deaths? Then a terrible realization struck him. The Inquisition had been harvesting this demon's body for decades. It was likely most of the fingers hanging on the racks of the message room had been cut from its hands. If the demon was still magically bonded to those bones as they were to one another, how many other secret messages had it spied on over the years? Omand didn't know if that was the case, but if so, such knowledge could prove useful. He would have to test the theory later. For now he hid that thought from the demon.

"You lied to me, wicked beast."

*False source punish*

If demons were capable of laughter, it would have mocked him. Omand's greed and haste had caused this. The lesson stung. The demon would settle for nothing less than the total extermination of the casteless before giving up its secrets. Several Inquisitors and a hundred warriors had just been torn to bloody shreds and fed into a multiplying demonic engine, simply to remind Omand that their arrangement was a partnership.

"I should kill you for this."

The demon showed him another image, once again, from above, falling through the clouds engulfed in fire. It was the same as before, only now it was speeding toward the western side of Lok.

Was this at long last the real path the ancients' forge had taken when it had been cast from the sky?

The new vision ended abruptly.

*True source upon kill*

Omand was not easily stirred to emotion. The temporary thwarting of his life's work had angered him, but already he couldn't help but calculate how he could capitalize upon these sudden events. A scourge from hell had been loosed upon Great House Vadal. Thousands would die. So be it. Their suffering could be of use politically. Omand would learn from his mistakes and press forward, wiser.

It was rare that Omand was outplayed in the great game and never before had it been by something inhuman... He would savor this rare education.

"I assure you, all the blood of Ramrowan will perish. The extermination has begun. I will expedite the process. You will see. Then the next location you show me will be the real one, or our agreement is over. If our arrangement ends, abandon your dreams of freedom, for you will be nothing but parts to be harvested... forever."

Omand broke the spell and stepped away from the tank. The two of them stayed there, watching each other through the heavy pane of glass for a very long time. The reflection of the golden mask of the Law was superimposed over the demon's flat black skull.

"This is not finished, old friend."

It swam away, leaving Omand alone.

By the time Omand left the tank room he had already formulated a plan. "Taraba, send messengers to alert the Lord Protector, and summon all the judges. We must convene an emergency session in the Chamber of Argument immediately."

The demon was clever, but not as clever as it thought. This was not a defeat. It was an opportunity.

# Chapter 20

Jagdish was uneasy. This errand had already taken him away from his duties at the border for longer than he liked. He had left solid officers in charge of the defenses, but they weren't him. A warrior shouldn't let his pride dictate his actions, yet if he let this level of offense pass, he wouldn't be much of a warrior at all. Troubling him also were thoughts of his daughter, currently traveling toward the relative safety of Vadal City. Pari had her maid and guards and would surely be excited to go on such a journey. She'd probably miss him, but she was brave like her mother.

Being away from family was a warrior's lot in life.

The northern woods were thick, overgrown with moss, and teeming with game. The fact they saw no hunters told him that Joshi's assessment was accurate. The workers of Vadal weren't hungry enough to hunt someplace they thought to be haunted.

Like all Law-fearing men, Jagdish had no use for such myths, but if things went bad with the Inquisitors, he'd happily leave a few more dead bodies to haunt the place. Except he'd have preferred to tend to that sort of affair in front of loyal warriors only and without outside witnesses. Rada and Karno had complicated his life once again.

As their horses plodded down the uneven trail, Jagdish turned back to check on his guests. He was honor bound to help Rada because she'd saved his life—and he genuinely liked the curious woman—but her presence now was unfortunate. It was one thing to have a member of the first poking her nose into disreputable warrior business; it was another to have her accompanied by an unbending servant of the Law.

Karno was the second Protector he'd ever dealt with. The first had been a difficult man to get to know, but in comparison this one was an absolute cipher. Karno made Ashok seem talkative and friendly. If there were ever any gregarious sorts obligated to that particular Order, they must have beaten it out of those children in their cold mountain fort.

Rada was busy identifying all the butterflies based on illustrations she'd seen in a book, but Karno caught Jagdish watching and gave him a small nod. Their agreement would hold. The two of them were to stay back out of sight when the time came. Or at least that's how Jagdish took it, since the man of few words managed to convey a great deal with very little.

The Protector's presence simply meant that Jagdish would have to be more careful than he was normally inclined to be, but he was still in the right here. The Inquisition was frightening, especially to a regular soldier, except Jagdish had to remind himself that he was no longer a regular soldier. He was a man of rank and status now, recipient of Vadal's highest award for valor, and the wronged party. Inquisitors weren't above the Law and couldn't go about ruining a great house's defenses with impunity. This confrontation was a necessity. Jagdish knew that he was sometimes hasty in his decisions, but not on this one. Declaring offense was a calculated move, because how else could he demand respect from his soldiers if he let the willful endangerment of their home go unanswered? How could he expect his men to fight the wolves of Sarnobat if their leader let Inquisitors stomp all over his dignity?

Also, with *two* angry phonthos, their offense became even more undeniable. Insulting him and Gotama was like unto insulting all the army of Great House Vadal, and by extension, their Thakoor himself. Harta Vadal may have despised him and was surely planning on putting the blame for their impending illegal war on Jagdish's head—only that also meant he needed to keep Jagdish around until then. Surely Harta would back his phonthos in their disagreement against these Inquisitors.

Jagdish had never fancied himself a political man, but he was learning it wasn't that different from regular war...just more dishonest.

If the Inquisition leader was prideful, then they would settle this affair the proper way, and either apologize, or take personal offense and duel. If he was unreasonable and tried to force a greater confrontation, Gotama's men would happily forsake their obligation to the hated Capitol Order after one word from their beloved commander, leaving the Inquisitors terribly outnumbered, and *then* Jagdish would challenge whichever idiot had left his house unprotected to a duel. Sure, he'd never fought a witch hunter before, but he'd battled wizards and even Ashok Vadal. Compared to those, what was some mask-wearing fop?

The trail was so poor that they often had to dismount and lead their horses. Roots waited to trip them. Parts of the trail had been washed out by the rains. Havildar Mohan and Nayak Joshi were in the lead, a mere twenty yards ahead, but the path curved back and forth so much, that they were often much closer, though the underbrush was so thick that Jagdish could only catch glimpses of them through it.

"Stay alert, boys," Gotama warned. "This is tiger country."

"Natural and unnatural both," Karno muttered.

When the old man turned back in his saddle toward the Protector to inquire what he meant by that cryptic warning, Rada supplied, "Witch hunters can turn into tigers."

"Ah, come now, my lady. That's just stories to frighten Law breakers."

"On the contrary, it is one of their wizardly abilities. I've seen them do it with my own eyes."

Jagdish scowled, as he'd not thought about having his opponent shape-shift into a tiger. That would certainly complicate a duel. "You seem unconvinced by her words, Gotama, but I know Ashok fought a wizard who assumed the form of a giant snake once, and another who turned into a swarm of insects. I myself have seen men transform into giant birds to flee the battlefield."

"Hmmm...Then I accept your tale as true, Lady Rada, and please forgive my incredulous nature, for I am but a poor country soldier, unaccustomed to the wily tricks of wizards."

As they continued their journey deeper into the woods, Jagdish's unease grew, and not just because of any potential duel. The lush forests of Vadal were always vibrant with the sounds of life. When they'd started down this trail they had seen a multitude of birds and animals, but as the hours passed, an unnatural stillness had fallen over the place.

Something tugged at the back of his mind. Not fear, as it was a deeper instinct that was troubling him. Their horses had grown skittish, and hesitant to continue onward. Jagdish could tell the men were feeling it too, their eyes flickering back and forth, nervous, and not just because of Gotama's tales of hunting tigers in terrain like this. The closer they got to catching up with the stolen paltans, the worse that skin-crawling sensation became.

The last time Jagdish had felt a sensation like this had been on the far end of the continent, in the awful swamps of the Bahdjangal...where the Sons had fought a demon. That was impossible, though, as there were no rivers deep enough to hide a demon near here, and they were still many days from from the coast.

When they stopped to let the horses rest and graze, Jagdish watched the tiny stream they drank from suspiciously, as if waiting for a mighty demon to leap from its hiding place in less than a foot of water.

Karno joined him at the edge of the water and spoke quietly. "I said we would hold back when you confronted the Inquisition."

"Do you wish to change that plan?"

"I do." The Protector must have been sensing the danger as well. "I feel an evil ahead."

"If you want to take Rada and turn around, none here would think less of you." Not that a man like Karno cared about the opinions of mere warriors, but Jagdish felt it had to be said anyway. "The rest of us must continue."

"As do we."

"Why? Why are you even here, really?"

The Protector glanced over to where his charge was carefully checking her horse's hooves, laboring in a very un-first-caste-like manner. "Rada believes her presence will be required."

"For what?"

Karno shrugged.

"That's helpful. Protectors take orders from librarians now, do they?"

"No...But I trust her."

That was rather surprising. "I'd wager the list of people you trust isn't a long one."

"It was short even before most of those on it died." Karno continued studying Rada. "She is not like most of our caste. Rada is without guile. She believes her presence will be needed to prevent a great harm, so I believe her."

Jagdish sighed. Rada *preventing harm* was the only reason he was alive and with this rank. "Maybe librarians are good luck. Alright, you'll do whatever you will regardless of what I say on the matter, but when it comes time to confront the masks, I won't have time to be stumbling over the finer points of the Law. Understand?"

"I do, warrior. Except it is not the stink of witch hunter that raises the hairs on the back of my neck today."

The Protector's words chilled him, for that Order dealt with the unnatural things that dwelled in the darkest corners of the continent. "There's something out here, alright, and it's violating more than just the Law. No wonder the locals say this place is cursed."

"The pall we feel is not always this strong here. For if it were, they would have summoned my Order to investigate."

"Lucky us, there's one of you here now." Then Jagdish raised his voice so all would hear. "Break is over, boys. That's enough lollygagging. Ready up. Stay sharp. Let's go fetch our brothers and have a few words with the masks about their unrighteous ways."

As they got closer to the end of the trail, an oppressive gloom fell over the group. It was a struggle to keep their horses from bolting. Warriors who were accustomed to showing their bravery were clearly having a difficult time maintaining their composure. The temperature was pleasant in the shade of the trees, yet Jagdish was sweating like he'd been sparring for hours.

"Easy, lads," Gotama urged his men. "These Inquisitors must be carrying a great deal of demon magic upon them to cause such a malignant spell over this place."

"I carried tons of the stuff all the way from the mouth of the Nansakar to Vadal. This isn't demon bones causing this." Jagdish glanced back toward Rada, to find that she was pale and nervously clutching her satchel so tight that her knuckles were making the leather audibly creak. "This is something different."

According to Joshi's knowledge of the area, they should be nearing the ruins. The obligated warriors should have left lookouts, and even if they had been well hidden—which would be easy in a forest so thick—surely they would have identified themselves when they saw their phontho.

"Gotama, are your missing risalders smart?"

"Smart enough they would've posted guards along the only way in. Their lack is troubling...I'm thinking your offense can wait, Jagdish. Let's get my men and go home."

Mohan called out a warning. They had reached the end of the trail.

As they caught up with the point riders, Joshi's and Mohan's mounts were stomping nervously, not wanting to get any closer. There was a clearing ahead, man-made from the look of all the stumps. Those trees been cut down years ago to build the few crumbling shelters that were visible, and the rest had probably been used for firewood. This was where the workers had lived while they were looting the ruins.

There was no sign of life.

Jagdish's horse balked and he had to fight to control him. These were Vadal war horses. They weren't Zarger's massive beasts, but they were bred to handle the stress of combat and the smell of carnage. They weren't easily spooked.

"Gotama, they're your men. How do you want to proceed?" Jagdish asked.

"The only way I know how. Directly." Gotama stood in his stirrups and shouted. "I am Phontho Gotama of the Mukesh Garrison! I have come to reclaim my seventh and tenth paltans from their illegal obligation. Show yourselves, Inquisitors!" Despite the old man still possessing a proper commander's bellow, and the sound echoing through the woods, no answer came. "Oceans. Where is everybody?"

They couldn't explore on horses near to panic. "Half of us will stay here, while the other half checks it out." Then Jagdish dismounted so there would be no question which group he belonged in. He wasn't the sort of phontho who sent men into danger while he stayed safe in the back.

Apparently neither was Gotama, as he quickly joined Jagdish on foot, a fact that surely distressed all of their bodyguards to no end. "Abhir, Tarsh, you'd better not let my horse run off. I'm not going to march home on my bad knee."

Jagdish signaled for two of his to remain as well, before Karno got off his horse, took up his war hammer, and told Rada, "Stay here."

She gave him a worried nod, still clinging to that leather satchel as if her life depended on it.

They started across the clearing, wary. To Jagdish, it felt like they were walking into an ambush. "Don't lose sight of the men next to you."

The ground was churned up near where the paltans had watered the animals at a nearby stream. The dirt was dry and soft, and each step kicked up just a bit of dust. There were fresh tracks everywhere—horseshoes, standard Vadal-issued boots...and something else. Jagdish tried to understand what could have made the strange pattern. They looked like a path of symmetrical holes, like when he'd seen workers planting seeds in a line with one of their new-fangled tools, only there were two parallel lines, and these holes were staggered, with an empty space between them wide as his palm.

"I've found blood." Zaheer squatted down, touched the drying mess, then examined his fingertips. "It's soaked into the dirt but it's only a few hours old."

Jagdish drew his sword, and the rest followed his example. As they continued moving toward the center of the clearing, they spotted more blood, both pooled on the ground and splattered on the stumps. Blood always told a story. Every man here was a seasoned combatant, so they recognized the spray of a severed artery, or the meandering trail of a man who'd just had his throat cut before it turned into a puddle where he had finally fallen and bled out.

None spoke, but they were all thinking the same thing: There had clearly been a battle here, but there were no bodies. Where were the severed limbs? The dropped weapons? The scraps of cloth or broken bits of armor?

The tracks had changed. There were far more of the strange lines of small holes, and worse, bloody drag marks. And every single one of those appeared to be going in the same unerring direction to the back of the clearing.

Toward the ruins.

"Wait here," Jagdish ordered, forgetting in the moment that he was the leader and the men at his side were supposed to be guarding him, not the other way around. He began creeping forward alone, only to be joined—unsurprisingly—by Protector Karno. The two of them followed the many drag trails; it was clear from the clawing finger marks in the dirt that some of those being carried along had still been alive at the time.

"There's blood, but no flies drink it," Karno whispered.

"What does that mean?"

"It is unknown. I have not seen this before."

It was a Protector's duty to understand such things. What manner of evil would be a mystery to the likes of that imposing supernatural Order?

As Joshi had said, the ruins were small: just a pile of stones that might have once been a small pyramid, barely ten feet tall. Nothing compared to some of the vast ancient structures inside and around Vadal City. It was clear that the stones had been intricately carved once before the Inquisition had come along and chiseled away anything that might have featured illegal religious icons.

What had been carved upon those walls so long ago? Perhaps it had been a warning sign?

Over the years many shallow holes had been dug around the pyramid by treasure hunters. It was clear those were old because they were now overgrown with moss and weeds. However, there was one pit, far larger and deeper than the others, and around it were vast piles of freshly turned dirt. The new excavation also differed from the others in one other profoundly disturbing way: all the drag trails disappeared into it.

Jagdish had been a fine border scout, stealthy as a fox. Despite his massive size, Karno proved to be Jagdish's equal, and the two of them made almost no sound while they approached the pit. As they crept up to the edge, Jagdish heard a noise coming from inside the hole that was unlike anything he had ever heard before. There was a rending, tearing, cracking, like a dog going at a bone, but not one bone and set of jaws, but hundreds, and combined, it made a noise that reminded him of bees swarming.

Slowly, uneasily, Jagdish lowered himself into the soft dirt and crawled forward, so as to not silhouette himself against the sky and display himself to whatever was in the hole making that awful noise. Once at the edge he peered into the pit...and then tried to comprehend the sight below.

They had found Gotama's seventh and tenth paltans, as well as many workers and Inquisitors and all their horses, though it was difficult to tell what was what, with all the bodies being in so very many pieces.

The pile was covered in a swarm of scurrying insects. Thousands and thousands of them, except each one was easily the size of his hand and dark as demon hide...and then Jagdish's growing terror was interrupted by the realization that these were not mere insects. *They were demons.* Or at least somehow related to those awful soldiers of hell, sleek and black, with four spidery limbs that each ended in a wicked point.

There was no way so many bodies could fit into a pit this size, but the demonic insects were rendering them down, rapidly and efficiently, into their component bits, and then spearing and carrying the chunks down a central hole, from which came a strange pulsing light. It was almost as if they were feeding fuel into some manner of demonic furnace buried there.

Jagdish wasn't going mad or suffering from delusions, because Karno was clearly witnessing the same unspeakable evil. Even the unflappable Protector recoiled in disgust.

Somehow the demons sensed them. The buzzing stopped. A thousand featureless heads turned their way.

"Run."

Jagdish and Karno sprinted across the clearing.

His men saw their leader's fear, and lifted their blades, ready to fight the unseen enemy.

There would be no stopping this enemy with blades. The seventh and tenth had tried that and ended up in the hole, being fed piece by piece into a demon light. "Get to the horses! Retreat down the trail! Go! Go!"

The demonic scourge erupted from the pit behind them.

Jagdish turned back just long enough to see a mass of tiny demons gushing forth like spilled oil. Thousands of sharp feet piercing the dirt made a sound like the raindrops of a thunderstorm as they scurried after the fleeing warriors, nearly as fast as a man could run. He had to turn around to keep from tripping. Falling meant dying. Those legs had been slicing bits off of dead men easy as a butcher carving a hog.

Despite his size, Karno easily outran Jagdish. The Protector leapt over a fallen log, then crouched on the other side and waited for Jagdish to pass. With a roar he hoisted the heavy log chest high and hurled it toward the monsters. As it bounced and tumbled through them, the impact sent some of the tiny demons flying away, but it crushed many...that popped right back up out of the soft dirt, seemingly unharmed, to resume the chase.

Jagdish caught up to the others, but unfortunately they weren't yet running, and then Jagdish realized why. The ground throughout the clearing was shifting. There had been more demons burrowed into the dirt and they were beginning to stir.

"What manner of evil is this?" Gotama thrust his sword hard into a squirming patch. When he lifted the blade there was a creature impaled on the end, about the size of a kitten, but with a black triangular body and four barbed limbs. Milky blood ran down the steel as the thing thrashed. Gotama flicked it away in disgust.

Hundreds more of the tiny demons erupted from the ground all around them. The warriors were ready to fight, but they hadn't seen the black mass of evil that had been vomited up from the pit, and it was closing on them fast.

"If we fight here we die! Get to the horses!" Jagdish shouted and thankfully Gotama wasn't too proud to heed the words of a younger warrior. "Retreat!"

As they ran, all the demons went after them.

Thankfully, unlike many phonthos, Gotama had not gone to laziness and fat, so could still run like a proper soldier. "Where are my boys?"

"Dead," Karno stated.

The giant horde of demons was gaining on them. "As we will be if we stop!" Jagdish urged.

And sure enough, because fate was a fickle whore who delighted in tormenting warriors, a few yards later one of Gotama's men tripped over a root and crashed face-first into the dirt. Jagdish cursed himself for giving that evil bitch ideas as he spun around and went back for the fallen man.

Only the monsters surged forward, engulfing the warrior even as he sprang to his feet. They clambered over his boots and climbed up his legs, every movement cutting like razors. He cried out and fell to his knees, one hand reaching for Jagdish, but then bugs were swarming up his back and hips and he was stabbed dozens of times, with legs striking faster than Jagdish could blink. The vile things scurried onto his head, and crawled down his extended arm, slicing all the way. And then the warrior was just *covered*.

The demon pile sank to the ground, the screams beneath muffled. By the time Jagdish realized there wasn't a damned thing he could do to help, the lump with the dying warrior inside was already heading back toward the pit.

That killing had slowed the horde only for the briefest instant, before the rest were back after them.

Their horses were panicking, crying and rearing, and the men they'd left behind were doing their best to control them. This was why warriors never tried to fight real demons on horseback! Animals simply couldn't handle the presence of hell's minions.

"Where's Vithu?" one of Gotama's men asked, looking around desperately for his missing friend.

"Gone. Everyone down the trail, fast as you can."

"Is this what you came for?" Karno asked Rada.

The librarian was fighting her bucking horse, but she kept her head enough to answer, "It's not said anything yet!"

"Then go." Karno grabbed her horse by the bridle, forced the entire animal in the correct direction, and smacked it hard on the rump. The horse sped off, with Rada holding on for dear life.

"What's not said—" Then Jagdish flinched as something hit him in the head. A big piece of bark had bounced off his turban and was lying at his feet. He looked up to see there were demons above them, high in the branches of the trees. "Above us!"

Except his warning was too late, and men and horses screamed as the bugs landed on them and immediately hooked their deadly limbs into flesh. They ripped through skin and muscle like a worker's saw.

Jagdish had seen a great many men die in his life, but never like this.

"Someone must survive to warn the great house!" Gotama shouted as he climbed onto his mount. "Stop for nothing!"

The great wave of bugs was nearly upon them, so thick in number they were turning the clearing black. The way out was too narrow. The demon tide too fast. They weren't all going to make it. Jagdish drew his sword and began slashing through the ropes their packhorses were fighting against. They tore free and began to run desperately around the edges of the clearing, searching for a way out. Whichever direction a living thing moved a line of demons followed. Man or animal, the demons didn't seem to care. All Jagdish could do was hope that distraction would be enough to spare the rest of them, as he caught his horse and vaulted into the saddle.

"Protect the phontho!" Havildar Mohan shouted.

"To the ocean with that!" Jagdish shouted. "Ride for your lives!"

The great wave broke around some of the loose horses. They

snorted and kicked and Jagdish couldn't bear to watch them die. Joshi yelped in surprise as his horse reared back, demons clambering up her flanks. Luckily Zaheer rode alongside just in time for the younger bodyguard to grab onto his brother's arm and leap free. Joshi's horse fell backward, monsters clinging to its belly like vicious ticks, and then she was gone into the swarming demons as two of Jagdish's bodyguards rode away.

The rest of the warriors had reached the trail, but Jagdish saw Karno was still on foot, hammer in hand. "What are you doing? Ride, you fool!"

Most of the swarm was distracted ripping apart Joshi's steed, but one of the little demons lurched toward Karno. A log didn't flatten them, but the concentrated force of a war hammer smashed the thing flat, splattering white blood everywhere. "I will bring up the rear."

*Oceans! Every Protector is a madman!*

Karno smashed another bug, and then sprinted after Jagdish, and somehow he kept up with the horses. Protectors might all be brave lunatics, but they were also the greatest athletes in the world, empowered by whatever secret rites it was their Order bestowed on them.

It was a mad rush through the forest. Branches tore at their faces. Jagdish could barely see Mohan just ahead of him through all the dust that had been kicked up. The trail was narrow and rugged, and every time Jagdish looked back, the demonic horde was still in pursuit, a churning mass of black razors. Karno would turn, kill a few more, then flee, doing this over and over until Jagdish lost track of him through the trees.

There was a crash ahead. One of the horses had tripped, going end over end in a cloud of dust. It was a brutal tangle of broken legs. Luckily the rider wasn't crushed beneath but was hurled hard into the grass instead. The other warriors were too close behind and going too fast to stop and help.

The downed rider was Rada.

"Whoa!" Jagdish pulled hard on his reins, fighting a mount with the smell of blood in her nostrils and fear in her heart, but he wasn't about to let his honored houseguest get killed.

"I'll get her, Phontho!" Mohan shouted. "You must escape!"

His bodyguards had an obligation to fulfill, but so did Jagdish, and besides, he was closer. "Rada, get up! Give me your hand!"

She was shaken and bleeding from a cut on her face, but the librarian was made of sterner stuff than she looked, because she struggled to her feet and stumbled toward him. Jagdish caught Rada by the wrist and swung her up behind him on the saddle. "I've got her!" His steed needed no urging and sprang forward.

They'd made it only a few feet before Rada let go of him and desperately began grasping at her clothing. At first Jagdish thought she was checking for injuries or was panicking because she thought there was a demonic bug clinging to her garments, but then she shouted in his ear, "The mirror! I've lost the mirror!"

*"What?"* When he looked back over his shoulder he saw Rada's injured horse was thrashing about because it already had half a dozen demons clinging to it.

Karno was running along behind them. "I'll get it." And he *turned back.*

The Protector went in swinging, flinging demons in every direction. The horse's rolling and kicking seemed to be attracting most of their attention, but several of the tiny creatures flung themselves at Karno. He batted some out of the air, but others made it through, and Karno grimaced as he was stabbed. Karno stomped them beneath his boots, he killed more with his hammer, he ripped a bloody one from his side and then squeezed it with his bare hand until it popped, but they kept coming. When Rada's horse stopped fighting, more of the creatures turned their attention upon the Protector. Despite that, he reached Rada's satchel and snatched it up by the broken strap.

"Run, Karno!" Rada screamed.

The Protector did, but the demons were all around him. He wasn't going to make it.

"Hang on." Jagdish's instinct was to wheel about and try to rescue Karno, but suddenly Havildar Mohan cut them off.

As he rode past, the bodyguard gave Jagdish a look as if to say *Let me do my damned duty for once, Phontho.* Then Mohan went straight toward Karno, screaming their battle cry, *"For Vadal!"*

He made it most of the way there before his horse realized it was about to run into a field of knives and recoiled in fear. Mohan was thrown from the saddle, but got up fast, sword appearing in hand.

There was nothing Jagdish could attempt without endangering Rada, and he was far too honor bound to do that. "Saltwater."

Mohan laid into them, cutting a swath through the creatures, but then they were on him, ripping and tearing. Bleeding profusely, he somehow managed to reach Karno and accurately slash a pair of demons from the Protector's back. For a moment, both men disappeared through the haze of dust and demons.

But then Karno crashed through.

He was moving faster than any man Jagdish had ever seen. Karno *caught up* to Mohan's running horse, took hold and leapt into the saddle. The Protector still had demons latched onto his arms and back and he yanked the things off and tossed them aside in a bloody spray.

Mohan was gone. They rode like mad.

When they had a small lead, Jagdish slowed enough for Karno to get alongside. The Protector was covered in lacerations and punctures of unknown depth. He handed back Rada's satchel, then told Jagdish, "Take the reins if I pass out."

Jagdish knew enough about the Protector's ways to realize their magic could only heighten one physical ability at a time. He'd seen Ashok survive the unsurvivable, climb the unclimbable, hear the unhearable, see impossible distances, and perform inhuman feats of strength, but he had never seen Ashok do more than one of those at once. It appeared Karno was the same and currently needed to concentrate on not bleeding to death.

They continued down the twisting path, faster than the demons, but those things seemed to be tireless in their pursuit, while their horses were laboring and lathered in sweat. Worse, the trail had many switchbacks, while the demons moved in a straight line, seemingly unburdened by passing through the thick brush.

"They're ahead of us!" a warrior cried. A horse screamed and branches broke as someone collided with a tree.

Riders were coming back up the trail, Gotama among them. "There's too many. We're cut off."

Either the demons possessed some form of intelligence to circle ahead of them, or there were just so damned many of them they could fill the entire forest. The group milled around as the enemy closed in. It was distressing to see they'd lost half their number and with trees close on all sides this was an awful place to make a stand. Jagdish spotted a jutting pile of rocks in the distance. "Abandon the horses. We'll take that high ground."

"It's more defensible than this," Gotama agreed.

Jagdish dismounted, then helped Rada down. It was clear

that fall had bashed her head, but hopefully the librarian wasn't too dizzy to run.

Karno seemed to snap out of a trance, and pronounced, "Good enough." Then he went to Rada's side. "I'll see to her." And by that Jagdish assumed that he meant he'd bless her with a quick and painless death rather than let her be carried back to that pit of light and flesh.

"Good luck," Jagdish told his horse in farewell, and then fled through the trees.

The demons were right behind them. Joshi and Zaheer placed themselves close to Jagdish, determined to die as righteous bodyguards should. The undergrowth tangled with flowering vines waiting to trip them. Fine Vadal blades were dishonored and used like machetes.

A warrior bellowed as a demon dropped onto his face. Gotama's reaction swing was so fast that the bug didn't even have time to strike with its legs, and so clean that he didn't so much as nick his own man's skin. Perhaps it was good that Jagdish had not dueled the old-timer after all!

The brush thinned as they entered a rocky field. The boulder pile Jagdish had spied wasn't much, but some high ground was better than nothing. "Get to the top." He turned back to check, only to discover they were down another man. He'd either got turned around in the woods and separated from the group, or the demons had taken him down so quickly that he'd died before he could scream. "Climb, damn it! Climb!"

The rocks were slick with moss, but there were no trees above them, so the demons could only attack from below rather than fall on them. They scrambled up the rocks, constantly having to pause and hack the fastest demons that were slashing at their heels. The pile only rose twenty feet above the field, but it still felt like climbing a mountain.

The summit was only a few yards across, barely big enough to fit them all.

One of Gotama's men slipped down a boulder, and before he could right himself, a demon attached itself to his leg. In a flash it burrowed deep into his thigh. Zaheer caught that screaming warrior by the arm and dragged him over the top. Karno grabbed the demon, tore it free, and hurled it against the rocks so hard that it splattered everywhere.

Jagdish grimaced when he saw the ghastly wound, muscle torn free clear to the bone. "Pick a spot and hold the line," he ordered as he took off his sash and tossed it at Rada. "Librarian, use this to tie off his leg, just above the wound, hard as you can, then stuff the rest in the hole."

She caught the sash, seemingly unsure at first, but then went to work trying her best to save the crippled warrior.

The green and gray of the boulder field was slowly turning black from all the churning bodies.

Gotama glanced his way. "Any ideas, Jagdish Demon Slayer?"

Of course he didn't have any ideas. They were surrounded and doomed, but Jagdish would never say that in front of his men. "Fight until we win."

"That's the spirit. Let's show these demon scum what Vadal men are made of!"

# Chapter 21

The usually haughty judges were nervous. These were important men who delighted in being one step ahead of their political adversaries. They'd not expected to be called here today, and that upset them, for the Capitol did not care for surprises.

Devedas enjoyed watching their discomfort.

An emergency session in the Chamber of Argument was an extremely rare event. Only a handful of individuals had the authority to call for such a thing, such as the Chief Judge—the office of which was still vacant due to the assassination—a great house Thakoor, or the head of a Capitol Order, and in that last case it had better be for a damned good reason, like a terrible crisis that needed to be dealt with in an expedited manner. To call for an emergency session was to risk your status, and no one in the Capitol was foolish enough to do so lightly.

The judges were already conspiring, trying to figure out who had called for this sudden meeting and why. Devedas called upon the Heart of the Mountain to sharpen his hearing and listen in on their whispered conversations. There was war in the west. War in the east. Rebels everywhere. Casteless exterminations. Looming starvation. Economic collapse. So on and so forth. Their speculation was endless.

Devedas didn't know why they were here either, but unlike

the rest of these fools he at least knew who had invoked his authority to force this meeting. Omand's coded message had not elaborated why, but he had warned Devedas that his presence would be vital.

The chamber was not nearly as crowded as usual. Messengers were still trying to track down all the usual attendees. When the judges couldn't be found or were off on holiday, they'd called for the secondary representatives from each house, and if those were unavailable, then the chamber obligated the highest-status man available from each great house delegation to serve. Devedas had worked in this hedonistic city long enough to know that for many of the absent judges it was because they were too drunk, under the influence of the poppy, or off doing some manner of illegal debauchery in one of the Capitol's pleasure houses. Devedas had executed bandits with more honor than the typical Capitol judge.

The gallery for non-voting spectators was filling in as well, representatives from various Orders. And beyond them was the section for the lower castes. The chamber hadn't sent for any warriors or workers to testify, but these high-status individuals must have heard and come out of curiosity. Devedas saw the colors of every great house army in the seats. If the meeting was about illegal house war, they'd need to know, either for self-protection, or lucrative opportunity. There were also a great many rich and important workers, though Devedas had never bothered to learn what all their insignia meant. Bankers most likely. Devedas found that the workers who printed and loaned the Capitol's money supply were too self-important for their own good, and often forgot their place.

The runners must have successfully scrounged up enough high-status men from each house to form a voting quorum, because the presiding judge banged the staff against the floor to call the session to order. That feeble old figurehead had no idea why they were there either, so he quickly and gladly offered the staff over to Grand Inquisitor Omand.

As Omand rose from his seat in the gallery and walked toward the podium, there was a great deal of murmuring from the judges. Omand was loved by none yet feared by many. Some of these men he had cowed into subservice, through threat or blackmail. Others had avoided the spiderweb entirely thus far, but they had to know that Omand was a force to be reckoned with in these halls. Despite his importance the Grand Inquisitor rarely spoke within the chamber and had never once called for an emergency session in all the years he had been master of his Order. Why would he do such a thing now? The curiosity was too much for them to bear, and the chamber fell silent.

Omand took the offered staff, then faced the audience, enigmatic and faceless. "Honored judges, as your humble servant, I shall not waste any more of your valuable time than is necessary." The golden mask of his office gave Omand's voice a haunting quality. "I bring warning that a grave danger has risen in the north."

The judges shared confused glances. Devedas listened as scribes were quietly questioned by their masters. Could this be about the looming war between Vadal and Sarnobat? But that made no sense. House war would be Protector business and bringing it up in such an uncouth manner would bring shame onto both great houses *and* the Grand Inquisitor.

"The threat I warn you of today is not natural, but demonic."

There were gasps from the audience. "Are the demons attacking?" someone shouted incredulously.

"Yes, but not by sea. This is not merely some raiders who have trespassed onto our shores. A terrible demonic plague—deadly beyond comprehension—has been unleashed within the borders of Great House Vadal, in the forests between Mukesh and Goda."

The delegation from Vadal blanched at that, then began speaking amongst themselves, as this was clearly the first they'd heard of such a thing. "How?" their ranking judge demanded.

"That is unknown at this time, but the Inquisition suspects that this is some manner of demon weapon left hidden since ancient times that has been disturbed—probably by Law breakers—and awakened. A group of Inquisitors was dispatched to investigate, and they perished, along with many obligated warriors, when the scourge revealed itself. They died bravely, and their last heroic act was to send word by magic to me of what they had discovered. The scourge is like unto a vast swarm of locusts, which will multiply and devour everything in their path, leaving nothing but ruin. I immediately moved to warn the chamber, for I assure you, honored judges, this is a menace the likes of which we have never seen before."

Devedas found himself leaning forward in his seat like everyone else in the gallery. This was unexpected. He'd thought that Omand would have some politician's trick up his sleeve to gain more power and further the conspiracy's goals, but this was something else entirely. The Grand Inquisitor couldn't fabricate a demon incursion, nor could he risk lying about the existence of one. This had to be real. Devedas' mind began to race, for dealing with demons was Protector duty.

"I have called this session because we must act swiftly against this menace while we still can. Demons cannot be allowed to gain any foothold upon land. A united force must be sent into Vadal lands to stop the menace immediately."

One of the judges from Vadal stood. "I intend no offense, Grand Inquisitor, but you speak of trespass in my beloved homeland, of which we've yet to see any evidence, and your proposal is *invasion*?"

"Not invasion. Rescue. I am afraid there is no time for this body to gather evidence and debate as is your usual tradition. Time is not on our side. Does the Law not require us to act decisively against any demonic threat? I seek authorization to temporarily lift the restrictions on obligation numbers, so that we may quickly raise a mighty force—unified from the many houses represented in this city—that will ride to the defense of Vadal."

"That is a most unusual request, Grand Inquisitor," the presiding judge said.

"This is an unusual threat, Your Honor."

Devedas knew the presiding judge wasn't a bad man, but he was not nearly as intelligent as his predecessor, and he demonstrated it by saying, "This is terrible news, but how can we act? Normally, when the Capitol is faced by a grave and immediate peril, it falls upon the Chief amongst us to make timely decisions, and then for the chamber to review those decisions afterward to make sure they are appropriately lawful, but alas that office has been unfilled since a vile casteless assassin took our beloved Chief Judge from us. Elections are not to be held for another two months so that each Thakoor may have their say. This vital process cannot be rushed."

"I am afraid Lok does not have months." Omand shook his head with exaggerated sadness. "We will be lucky if demons aren't scratching at the gates of Vadal City by then. We must strike as soon as possible, or millions will die. Vadal will be destroyed."

"Good," somebody from the Vokkan delegation muttered.

Somehow Omand heard that, and he stared at the representatives from his own house. "And then we will be next, for demons do not understand house borders. After Vadal, they will spread, who knows what direction? As we dither, they will multiply. Picking us off, house by house, until the slopes of Mount Metoro are blackened by demon hide and the desert is watered with our high-status blood."

"We've seen no evidence of this attack!"

Omand looked across the seats, probably trying to discern who had questioned his word, but if the Grand Inquisitor was offended, it couldn't be heard in his tone. "I understand. Grave allegations require great evidence. You did not hear the troubling reports that were delivered to me by rapid magical means. I wish there was time for every one of you to confirm them for yourself, but sadly there is not. However, to assure you that what I say is true, I hereby stake my reputation upon this report. Send for your spies and wizards. Collect your eyewitnesses. I swear upon the Law that in the coming days it will become obvious what I say here is valid. If my words prove false, then I will resign as Grand Inquisitor and leave the Capitol in shame forever."

Making such a public vow was incredibly risky. There was no turning back from such a thing for a high-status man. If he was wrong, then he was finished. Omand being so bold in his declaration probably convinced more judges that their nebulous fear of unseen demons.

"The Capitol does not have an army for a reason!" shouted one of the Uttaran judges. "The Law forbids the creation of a central army, so that the houses may remain free."

"That is great wisdom," Omand agreed. "The Capitol does not have a standing army, yet it has Orders that are responsible for the safety of the Law and all the houses. Those Orders, such as the one I lead, are not many in number. Which is why the Law allows us to temporarily obligate warriors and workers to aid us in our duties. This is simply that same principle, only scaled up to meet a correspondingly greater threat. That is all that I ask."

There were many judges nodding along at that wisdom, but the Vadal judge was clearly growing angry. "And I'm sure you would volunteer to lead this army into my house, Omand, who has repeatedly been a thorn in the heel of our noble Thakoor, Harta Vadal, who just happens to be away on important business as you conveniently call this meeting."

Omand lifted his hands apologetically, but before he could

speak, a judge from Sarnobat shouted, "Alas, Omand did not choose the day or hour that Vadal Law breakers would decide to consort with demons!"

"How dare you!"

The Grand Inquisitor banged the staff hard against the floor to cut them off. "Judges, please. I beg of you to be wise. This is more important than traditional rivalries. Do not fight amongst yourselves while there are demons at our door. To assure the parties concerned about potential bias, I will recuse myself and my entire Order from being considered for any leadership role over this proposed force." Omand made a big show of returning the staff to the luckless presiding judge, who was obviously hesitant to take it back. "I am merely the messenger. Let the Inquisition gain no power from this endeavor. However, the Vadal delegation brings up an excellent point. Someone must lead this response. Battling the scourge of hell will allow us no time to rule by committee."

*You clever bastard.* Now Devedas understood the real reason his presence had been requested here.

"Then who among us should be in charge?" someone else demanded.

"That is your decision," Omand replied. "Create a special office for this position, empower it to do whatever must be done to save us, and the Orders will serve whoever you choose. Though, I would counsel you to place within it a man of honor, wisdom, and courage...For if he falters, we are all in danger."

"Devedas!" a woman immediately exclaimed. "Send Lord Protector Devedas."

Devedas recognized that voice. Artya was one of Omand's conspirators from Zarger, but then a few other judges quickly echoed her words. The entire chamber erupted.

"The hero who defeated Black-Hearted Ashok!"

"He belongs to no house, and only has loyalty to the Law."

"Protectors know how to fight demons!"

It was rare to hear such agreement from a group so contentious. Devedas sat there, stone-faced, as the praise rolled over him. The Capitol had fallen in love with what they imagined him to be. He was the legend who had killed the most feared criminal of modern times. Even the most suspicious judges believed Devedas to be Omand's greatest political rival, and who better to check the Grand Inquisitor's possible ambitions than the Lord Protector? Of course, those who believed that didn't shout that particular idea aloud.

The presiding judge banged the staff against the floor until the chamber quieted down. "Lord Protector Devedas, what say you? Would you take command and make decisions to act on behalf of the Capitol in an emergency capacity until this crisis is past? And if Grand Inquisitor Omand's report is mistaken, willingly forsake this mantle, and return to your regular duties?"

Devedas stood and surveyed the entire room from his position in the outsiders' gallery. In their haste, these pampered fools were creating the very thing that would destroy them.

"I will do what the Law commands."

# Chapter 22

Rada was covered in blood. Her clothes were practically soaked in it, red from fingertips to elbows. Yet the poor warrior she'd been trying to help had died anyway, and from the look of things the rest of them would be following him into the great nothing momentarily.

"Keep fighting!" Jagdish roared.

The warriors were panting and drenched in sweat, but they kept going, long past any rational man's breaking point. Rada didn't know for how long they had fought—it seemed an eternity, hunched over, legs cramping, backs aching. The demons kept clambering up the rocks, and the warriors kept hitting them with their swords. Yet it seemed for each one they cut or smashed, two more were ready to take its place.

"No man quits!" Gotama shouted as one of his men faltered. He grabbed that warrior by the neck and shoved him back toward the edge. "Did I grant you permission to die yet, Nayak Tarsh?"

"No, Phontho!"

The old man sliced a tiny demon in half, then kicked both pieces over the side. "Then get back to work."

Karno ranged back and forth across their narrow perch, tirelessly picking up the slack whenever a warrior's arm failed and he was about to be overwhelmed. He must have killed hundreds of the things with his hammer by now, and was as covered in white blood as she was in red. Yet there was no pile of demon corpses below them, because the demons were as quick to carry off their own dead as they were human bodies. For what dark purpose, she couldn't understand.

"Rada, does the mirror speak?" Karno demanded.

"Nothing."

"Then make it."

"I can't."

Karno stopped his relentless killing to come to the center of the circle, where she was still kneeling next to the warrior she'd been powerless to save. He placed one hand on her shoulder. "Look at me."

She did.

"If it wanted you here, you are its bearer. Take command."

"How?"

"You are the smartest person I know. Figure it out. Do so quickly or we will all die."

Then Karno went back to smashing demon bugs with his hammer.

With shaking hands, Rada opened the torn satchel and dumped the piece of priceless black steel onto the bloody boulder. It sat there. Reflective side down. Pitch black and fearsome.

She'd not experimented with the thing. Oceans, she'd barely looked upon it since taking possession! When last freed it had absorbed a man's arm. The last time she'd stared into it, something inside had stared back. Vikram Akershan had cautioned her to never touch it with her bare hands, because just like a black steel sword, it would judge her worthiness, and there was no mercy upon those it found lacking.

A warrior screamed in pain. A demon had gotten through.

"I can do this." Rada picked up Asura's Mirror in both hands, cringed, then closed her eyes tight, waiting for it to punish her for her insolence.

When nothing happened, she slowly opened her eyes.

Then the damned thing *bit* her. She yelped in surprise more than pain, but the warriors were too busy fighting for their lives to notice her minor injury. It had pierced her palm, deep enough to draw blood, but it seemed to have stopped there. She imagined it cutting off all her fingers and blood spraying from the stumps, but it just sat there, seemingly content.

Rada hurried and flipped it over, revealing the polished side. All that was looking back at her was her own battered, filthy, blood-splattered reflection.

Just like the first time, the longer she looked into the mirror, the more it seemed to draw her in. Even as warriors fought desperately all around her, the sounds of violence faded. The blue sky behind her reflection seemed to darken, until it was like unto the night sky, filled with stars.

It was as if she was alone in the dark.

Then that *thing* was there, watching from inside the glass.

*The Asura.*

It had form, but not substance. There was a suggestion of a beautiful woman's face, but coldly emotionless, seemingly unmoved by their terrible plight.

Black steel had incredible powers, but there was no record of this device in the Capitol Library, so she had no idea what it was capable of. It had to be able to do *something*. "You wanted me to come here. Now we're surrounded by demons. Save us, please."

As before, it didn't speak with words, as much as fragmented whispers that were in the mind rather than the ear.

The mirror needed to be here because of the demons.

*Containment initiated.*

"Wonderful. Please, hurry. The warriors can't hold much longer."

Except then Rada got the distinct impression that the mirror didn't care what happened to them in particular, only that it be delivered to where the demons would be.

"What about us?"

The Asura had tested her blood . . . *and found it lacking.*

*Denied.*

"I've tried to live an honorable life. I've fulfilled every obligation ever given to me." And then all of her guilt over the casteless genocide came crashing back. That had to be why the black steel thought she was unworthy. "Is that it? I did what I could! I tried to make that right. I tried to tell the truth. Please, don't condemn these men because of my weakness."

Except the Asura ignored her pleas. The ancient thing was without pity. She had to try some different tack. She thought back to everything she'd ever read on the topic. Black steel would destroy itself rather than fall into evil hands, and there was no greater evil than demons. "Help us that we may help you."

The mirror seemed agreeable to that.

"Oh thank you, mighty Asura!" Then Rada realized that words had appeared on the polished black steel, superimposed over her image. "What're these?"

*Partial access.*

The words moved and were then replaced by more words. To someone who loved books more than life itself, this was the most miraculous thing Rada could imagine. It was a page that *changed*. It was like many books in one. How many words could one piece of black steel hold? What could the Library do with magic like this? Unfortunately, without her glasses the words were too blurry to read.

Thankfully, the ancient being that lived in the black steel device must have had some small measure of mercy, because it sensed Rada's frustration at being unable to read it and made the words larger so that she could see them. "Thank you."

The letters and numbers were archaic, the ancient predecessor to the current legally mandated alphabet. Fortunately for Rada, she was a Senior Archivist, and a damned good one, schooled in older texts, so with effort she could decipher all the words.

A warrior fell atop her, crashing about, desperately trying to keep a demon's razor legs from his throat. She was knocked over and crushed beneath him, but that pain seemed far away, and she remained focused on the mirror, even as Karno killed the demon and hoisted the warrior off her. "Are you alright, Rada?" he shouted, but his voice seemed to be coming from very far away. Karno's stone face broke, displaying concern for her well-being, but he had no choice but to leave her lying there and return to the battle.

Rada could make no sense of the rapidly moving words. There were numbers at the top, which she recognized well enough, and they seemed to be subtracting. Three hundred. Two hundred and ninety-nine. Two hundred and ninety-eight. And so on. "What's that for?"

*Containment.*

From the speed the numbers were changing, they'd probably be dead long before those numbers ran out. The warriors were gasping and wheezing. Their arms had to be on fire. "You told me what to do before, when the raiders attacked. Tell me what to do now."

But the Asura did not have an answer, for it didn't know either. Except Rada was beginning to realize that this thing was somehow *broken*. Maybe the Asura trapped in the black steel had decayed with age, like an elder whose brain had gone to fog. Its abrupt warnings to keep her from being murdered by the wolves of Sarnobat must have been some leftover instinct. In this more complicated situation, the Asura seemed almost as overwhelmed as she was.

"Then why'd you send me here?"

*Probability.*

Warriors were being cut. Blood droplets landed on the mirror. *Two hundred and fifty-five.* There was no time to fully decipher the words that were rapidly crawling across the mirror beneath the numbers. She focused on one but was once again denied as unworthy. The Asura made an unapproving tone, as if to say that would require full access to its powers, foolish unworthy child. Rada hurried and picked another and received the same negative answer. "Oceans! Do something."

The Asura had fulfilled its purpose. Now it could only be directed to act.

Rada had to calm herself and focus. The letters may have been archaic, but she could make out enough of them to reason out their meaning. The mirror had given her promptings before, telling her when to duck or fall. She'd been worthy of those blessings. Perhaps there were more blessings that existed at that same level?

"What part of you did that?"

One word seemed to float above the others, and Rada was fairly certain that it would translate to *defense*. "Yes! Perfect." From the warrior's distant cries, Rada knew they were out of time, so she picked the very first words that appeared.

*Execute.*

The world came rushing back, and Rada found herself lying flat on her back, next to a warrior's corpse, with the Asura's Mirror resting upon her breast.

The fighting had stopped.

"What in the salty hell is this?" Gotama whispered.

The fighting had stopped, but not from the demon's lack of trying. The vicious things were still scratching their way up the rock, only they couldn't seem to make it over the edge. The remaining warriors were shoulder to shoulder, and as they struck at the demons their blades bounced off something unseen. It was as if a barrier had been inserted between the two sides, made out of the world's hardest and clearest glass. Rada stood, and slowly turned in a circle, realizing as she did so that the impassable barrier seemed to form a circle around them.

"Don't hit it!" Jagdish shouted. "Calm yourselves. It's protecting us."

The warriors were clearly terrified of this witchcraft, but it beat being ripped to pieces. The demons kept coming, only now they were crawling over their own bodies, and *up* into the air, the terrible points of their claws clacking hard, against a wall of hardened air. They kept swarming, and the mob of bugs kept rising around them, seemingly hanging onto nothing at all.

"Did you do this?" Karno demanded.

"I think so," she answered.

Every warrior took an unconscious step toward the center, as the demons continued crawling up air. They were now surrounded ankle high, and more demons were still angrily trying to get in.

"I've heard of something like this," Jagdish said. "It is some manner of shell, where a thin layer of air becomes hard as steel. Ashok's woman, Thera, supposedly created such a thing in the graveyard of demons using her illegal god powers. She was safe in the center of a clear dome that even Ashok wasn't strong enough to break through."

"How long does this effect last?" Karno asked.

"Who knows? Enjoy the opportunity to rest our arms and bandage our wounds."

The warriors were all drenched in sweat and struggling for breath. Frightening magic or not, they'd be thankful for the lull. Except the demons were still accumulating against their barrier, and they were now waist high. The triangular creatures were repeatedly slamming their underbellies against it, and Rada could only hope that it held up under their increasing weight.

"Karno, Jagdish, come and look at this," Rada said, holding out the mirror.

"Is that black steel? Did you have that in *my house*? Are you a *wizard*?"

"Later." Karno held up a hand to silence Jagdish. "What did it tell you, Rada?"

"It's confusing, but I think it knew these things would be here, or at least the probability of them. Something like that. It's here to contain them no matter what. That's what it cares about, but I think I persuaded putting this defensive magic over us first."

"What does this mean, *contain*?" Karno asked suspiciously.

Rada turned the mirror so the two of them could look into it. "Careful, don't touch it. The Asura gets angry."

The demons were now chest high and climbing. Gotama rapped his knuckles against the invisible wall, then gave an appreciative whistle. "Librarians are certainly far more capable than I was ever led to believe."

Jagdish was looking into the mirror, mouth agape. "I've never seen anything like this."

"The words it is showing now, I think, are all the ways it can defend itself or its bearer," she said as her eyes flicked across the mirror, mind desperately trying to record all the precious ancient knowledge in the still-moving words. "I don't know what the subtracting numbers are for."

It was nearing a hundred now.

"I think I know what that is." Jagdish reached into his uniform and pulled out his treasured pocket watch. He was inordinately proud of the little device and had showed it to her many times before. Flicking it open, he tapped the glass over the mechanical arm. "That's a clock like this, only in finer measurements, and counting down rather than up. But counting toward what?"

"Containment, I think. Whatever that is."

The noise of the demon claws was unbearable. It was a horrible, endless, *scratching*.

"If this witchcraft breaks, we'll be buried alive!" shouted one of the warriors, as panic began to overcome rationality.

Gotama took the young man by the arm. "Don't worry, lad. We'll only be buried *alive* briefly."

"Better to cut our own throats than be dragged away by that!"

Then Gotama smacked the warrior across the cheek. Not particularly hard, but enough to get his attention. "Enough. Keep your head. Tend your brothers' wounds and wait your chance. Let the wizard do her business. She'll get us out of this." Gotama turned toward her. "Right?"

"I'm doing my best." Rada paused, because for a moment she thought the growing darkness was her being sucked back into the mirror again, but then she realized it was because the demons had now covered most of the dome and were putting them into the shade. The idea of the terrible things blotting out the sun filled her with dread. Then the image within the mirror changed. "That's new. What is that?"

"A map," Karno stated.

It was like a beautiful painting, but marked with dots that glowed like fireflies, and covered in words of places that no longer existed. "My goodness. Not only can black steel become a book, but it can also be a book with pictures? Is there anything this marvelous material can't do?"

"*That* is what you're thinking about right now?" Jagdish said, exasperated, as bloodthirsty demons scurried around on top of the invisible dome only a few feet overhead, and an ancient device counted down toward some mysterious end. "I know those shores. That's the northern coast of Vadal, so that red light is where we are...but what the hell is *that*?"

A bright line was growing across the map, heading toward the spot that Jagdish had indicated as their location, as if watching an artist dragging a paintbrush perfectly straight. It couldn't possibly have represented a real thing, because nothing in the world moved that fast. The line crossed much of the continent over the span of a few heartbeats. It appeared it would reach the red mark...

*Twenty.*

*Nineteen.*

*Eighteen.*

...just as the mysterious counter ran down.

"Look!" A warrior pointed upward.

It was difficult to see through all the wriggling bodies, but there was *something* high above them. The boulders began to tremble beneath their feet. The light that was sneaking between the demons turned into blinding beams.

The horde must have realized something was wrong, and as one they stopped their incessant attacks against the barrier and looked up as they sensed their impending doom.

*Seven.*

*Six.*

The line upon the map hadn't been a representation. There really was something ripping a hole through the sky while crossing the entire world. It was a spike made of coiled lightning, trailing hurricanes.

*Four.*

*Three.*

The earthquake knocked them from their feet and scattered the demons. Karno moved his body between Rada and the incomprehensible wrath from the heavens. The act would make no difference against such force, but he was a Protector to the end.

*One.*

The world turned to fire.

# Chapter 23

Everyone in the Cove had rushed outside once they'd heard the strange noise, so they all saw the strange beam cutting across the sky. It was bright as the sun, but stretched out, creating a line of light that lingered even after the eyes were closed.

Keta stood on the roof of the headquarters of the Sons of the Black Sword, along with Thera and her risalders, awestruck by what they were witnessing. He could yell to the people on the terraces below about how this was prophecies being fulfilled, only no one would hear him over the continuous thunder.

Following the beam were violent whirling clouds, as it boiled the unfallen rain into steam.

The Keeper of Names looked to his prophet, knowing that she had seen a sign like this once before. Thera had only been a child when the bolt from heaven had struck her down, but from what he'd been told there had been similar violence in the sky. The thing that had hit Thera had been tiny. The projectile was still sufficient to fell a daughter of Vane, splitting her skull and putting her in a coma, and the Voice had dwelt within her ever since.

"Is this like what your people saw when you were young?" Keta shouted.

"This is bigger!" Thera answered. "This is no bolt from heaven."

This was a flaming spear, hurled by an angry god.

This sign wasn't just for the population of the Cove. Surely the whole world would see this spectacle. The faithful fell to their knees, praying for mercy, begging the Forgotten to spare them. Even the mighty Sons, fearless in battle, cowered beneath this display of heavenly might. It was a fire sufficient to smite them all.

The tip of the spear vanished behind the mountaintops, heading for some distant point far over the horizon. The thunder died to a rumble.

"The Voice warned of us this day!" Keta bellowed, hoping his people could heed his words over the sudden wind. "All will see this sign. Be not afraid, for we are the chosen people who—"

The northern horizon flashed red. Children wailed. Animals stampeded.

Thera swooned as the Voice came upon her.

The brave bodyguard Murugan caught hold of her arm to keep her from falling, but the sudden manifestation of the gods hurled him violently away from his charge.

Thera was consumed in light, blinding as the thing in the sky.

*The time of war is upon you.*

As the Voice hammered the insides of their heads, everyone in the Cove went to their knees.

The light dimmed just enough for all to see that the Forgotten had appeared in their midst, insubstantial in form, a giant made of fog and light, towering over them. It swept one mighty hand toward the north.

*The final arrow has flown. Upagraha's quiver is empty.*

Keta had to lift his hand to shield his eyes from the glory. Deep within the center of the giant was Thera, head down, limp, floating helpless, while she served as a conduit for the gods.

*Only the Sons of Ramrowan can save man from the demons now. Only my chosen servants can save the Sons of Ramrowan from the Law.*

In all the times he had served as witness, Keta had never questioned the gods before, but desperation overrode his fear. "But how? We have tried to protect the casteless! What would you have us do? Oh, Forgotten, please show us the way!"

The glowing giant turned to regard Keta, and for just a moment, the Keeper of Names looked into the eyes of a god.

*Without water they will fall.*

# Chapter 24

Once they had been alerted to the strange phenomena in the sky, the special session had been adjourned, and all of the judges had rushed from the Chamber of Argument to see the thing in the sky for themselves. After it had gone from their sight, a tremor had shaken the Capitol.

Two men stood apart from the frightened others.

"What have you unleashed, Omand?" Devedas demanded, as they watched eerie lightning dance across the unnatural red clouds to the northeast. Never before had any of them seen such a worrying sight.

"You flatter me but creating such a spectacle is beyond my capabilities."

"Do not make jokes at this time. If we felt the impact from here, who knows what state the north is in."

Omand gave a small bow of apology. "This was not my doing. My report about the ancient demonic weapon being awakened in Vadal was true. This is something else." Then he noted that their position upon the steps was near where the Chief Judge had been felled by an assassin's bullet, and that thought made him smile.

"By the compass, it is no coincidence," Devedas muttered. "This is some form of magical assault against us."

"Whatever it is, dealing with it is your responsibility now,

Lord Protector . . . Or rather, I should use whatever your new title is, once these judges return to their debate over what to call their new emergency leader. The deed is done. Now they simply have to give it a name. It has been a long time since any one individual has held such unchecked authority."

"That title will not be king."

"Not yet . . ." Omand nodded his golden mask toward the frightened judges. "But see how they are scared?"

"They should be."

"Crisis presents opportunity, Devedas."

"How can you still scheme at a time like this?" Devedas turned toward Omand, incredulous. "We must set our plans aside for now. This changes everything."

It changed nothing, but of course Devedas would think that way. He was a man of strict responsibility. Even his maddest ambitions were tempered by a sense of duty. Devedas would overthrow the government and crown himself king, but only because he truly believed he would be better than all who had come before. Such predictability would keep him manageable.

"Then go, Protector. Gather your army and rally the Orders. Obligate warriors. Take what you need, then do whatever must be done in the north. I will remain here and make sure the Capitol fully supports your endeavors."

"I shall." Devedas gave him a grim nod and began walking away.

Troubled yet determined, with that handsome face scarred by black steel, Devedas cut such an imposing figure that even the most prideful judges were quick to scurry out of his way. Here was a real leader. Some judges offered Devedas encouraging words, saying that all of Lok was counting on him, and to go forth and be their champion. *The Law's champion.* When they saw their idealized protector going off to face the storm in the north, they even took up a chant.

*Devedas. Devedas. Devedas.*

For just a moment, Omand felt a pang of jealousy. What rubbish. In all his years in the Capitol, Omand had never imagined the judges acting with such indignity. Despite all he had done for these ingrates, they had never once cheered for him. Perhaps they should have . . . then he wouldn't need to overthrow them.

The Grand Inquisitor turned his gaze back toward the distant storm. He didn't know for certain what had happened in Vadal, but he had his suspicions. It would be necessary to speak with the Astronomers Order. The giant spyglass in their observatory on the other side of Mount Metoro would be able to confirm it, but he suspected the old illegal gods had just stomped on his prisoner's clever ploy.

Religion was for fools, but nonetheless, he had been blessed.

Omand's dreams had begun with a tidal wave and would be achieved in a pillar of fire.

# Chapter 25

〰️〰️

Far beneath the sea, Ashok's journey continued.

At one point a deep rumble passed through the tunnel.

"It's a quake," Moyo warned, as he braced himself against a wall. "Hang on."

Dust fell from above and the watery trench running down the center of the tunnel rippled, but the tremor didn't seem too dangerous...but what was a dangerous quake while beneath thousands of tons of rock and millions of tons of water? Ashok waited for the shaking to subside, before asking, "Does that happen often here?"

"It's rare. That wasn't a big one, thank the gods. You can see the breaks where those have hit over the years. Just imagine what would happen if the ground split above us and the whole ocean came rushing in!"

Ashok would prefer not to think about that.

"Don't worry. We wouldn't drown. We'd be squished to death long before we could drown. Worse, if the down below were to flood entirely my guild would be out of work. Future collectors would need to grow gills if we were to keep up on our duty. Ha!"

They made good time, despite Moyo often having to stop and carve new guild signs where cracks had formed, and he once nearly fell down a hole that hadn't been there before. It would be easy to slip and break a leg. Alone, that would be a death sentence.

At one point they passed a shaft in the center of a big room that had a unique sign, with the points of three triangles meeting in a circle. Moyo said this hole was notorious among his kind, for at the distant bottom there was stored a vast treasure of metal that did not corrode. Except it was a trap, as anyone who carried this metal would gradually sicken, their hair falling out and sores appearing on their skin, until they inevitably perished. The other collectors couldn't even carry those bodies back without getting sick themselves, so they had been tossed back down the hole.

After several more periods of what felt like days, the tunnel changed, widening out and branching off in two different directions. It was the first true fork in the road that Ashok had seen thus far. Moyo had warned him about this place previously—just in case he had fallen down a hole and left Ashok on his own—that he was to always stick to the rightmost tunnel. Doing so would get him back to Lok eventually.

There was a cache hidden at the fork where a portion of wall had crumbled, revealing a few small rooms that had been picked clean hundreds of years before. There was food and drinking water left in casks sealed with wax. The rations were dried meats and a kind of unleavened bread crusted in honey and salt—hardy stuff meant to keep a traveler alive, and which would last a very long time.

Moyo declared it a good place to rest, so they set down their packs, gathered some food, and then put out their lanterns to conserve oil. Even though the odd Fortress fuel seemed to last a very long time, sputtering with a steady orange glow, it was best reserved for movement. It was not needed to provide warmth. If anything, the underworld was surprisingly temperate, even somewhat humid.

"Once a year, when it becomes too cold and snowy to collect along the shores, all of my guild in Xhonura gathers for a mighty expedition down below. We refresh all the caches and push a little bit farther into the dark to see what we can find."

"How many times is this for you?"

"I've been on twenty expeditions."

He had been a Protector for twenty years. "That's a good number for an obligation."

"Yes. Twenty proper, and one forbidden trip, with just me and a fugitive who is most likely a god reborn."

"You're still going on about that? Fortress breeds stubborn men."

"It has to." Moyo's face couldn't be seen in the darkness, but Ashok could hear the melancholy enter his voice. "We're a dying people."

"What do you mean?"

"Every year, we make do with less and less. The belts get tighter. We've used up what the ancients left behind, and our land is poor. There are fewer and fewer children born. There are houses that were filled for generations, only they're quiet as this place now. I'm no trader. I've never been to your infidel land, but I've heard tales about it. Rich. With forests full of lumber, and fields full of wheat, far as the eye can see."

"In places, it is like that. In others, it is not."

"But those have something to trade still, don't they?"

"I suppose."

Moyo sighed. "We have no real trade. We have you. With a Law that hates us and wants us to die for our beliefs."

Ashok chewed his dinner in the dark for a while before suggesting, "It is likely if Fortress surrendered to the Capitol, they would trade."

"It is said our people will unite someday, but as equals. Not as your slaves. They'd take our beliefs away. We wouldn't be us no more. That's dying either way, and I suspect you know it."

Ashok could only nod, a pointless gesture when neither of them could see. Perhaps Moyo was right. Thera's rebels only wanted to live their own way. The Law could never allow that. Why would these people be any different?

"We give your criminals guns and get back seeds. We're just surviving, waiting for the day the Workshop can fulfill its purpose."

"What is it you wait for, Collector Moyo?"

"You, Avatara."

The two men sat there in silence for a long time, eating their dried-out food and drinking stale water until Moyo spoke again. "As a boy, my first expedition through these caverns was my grandfather's last. His rope snapped; he fell down a shaft and broke his neck. Then my father died trying to find another way into the forbidden section. As did my son ... upon his very first expedition."

Ashok had never been good at offering comforting words. "There is honor in dying while fulfilling your obligation."

"I hope so because dying is a family tradition..." Moyo abruptly stood up. "Come on. Light your lantern. I must show you what my people hope and die for. It is not far."

Ashok took up his lantern and followed Moyo down the warned-against left fork of the tunnel. At first it didn't seem so different from the one they had been following to get here, but then he began to notice how much guild sign had been scratched into the walls. Ashok traced the carvings with his fingers as Moyo had taught him. *Danger.* There were more and more warnings as they went along, many of them including symbols he had never seen before. It appeared some had been struck quickly, hurried and imprecise compared to the rest.

There was a broken pick lying on the floor, rusted and unusable. It was the first time Ashok had seen something salvageable abandoned like that.

"My people don't like to linger in this area." Moyo gestured with his lantern. "The reason is just ahead."

The tunnel passed through a threshold of sorts. Ashok had seen such structures many times along the way, but this one was different, for it had been garishly decorated with bones, thousands upon thousands of them. Somehow bodies had been fastened to the wall and left there dangling. Some were whole, others fragmented, and a few appeared to have been torn apart, and then reassembled wrong.

"Is this another tomb? Like at the beginning of the caves?"

"No. We didn't make this. The Dvarapala made this from us. The tomb you saw was made to respect our lost. This is a mockery."

Ashok lifted his lantern high to try to take in the entire thing, realizing as he did so that the bones hadn't been left haphazardly. There was an order to them. They had been arranged in geometric patterns. It was a design made out of death.

"What is *Dvarapala*?"

"It's an old word. It means *it guards the door.* Stop!"

Ashok had been nearing the threshold. "Beyond this line is trespass?"

"Aye. You might make it a hundred feet. You might make it one. But the Dvarapala will be angered, and it is a mighty thing. Strong, even like unto the gods who gave it life. Even demons fear it. Many collectors have dared cross. Very few have lived to tell of it. Those who have seen it say it is a giant from before the kings and it has lived here since the ancients carved these tunnels."

Glancing down, Ashok scowled as he realized not all the bodies were human. At first he thought the desiccated remains belonged to a child due to the size, except the skull was shaped like an opossum, and it had long fingered hands that ended in claws. Instead of toes, there were hooves like a goat.

"What is that?"

"The reason I hum while I walk, so they can hear me coming, and I do not surprise them."

Looking at the sharpness of those fangs, Ashok would never again question the handed-down wisdom of the Collectors Guild. He stepped away from the arch. "What is on the other side that makes it worth such risk?"

"Hood your lantern. You will see."

Ashok did so, and as his eyes adjusted, he could make out a strange illumination in the distance. It wasn't fire, nor was it the dim sunlight he'd seen filtered through the ocean in the clear.

"At the end of this tunnel is the broken city, the last section of Ramrowan's workshop. It is a vast cavern, abandoned since the first king, but somehow lit as if it were day. Those who have seen it speak of wonders, tall buildings full of treasure, including precious black steel, more than enough to make our island wealthy and strong again. Except Ramrowan ordered the Dvarapala to guard and keep his workshop safe until he returned."

Ashok opened the hood on his lantern. "Yet you keep testing it."

"There's always someone who claims to be Ramrowan reincarnated. So we collectors think, maybe this will be the time? Then some of us end up on the Dvarapala's wall, and the rest know it is not time yet. I still think you're the Avatara, myself. Maybe we should try again, eh?"

"All treasure hunters are fools. I am not your god reborn. There. I have spared your life... Have your warriors tried to kill this beast?"

"Oh, so many!" Moyo laughed, and then abruptly quieted himself, as the sound echoed. "Not a single one of those has ever made it back. Come on. We must return to the cache. This is not a good place to rest."

# Chapter 26

The little casteless boy scrubbed the blood from the floor. With bucket and rag, he worked until his flesh was raw and his hands ached. The black sword lay nearby, clean, despite the multitude of lives it had taken.

It had been repeated countless times, except there was something new in Ashok's dream. A shadow grew within Great House Vadal, until it loomed over the blood-scrubbing boy. Thick and oozing, like smoke from burning oil, the darkness expanded. Seething rage could be felt coming from the shadow, hot as the fires his father had used to cremate bodies. Unlike the man he would become, the boy could still feel fear, and he spilled the bucket of pink water as he tried to escape.

The shadow followed.

*"This insect is what you chose?"*

The shadow wasn't addressing the boy, for he was too far beneath it. That terrible anger was directed toward the black sword.

*"I was forsaken. A thousand years of torment, for nothing."*

The boy tried to run, but the shadow effortlessly encircled him.

*"I will tear down all you have created."*

An unknown noise brought Ashok instantly awake. Placing one hand on the sword lying next to him on the cold stone floor, he waited, but sensed no movement. The only sound was

Moyo's snoring. Even Ashok's abnormal eyes could see nothing in the pitch black of the down below, so he used the Heart of the Mountain to sharpen his hearing. He almost expected to hear the click of goat hooves, but there was nothing. They were alone in the small room the cache was hidden in. There wasn't so much as a mouse breathing within twenty feet.

Then someone whispered in his ear.

*"Ashok Vadal."*

He was certain there was nothing there. Even a man without fear could still be made uneasy, so he slowly, quietly drew the stolen Fortress blade from its sheath.

The voice came again.

*"Fall."*

The whispered name wasn't his mind playing tricks on him. It came like a serpentine hiss that made the hair on his arms stand up. The Law had always taught him that ghosts were a myth, but that hadn't stopped them from speaking to him upon occasion.

*"Arise and be tested."*

Suddenly, Ashok found himself standing in the tunnel outside the cache, drawn sword in one hand, lantern flickering in the other, and no memory of lighting it, or how he had gotten here. From the noise, Moyo was still inside, asleep and unaware.

Had he unknowingly moved himself? Or had it moved him? Either way, it made Ashok furious.

"What are you?"

*"Judgment."*

The whisper was in his ear, but somehow he knew that it had come from down the hall, from the left fork, beyond the monument of bones. The Dvarapala was calling him. Challenging him.

Ashok blinked, and somehow now he was standing before the threshold of trespass, with no recollection of walking here. The lantern cast strange shadows across the multitude of skulls. They seemed to turn, as if watching him. Ashok despised thieves, and this creature was either stealing his time, or his very will.

"Get out of my head."

*"Comply and face judgment, Fall."*

It wasn't in his nature to refuse any challenge. A bearer was required to accept all duels. Except with Angruvadal broken, Ashok was no longer bound by those traditions, and meeting some horrible being from the ancient world would not help him get back to Thera.

"I have no quarrel with you."

*"Angruvadal does. It was Angruvadal's master who condemned me here."*

The whisper was growing sharper, angrier.

*"You are Angruvadal now. You must pay its price."*

A shard had been embedded in Ashok's chest when it was destroyed, but he was not his sword. Being alone underground for so long must have driven the thing insane. "I have no time for the ramblings of a mad god."

Ashok turned and began walking away, but only made it a short distance before everything went black, and he found himself once again standing before the threshold, with the last few seconds of his life missing.

"A coward's magic trick," Ashok snarled. This time the effect had left him dizzy. There was growing heat in the center of his chest, as the shard buried there came to life.

*"Behold. Your owner hungers for battle."*

Except how could he fight something so powerful that it could take control of his very limbs? The will of black steel was inscrutable, its peculiar code a mystery to man. Except in that moment, Ashok knew with absolute certainty that Angruvadal wanted this thing to *die*. This was a grudge beyond mortal comprehension. Having used Angruvadal to slay a multitude of his enemies, it seemed only fair he return the favor now. He could only hope that the remains of his oldest friend would be sufficient to protect him from the Dvarapala's strange magic.

"I was Angruvadal's final bearer. If someone has to answer for offense given a thousand years before I was born, so be it. Show yourself, foul thing that lives beneath hell, so I can put you out of your misery."

A ball of light appeared on the other side of the threshold, far brighter than his feeble lantern, so intense he was forced to shield his eyes. It was just a blob, without form, floating in the air. Then the light began drifting down the tunnel, showing him the way.

Ashok crossed the threshold and followed.

The sword he had procured was similar to the Uttaran style, had decent balance, and seemed to be of solid quality. From what he had seen, Fortress produced incompetent swordsman but armed them with decent steel. It was no Vadal blade, but it would do.

Would it be enough to slay an ancient being that had supposedly killed warriors by the legion? He would soon find out.

The beacon led him farther down the tunnel into the strange illumination Moyo had shown him earlier. White as Canda's moonlight, it seemed to come from above, though there was no source. He no longer required his lantern to see and entertained the thought of putting out the flame to save the oil. Assuming he survived, he would need it on the way out. However, it would be foolish to trust that an unknown magic would not betray and abandon him when most needed, so the lantern stayed lit.

The mysterious brightness grew until it was like he was walking on the surface on a dim and cloudy day. Many would consider such magic miraculous, but Ashok found it deceitful. What manner of loathsome thing hid from the sun so much that it needed to create a fake one?

The tunnel gradually widened into the largest space Ashok had seen in the underworld so far. Moyo had called it a cavern. That was incorrect, for this place had clearly not been made by nature. It felt as if he was inside a great hollow cube, so vast the light cloud could not touch the distant ceiling.

His magical guide drifted toward the side and up what had probably been stairs once, except dripping water had eroded them into a bumpy ramp. Ashok climbed until he saw there was a wide platform to the side, so he leapt up onto it for a better look around.

There was a city inside the cube, made of featureless rect-angular buildings, each of them taller than any structure in the Capitol—dozens of them, stretching forward in orderly rows. Their walls were covered in strange moss, and fields of black mushrooms grew in the wide, damp streets. Ashok knew nothing about architecture, but these grand structures beneath the ocean were the largest he had ever seen, magnificent despite being coated in a film of mold and decay.

Though the guide light had stayed close to him in the tunnel, it seemed content to continue onward now, leaving him behind. As marvelous as the spectacle of an underground city was, Ashok had an ancient god to kill, so he continued.

His sandals splashed through puddles. Cracks and holes in the ancients' roadway had turned into dirty lakes and streams, wherein pale eyeless fish swam. He could hear small animals fleeing the light. Something flapped above. He assumed it was bats, but in this cursed place, who knew?

The light led him into an open square between four large structures, where something he couldn't understand had been placed in the central courtyard. At first he thought it was some manner of banquet, as there appeared to be a dozen men seated around a low table, attended to by servants, except as he called upon the Heart to focus his vision, he saw that they were corpses arranged in a grotesque mockery of life. Set before them were plates of small animal bones, a parody of a meal. As the light expanded to fill the central space, more bodies were revealed, propped upright somehow, like scarecrows in a worker's field. There were retainers in ragged capes and bodyguards in rusting armor with blades sheathed in rotting leather. With revulsion he realized that there was even a band, with corroded instruments clutched in fingers of bone, and skeletons that had been stuck together as dancers, frozen forever in mid-twirl.

*"Welcome to my celebration."*

Some of the bodies were clearly ancient, bleached bones crumbling. Others were far newer, probably collector dead, though they were not dressed in the practical manner of Moyo, but rather in strange courtly garb, once opulent, now faded and rotting. That clothing was unlike anything he had seen in Lok or Fortress. Which meant the Dvarapala must have dragged the bodies here and dressed them in the ancients' attire, before arranging them in this sick façade, like a child's dolls.

*"Join us, Fall."*

His whole life he had been taught there was no life beyond this one, but such disrespect for the dead filled him with disgust and revulsion. He didn't need the Law or gods to tell him this perversion was the worst type of crime.

*"You are not here to judge me. I am here to judge you."*

The whispers seemed closer somehow, and Ashok slowly turned, searching for his foe. "Why have you done this to them?"

*"I tired of being alone."*

Then the Dvarapala revealed itself.

It came from above, crawling down one of the edifices on the far side of the square, defying gravity as if it were a gigantic spider. Its skin was blue beneath the strange light, similar to the cold flesh of a Dasa. It was shaped like a man, but far larger, and

with an extra set of arms. Its head was pointed downward as it
clambered effortlessly across the slick surface, until it neared the
ground, and then bent at the waist—at such an impossible angle
it would have broken a human spine—to place its feet upon the
ground. When it straightened itself and lifted its head, it was
several feet taller than Ashok.

*"They should not have left me here alone. I was corrupted."*

"Expect no pity from me. Not after seeing this." Ashok set
his lantern upon the banquet table in order to have that hand
free. "You had your obligation. I have mine. You should have left
me be so that I could fulfill it."

*"My purpose here is lost."*

"If your obligation is done, end your life with dignity, and
spare me the trouble."

*"I do not have that authority. Only the master has that power.
Are you he?"*

"No."

*"Inconclusive."*

The Dvarapala stalked toward him. It was a hulking thing,
muscled like a bull, and like a bull, it had horns, but too many.
Its four arms each ended in a gigantic hand that looked strong
enough to rend Ashok's body in half. Just like the far smaller
Dasa, its face had no features at all, just a membrane of blue
skin stretched over the bones beneath, though whatever shapes
lurked beneath there, they shared no relation to the face of man.

*"All things degrade in time. Even deep within the world, unseen
particles bombard us. Centuries pass. Rot. Memories are lost. Rot.
Errors are made. Rot. Commands are forgotten. Rot."*

It stopped a mere twenty feet away. Though it was nearer
now, its words remained a whisper.

*"I no longer know my purpose. All I have left is my hate."*

"Hate alone will not sustain you." Ashok raised the sword
and subtly shifted into a duelist's stance. "That is something I
learned in my own dark prison."

The two combatants studied each other for a moment. The
Dvarapala had killed many warriors of Fortress, but it was
doubtful any of those had a fraction of Ashok's skill. Ashok had
defeated man and demon—more than anyone else alive—yet the
capabilities of this thing were a mystery. The Heart of the Mountain had returned him to his former strength, and the shard of

Angruvadal burned with a cold rage, the likes of which Ashok had never felt from it before. It began to feed instincts into his mind, of dangers and potential angles of attack, just like old times.

The beast came at him, stooping as it ran, until it used its lower pair of arms as extra legs. It was like dodging a charging cavalry horse. The arm that swung for him was as long as a lance. Ashok spun out of the way, slashing as he did, striking deep into the blue flesh. The Fortress steel struck true.

They parted. The Dvarapala circled, still low to the floor, cautious now. The wound in its side didn't bleed. The skin hung open and dangling, like parted fabric.

The footing was slick, treacherous. The monster weighed far more than he did. That extra mass would anchor it. So Ashok ground one sandal into the muck until it found good purchase, raised his sword, and calmly waited.

*"I was not always this. They made me into this thing you see before you."*

"I understand that more than you know."

This time when the Dvarapala attacked, it was clever, feinting right, then lunging toward him, multiple arms coming at him lightning quick. Ashok pushed off, leaping aside, striking at one of the limbs. The impact was solid, and he pulled through the cut as he moved back.

That hit would have severed a man's arm, but the Dvarapala's bones must have been hard as demon. It stepped back, testing its fingers by repeatedly making a fist.

*"You exhibit enhanced reflexes, strength, speed—"*

Ashok interrupted the whispers, thrusting at the monster's broad chest. It moved with surprising speed, shifting aside, and then bringing one of its upper arms around to knock away the follow-up strike.

*"—and aggression... What generation must you be?"*

"You speak in riddles. Be silent and fight."

Ashok went at the beast with everything he had.

The Dvarapala reacted with an explosive fury, intercepting each of his attacks with one of its many arms. It must have been toying with him earlier, as it pressed its tremendous size advantage now, driving Ashok back. A lesser swordsman would have been overwhelmed and crushed underfoot, but Ashok stayed ahead of the furious blows. The two of them splashed through the muck, before its third arm came from underneath to nail him in the hip, landing with such tremendous force it sent him crashing back into the banquet, scattering bones.

Ashok rolled off the table as a giant blue fist slammed into the spot where he'd just been. Managing to get in a fearsome draw cut across the beast's stomach, Ashok then had to duck to avoid yet another blow. Angruvadal warned him to put the table between them, and Ashok did so. That saved his life as another hand swept around to obliterate an ancient skeleton instead, and Ashok ducked through the cloud of obscuring dust.

The lantern was still burning on the table. Ashok struck it hard with the flat of his blade, flinging it at the Dvarapala's blank face. Glass shattered against a horn and the Fortress oil erupted into orange flames.

It didn't seem to notice that it was on fire.

The beast sank all of its hands beneath the table and wrenched tons of stone from the floor. It flipped the table toward Ashok, end over end, and all he could do was run or be crushed.

Ashok picked up a skull and hurled it. The monster knocked it aside, but Ashok had been right behind that distraction, and struck the beast upward, and then down, carving the sword through blue flesh. His third attack sliced through the back of its knee, but from the way the Dvarapala didn't topple, it had no tendons to sever.

Though he was able to avoid most of the impact, he couldn't escape the counter entirely, and even catching an edge of that mighty backhand sent him flying across the space. Dancers shattered beneath him, and then he was rolling through the muck.

The pain was incredible as dungeon-atrophied muscles screamed in protest, but none of his bones broke, and no arteries were severed, so the Heart could keep feeding him strength. Ignoring the agony, he leapt back to his feet as the burning Dvarapala closed in.

The instincts of Angruvadal's prior bearers were no help here, as none of them had ever faced a being like this, but the shard itself somehow knew this creature well, and actual images cascaded through his mind. It was like looking at a master artist's meticulously crafted drawing of the Dvarapala, and all its strange inner workings.

Angruvadal showed him that though it was fearsome, it was not indestructible. There was a weakness.

One of the nearby corpses had been placed as if he was protectively watching over the inhabitants of the square. From the level of decay he had only been here a handful of years, and there was another Fortress-forged sword at his side. Ashok rushed over and pulled it from the crumbling sheath. It came free but trailed a long strip of cobwebs after. The blade was covered with rust, but it would have to do.

Four arms versus two swords, Ashok turned back to meet the Dvarapala.

It tried to encircle him with its incredible reach, but he slashed his way free. When it came at him again, he struck, then moved, sliding across the slick floor. If he slipped, he would die. If it cornered him, he would die. Using the western two-blade style, he kept ahead of the thing, constantly striking. The rusted blade did not cut well, but he could still use it to redirect those terrible fists away from his body. The other blade was wickedly sharp, and he put it to work. Each impact caused bits of flaming blue skin to break off and float away.

With certain knowledge, this could not continue. Even with the Heart, he would tire. One mistake. One good hit. And Ashok would surely die. He was methodically slicing the Dvarapala to ribbons, yet he couldn't reach its vulnerability.

Then his foot slipped.

That was enough, and the Dvarapala struck him down. Ashok felt the ribs on that side break as it slammed him against the stone floor. Swiftly, he ran his sword up the inside of the monster's leg, flaying it wide open, but then the other leg kicked him in his damaged chest.

Ashok skidded through the scattered bones until he crashed against the remains of the table.

In a life of endless combat and misfortune, that was the hardest he had ever been hit.

There was no air. He couldn't breathe. When he looked down and saw the huge footprint denting in his chest, it was no surprise his lungs wouldn't fill. They'd been absolutely flattened. Such an injury would have instantly killed a normal man. Magic had made Ashok more than man, but this was grim even by his standards.

*"I want to die, yet you are unworthy to slay me."*

The Dvarapala walked toward him. The oil fire had gone out, leaving its strange head blackened and charred. The rest of it was falling apart, cut so many times it was like one of the Protector Acolyte's training dummies. Only instead of stuffing falling out, it bled something that looked like sand. Rectangles of silver bone could be seen through the multitude of holes, and there, deep in its torso, was the target Angruvadal had revealed.

For a moment he thought the magical light was dimming, except that was simply his brain running out of precious air. It was like looking through a narrowing tunnel, and at the end of that was the Dvarapala. A man without fear could still be urged to desperate haste, so Ashok dropped the rusty sword and pressed that hand hard into his flesh, grasped a broken rib, and wrenched it back to what he thought was the correct place. It caused a pain the likes of which he had never imagined. Despite that, he methodically repeated the process, rib by rib, concentrating the Heart of the Mountain toward controlling the bleeding, and then made himself breathe by sheer force of will.

With an incredibly violent cough, he hacked up a fountain of blood.

Much better.

*"I was not always this thing. I am the mind of a man etched onto black steel. I do not know if I am still real. How could you allow this?"*

The effect was briefer, but more noticeable than last time, as something once again took possession of his body. *"You volunteered,"* Ashok answered, with a voice that was not his own.

He didn't know where those words had come from, but they seemed to enrage the Dvarapala. *"Lies! Lies!"* The thing sank down next to him, lowering its charred, faceless head, until the sharp tips of the horns were only inches from Ashok's eyes. *"Rot and lies!"*

Ashok drove the sword through a narrow juncture of silver bones, straight into the Dvarapala's black steel core.

It exploded.

An unknown time later, Ashok slowly blinked himself back to consciousness.

His vision was swimming, but it revealed the mighty Dvarapala was lying a few feet away, split nearly in half. The damage was almost like one of Thera's powder bombs had gone off inside its chest. One leg was kicking spasmodically. Silver bones had sheared.

Its powdered blood had been spread everywhere, and some of it hung floating in the air like motes of dust. The destruction was similar to when Angruvadal had shattered, only this time all that energy had been contained inside a body.

The beast was done for.

Ashok could barely move. If it hadn't been for the Heart of the Mountain, he'd be joining the monster shortly, but his wounds would heal. In the meantime, all he could do was lie there as the creature kept whispering the same message, over and over, weaker each time.

"*A fatal error has occurred.*"

He felt no anger. Only pity. "Your obligation is fulfilled. Be at peace, guardian."

His words seemed to shake the thing from its mantra. The horned head was partially submerged in a puddle, but it wasn't looking at Ashok anyway. It was staring into the great nothing beyond.

"*I remember who I was. I vowed to Ramrowan I would protect this place as long as necessary. I would not let them squander the future. This is how they can rebuild. I remember now why I made this sacrifice.*"

"Was it worth it?"

"*That will be up to you.*"

The whisper tapered off, and the mighty Dvarapala was no more.

The light that had guided him here winked out of existence, leaving Ashok alone and crippled in the dark.

Having his chest crushed had nearly ended Ashok's life. All he could do was lay there among the dead and let the Heart of the Mountain repair his body. Sapped of all strength, for a time he drifted between sleep and reality. Both places were pitch black.

Ashok was troubled, not just by splintered ribs, ruptured organs, and internal bleeding, but by the knowledge that it had not been the Dvarapala that had taken control of his body and sent him down that fork. It was not the work of a mad god to force him back to the threshold when he had tried to walk away.

It had been Angruvadal.

His life was what it was, all because one of the most powerful magical devices in the world had picked a casteless blood-scrubber boy as its bearer. He had lived, trying his best to honor the will of the sword. It had been his companion and oldest friend. Devedas had been his next. Now both of those had betrayed him. Angruvadal had once stopped Ashok's heart to spare Devedas from his wrath. This was worse.

Whether it was pronounced dreaming or awake, aloud or in his head—he didn't know—his ultimatum was delivered.

"I have been your bearer. First by hand, then by heart. I have served. But know this, Angruvadal, I am not your slave. I have done all that is asked of me, but I will not be forced again. I kept the Law by choice, just as I choose my own way now. If you have need of my service, ask, and we will remain of one purpose. However, if you ever seize control of this body again, I will rip you from my chest, and even as that wound ends my life, I will hurl you into the sea. This I vow."

The shard was still. Ashok would take that for compliance. It knew him far too well to doubt his conviction.

Later, Ashok was awoken by an approaching light and hesitant footsteps.

"Avatara!"

Ashok slowly, reluctantly sat up, cringing at the hurt. His bones were no longer as shattered as the glass of his lantern, but they were still riddled with cracks. Every breath was like inhaling fire.

The light bounced as the collector ran toward him, and then he suddenly skidded to a stop when he saw the remains of the Dvarapala. Moyo stood there, wide-eyed and gaping, as he took in the destruction.

"You are a brave man, Collector Moyo. You crossed the threshold, despite not knowing the Dvarapala was dead." He would have tried to give him a respectful bow, but Ashok didn't think his torso was ready to bend just yet.

"Is all that your blood?"

"It is." He glanced down, as the comparatively feeble light revealed just how much he had lost. No wonder he felt so weak. "I will make more."

"It's done...I can't believe it." Moyo walked toward the blue body, kicked it, and then quickly retreated. When it didn't leap up and tear him limb from limb, Moyo shouted, "It's really gone! This is it?" He glanced around the huge space, as if trying to comprehend it all, and failed miserably. Moyo began shaking so badly his lantern rattled, and the oil inside sloshed about dangerously. "You really are the one!"

"Steady, Moyo." The last thing Ashok needed was for his guide to drop his lantern and set himself on fire. Crawling his way back to the cache blind would be a challenge. "Calm yourself."

"My guild has been preparing for this day for centuries. I can't believe this is happening." The collector carefully set his lantern down—thankfully—and then sank to the floor and began to weep.

Generations of his family had given their lives toward this goal, so Ashok let Moyo be. It was customary for the warrior caste to show great passion during moments of triumph or failure. Why should it be any different for the scavengers of Fortress? Let him be overcome by emotion for a time. Ashok was in no condition to march yet anyway.

After some sobbing, Moyo managed to wipe his eyes and tried to compose himself. "Oh great Ramrowan, what would you have me do?"

"I remain Ashok, the same man you've walked beneath half the ocean with. All I would have is your continued help getting home."

Yet Moyo was still reeling. "Sure, Avatara...I mean Ashok. But this changes everything. All of Xhonura has been waiting for this day. All our priests and gurus have been preparing us for your return. The guilds stand ready to fulfill our purpose."

"If you need to return to your people to tell them this door is no longer guarded, so you can begin looting this city, I understand, and will take no offense. I am certain I can read your guild sign well enough to make it the rest of the way on my own."

"I don't think you understand...I can't believe I'm correcting the gods' right hand, so let them strike me down if I am anything but honest." The collector took a deep breath. "Alright. This proves you are Ramrowan. There can be no doubt! Ramrowan is the rightful master of Xhonura. All our weapons are yours to use. All our guilds must serve your will. The Workshop, the island, it all belongs to you."

Ashok thought that over. It sounded absurd, but these Law breakers were an absurd people. "That is your Law?"

"It is."

"So I am the king of Fortress now?"

"Yes! Well, the Ram. The current Ram will require some

convincing, of course. Except this is undeniable proof!" Moyo gestured wildly at the body. "Ram Sahib is sure to concede and step down. The Workshop will be yours to command."

He had been rushing back to Lok, hoping to find Thera. It was his duty to protect her, but how could one man save her from the might of the Capitol and all the great houses? She would never abandon her rebellion, or the casteless it was trying to free. It was a futile battle, and no matter how hard he fought, their failure was inevitable.

*Unless...*

"How big is your island's army?"

# Chapter 27

"Next to present her eyewitness testimony concerning the destructive events in Goda province one week ago will be Senior Archivist Radamantha Nems dar Harban, of the Capitol Library."

"Good luck," Luthra of the personal guard of Great House Vadal whispered as he parted the curtain for her.

Rada walked into the opulent meeting room, which she had previously visited a great many times before while staying in the Great House in Vadal City, though she had never seen this many important dignitaries gathered before. There were arbiters and other high-status members of the first caste, as well as warriors in their finest uniforms of Vadal gray and bronze, and even wealthy workers of unknown duty but extremely fine garments.

Karno was present as well, having been the last to testify before her, but he was the only friendly face she saw among the crowd, not that anyone had ever accused Karno Uttara of excess friendliness.

Last of all Harta, the Thakoor of Great House Vadal himself, was present. His expression was unreadable, which made Rada very nervous.

All the very important people sat upon cushions, watching, as she took her place in the middle of the room. She had been given a fine dress and had tried to make herself pretty using all the tricks her sister Daksha had taught her. If she were to be condemned for her actions, then at least she would do so while looking stately and respectable.

"Oh yes, Rada and I are acquainted," Harta Vadal said with a very annoyed tone. "Hello again, Librarian."

Rada gave him a very appropriate bow in the northern style. "Thakoor Vadal."

Harta waved one hand dismissively. "Proceed with your testimony."

She cleared her throat, and then began her prepared remarks. "Upon the date in question, I was journeying through the Vadal woods, peacefully minding my own business, when—"

Harta cut her off. "This council does not care about your travels. We are here because nearly two hundred square miles of Vadal territory was obliterated, along with many of my subjects and property. Nor do we wish to hear a librarian's take on battling swarms of miniature demons after we've already heard the testimony of two phonthos and a Protector of the Law about that matter."

He may have been the Thakoor of this house, but Rada was too weary to put up with Harta's manipulative games. "Then I should go?"

The other important men were taken aback by her flippant tone, but Harta seemed unmoved. "What an improvement in manners, as you didn't bother to ask my permission last time you abandoned my protection."

"Is it normal etiquette in Vadal lands for guests to have to ask their host's permission to leave? That seems more how one would treat a hostage than a guest." To be fair, she'd been alone, with nowhere else to go, and been depending on Harta's mercy to not sell her to the Inquisition. This time she had the fearsome Karno Uttara sitting a few feet away, watching the proceedings in his usual impassive yet somehow threatening way. Life was easier when you had a hulking bodyguard who represented the might of the Law.

"I see our time apart has straightened your spine and sharpened your tongue. Good. I tired of your obsequious ways. Gotama and Jagdish have already regaled us with their tales of valor, but what transpired next was beyond their warrior comprehension. You, on the other hand, are a trained scholar with a Capitol education. Tell us of the pillar of fire."

Despite having relived those horrible moments over and over in the days since, the thought of it still made her shiver.

"You stood within a furnace, yet were not consumed," said one of the court wizards. "How?"

"We were saved by a magical pattern of unknown type. Forgive my lack of specificity, for I am no wizard. All I know is that this impenetrable barrier that saved us was created by a black steel artifact known as the Asura's Mirror, which had been given to me for safekeeping by Senior Historian Vikram Akershan."

"Bring forth the damaged object," Harta commanded, and a warrior of the personal guard immediately appeared from behind the silk curtains, carrying a wooden chest that he placed on the floor in front of his Thakoor, before hurrying out of the way. Harta leaned forward and opened the chest, revealing the Asura's Mirror, and the jagged crack that now split the middle of it.

"That's the one. When these proceedings are over, I would like it returned to me, as I am still legally obligated to be the artifact's bearer."

"My wizards say it is broken and unresponsive, which would make it no longer classified as an artifact, and thus not the jurisdiction of the Library or the Museum. Black steel fragments become the property of the great house that possesses them."

"Your wizards are wrong. Historically, when black steel artifacts are destroyed they shatter rather spectacularly. The mirror did not, which means it is merely damaged, not destroyed, ergo it remains property of the Capitol Museum, on temporary loan to the Capitol Library."

"You speak on behalf of your Order?"

Rada made a show of looking around the chamber. "I see no other librarians here."

Harta just shook his head and chuckled. "I can't believe you brought this dangerous thing into my home. For that audacity alone, I would seize it."

"I strongly protest."

"I don't care." Harta closed the lid on chest. "Continue your report."

Rada looked to Karno for support, but he was just sitting there, stone-faced. Karno's obligation wasn't to the mirror. He'd fight a whole army by himself to protect her life, but he didn't give a demon's damn about protecting the honor of the Capitol

Library. What else could she do? Throw a tantrum and deprive the Library of even more dignity? The Thakoor was the supreme leader of his house. The matter was settled.

*For now.*

"The barrier stopped the demons, and then it held back the explosive force and the heat as well." Which was the best way she could put it for these people, since in her experience courtly types were simpletons. The reality had been far more incomprehensible.

"Tell us of it," an arbiter demanded. "What was it like?"

Rada took a deep breath. "The force was beyond imagination. First it burst in the sky above, which flattened the entire forest in the blink of an eye, pushing down trees like grass in a strong breeze. Then a continuous stream of molten fire poured from above. Boulders and trees were flung on fiery gusts to shatter against our shield."

It had gone on so long that Rada's terror had eventually subsided enough to be overcome by academic curiosity. One could only scream their lungs out for so long before growing hoarse. Though none of the surviving warriors would ever admit to it, she hadn't been the only one crying inside the Asura's shield!

Some of the high-status men clearly didn't believe her, or lacked the faculties to process the information, but a few appeared intelligent. Her observations might actually be useful to them, so she pretended she was giving a normal scholarly report and continued.

"According to Jagdish's mechanical pocket watch, the blast itself lasted approximately one minute, during which little could be seen beyond a fiery haze and vague shadows indicative of destruction. Despite such incredible heat that the rocks around us seemed to soften and deform like a Devakulan volcano, the barrier remained cool to the touch."

"You should have roasted like meat in an oven," said one of the warriors.

"Clearly, we were not. Everything inside the barrier—which I assume to be spherical—was unharmed. The forest continued to burn for quite some time after the fury subsided." Rada didn't add the part where she had started to panic, because she imagined them running out of air inside the shield, like in a lurid book she had once read about the effects of being buried alive, except somehow their breathing had never been interrupted either. "As the fire died off, it revealed an ashen nightmare. The demons were gone. The forest was now charred-black and laid-flat logs, rendered into glowing hot coals, as far as the eye could see. However, I recognize that I have notoriously poor eyesight and had previously lost my fine glasses, so in the interests of providing truthful testimony I would corroborate this part with another witness. How bad was it, Karno?"

"It is as she says."

The high-status men nodded at that, because no one righteous would ever doubt the word of a Protector in public, especially about something they had seen, as everyone knew Protectors had eyes like eagles, the better to seek out criminals with.

"The shield remained protecting us until the evening. At some point, overcome from the day's excitement, I fell asleep." In truth she had been so emotionally devastated that she had used a rock for a pillow and passed out until dawn. "The next morning the barrier had vanished, and the ground had cooled enough for us to march out. It was a most unpleasant journey."

"How did you operate this black steel device?" Harta asked. "The warriors' testimony made it sound like the thing spoke with you somehow."

"I didn't so much operate it, as I asked it for help, and it granted that small mercy."

"Did the black steel device call the fire from the sky to smite the demons?"

"I am unsure, but that is most likely."

"Or was it *you* who inflicted this wound upon my lands?"

"No." Rada blinked a few times, as she'd been very much hoping to not be condemned to death today, but with Thakoors who could guess? "Of that, I am certain. As Karno and Jagdish may attest, the . . . whatever it was . . . the fire was already on the way when I begged the mirror for aid. The only boon it granted me was the barrier that saved us from the destruction it had already summoned."

"I see." Harta stroked his beard. Ever the statesman, his mood was inscrutable. "This testimony will be sufficient for now. The council is adjourned. Mulgar, Rajden, Saksham, and Tukaram will stay. The rest of you I will send for if I again require your presence."

The rest of the important people got off their pillows and quickly fled the room. Rada tried to as well, but Harta's eyes narrowed as he shook his head, and that was all the confirmation she needed to know that she had not been among the dismissed. She was of high status, from a different house, and obligated to a prestigious Capitol Order, but within the borders of the Great House Vadal, Harta might as well have been one of the forgotten gods for how much power he held, and Rada's firm hope was that this malevolent god wasn't going to require a sacrifice today.

On that note, she'd not seen Jagdish, and Harta disliked him *far* more than her. If Harta needed someone to blame, it would probably have been Jagdish. Oh, who was she kidding? He'd probably have them hanged together, his most troublesome phontho *and* an ungrateful guest who had brought a black steel weapon that burned whole forests to their borders.

Despite not having his name listed among those to stay, Karno had not gotten up. Harta saw that, yet he said nothing. It appeared even Thakoors were hesitant to try and boss around Protectors. As the supreme arbiter of the Law in his lands, if Harta wanted to declare Rada a foreign witch, there was nothing to be done about that, and then Karno would have to choose between his loyalty to the Law and the oath he'd given to Devedas. She trusted that Karno, being a good man, would choose righteously, but she'd prefer not to test that theory.

When only a handful of them remained, most notably among them the highest-ranking warrior, and the house wizards, Harta asked her the most important question. "Do you think someone could use this device to call fire from the sky again?"

"So you send away every witness you can't trust, before asking if I can deliver Vadal a powerful weapon?"

"Of course. Which of your history books taught you to expect this?"

None, actually. Rada had anticipated this on her own. She must be getting better at politics. "I do know more about the mirror than I have said."

"As expected," Harta replied.

"And my forthright answers about the mirror can save you a great deal of time and expense from having your wizards puzzle it out on their own, assuming they even know how to decipher the ancient language at all. In exchange I would ask a favor."

"I'm glad to see you did learn a few things about how to be a proper member of the first caste while being in my company." Harta actually laughed at that, and it even seemed genuine. "Life is give and take. Well done, Rada. However, you also forget your place. You are not in a position to make demands of me. I could always just make you tell me whatever I want."

"As you could have before, but did not, because that isn't your way. You prefer coercion to violence." She nodded toward her bodyguard. "Plus, this time I have Karno."

The Protector just looked at her with his heavy-lidded eyes, as if to say that he didn't appreciate being used as a bargaining chip in her schemes.

"True," Harta said. "Which is why I've had four members of my personal guard hidden in the curtains above with extremely powerful crossbows aimed at him the entire time."

"Five," Karno corrected. "I can hear the creaking of the strings. From the smell, the bolts are poisoned as well."

"I will defer to your superior senses, Protector. I intend no offense. They are my insurance. My family hasn't had the best experiences with members of your Order in recent years."

"Of course." Karno seemed unperturbed that Harta had been ready to skewer him the entire time.

Harta turned back to Rada. "I do have my preferred methods. Force is the lazy path. I am a diplomat... as long as it suits me. You can be perceptive, Librarian. Enough that I have on occasion missed your counsel and have been forced to make do with these unimaginative fools since you left." His closest advisors looked down in shame as Harta said that. "So what would you ask of me in exchange for this secret knowledge about the pillar of fire?"

Her request was immediate, for she had been hoping for this moment. "Ignore the Capitol's order to exterminate the casteless in Vadal. Promise to spare your non-people."

Even a master politician could be surprised. "Really? You want to save the fish-eaters?"

"Yes." Vadal was only one of twelve houses, but if she could save even a fraction of the non-people her cowardice had endangered, it was better than none at all. "Vow it and I will gladly tell you everything I know."

"An unexpected request." Harta thought it over for a moment. "A Thakoor does not make vows to anything other than his house and the Law, and this might put me at odds against the latter. However, my armies are otherwise occupied anyway. Sarnobat has used this destruction to their advantage and launched a large offensive, and I believe Vokkan will not be able to resist the temptation to do the same. Phontho Rajdan?"

This one wore a much fancier sash and turban than Jagdish, with several more stars on his sleeve. He was Vadal's chief warrior and had been present the night that she had taught Harta's council about the history of broken and stolen ancestor blades in relation to the rise and fall of great houses.

"Without question, Thakoor. The wolf and the monkey give us all the excuse we need to ignore the extermination order for now, Thakoor. Defending our borders takes precedence over a whim of the judges. No one will question the honor of such a decision."

"Thank you, Phontho...Very well, Rada. Your cooperation will buy the non-people at least a few seasons, and once this war is settled, then I will reexamine the issue—while keeping your plea for mercy in mind, of course."

"I am no arbiter," Karno stated flatly, "but that is the best he will give you."

"Listen to your Protector, Rada, for he understands the terrible things someone in my position will do to protect his house."

It would have to do. Rada didn't enjoy the idea of being tortured either. She'd read enough books on the topic—which, even if exaggerated to shock the reader, made the process sound extremely unpleasant. "Then we are agreed. The casteless live a few seasons."

"It is done." Harta gestured toward the chest. "Now, can this be used to cause great destruction again?"

"I don't think so," she answered truthfully.

"She's just saying that to keep us from using it against our enemies," snapped the warrior.

Harta ignored him. "Expound, Rada."

Since she knew for a fact that Harta had a surprisingly keen intellect, she did. "Before the mirror cracked while the fires around us cooled, it showed many images upon its surface and a great deal of writing in the ancient tongue. The equivalent of hundreds of pages, each one flashing by in an instant, like flipping through a book. Since it takes time to decipher the old styles of lettering, I wasn't able to read everything at the time, but I have been pondering on the rest since and I believe I have an approximate translation of much of it."

"Impossible," muttered one of the wizards. "Nobody can memorize such a thing so quickly."

"I have seen her memory tested before," Harta said. "Continue."

"The destructive fire was sent from the moon."

The wizards and the warrior exchanged incredulous glances, and then began to laugh.

Harta held up one hand to silence them, and they stopped the instant they realized they'd drawn their Thakoor's ire. "Canda or Upagraha?"

She named the smaller of the two moons. "Upagraha. I don't know if Canda possesses fire. It was not mentioned. The words were difficult to understand, and for a great many I believe there are no modern equivalents in existence. I fear what I say may sound like religious babblings, but I assure you I am a Law-abiding woman."

"There are no Inquisitors here." Harta turned toward his other guest. "Protector?"

Karno shrugged. Rada had already told him anyway.

"The fanatics would say this fire was sent by the gods to crush their ancient enemies. The demons we encountered were not the same as those which rise from the sea. These were like a swarm of insects, only instead of sleeping in the ground for seventeen years like some types of Gujaran or Vokkan cicadas, these slumbered for a thousand years until they were accidentally awakened by the Inquisitors."

"Why do you assume it was an accident?"

"If you had seen how these things kill, you would not ask that," Karno answered.

"Regardless of what brought the Inquisitors to those particular ruins, they did not expect what they found beneath. I believe if the old writings had not been scrubbed from the stones, they would have been a warning sign to leave that place alone. Once awakened, these particular demons would have spread far and wide, feeding, multiplying, and killing many. My assumption, from seeing how quickly they carried off our dead, was that they were to be immediately consumed to somehow grow the swarm. The Asura, by means I cannot understand, told Upagraha about this, and it *contained* the threat."

"The moon... is alive?" a wizard asked.

"Whether it is itself some manner of being, or wizards of unimaginable power live upon it, that answer was not in the pages I saw."

"This mirror told Upagraha to smite my lands, but you don't think it could be directed to rain fire down upon some other house in the same manner. Why?"

"That was the last of its fire. It only had so much to begin with, but it used up the rest fighting the demons long ago. This last weapon had been held in reserve, against a threat such as this. That is why the mirror needed to be present. It had to be certain, so as to not waste it."

One of the wizards cried, "Our lands have been stung for nothing!"

Except Harta just shook his head, for as expected he must have realized that Rada would not have asked for a favor that could be spitefully revoked if her news was of no use to him. "Calm yourself, Saksham. She has more."

"I do. I believe there is an entire library worth of ancient information in that mirror. I saw but a tiny fraction of it. Assuming I was translating it correctly..." Harta's assurances aside, Rada had to tread carefully here, so as to not say anything inadvertently religious. "*Whoever* created the mirror and put Upagraha in the sky had prepared other defenses should the cleansing fire fail. From the maps it showed, some of these appeared to be hidden here, in the north. I speak of weapons made of black steel."

"Another ancestor blade?" Even skillful Harta, the consummate politician, couldn't disguise the eagerness from his voice at that idea.

"It didn't specify the type, but help save the casteless from the wrath of the Law, and I will show you the way."

# Chapter 28

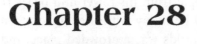

Four decomposing bodies hung from the gateposts.

Ashok knew them.

They had been among the monks who had fed him, clothed him, and given him a place to rest and heal. From nooses around their necks, they dangled high above the road into the squalid city. With bones broken, and flesh torn by whips, their once bright robes were darkened with dried blood and hung in tattered strips that whipped in the cold Fortress wind.

"Corpses left as warning." Moyo spat. "Ram Sahib's decorations are not so different from the Dvarapala's."

"Why are they here?" Ashok asked, but Moyo only shrugged. So he looked to one of the nearby merchants peddling his meager wares along the road, and demanded, "Why are these men here? What was their crime?"

"Who knows? They angered Ram Sahib somehow," the merchant replied. "I wish they hadn't. The smell drives customers away from my stall. Would you care for some potatoes? I have not seen you around before, tall stranger."

"He is a new collector from the south shore," Moyo said as he grabbed Ashok by the arm and pulled him along with the crowd. Once they were away, Moyo whispered, "Mind your tongue until you make your case to the Ram. You are a wanted man here, foreigner."

Ashok took one last look at the dead monks, and then pulled his hood down lower to conceal the anger in his eyes. With a heavy canvas sack over one shoulder, he followed Moyo the Collector into the capitol of Fortress.

The streets were mud. The homes were brick. It stank of shit and coal. The people were thin and haggard, barely surviving, and Ashok was about to ask them to go to war for strangers on behalf of a prophet they'd never met . . . of a god he didn't believe in.

"We must hurry. It is almost noon. That's when the Ram addresses the people from his tower and hears the petitions of the guilds. There will be many witnesses for our triumphant return!"

The City of Guilds was a crowded place, industrious as Neeramphorn, poor as the ghettos of Rangsiman, and cold as Dev. There were signs of indifference, beggars and lepers, and the most common greeting was an unfriendly glare. Windows had been broken but not repaired. Paint peeled. Cracks went unmended. Weeds grew wherever feet didn't keep them trodden down. It was a struggle for Ashok to understand the nature of man, but even he could sense the uncaring attitude of this place. This city was a sick beast, waiting to die.

Like the monastery and the village he had seen, the buildings here were also bland, squat, and featureless, with colors ranging between mud and stone. It was very different from Lok, where even the poorest among them sought out color and decoration, and where art was carved or painted onto any surface that allowed it. Even the casteless made art when their circumstances allowed. Ashok would never have thought about such things without seeing a place totally bereft of it.

"The city wasn't always like this," Moyo apologized as they had to step over a blind cripple. "In my grandfather's time the City of Guilds was the pride of Xhonura. As things run out, the guilds fight harder and harder over less and less. Your opening the last part of the Workshop will free us from that. It will make us rich and fat! My people will be excited again. You will be their hero, Avatara, and I will be rewarded for showing you the way."

Ashok did not share the collector's optimism.

The city wasn't a large one by Ashok's standards, accustomed as he was to the ever-expanding cities of Lok, so it didn't take long for them to reach the center. The public square was surrounded by large houses, each bearing some symbol indicative of a guild.

In the middle of the square had been erected a four-story tower with a platform atop it.

Hundreds of people were assembled in the square, awaiting the words of their Ramrowan reborn, and hoping to ask some favor of him. The guilds were the same, only their representatives stood upon the balconies of the houses, above the grime, slightly closer to the representative of their god. To Ashok these seemed just like the beggars he'd seen in the street, only more organized. People continued to arrive, packing in until they were standing shoulder to shoulder, and those behind Ashok complained about being bumped by whatever the hard thing was he had in the sack thrown over his shoulder.

At a specified time a bell was rung, and the crowd took up a chant. Not just those in the square, but it was as if all in the city stopped and turned toward the tower to pay their respects. Some showed genuine devotion, while others clearly only did it because it was expected of them. Even Moyo began to sing along. Ashok could not understand these words.

A man in yellow robes walked to the edge of the platform, carrying a ram's horn. It seemed odd to Ashok that in a land so bereft of color—probably because they had so few things that made good dye—that whatever pigments they did have were used up on the robes of their clergy.

When the priest blew the horn, that must have been the symbol for the chant to stop. As one, the entire city declared, "Glory to the Workshop, in Ramrowan's name."

"They're going to love you," Moyo whispered.

The horn blower shouted, "Heed the words of Ram Sahib!" then moved out of sight.

The mob fell silent, desperate to hear. A moment later another man appeared atop the platform, also dressed in yellow, but wearing an ornate crown and using a golden Fortress rod covered in rubies as if it were a staff. Even the powder horn worn at his waist was encrusted with gems that reflected the sun.

Sharpening his vision to assess the supposed god reborn, Ashok could see that the Ram was near his age, but soft from a comfortable life. Somehow plump, in a land where everyone else was skin and bones. There was a smirk upon Ram Sahib's face as he surveyed the adoring crowd. He leaned upon the ceremonial weapon, not because he was old or feeble, but because he was lazy. He was a comfortable master. Unchallenged, while his people dwindled and his country rotted around him.

Ashok had already been inclined to dislike this Ram even before seeing the bodies of four of the humble monks who had offered him shelter. Dislike turned to disgust.

"Greetings to Xhonura and all the faithful children of the workshop." Ram Sahib addressed the crowd, and was clearly an orator who knew how to make his voice carry a good distance. "Before I hear the day's petitions, there is but one announcement: The apostate Dondrub has been captured and will be executed in the morning."

There were many gasps and cries from the crowd, but those quickly bit their tongues or covered their mouths. That behavior was familiar to Ashok. They were silencing themselves so as to not be looked upon as collaborators or traitors. He had often seen similar reactions while making unexpected pronouncements of Law. Accused criminals had no friends, at least not in public.

"Any among the people who have ever listened to Dondrub's false teachings must repent and ritually purify themselves. Any who questions my rule is committing blasphemy. From this day forth, the penalty for blasphemy is death. I have spoken."

Disgust turned to hate.

"Is this what a king is, then? All the failings of the Law, compressed into a single man?"

Ashok had no issue with making his voice be heard either. Every head in the square turned to see who had spoken, as apparently nobody ever interrupted their leader's daily speech. Those nearest to him recoiled away, so as to not be tainted by his insolence. Only Moyo remained, except his eyes had gone wide with fear, as he finally comprehended the dangers inherent in his plan.

"Was blasphemy the crime of those monks who hang from your gate?"

"They assisted an infidel heretic." Then Ram Sahib shielded his eyes from the noonday sun and squinted to see the identity of the fool who had just sealed his fate. "Who dares question the Ram?"

Ashok pulled back his hood to reveal his face. "The infidel heretic."

There were gasps. A woman screamed. Now there was space

around him, as those closest struggled to get away, either to avoid being tainted by a filthy mainlander, or to not get shot by the guards who were hurriedly readying their Fortress rods. Even Moyo was swept away by the rush of the crowd, and for that Ashok was grateful, because the collector had done no wrong.

"For months I was kept in the dark and starved, and the only people who would share their bread with me died for it. What petty god would command such a thing? You are just as cruel as the Law, but without the dignity."

"Kill the trespasser!" the Ram bellowed.

There was nothing Ashok could say that would sway them not to try, but he had something Moyo was certain would convince them. Reaching into the sack, he took hold of one of the Dvarapala's horns, and lifted the severed head high over the crowd with one hand.

The guards froze. The mob became somehow even quieter than when they'd been waiting breathlessly to hear the words of their king. They all knew what it was, for legends of the beast had haunted the island for centuries. Ram Sahib reflexively lifted one hand to touch the many-horned crown on his head, and Ashok realized that it had been carved in the Dvarapala's image. Of course. Here the guardian creature was a symbol of fearsome eternal power, much the same way the Protectors wore the face of the Law over their Hearts.

"The one who guards the door!" someone shouted.

"The door is open now!" Moyo pushed his way through the awestruck crowd to stand defiantly at Ashok's side. "The true Avatara has returned."

The blue head was so heavy, dense with black steel and bones of unknown material, that the muscles of Ashok's arm bulged as he held it overhead, but he slowly turned the trophy so all could see.

"Impossible! No bullet can pierce the many-armed guardian!" The man who said that stood on the balcony of a house that bore the sign of a Fortress rod on it. "We have tried!"

"I used a sword."

"It is a trick!" the Ram shouted. "Do not be deceived! I am the Avatar of Ramrowan. It is not yet time to open the path. In time I will—"

"*Enough!*" Ashok roared loud enough to silence a king. "I

have already taken one god's head. Tempt me and I will gladly take another."

The Ram retreated from the edge.

"Heed my words, people of Xhonura, for I am Ashok Vadal and I have slain your Dvarapala. I do not know your ways. I do not want your crown. I have returned only to ask for your help." He flung the head to the ground. "Guru Dondrub told me that your people believe in the old gods, so I will tell you that they have again chosen a Voice. There is a prophet in Akershan, leading a rebellion against our Law. It is my duty to protect her. If you truly believe Ramrowan left this island so that it would be ready to finish his war, that time is now."

It was too much, too fast. The people were struggling to understand. Some of them were asking, *Could it be?*

"Hear him!" Moyo urged as he began circling Ashok, pointing at his champion. "I found this dead man frozen on the beach, blue as any corpse, but saw him come back to life with my own eyes. He could not drown. He did not freeze. The guildsmen threw him in the hole and famine didn't end him. Stronger than the Dvarapala, *he* is the true Ramrowan. The path is open for us. I have seen the broken city beneath and the treasures it holds. The Workshop is free—"

Blood hit Ashok in the face.

The collector looked down at the red hole that had been torn through his chest, then back up at Ashok, confused.

Ashok caught Moyo before he could fall.

Ram Sahib stood atop his tower, wreathed in white smoke, the golden Fortress rod still at his shoulder. That ball had been meant for Ashok, but Moyo had unwittingly stepped in front of the intended target.

Ashok's hate turned to...something else...something that had been building in him the entire time he'd been chained in the darkness.

"Take what's yours, Avatara," Moyo whispered.

Ashok gently lowered the collector to the ground, then he rose, and started walking toward the tower. His eyes met Ram Sahib's, and the king of Fortress knew fear.

"Kill him! Kill the trespasser!" Except the guards hesitated. Their entire lives they'd been told legends of Ramrowan reborn, and surely, deep down, they knew their current master was unworthy. How could they gun down this stranger who fulfilled their prophecies, who had brought them the head of the legendary beast that lived beneath the sea? When no one would do his killing for him, the Ram pulled the ornate horn from his belt and began the cumbersome reloading process of his ceremonial weapon.

Ashok began to run.

The crowd tried to get out of his way. Those who didn't make it, he hurled aside. Calling upon the Heart, he moved faster and faster, until the last of them he simply leapt over.

He landed in front of the warriors guarding the stairs. There were at least a dozen shaking weapons pointed at him.

"Move aside and live, or fight and die. It matters not to me which you choose but do it quickly."

As frightening as Ashok was in that moment, they still looked toward one of the guild houses, specifically the one marked with the sign of a Fortress rod upon it. The man standing upon that balcony hesitated for only a moment, before giving a sign with his hands that Ashok did not recognize.

The soldiers lowered their weapons and got out of the way so Ashok could pass.

He rushed up the narrow curling staircase inside the tower, fast as the Heart could drive him. Above him was the metallic *clack* of a Fortress rod being cocked, and Ashok threw himself hard to the side as it was fired. The soldiers were standing down, but not the yellow-robed priests. He was upon that priest an instant later, took him by the neck, and hurled him down the stairs. Another behind him didn't even have time to fire before Ashok reached him and bashed his head against the stone wall.

A few heartbeats after he entered the tower, he walked out onto the platform. The monk who had blown the horn was begging for surrender, while Ram Sahib was still readying his ornamental Fortress rod. Panicked, the Ram raised it, trying to track Ashok as he stepped to the side, and ended up shooting his own man in the back.

Ashok stepped over the dying priest as he gurgled and choked on his own blood. The Ram took up the powder horn as he backed away, clumsily trying to reload his weapon, but when he realized he wouldn't have the time, he instead swung the ornate thing like it was a golden club. Ashok caught the powder horn with one hand, wrenched it away, and smashed the Ram over the shoulder hard enough to shatter bones. Then he kicked the Ram's legs out from under him, and his landing shook the entire platform.

As the entire city watched, Ashok stood over their broken ruler. He looked out over the smoky gray of Xhonura and found that the entire multitude was staring at him, some terrified, but most expectant. Ram Sahib had been feared, but that was all. No one loved him enough to fight for him. They had been afraid to rise up against him, but none would lift a hand in his defense, while he lay there, pathetic.

"Spare me, foreigner." Ram Sahib cringed, unable to move his body from the pain. "Whatever you desire, it is yours. Treasure, women. Name it."

The jeweled horn had cracked, so Ashok turned it over and poured the Fortress powder onto Ram Sahib's face. He cried out in surprise as it got in his eyes, and then gagged as it fell into his mouth. Ashok kept the horn turned until it was empty, and then tossed it aside. As Ram Sahib coughed out a cloud of black, Ashok squatted next to him, reached into his cloak, and took out the fire starter that Moyo had given him to make sure he could always light a lantern in the down below.

"You should not have shot my friend."

The Ram's eyes went wide and white upon his powder-darkened face as he watched Ashok drag the steel rod across the flint. Sparks rained down. The Fortress powder ignited with a hiss and flash. The foul, angry stuff burned fast.

Ashok listened to the screaming for a while but, still unsatisfied, he kicked the burning Ram over the side.

The screaming stopped abruptly.

It was quiet. The City of Guilds watched, waiting for him to say something.

"Is the collector alive?"

The crowd there parted, enough that Ashok could see a few men were tending to Moyo, probably brothers from his same guild by the look of their clothing. Their distraught look told him the answer. Ashok closed his eyes and sighed, unexpectedly shaken by that. It seemed without the Law to tell him what to do, whenever he tried to make things better, good men died. He had agreed to Moyo's plan because it was his country, his people, but Ashok should have known better. For him, there was proving to be no such thing as peaceful solutions.

"Which of these houses belongs to the Collectors Guild?" Many hands pointed in the same direction. It was one of the smallest buildings, but there was the sign of the shears, pick, and lantern. Every balcony around the square was full now, but that one especially groaned beneath the weight of all the bodies that had turned out to see the commotion.

"Your man spoke truth. The path below is open. Send your expeditions and you will see." Then Ashok thought of what Moyo had told him. "When you do, let this whole island know that Moyo was the one who found me, and showed me the way. Remember his name."

Now that they had begun to realize the magnitude of what had just transpired, the crowd changed. Ashok could only assume that those who were fleeing had been loyalists to Ram Sahib, or had somehow benefitted from his cruel rule, and were trying to escape the inevitable purge. Others seemed overcome by a religious furor. There was a great deal of crying and shouting at the sky.

"Avatara, what will you do?"

"I am going home."

# Chapter 29

Ashok was tired of this gray land. Tired of its strange people. His message had been delivered. It was time to go. The same sack that had carried the Dvarapala's head was now filled with supplies. The people had been happy to give away their goods when asked, either because they actually thought he was their hero reborn, or because they knew he wasn't and were happy to help him leave.

As he walked out of town, a mob followed. He had told them to go away, but all fanatics were fools, no matter what nation they came from. Moyo had taught him enough guild sign that Ashok believed he could get himself back to Lok, but he couldn't do it leading this ragtag bunch. Thera needed warriors and weapons, not more bodies that were basically casteless by some other name.

"If you want to come to Lok, join your army first. You are useless to me like this."

He didn't understand the strange government of this place, but they would believe him and send help, or they would not. Either way, he could afford no more delays. Watchers stood at every window, pointing and gossiping. Making his way down the muddy streets, the curious crowd behind him continued to grow, as did his annoyance.

"Are you deaf? Convince your leaders to help fight." There

271

were men, women, and children, priests in different color robes, and various strange uniforms and outfits that he had never seen before. They kept trying to touch him, as if expecting some kind of blessing. Many of them shed tears of joy.

"Leave me be."

If they were still with him very far out of town, he would be forced to throw rocks at them until they fled, like stray dogs following a caravan full of food.

Moyo had believed they would make him king, but he was discovering that Moyo's optimistic outlook extended to more than just spelunking. The collector may have been a genius at surviving in the down below, but he was naïve in the ways of politics. The reaction Ashok had been given was one of confusion more than adoration. It appeared some of these sects were ready to welcome him. The orange robes had even tried to present him with Ram Sahib's burned and dented crown. The blue robes seemed nervous but accepting. The green were outright hostile, while the yellow robes of Ram Sahib's faithful had seemingly run for the hills. Religion was all very confusing to him.

The guilds seemed as varied in reaction as the sects. Only the collectors had seemed genuine in their enthusiasm, as Moyo had convinced a great many of them about Ashok's coming back to life after finding him on the beach. They had promised him that Moyo's body would be given a place of honor in the collectors' ossuary. They seemed very excited about the prospect of launching a new treasure hunting expedition into the city that had been off limits and were eager to begin. The other guildsmen he'd spoken to seemed confused and divided, angrily arguing over the legalities or sense in adopting a foreigner as their leader, and as their debates grew heated, Ashok was able to understand less and less of their dialect, so he had walked off without fanfare.

No matter. He was done here. Let Fortress fight one another or the Law, it was out of his hands now.

There was a contingent of gunners waiting at the gate. Their weapons remained shouldered when they saw Ashok and his mob, so at least it seemed they didn't want to fight him. It was hard to tell with these people. They wore the symbol of the rod, and one of them stood apart, with unique, compact Fortress weapons hung through scabbards tied to his belt. That one clearly carried himself as the leader, and Ashok recognized him as the one who had stood upon the balcony and given the signal for the tower guards to stand down.

Like everyone in Fortress, the gunner leader was short compared to Ashok, and wore lenses of glass over his eyes. Ashok had seen some of the first caste in the Capitol wear such things to improve their vision. It seemed a poor trick compared to what the Heart of the Mountain could do.

He greeted Ashok with a respectful nod. "I am Sachin Chatterjee, master of the Weapons Guild. May I speak with you, Avatara?"

"As long as you do it while we walk. I am done with this place."

"As you wish." Sachin fell in beside him, and it was clearly a struggle for him to match Ashok's long strides. "This is a momentous day."

"For some more than others."

As they passed beneath the gate, Ashok noticed that the monks had been cut down. Members of the Weapons Guild were respectfully wrapping the bodies in blankets and placing them upon a cart.

"They will be returned to their monastery for burial," Sachin said.

"That is your doing?"

"Yes. It seemed appropriate."

Ashok appreciated that. Today wasn't the first time that disrespecting the dead had provoked his emotions and the resulting ire had caused him trouble. He didn't understand why such behavior galled him so. They'd gone to the great nothing beyond. What did it matter?

Yet . . . it did.

"Thank you, Weapons Master."

They continued walking down the road with the mob still tagging along. Even the cripples on their crutches were trying to keep up. "Begone!" Ashok shouted again.

"Do these followers trouble you? I could have my men drive them off."

"You'd shoot them over my annoyance?"

"No. Lead and powder is expensive, and these men are already skilled, so there is no value to them practicing at such close range. I'd have them fix bayonets and poke at a few until the rest got the message."

"That is unnecessary for now. What do you want?"

"To meet the man who cast down the tyrant Sahib."

"He went from hero reincarnate to a tyrant in the span of a few hours."

"Xhonura doesn't breed a sentimental people. Sahib was too aggressive, too interested in consolidating his own power. He still retained the support of many important guilds, but his popularity had been on the wane. His replacement was imminent no matter what."

"So your new king is whoever is brave enough to murder the old?"

Sachin walked with his hands clasped behind his back. "Hardly. The Ram does not rule without the support of the guilds. We can't afford to throw the whole island into upheaval each time someone makes a claim. There is a process. Of those who claim to have the spirit of Ramrowan, only those supported by a sufficient number of the guilds are heard. For the others who make such claims, there is a separate process."

"I have seen your process. It involves starvation and being bitten by rats. I did not care for it."

"It is said if they are holy, they will survive."

"How often does that happen?"

"You are the first ever. Which is why I am walking with you, instead of having my men shoot you hundreds of times."

"I thought lead was too expensive."

"For you, we would spare no expense... Yet you did survive that trial, which intrigued me, and when I saw the head of the Dvarapala, that was enough for me to signal my men to let you pass so that I could see what would happen."

"You saved their lives."

Sachin looked Ashok over, calm and analytical. "I believe that to be true. The rest of our discussion will require privacy." He came to an abrupt stop, then turned and ordered his gunners. "Chase these people away."

His men drew forth the odd knives that attached to the ends of their guns.

"Do not harm them," Ashok warned.

Sachin cocked his head to the side, curious. "Nothing I heard about you suggests you possess a gentle nature."

"If there is killing to be done in my name, I will do it myself."

"Of course... Escort these back to the gates. Anyone who spills blood will be severely punished." Then Sachin waited while his men sheathed their strange blades, then began herding the faithful away. "Now we may speak freely."

Ashok kept walking. "You are the master of weapons for this whole island?"

Sachin rushed after him. "Yes."

"The rebellion I fight for requires weapons and men who know how to use them."

"You are familiar with our guns?"

"They are distasteful, dishonorable things, but their effectiveness is undeniable, and in sufficient numbers make even casteless equal to experienced warriors in battle. We have sixty gunners."

"I have six thousand."

Ashok was surprised by that number, but Sachin didn't strike him as a liar. Even without the ocean between them, the Law never would have been able to break this place. "Such a force would be sufficient to match the entire army of any one of the great houses. What would it take to bring them to my country?"

"It would require the majority of the guilds to come to an agreement. This will take time and much discussion, the nature of which will all depend upon what the collectors' expedition finds below. You must understand, Xhonura is a poor land. Our iron is fine but limited in quantity. We lack copper, brass, and lead. Our guns do not remain simple because we are too simple to innovate, but rather too poor to replace the materials. We barely grow trees sufficient to carve stocks. Our soil is as poor as our mines. Food is scarce in the best of times. We are a few bad winters from affording no army at all."

"Then it is a difficult proposal."

"Yet the gods will it, or so Guru Dondrub tried to convince me before he was arrested for blasphemy. He was rather convinced of your destiny."

"I am not."

"Then why do you do this?"

"For a woman."

"Ah..." Sachin said, as if that made all the sense in the world. "As fine a reason as any."

"You should free Guru Dondrub."

"I have already ordered it. If Sahib were truly Ramrowan,

then the gods would not have allowed you to burn his face off. You cannot blaspheme a fraud...On that note, the presence of such a compelling Ramrowan as yourself would complicate the negotiations. Your abrupt foreign ways would upset the more conservative guildsmen. It would not do to replace a tyrant with a barbarian. It is better for them to imagine a distant idealized Avatar, represented only by the compelling tales your ally the Guru tells."

Ashok wondered about that. "Is he my ally?"

"Far more than you know."

"And you, Weapons Master?"

"I am undecided, but I am not your enemy. I spend my days surrounded by vats of volatile compounds that explode if handled incorrectly. Such a life does not promote the making of rash decisions." Sachin extended one hand, similar to the southern style of goodbye used in Dev. "You will know our answer in a few seasons."

Ashok paused long enough to shake on it, and without another word, turned and continued walking back toward Lok.

# Chapter 30

~~~~~~~~~~

*Without water they will fall.*

Those words had sent Thera and the Sons of the Black Sword on a mission of righteous vengeance.

For weeks they had ridden along the slopes of the Akara River Valley and into the mountains of Thao, northward toward the high desert. It was rugged, desolate country, and they saw very few people, none of whom were foolish enough to question the identity of the numerous and well-armed band.

Thera often cursed the Voice. In the rare times it manifested it tended to be cryptic, confusing, often communicating in riddles that only became clear after the events the gods had predicted transpired... but this time, the god who was living in her head had given her a good idea, an actual workable course of action, where even a force as small as the Sons could strike against the Capitol and make the first caste feel the cost of their decisions.

After the Voice had come upon her, she had awakened on the roof of the barracks, surrounded by worried faces. Serving as the gods' mouthpiece always left her dazed and weak, a state not too different from the seizures that had plagued her since the bolt from Heaven had first struck. It was Keta's duty as Keeper of Names to record the Voice's pronouncements, except this time nearly the entire population of the Cove had seen and heard the manifestation of the Forgotten.

As soon as Keta had repeated the words, she had known exactly what to do.

*Without water they will fall.*

It would be risky. Not just because of any great house forces they might encounter along the way, but it would be difficult to make the journey there and all the way back to the Cove before the first snows of winter blocked off the mountain passes. If the weather turned early and the Sons were still on the Thao side of the mountains, it would be difficult to elude the forces the Capitol was sure to send after them.

When Thera had told her officers that she had been inspired with a way to strike back against the Law, but that it would be a long, exceedingly dangerous journey, they hadn't cared about the risk. The faithful had been gripped by such a religious fervor after seeing the Forgotten's image that every last one of them would have marched against the Capitol itself armed with nothing more than their belief that the gods were on their side.

Compared to that, what was destroying an aqueduct?

Thera and her officers sat around a campfire made from sagebrush, so exhausted from another long day on horseback that none of them talked. They just ate their rations and stared into the distance, tired beyond caring. Even a gods-inspired fever can only last for so many days in the saddle before it is replaced by a kind of weary numbness, where you don't think, you just ride.

They were in the high mountains now, and ahead of them lay the desert, home of the mighty Capitol, the beating heart of the first caste. The mighty Akara was nothing more than a turgid stream here, and within another week, the city that shared that river's name would be in their sight.

The Sons had followed her, trusting, even though she hadn't yet revealed their actual destination. She had three hundred men sneaking across the borders of multiple great houses, any of which could crush them like bugs. All they knew was that they would strike at one of the Capitol's most precious resources. She'd not yet told them what the specific target was for a reason she couldn't even divulge. Only a handful of her wiliest followers knew there was potentially a wizard spy among them.

There would be no room for error. And with faith being gradually replaced by fatigue, she needed to raise their morale. Thera had been raised by the greatest raider the west had ever seen, and she'd watched how he took care of his people. She knew when it was time to get a warrior's head right.

Thera looked around the leader's council. There was Murugan of Thao, dedicated bodyguard, close and wary as always. There was Gupta, worker of Jharlang, risalder of gunners; Shekar of the Somsak, risalder of skirmishers; Toramana of the swamp people; risalder of archers; Eklavya of Kharsawan, risalder of infantry; and Ongud of the Khedekar, risalder of cavalry. She had requested one other advisor to come on this mission, and that was Javed of the caravan people, merchant turned priest. She had ordered him to accompany the Sons because he was among the few in the Cove who had traveled extensively through the central desert. Such knowledge could prove invaluable.

Only by taking one of their priests, it had made sense for the other one to stay and lead the people of the Cove. Of course, Keta had hated that. Nor had he liked the idea of Thera putting herself in danger by personally leading this raid. She could see Keta's logic, but how could she ask the Sons to risk so much, based on the cryptic words of the god in her head, and not be there with them? The Sons no longer had unstoppable Ashok to inspire them. Keta wasn't fit for such a role. Frankly, neither was she, but the *idea* of her could serve. She'd finally told Keta that if he didn't like it, next time he could be the one to get stabbed in the brain by the gods, so he would stay, and that was final.

"Javed."

The priest looked up from his meal. "Yes, Prophet?"

"You have been to the Capitol. Tell us about it."

"Is that why we're here?" He blinked a few times, too tired to comprehend. "We can't possibly be attacking the Capitol..."

"Humor me. What's it like?"

Javed thought it over. He was a handsome, well-groomed, confident man, which seemed odd for a priest, probably because the only other priest she had ever known was Keta, who was small, odd-looking, and intense. "I've been to the markets there mostly, as a worker of my status would never be allowed inside the more important distracts. Yet any part of that city is a remarkable sight. They say it is the most beautiful city in the world, and having traveled across every great house, I believe this to be true."

"It is a place for fat firsters to roll about in all the bank notes they stole from vassal houses as taxes," Ongud muttered.

"That is probably true, my friend, but what notes they don't use for beds they spend on architects and gardeners."

"And whores!" Shekar added.

Most of them laughed, though Eklavya reached over and thumped Shekar hard in the arm. "The Prophet is a lady!"

"A lady from the warrior caste of House Vane, who whipped every other house in the west." Thera loudly cleared her sinuses and spit into the fire to show that her feelings were not so delicate. "Trust me, Risalder, if I was ever offended by the shocking idea that soldiers enjoy the company of pleasure women, I wouldn't hesitate to let you know."

Their smiling at that was good. Each time something miraculous happened to remind them that she was the Voice, they usually spent the next few days being obnoxiously careful around her, as if she was made of glass, and might fall over and break in a stiff wind. She needed them inspired, but it was a fine line to walk, and she had a rebellion to run. There wasn't time for such coddling nonsense. It was good to remind them that she was just flesh and blood, same as the rest of them, and she'd been a criminal longer than most.

Javed was looking at her curiously, though, and she had to remind herself that this last event was the first and only time he had ever seen the Voice actually manifest. It appeared that even someone faithful enough to become only the second priest in the whole world still needed time to ponder upon seeing something like that. But then he shook his head as the spell was broken and went back to his tale.

"It is vast—I believe the only city more populated is Vadal City, but that is a sprawling, chaotic swirl of colors and styles that seems to go on forever. The Capitol is stark, sitting alone in the desert, surrounded by walls of sandstone, and the buildings within are taller than you can imagine, with each Order competing to be more magnificent than its neighbors. Even their slaves go about dressed in the finest silks and jewels, because no family can stand being seen as poorer than anyone else. A curious mix of wealth and indolence, the Capitol is unlike any other city you've ever seen."

"I have never seen a city at all," Toramana said. "I thought the ones we captured were cities, they were so big, but I am told those are merely towns."

"All of Chakma would fit inside the Capitol's grand bazaar with room to spare. The streets are so wide that elephants lumber down them side by side, even though it's too hot for elephants there, and the creatures are miserable in the sun. The judges don't care." Javed seemed to be enjoying telling stories, and the risalders had awakened enough to pay attention. "There's a theater with ten thousand seats, and even that isn't big enough to satisfy their desire for constant entertainments, so they hold plays in the streets, and there are musicians on every corner. Every night, some family is throwing a feast, and they compete to see which is the greatest. There are fountains and statues, and they even have a zoo, filled with animals captured from every corner of Lok."

"My son Rawal always wanted to see a city." Toramana said gruffly.

Javed fell silent, but then rested a comforting hand on Toramana's shoulder. "Rest easy, noble chief. As one of the faithful your boy resides forever in the city of the gods, the glory of which makes the Capitol look like a casteless shack."

That actually seemed to comfort the big man. "So the Keeper has said."

Thera didn't know if that paradisical afterlife was one of the things Keta had made up, or one of the things taught to him by Ratul, who had also probably made it up, but the idea seemed to ease a father's grief, so it was good.

"As the prophet, I declare those boys will be remembered as full Sons of the Black Sword, because if they hadn't been taken too soon, they would've surely served, brave as the rest of you." Thera had only told the slyest of her warriors—the crafty ones she could be certain would keep their mouths shut—about her suspicions that those boys hadn't been killed by any natural beast, but that was best left unsaid for now.

"To Parth and Rawal." Ongud lifted his canteen. "They never saw the Capitol, but the rebellion will defeat it for them just the same."

Everyone joined the salute, raising whatever container it was they had to drink from, half of which were already empty, but such was the nature of being on a long journey.

"Now, Javed, tell us of the aqueducts."

"The aqueducts? They're massive stone constructs, like rivers raised high above the desert. It is said that the first caste built their city in the middle of the continent, because it was the farthest place from the impure ocean, but the Capitol has few wells, and you have to dig incredibly deep to get any water at all. So the aqueducts are what keep it alive. They're so big that when merchants pass beneath in the summer, our entire caravans sometimes stop to enjoy the shade. There are three." He reached over and picked a stick from the ground, and then used that to draw a star in the sand before him.

"That is the Capitol." Then he made a line above it. "The first aqueduct ran from the Nuanjan in the north, along the border of Vokkan and Zarger, but as the Capitol grew that was insufficient for its endless thirst. So next they turned their eyes to the west, drinking from the swift Tunka and passing through Karoon." A second line to the left. "Last of all, they sipped from the icy runoff of the Devakula glaciers, running west of the city of Akara, following the border of Devakula and Makao." A third line below.

The priest was no fool, and he paused for a long time after he suddenly understood the target of their mission. "And today"—he stuck the stick into the sand down and to the right of the third line—"we are about here."

The men on the opposite side of the fire had stood so that they could see. Once they were out of the mountains, it would be a straight shot to Akara.

"Without water they will fall," Javed muttered, staring at his map.

The leaders understood now, and all eyes turned toward their prophet, surprised by the audacity of their mission. This was no mere raid. This was a crippling blow.

"I've spoken in private with a few of you already. Eklavya?"

"Yes, Prophet?" The young risalder snapped to parade quality attention. He couldn't help himself. Such was the orderly nature of the Kharsawan... The other thing their warrior caste was renowned for was their love of engineering, especially building—or more importantly, tearing down fortifications.

"Have you given any more thought to our earlier discussion?"

"As to how to destroy such structures? I have several ideas."

"I helped," Gupta added.

"Gupta helped," Eklavya agreed. "Miners spend a great deal of time worrying about why things collapse. Between us we have multiple strategies that should work, though we won't know for sure until we lay eyes on the thing. As directed, I gathered another twenty strong workers, used to hard labor, and placed them among the infantry."

"We have stone breakers among them," Gupta said. "To see what they can do by hammer and spikes alone is miraculous. And if necessary, my gunners' powder can be used to make a small crack a very big one, very quickly."

"I'd prefer to save the powder so that we can shoot whoever comes after us instead."

"As would I and my gunners, Prophet. Shooting has spoiled us. Swinging them like clubs would be much harder work and not nearly as satisfying."

"Oceans," Ongud said, clearly awed by what they were trying to do. "We'll need those guns. Such important works are sure to be well protected. Make sure to tell your smartest men these plans of yours, so if either of you die or are indisposed we can carry on without you."

"I was just awaiting the prophet's permission." Eklavya looked to Thera, and she nodded. "It will be done."

"How well will this sky river be guarded?" Toramana asked.

That was one thing Thera did know. "They stretch for far too many miles for warriors to watch the whole thing at once, but there will be patrols on both sides, Devakulans on the east, Makao on the west. Vassal House Vane had to obligate warriors to that duty every year."

"Then we will surely have a battle." The swamp man smiled. "Excellent."

"The likelihood of that depends entirely upon how fast we can destroy the thing," Eklavya said. "They're huge and constructed to last for centuries."

Not all of them were convinced. Shekar was Somsak, who were legendary raiders, but they tended to loot and run without thinking about the long-term strategy. He gestured at the other two lines. "So we break one and water the desert, but the other two are beyond our reach. They'll still be able to drink."

"Don't think like a warrior." Murugan stood behind Thera, the only one not looking at the map, carefully keeping his eyes away from the fire so as to not damage his vision in the dark. "We're used to tasting dust. Think like the first caste."

"I am incapable of such softness." And since they had all seen the tattoo-faced warrior fight like a wild beast, that was easy to believe. "Even their men are made of flowers."

"Exactly," Thera said. "The first are used to a life of easy comfort. They have fountains that vomit water and public baths to lounge in and lawns of green grass in the middle of the desert. Once we deprive a city of nearly a million people a third of its water supply, all that is gone. They won't die of thirst. Oh no. But for the first time they will be afraid they *could*. They thought they could order the deaths of all the casteless with impunity, but now they'll realize that their actions have consequences. Their damnable Great Extermination has a cost."

"Hmmm...We damage their morale, but also after we destroy this one, they will have no choice but to send many more troops to guard hundreds of miles of the other two, which means many more warriors who won't be hunting non-people." Then Shekar caught himself. "Casteless. Sorry, Prophet."

"You're smarter than you look, Somsak." Thera studied all the faces clustered around Javed's clumsy map. It was obvious their enthusiasm had been reawakened now that they understood the purpose to this journey. "Alright, then. Now your duty is to go back to your paltans and make them understand exactly what's at stake. We're not just giving the Capitol a split lip because we can. We're teaching them as long as the casteless aren't safe, neither are the first. This fight is bigger than our rebellion. It is our chance to break the Capitol's will so we can save the lives of millions. *The gods sent us here*. Do you understand me, Sons of the Black Sword?"

There was raucous agreement. The first caste was cursed. These were proper soldiers.

"When the battle comes, I expect my risalders to lead with the wisdom of Jagdish, and every last Son to fight with the ferocity of Ashok. Let's bleed the Capitol and be home before it snows."

"We will not fail you, Prophet," Ongud promised.

"I know you won't. Now go to your men."

Only Javed and Murugan remained, as neither of them had a paltan to lead and hearts to inspire.

"That was...unexpected," Javed said. "The Capitol takes the

aqueducts for granted. Even when great houses clash with the Capitol, they'd never attack such symbolic monuments because every other great house would turn against them and destroy them utterly. And no criminals have ever been so brazen. It's a bold plan. Are you sure this is what the Forgotten meant?"

Thera sighed. "You can never be certain with the Voice. I wish it were otherwise, but we do our best and hope."

"You're telling the truth," Javed marveled. "I mean, I believed before enough to walk across half the continent to find you, but... the Voice was not what I expected. Everything Keta told me is true. You really don't know why it says what it says and you've got no control over it."

Thera chuckled. "Keta's right. I'd tell everybody how it really works, but Keta thinks it would scare the faithful too much. I'm sorry, but I'm afraid you volunteered to serve a very fickle god."

"The Keeper prefers to call the Forgotten's nature *inscrutable*. Who are we mortals to question? No matter. Now that I know where we are going, I can help serve as a guide, and range ahead to scout. In a few days we will reach the high desert, and I know it well."

"Thank you, Javed. Now if you'll excuse me, I've got to get some sleep. I'm exhausted."

"Of course." Javed placed his palms together in a sign of respect, and then stood and began walking away, only he hesitated, just outside the firelight.

"What's troubling you, priest?"

"I'm sorry, but have you heard of Shabdakosh?"

"Vaguely."

"It was a desert village. A waypoint for merchants and the first traveling to the Capitol. The residents there were slaughtered by a casteless uprising, wells poisoned, homes burned. Many innocents perished." His voice grew distant. "It was a tragic day."

"I heard about that afterward. They blamed Ashok but he had nothing to do with it. Why do you bring it up?"

The priest paused there in the darkness, as if mulling over his words. "The closeness of that violence shook the Capitol, much like what we intend to do... Only the first caste's fear made them worse. More reactive. More vindictive. Without that massacre, they might not have ever voted for a Great Extermination."

Thera didn't know much about the Capitol's internal politics.

She tended to just think of the judges as a distant but malignant force, but what else could the Voice mean? Andaman Vane had been inspired to rebellion because of the Voice, except the rebellion it had promoted hadn't been the one he had started. Her father had died as a direct result of believing the prophetic words that had flowed through her.

"Do you think I've got it wrong?"

"That's not my place to say. I don't know. It's just a random thought. We all make mistakes . . . but some mistakes are greater than others. Good night, Prophet." Javed walked away.

When he was gone, Murugan said, "Our rice merchant seems troubled."

"He wasn't raised warrior caste. Our people are taught since birth to never hesitate, it's pick a direction and run."

"That makes us effective."

"It also makes us rash sometimes. Workers tend to be deliberate, but to be fair that organized merchant mind of his is probably the main reason the faithful haven't started eating one another in the Cove." Thera signaled for her servant, who had been waiting in the background. "Laxmi, would you bring my bedroll?"

Only Thera, her bodyguard, and Keta knew about the *unquieting of the minds*, and that the House of Assassins' slaves could think and speak again. As far as the Sons knew, Thera had brought silent, unobtrusive Laxmi along to serve as her maid. It seemed an appropriate thing for a prophet to have a servant. Only Thera and Murugan knew that the girl was their wizard.

When Laxmi handed her the blankets, Thera whispered, "Any luck?"

Laxmi shook her head no.

Very few people were as gifted at sniffing out magic as Gutch had been, so she couldn't just tell if somebody had a bit of demon in their pocket like the big worker could. But Laxmi was confident that if anyone used magic nearby, she would be able to tell. The spy might still be in the Cove, but if he was among the Sons of the Black Sword, Thera intended to flush him out. Now that she'd revealed their target, a spy was almost certain to try and alert his masters.

And once she caught him, after she cut the spy's hands off so he couldn't do magic anymore, she would turn him over to Toramana and let him avenge his boys.

# Chapter 31

Bharatas had ridden Kurdan into the valley. Though he had his pick of the finest stock in Akershan now, she had been with him when his vendetta against Ashok Vadal had begun, so it seemed appropriate she would be his steed at its potential end.

He dismounted at the edge of the lake and watched as a few low-status soldiers had to suffer the indignity of floundering about naked in the dark, icy water, searching for the supposed secret path. Very few whole men knew how to swim. Swimming was for lowly impure things, like fish, or casteless.

Other soldiers of Akershan stood all along the shore, torches held aloft. Eager. Was this the end of their long hunt? Could the rebels really be hiding on the other side?

"Have you found anything yet?" Bharatas demanded.

One of the poor freezing warriors had struggled to a spot where his feet could reach the bottom. "Not yet, bearer."

"Keep looking." Then he nodded toward one of the risalders. "Bring up the prisoner."

The lake wasn't that big, the water wasn't that deep, and the mountain runoff was clear enough there was surely no demon concealed in it, but if what the prisoner had given up after many long torture sessions was accurate, this was one of the finest defenses Bharatas had ever heard of.

While Bharatas waited, he fed Kurdan a carrot from his pack, and then scratched behind her ears, as she liked. The prisoner was in such terrible shape that he couldn't walk, so was dragged by each elbow by a pair of warriors. Since all his toes had been snapped and his shins beaten with rods, he couldn't even stand on his own, so they had to hold him up before their leader.

"This is it?"

"It is." It was hard to understand their captive, since all of his teeth had been smashed out. "Just kill me."

The worker had held out a surprisingly long time, but as predicted, all men break eventually. Well, perhaps not Ashok Vadal. That one Bharatas assumed he would just have to kill, and with ancestor blade in hand, he would actually have a chance. Angruvadal versus Akerselem. Their battle would be legend. There were rumors Angruvadal was broken, but Bharatas would assume the worst.

"Where is the tunnel?"

He pointed with one shaking hand, but since each of his fingers had been repeatedly smashed until they were just crooked lumps, it was hard to tell exactly where the prisoner was pointing. It would have to be close enough for the unfortunate swimmers. "Search more to the left," Bharatas ordered.

"It's deeper there," a warrior wailed. "It's too cold. We'll drown."

"The blood of Chakma cries for vengeance!" he shouted back. "Better to drown than let that insult against our house stand."

The men took deep breaths and swam out into the darkness.

The swimmers weren't the only ones holding their breath. The finest warriors in Akershan waited to see if they would finally have the chance to restore their honor. Every man was quiet. All that could be heard was the occasional snort of a horse, the crackle of their torches, and the prisoner begging for death.

A short time later a warrior came desperately splashing back. It was hard to understand him over the chattering of teeth. "We found it! It's just as he said!"

The torturers had been told the only way in was a long cut through the mountain, usually filled with water, which ended in a reservoir elevated above them, overlooking a bounteous secret valley populated entirely with religious fanatics. It was a veritable rebel paradise, free of Law or caste.

And now Bharatas would destroy it.

"You'll never get inside." The prisoner had found the strength for one last taunt. "These mountains can't be crossed. No man can hold his breath long enough to reach the other side."

Except Bharatas had already thought about the challenges of besieging such a place and had requisitioned a great number of tools. "Alright, men, this is the place. Get to work."

"You heard the bearer! Seventeenth paltan has the first shift!" an officer shouted, and warriors rushed forward carrying shovels and picks.

"You fools can't dig through the mountain!"

"We don't need to," Bharatas assured the captive. "I'd bring the entire might of Akershan down upon this place if I needed to, but once you described the nature of it, I knew all I really needed was time and gravity."

The prisoner was barely still alive, but as the warriors began laboring, the realization of what they intended to do truly ended him. In his delirium of pain, he had probably convinced himself what did it matter if he talked? They'd never get in anyway. By the torchlight Bharatas could see the man begin weeping, for he finally accepted the truth, that he had brought death upon his friends.

"Kill me, please."

"Do it yourself or ask your gods for help. I am a man of my word..." To the guards he said, "He told me what I wanted to know. As agreed, give him blankets and rations, put him on a strong horse, and point him toward Dev."

As they carried the screaming worker away, Bharatas returned to filling his vow.

"Drain the lake."

# Chapter 32

The Keeper of Names was awakened by shouting.

Keta had been updating the sacred book, which had been entrusted to him by Ratul, when he had fallen asleep with it still clutched in his hands. Since it was coated in demon hide, silky smooth when rubbed one direction, but sharply abrasive the other, he had been lucky he'd not cut himself on it. The candle that he'd been working by had gone out. He didn't know the time, but it felt late. By the light of Canda coming through the window, he saw that the notes he had taken interviewing the most recently arrived casteless refugees about their genealogy had been blown all over the floor, probably by a gust of wind.

It was very unbecoming for the Keeper of Names to fall asleep while conducting such a sacred duty, but it was hard work tending to the needs of so many faithful. It was easy to forget just how much work he had delegated to Javed over the last year. Between his overwhelming duties and the constant fretting worry about Thera's safety, it was amazing Keta survived on as little sleep as he got.

Then he heard the shouts again and realized why he was awake.

"Let me in! I must speak to the Keeper of Names. It's an emergency."

Whoever it was sounded very upset. Keta scooped up the

meat cleaver he kept by his sleeping mat—an old habit—and leapt to his feet. "I'm coming!" he yelled as he ran down the stairs.

His bodyguard tonight was a casteless lad who had drawn the honor of protecting the rebellion's priest from assassins and annoyances. "It's one of the watchers, Keeper."

The man causing the commotion was standing in the doorway, holding a lantern, and Keta recognized him as one of the faithful who had escaped Chakma, though just awakened Keta couldn't remember his name. There were just far too many faithful now to keep up on all of them.

"O thank the gods." The messenger was breathing hard, as if he'd run all the way from the lookout point. "You've got to come right now, Keeper. You must see this."

Still bleary with sleep, Keta asked, "See what?"

"There's lights in the valley. Torches. Heading toward the lake."

They were expecting no arrivals and weren't prepared to drain the tunnel. Could Thera have come back already? Even if all went well they'd still be a few days from Akara. Unless they had given up early and turned around for some reason? Perhaps the quiet slave girl had revealed their spy? Or maybe Thera had changed her mind? Had something gone horribly wrong?

"Is it the Sons of the Black Sword?"

"We can't tell, Keeper, but there's a great many of them. Please come."

Barefoot, Keta ran after the observer. It was late as he'd first thought, so the Cove was deep asleep. They went up the winding terrace road, and then turned up the steep path near the ancient reservoir. Keta followed the bobbing lantern, hoping that this was nothing. If it wasn't the Sons back early, then likely it was just some Akershani passing through.

Even though it was currently filled with water, there were always guards watching the tunnel entrance, and Keta saw that they too were nervous. They'd already been alerted about the torches in the valley. The rebellion always kept eyes on the lake below because the secret tunnel had protected them from the outside world. Secrecy was the only thing keeping all of these faithful safe from the wrath of the Law. The runner extinguished his lantern as they got closer to the top, because from this point on they were trained to never show any light that might give them away. By Canda's moonlight they made their way up the slope, fast as they could without tripping.

It was a fearsome climb, and Keta's lungs hurt. The air was so sharp in these mountains it cut the nostrils. Once they reached the top, they crouched and crept forward, instinctively quiet, though realistically they could probably bang a drum and sing a song from up here and there was no way they could be heard so far below, but he had taught them to take no chances. Other guards were waiting at the edge, watching, and one of them signaled for Keta and whispered, "Over here."

Panting from the uphill run, Keta approached the cliff. Far, far below, down the unclimbable rock face, was the valley. In the near darkness he could only pick out the lake because its waters reflected the moonlight. Around the lake's shore were torches.

Far too many torches.

It wasn't the Sons.

This was a different, far more numerous, army.

Keta watched the invaders. Did they know about the path? If not, this might just be a patrol, or some temporary encampment, who would eventually move on.

Fear gripped Keta's stomach. His first thought was to sound the alarm and wake the Cove, but what good would that do? They'd simply panic and rush around uselessly. Better to let them sleep. They could be terrified in the morning.

If the men did know about this place—perhaps the slave girl had been right about the tiger being a wizard—then they still couldn't get in as long as the tunnel remained fully flooded. The reservoir was nearly half full, and as long as the ancient spillway gate remained open a crack, it would continue to slowly feed into the lake below.

"It's alright," Keta assured the watchers, but mostly the words were for himself. "Even if we're found. They can stay down there and freeze all winter. We're self-sufficient. We grow plenty of food. We can outlast any siege."

"How will the Sons get back in?" one of them whispered.

Keta hadn't thought about that yet. "Thera won't be back for weeks at the earliest, but she's far too clever to walk into a trap. We'll think of something before then. Don't worry. As long as the tunnel stays flooded, invaders can't get in, we're safe."

Too late, Keta realized what he'd just said.

*Without water they will fall.*

# Chapter 33

Witch Hunter Javed had never really felt guilt before.

He could understand the concept, and act like he was feeling it well enough to convince anyone, yet guilt remained a thing that others experienced which he could not. When he was a child, he had always simply done what he felt like doing. There were always consequences to those actions, especially if he got caught, but at no point had he ever fretted about his deeds. He simply lied his way out of trouble. As he had gotten older, Javed had recognized that he was different, unable to feel emotions that others took for granted.

As a boy he had been told about a marvelous lizard that lived in the Gujaran jungles, called a chameleon, which could change its color and markings at will to blend in to its surroundings, allowing it to hunt its prey while avoiding its predators. That had struck Javed as a brilliant philosophy to live by, and he prided himself on adopting the chameleon's ways. Displaying his true nature marked him as odd, dangerous, and thus a target, so he had become extremely proficient at pretending to be whatever those around him required him to be.

There was always a need in the Capitol for handsome, charismatic, amoral liars. After Great House Zarger had obligated him to serve the Inquisition, Grand Inquisitor Omand had recognized

in young Javed great potential. Only the most cunning and magically talented Inquisitors could become elite witch hunters, and
even then it took most of them years to cultivate the devious
methods that came naturally to Javed. He quickly increased in
rank and status. He didn't care about the Law, but he enjoyed
rooting out those who would fight against it. They were goals to
be conquered. In challenge, he had found purpose. Infiltrating,
deceiving, spying, and assassinating were difficult activities, and
he took great pleasure in succeeding where lesser men would fail.

Javed had done a great many terrible things on his assignments, all untroubled by conscience . . . until this one.

"Hurry up before we're spotted, priest!" the warrior shouted
from the road below.

"There's dust rising to the north, Deng. I need to see if it's
travelers or a patrol." Javed leaned back over the edge of the cliff
to say that, and once satisfied that the warrior believed him and
would stay on the trail with the horses, he went back out of sight
to continue digging the sand out from beneath a rock.

There was no dust in the distance. Javed could have led the
Sons across the entire desert without being seen once if he'd
felt like it. However, he had needed a momentary distraction to
dig atop this hill without his companion noticing. Once Javed's
fingers found the clay pot, he pulled it free of its hiding place.
A scorpion crawled from beneath the boulder and scurried away.
Thankfully it didn't sting his hand. That had been an act of
respect, one venomous creature to another.

Javed removed the lid from the pot and found it empty, not
surprising considering how sparse the population was in this
region. There wasn't much for the Inquisition's informants to
inform on.

"Is it the army or not?" Deng Somsak demanded from below.

The two of them had been sent ahead of the Sons to scout
the path. The Somsak was an experienced raider, but this was
unfamiliar country to him, while Javed knew this land like the
back of his hand. It had been easy to steer Deng this way, and
then, of course, someone had to hold the horses while the other
climbed up the high ground to have a look around.

"One moment, friend."

He took from his pocket the note he'd hastily written in an
Inquisition cipher, and then paused. When the local Inquisitors

saw that some of the colorful banners along the trade route had been rearranged, they would know to check this drop location for a message. When they saw his priority marking, word would be sent via demon bone direct to the Grand Inquisitor's attention. If Omand willed it, the local garrisons would be mobilized, the aqueduct would be protected, and the Sons destroyed. Instantaneous magical communication was a powerful, albeit expensive, tool, and the Inquisition made better use of it than anyone.

Javed had brought enough demon with him to work such magic himself, but his instincts had warned him against using it. Something about Thera's demeanor recently had indicated that she was more suspicious than usual, and it had been ever since he had been forced to take the lives of those two boys. His instincts were seldom wrong, so he had hidden his demon bones in one of the gunner's packs, buried inside a pouch of Fortress powder, where it would be unlikely to be found until they engaged in battle, as the gunners were constantly admonished never to toy with the dangerous stuff. If he found out for sure that Thera did expect there was a secret wizard among their number, Javed would find a way to present that hapless gunner to her.

Luckily for him, the Inquisition had many other methods of sending messages.

Yet Javed hesitated.

The note was simple. It gave away the Sons' target, their numbers, and the makeup of their forces. It also indicated Javed could not be reached via demon at this time, and any further instructions for him would need to be given by other means. It concluded with an account of Thera's manifestation of the Voice, that she was not a fraud as suspected, and that there was some manner of unknown witchcraft working within her.

That last part was what had been troubling him the most.

He was a witch hunter. He'd seen every kind of vile, debased, and aberrant magic in Lok. The Voice had been something new and different. It was as Keta had said, an entity that spoke directly to his mind. At first he had dismissed the Keeper's tales as the mad babbling of a fanatic, but there was something to this Voice, and it had bedeviled him ever since he'd witnessed the thing. Tearing at the corners of his mind and keeping him awake at nights. Never before had he experienced bad dreams about anyone he had killed, and now he was plagued with them.

A priest in name only, he scoffed at such superstitious foolishness. Fanatics and their silly religion amused him. Except this... this was different. Thera had cured his uncurable poison. The faithful called that a miracle, though Javed had dismissed it as a trick, but after hearing the supposed Voice of the old gods, he was no longer so sure.

The rebellion it had inspired was not at all what he'd expected either. Keta may have been a madman, yet he was a good man. The Keeper truly cared for his people, especially the weak and useless ones, in a way that Javed could never understand, but had been forced to copy. Managing such a great undertaking as keeping the disparate people of the Cove united and flourishing had been beyond Keta's abilities, so as a chameleon does, Javed had become what was required, and begun managing the flocks and fields, and teaching the rebels how to thrive. He'd hated it at first, until he'd found that being a priest was just as challenging as being a witch hunter, albeit in entirely different ways.

Vultures circled above the desert, similar to those that feasted upon traitors atop the dome. Or perhaps they were even the same birds? No... for Omand kept those in the Capitol far too well fed for them to stray this far looking for meat. Regardless, the vultures' circling shadows were a reminder that there was a fine line between pretending to be a traitor and becoming one.

Javed had torn many things down, but he had never actually helped build anything before. The only thing he'd ever created were fake identities for himself, and chaos. For the last year he had helped an entire people forge a new identity for themselves. He had poisoned them, then helped tend their sick. He had comforted the families of children he had murdered. Usually by the end of a long assignment, he was eager for his targets to die, so that he could move on to his next challenge, his next stepping-stone. Yet he didn't hate these. In fact, he had come to respect this peculiar people, and he lacked the animosity that usually fueled him.

And this coded note would be all that it took to destroy them once and for all. The future he'd helped make would be dashed to pieces.

"Oceans, Javed, are you taking a nap up there? Someone's gonna come riding down this canyon and then I don't want to hear any priestly crying about me having to murder all the witnesses!"

Deng was joking, as he had learned that, despite their fearsome countenances, even the Somsak didn't enjoy being vicious to those who didn't deserve it. However, Deng had no clue that Javed had done exactly that, murdering witnesses, savagely ending the lives of some of the most innocent among them, all to protect a mission that he was now questioning.

"They're on camels," Javed smoothly lied about the nonexistent threat. "The warriors of Dev ride horses here, so they're probably just regular travelers. I'm on my way down."

"About damned time," the impatient warrior said. "Let's get out of here."

Alas, if the Voice was real, then Javed had already made himself its enemy by spilling the blood of its believers. The memory of the last two haunted him, more than all who had come before...but what was done was done. Javed put the note in the pot, put the lid back on, and buried it beneath the boulder for his Inquisition brothers to retrieve.

As they rode through the desert back toward the Sons of the Black Sword, Javed wondered if he had done the right thing. He was unused to having such thoughts.

# Chapter 34

～～～～

Omand watched out his carriage window as a judge's mansion was consumed by fire. The flames cast a flickering red light across the Capitol. There was a fearsome beauty to it. Such calamitous events were rare in this glorious city.

"It appears the fire crews are here to fight the blaze," Taraba said. "They cannot approach until our men let them through."

The two of them were the only passengers inside the luxurious carriage. "Eh . . . Let it burn for a while longer."

An Inquisitor ran to the side of the carriage to deliver his report. "Judge Bhaguri Vadal resisted arrest and was killed. A candelabra was knocked over and started the blaze, then he barricaded himself in his quarters and refused to come out. Apologies, Grand Inquisitor, he gave us no choice."

The golden mask of the Grand Inquisitor turned down toward his underling. "Unfortunate, but understandable. Vadal folk are obstinate and hard headed. Sadly, he was Harta Vadal's cousin and would have made a valuable hostage. And his family?"

"His wife and daughters were captured unharmed, sir. As well as a phontho obligated to serve as their senior military advisor."

Omand just shook his head. What was the world coming to that a warrior would let himself be captured while a judge would fight to the death? "Take them all to the Tower of Silence."

"To the roof?" the Inquisitor asked hesitantly.

"To the dungeon. We will see how much Harta cares about the rest of his relatives. And if he does not? *Then* they go atop the dome... You are dismissed."

That Inquisitor ran back toward the burning mansion, as another approached holding a messenger packet. Omand extended his hand through the carriage window and took the envelope.

"Taraba, have the driver take us to the next arrest."

As his right hand gave the orders, Omand opened the letter that had just been presented to him. Remarkably, the wood that had been imported all the way from Vadal to decorate the façade of Bhaguri's mansion burned so brightly that for a moment Omand didn't even require a candle to read.

The message room at the Tower of Silence had been very busy tonight. Not surprising, since he had just ordered the arrests of individuals across every great house and every caste. The sweep was intended as a systematic removal of the most troublesome elements.

There were, of course, a great many messages that had arrived via demon, documenting the relentless slaughter of the casteless, documenting that they were now extinct in many parts of continent. Omand skipped over those. His spy among the Akershan reported that the rebellion's hideout had been discovered and was under siege... *Oh well*. Omand had managed to conceal that location for far longer than he had expected. It appeared their usefulness was at an end.

And most importantly, Witch Hunter Javed had left them a dire warning of impending sabotage. *The audacity of these particular rebels was remarkable!*

The carriage began to roll, and Omand pondered how to proceed.

Devedas had departed for the north to contain the demon attack in Vadal, and as an emergency measure he had taken most of the warriors obligated to the protect the Capitol with him. After all, who could wait for reinforcements while mysterious beams of fire were shooting from the sky? Once that mighty force had gone, and many important men had been deprived of most of their bodyguards, Omand had turned his attention to purging the Capitol of any who might still stand in his way.

Normally, clumsy accusations of insurrection would be insufficient to arrest this many men of status, but that was the benefit of a crisis. In their fervor the judges had given Devedas a shocking amount of authority, and then he had delegated the safety of the Capitol to Omand while he was away. The handful who protested Omand's stern actions were quickly jailed, using the very powers that they had voted to give away.

The end of the Age of Law was upon them, and most didn't even realize it yet. Omand was having a splendid time.

"Interesting news from the southern desert, Taraba."

"Oh?" His assistant had sat back down across from him as the carriage swayed. "What is it?"

"Javed says the so-called prophet and her Sons of the Black Sword are on their way to destroy the aqueduct. They intend to drown the desert to make us suffer."

"A bold attack." The young man sounded impressed. "How old is this news?"

"According to Javed, they left the Thao mountains three days ago and are avoiding the trade roads to keep from being spotted."

"Then we still have plenty of time to mobilize the warriors in Akara. Or the alternative..." Taraba must have realized the Grand Inquisitor wouldn't have brought up the topic if he'd already made up his mind what to do about it. "You could continue to let these rebels be instruments of terror, as they were when Black-Hearted Ashok was still among the living."

Omand smiled behind his golden mask, because he had been very proud of that particular plan. The specter of Ashok and his vengeful black steel blade had unnerved the Capitol far more than he'd ever hoped for. When he had first set that broken creature loose upon the world, Omand had never realized just how far Ashok would go. Without a villain, their story never would have had a hero to turn into a king. Without Ashok's unwitting assistance, Omand might not have ever achieved his goals.

"I could let them continue to run wild... However"—Omand gestured out the window to where fiery shadows were still flickering off the vast stone edifices of the Capitol—"why should I allow them to harm a city I now own? If there is terror to be inflicted here, *I* should be the one to do it. Also, there is word from Akershan that their warriors have finally found the rebels' crater in the mountains. The Sons of the Black Sword will have no home or families to return to even if they were successful in harming our aqueduct. Let us spare them such sorrow."

"If I may be so bold as to make a suggestion..."

Omand was curious, mostly because he expected Taraba to be his successor someday, and he would like to make sure the Inquisition was left in clever hands. "Please do."

"Let them destroy the aqueduct first, *then* kill the troublesome rebels."

"And why would I do such a thing?"

"Our actions tonight—removing those who will be troublesome—will be seen as unnecessarily harsh by many. They will bristle against your strong hand. However, no one would ever believe mere rebel criminals are clever enough to destroy one of the Capitol's greatest works on the own, so *surely* they must have had collaborators within the first caste guiding them. Which makes this purge necessary and provides us a fine excuse to remove even more critics in the future. None will dare question you in public for fear of being seen as weak on traitors, or perhaps even traitorous themselves."

Omand mulled it over. "That is brilliant, Taraba. Keep it up and you will inherit my golden mask someday. Let the aqueduct fall, and its replacement can be the first great work our new king commissions once he is crowned."

"Of course, Grand Inquisitor," Taraba said. "Would you like for me to alert the garrisons along the aqueduct? We have enough time we could draw troops from Makao and Devakula. Both of those great houses are obligated to defend it."

"Yes. Alert both. There will be great honor to whichever house destroys such infamous rebels. Have whoever is our witch hunter in Akara oversee the operation. Take no prisoners except for their prophet. Javed confirms that she does have some unique form of magic, which may be useful to us."

Only then Omand recalled what he had learned about the fall of the House of Assassins. It had been Sikasso's attempt at capturing that odd prophetic power for himself that had resulted in his death, and Sikasso had been an extremely capable man. "Well, tell him to *try* and take her alive, but if that proves to be too much of a challenge, bring her corpse back to the Tower of Silence for dissection and study."

A short time later the carriage arrived at the scene of another planned arrest, and Omand was positively delighted to watch an Uttaran arbiter be dragged from her home, pronounced a practitioner of witchcraft without trial or evidence, and executed in the street.

# Chapter 35

~~~~~~

Thera's army was small in number, yet exceedingly deadly. One volley from Gupta's gunners had put the defending paltan into retreat. It was unlikely that these warriors of Dev had seen illegal Fortress rods in action before, and even if some of them had, they had been totally unprepared for the thunderous might of fifty-eight of the things.

It looked like only a handful of the enemy patrol had been struck—their guns were simply not that accurate against targets over two hundred yards away—but the smoke and noise, combined with the terrible wounds inflicted upon the handful who had been hit had put the fear into the rest, and the warriors had fled on foot, running toward Akara.

"Should we pursue and run them down?" Ongud had a keen mind for strategy, but he was still a cavalryman at heart. When something ran, he wanted to chase it. "Or do you want me to let them escape to warn their brothers how well armed we are, so the others hesitate long enough to let us finish our work?"

Thera looked toward the sky. It was early in the morning on what looked like it would be a clear, cold day, where sound would carry for great distances. Even if she had Ongud's horsemen chase the fleeing patrol, somebody else would hear or spot them, if they hadn't already. The border between Dev and Makao was

305

well traveled. The local garrisons would be alerted soon enough, but it would take time for them to mobilize a force sufficient to challenge the Sons of the Black Sword, and then more to get here.

"Let them go," Thera ordered. "Fear is contagious."

"Understood, Prophet."

Thera and most of her officers sat upon their horses on a bluff that had offered them a good place to watch Gupta's ambush. This position also gave her a commanding view of the terrain. The high desert to the southwest of Akara was a rugged canyonland of steep cliffs, mesas, and narrow canyons filled with yellow sand and sagebrush.

And through that unwelcoming wilderness stretched one of the most impressive structures in the world.

The mighty aqueduct that loomed just ahead of them was truly one of the most impressive things she had ever seen. It was a stark white line that stretched as far as the eye could see, gently sloping down from the mountains toward the distant unseen Capitol. It was hard to believe that this thing had been built by the hands of man. The Capitol aqueducts were often called rivers in the sky, which was a misnomer, since it was more of a great stone trough a hundred feet in the air, but that didn't make it any less awe inspiring in person. It was so big that she was having a hard time imagining how they were actually going to be able to break the damned thing.

"What do you think, Eklavya?"

The young warrior was looking through a spyglass and had been so enthralled by the great construction that he hadn't even watched the lopsided battle unfold below them.

"I've seen lesser aqueducts before, but this is ten times that size. I've read about the building of these things, but in person... Oceans. The conduit itself is an engineering marvel, wide enough an elephant could swim through it, yet angled so precisely that it's only dropping but a couple feet over every mile. Each stone in the pillars is huge and cut to such perfection it'll be tough to get a knife blade between them."

"We're not here to see the sights, Risalder. I only care if you can destroy it."

Despite his joy at seeing such a thing, there was no hesitation. "Absolutely we can. And I know right where to go." He pointed toward a spot where it crossed over a canyon. "There. That'll be the point of highest stress and if the whole section falls, the most time-consuming for the Capitol to repair."

"You're sure?"

"I am, Prophet. There're two channels inside the covered conduit, so that way they can keep one open while doing maintenance on the other. It's heavy but strong. We collapse one pillar, it might hold. We damage the two pillars that carry it over that gap, the weight will do the rest of the work for us. Both channels will go, and once it turns into a waterfall it might even damage other footings before they know to close off the flow from the mountains." Eklavya lowered the spyglass and looked her in the eye. "I've been fascinated by this sort of thing my entire life. I believe this day is why Mother Dawn told me to join the Sons of the Black Sword. I give you my word, that is the place."

He was just so damned earnest that Thera couldn't help but believe him. They might be fanatics, but they were her fanatics. And Eklavya was smart; if he hadn't been cursed by belief in illegal gods he'd probably be well on his way to a prestigious officer position. If he'd been born a worker he'd probably have ended up a banker, and of the first, a judge. So if Eklavya declared that spot to be their best target, she'd take that bet.

"How long will you need?"

"That, I don't know. I've helped bring down castle walls before, but this is an entirely different beast. We could be done by the afternoon if we're lucky, sundown if we're not, but I've got faith the Forgotten will aid us."

"I've got more faith in your wits and the strength of those stonecutters' arms than the blessings of the gods, Kharsawan. Get to work."

"Yes, Ma'am." Eklavya immediately gave her a crisp salute and rode off to gather his work crew.

The priest, Javed, watched Eklavya go, then said to her, "I should go with them. I might be of some help."

"No. Stay close to me. If our outriders see anything you'll be the best one for deciphering what it means in this land. And if we do need to fight, maybe you could do like Keta does and say a few inspiring words to the men before they go into battle. They get motivated by that sort of thing."

"Of course, Prophet." Javed seemed nervous. Which was understandable, considering they were currently a scorpion hiding in the Capitol's boot. They could sting it first, and still might get crushed.

Her officers had already begun moving their forces into the best defensive positions. Shekar had sent keen-eyed skirmishers to every vantage point. The question was not if the forces of the Law would respond, but when, and in what number.

Unfortunately, Thera got her answer less than two hours later.

The news was dire.

"It's got to be every warrior from Akara and then some. More paltan flags than I could count, both the colors of Dev, and vassal houses I don't even know," Shekar reported. "Easily the same number of foes we faced in Garo, if not more."

"We've won such a battle before," Toramana said with forced bravado. "Let them come."

"I wasn't finished," Shekar snapped. "That's closing from this side of the canyon. Another army rides this way from the west. Makao's coming for us as well."

"Saltwater." Makao had been the house that she had been married into, so Thera still held a special hatred for them. It was one thing to die, but it would be extra insulting to die at the hands of the perfumed peacocks of the Makao warrior caste. "How many from the west?"

"They're farther away so it's hard to tell, but my brothers guess it's probably a similar size force, just from how much dust they're kicking up, riding hard."

Their hurried meeting was in the canyon near where Eklavya's workers were busily trying to demolish the aqueduct. She had sent for all of her officers to hear the Somsak's bleak report. Most of them had arrived in time, and they were all sharing grim glances. The Sons were good soldiers, but against that many foes they'd be slaughtered for sure.

"How could they have gathered so many troops so quickly?" Ongud asked. "We're half a day's ride from the nearest barracks."

"They had to know we were coming," Thera said.

"How?"

She looked toward Laxmi, who was still standing by as if she was a normal servant, but the quiet wizard girl just shook her head. If the defenders had been warned it hadn't been by magical means.

"It doesn't matter now. If they knew there was an attack planned against the aqueduct, but not exactly where, they'd stage in the area and just wait for us to show ourselves. Where's Eklavya and Gupta?"

"I'm here." The young risalder ran toward their circle. Eklavya had taken off his armor to join in the labor with his men and was soaked in sweat and covered in dust. "Gupta was still swinging a pick last I saw."

"How goes the demolition?"

"There's so much weight bearing down on the stones, they're hard to split. Both pillars are damaged, but we need more time to bring them down. A couple more hours at least."

Shekar shook his head. "We'll be encircled with no chance for escape by then. If we run now, we might be able to make it."

"Could we hold them long enough?"

"With the gods all things are possible," Toramana said.

"We're sadly lacking in gods right now," Thera responded. "Counting on nothing but ourselves, could we hold off that many troops long enough to bring this thing down?"

"Against that many, in this maze of unfamiliar canyons? We will lose," Ongud answered.

"You lack faith!" Toramana roared.

"I take no offense at your words, Chief. If the prophet says to fight to the death, I will fight and die a happy man," their cavalryman responded. "But unless the gods see fit to come down and fight alongside us, this canyon will be our grave."

Toramana was cunning and fierce, but Ashok had told her that Ongud had the best mind for strategy among the Sons, and she had looked to him for ideas once Jagdish was gone. She had no doubt his take was the accurate one.

"How much time before we are cut off?" she asked Shekar.

He spread his hands apologetically. "Assuming there's not another flanking force out there we've not seen yet, you must decide now, or that decision will be made for us."

"We should go," Javed urged. "Scatter into the hills. Hide. Return to the Cove. Live to fight another day."

"The priest is right," Murugan said. "The Voice must live. Without you, there is no rebellion."

All eyes were upon her.

Surely the gods wouldn't have sent their own army to its

doom? Or was she just a fool who had made the wrong call? If they fled, the Capitol would feel no pain, and would continue its mad slaughter of the casteless until they were extinct. A fury built inside her. Rage at the helplessness, at the constant fear, at the impotent gods, and most of all against the terrible Law that had stolen so much from her.

This was the best chance she'd ever have to hurt it, to make the first get a tiny taste of what they had forced upon her.

"We stand and fight."

"No, wait!" Eklavya begged. "There's another way. Give me a bit more time and as much of the Fortress powder as you can spare, then go. With the stress we've already caused, if we pack it into the right places, it should do."

"How would you set it off?" Ongud asked.

"There are ways," Eklavya assured them, but Thera could tell he was lying. Having been a smuggler she knew far more about the dangerous material than the others. Eklavya intended to sacrifice himself, but Thera said nothing yet.

Ongud considered the ramifications, before saying, "The Sons can hold off the Dev advance while you do this, and then retreat before Makao arrives, but we must reposition our forces now."

No amount of righteous anger could keep things from spiraling out of control, and Thera once again felt that awful sensation of being overwhelmed, like when she'd been thrown into the sea. All eyes were upon her.

"Do it."

Her risalders sprang into action, running back toward their paltans and shouting orders.

Murugan began walking toward where their horses were tied. "You should be ready to—" Then her bodyguard realized that she was following Eklavya toward the pillars, and Murugan was forced to go after her. "What are you doing?"

"Helping. Laxmi, come with me." She waited long enough to make sure the wizard girl followed, as did the priest, who seemed confused but had nowhere else to go.

The cutters were working feverishly, breaking the gigantic stones at the base of the pillars by driving a line of steel spikes into them with hammers. Each time they struck a spike, it would go a little deeper, cracking the stone a bit wider. They were working in teams, taking turns so that there was no delay between impacts. It seemed to Thera nothing was happening at all, until with one more hit, the crack suddenly spread, splitting a stone in two hard enough to cause dried mortar to burst out around the seams.

Once he was beneath the shadow of the aqueduct, Eklavya began shouting orders. "Here! This one. Concentrate on this one. Now! Hurry!" The team of stonecutters immediately complied and did as they were told, setting their spikes and striking them into a central stone. "Gupta, get over here!"

The other risalder came running, totally covered in mortar dust. "Why are my gunners heading this way?"

"New orders. Gather their powder. Keep enough for a few volleys. We'll stuff the rest in the hole the cutters are making now. We're nearly out of time." The young man didn't realize his prophet was right behind him until he caught sight of Thera out of the corner of his eye, and spun about, surprised. "You can't be here."

"I've used Fortress powder more than any of you. I used to smuggle it, remember?"

Poor Eklavya was desperate. "It's too dangerous."

"Especially if you do it wrong. Listen, it needs to be contained tight. If it's loose, it'll blow outward and be wasted. You'll just get a big stinky cloud." She'd used that trick to escape the Law a few times over the years. "For the most boom, get it covered tight."

"Like it's contained inside the barrel of a gun to direct the force," Gupta said. "We know, Prophet."

Of course they had figured it out. They weren't fools, and they'd been thinking hard on this for a while, but offering needless advice hadn't been why she'd come down here. "I know what you're going to do, Eklavya, only you're not indestructible Ashok, and this isn't the House of Assassins. There's no coming back from being buried beneath this." She waved her hand at the wonder towering above them.

"I'll pour a trail out on the ground, light it, then get away before it explodes."

"The hell you will, Kharsawan. We both know that's not certain enough for you. You won't waste that much powder on the ground, nor risk it not going off. You intend to stay and stick a match in that hole yourself."

He was caught, but his lie had been to comfort her, not him.

The decision was made, and Eklavya was committed to his glorious warrior's end. "If we're to complete the mission, it must be done, so I'll do it. I'll not order another man to die in my stead."

The workers were busy striking the rock, moving between the embedded spikes with perfect rhythm. Gupta, seemingly unsurprised that his friend was willing to blow himself to bits, went about gathering most of his men's powder satchels and horns. If it was a warrior's path to seek the sort of death that they'd write songs about, then it was a worker's to make sure the job got done.

"No one has to die if we have a wizard who can make fire appear out of thin air from some distance away."

"Where—"

Thera grabbed Laxmi by the arm and pulled her forward. "Here you go."

"Your cook?"

"And wizard in training before the assassins made her into a mindless slave. That's broken now. She told me Omkar taught her three patterns. The fire pattern is one of them."

The poor girl looked as overwhelmed as Thera felt, yet she spoke with courage. "It has been a long time, but I can do this."

"From far enough away to not be blasted or crushed?" Eklavya asked, incredulous, and clearly unwilling to sacrifice some poor girl in his stead.

Laxmi gave him a resolute nod as she took one of the several bones Thera had given her from where it had been hidden in her coat. "With enough demon, yes."

"Thank the gods!" Eklavya broke into a grin. "I truly didn't want to die today, but I didn't see much choice."

Her father had once told her that you could tell the true measure of a warrior by what they were willing to die for. If that was true, the Sons were paragons of their caste. Andaman Vane would have been proud of her army, and hopefully proud of her as a leader. "Laxmi is under your command, then."

"Yes, Prophet!" the wizard and the warrior said simultaneously.

Murugan was looking at the growing pile of Fortress powder containers with increasing horror. When separate, it was not so fearsome. Together, it became powerful. The black powder was sort of like rebellion that way. "You need to be away from this," he insisted. "Now."

From her bodyguard's tone, she had no doubt that if she

stayed there any longer he'd pick her up and carry her off, status be damned. The boy had an obligation to fill and she certainly wasn't making it easy for him. "Agreed, Thao. Let's go back up the ridge so I can at least watch the battle."

Murugan clearly wanted to tell her that wasn't wise but talking her out of it would be impossible. He was lucky she didn't want to be at the front line, damaged hands and all. She was surprised when the priest didn't immediately go with them. Agitated, Javed was watching the line of gunners drop off their satchels. He reached for one that had just been put down, as if wanting to help.

"Come on, Javed. There's nothing you can do here."

Reluctantly, the priest followed.

High atop the ridge, Thera, her bodyguard, and her priest watched as the Sons easily held off the lead paltans of Dev. It was only small groups of riders for now, testing their defenses. Her risalders were keeping the Sons of the Black Sword clustered around the canyon entrance, while Ongud's cavalry was guarding their flank and making sure their escape route remained clear.

"Sparing that patrol earlier was the wise choice," Murugan said. "See how the enemy phontho holds back his infantry? I bet he was told about how many Fortress rods we have and he doesn't want to send his men in to get threshed like wheat."

"Maybe . . ." Only Thera was unconvinced by that. Infantry could only march so far in a day, and a goodly portion of the force arrayed against them was on foot. Which meant this army had already been camped nearby. With the armies of two houses headed their way, it was clear they'd been warned in advance, and if the great houses had known they were coming here, surely they would have known about their illegal weapons as well.

A chill wind had come from the south. It made the multitude of enemy flags dance. Thera's hood was down, and it caused her long hair to whip about in the wind. That was the closest thing the Sons had to a banner. A few hundred yards below the ridge, her men looked up toward her, and though she would be nothing but a darkened silhouette against the sky from there, they would still be comforted that the Voice of the gods was watching over them.

"Or the Dev phontho heard about what we did to the Akershani in Garo, and he's afraid of us," Murugan said. "As he should be. It's right across the river from their lands. He's probably scared."

"I admire your confidence, warrior, but don't let it outrun your sense," Javed warned. "They'll come for us. No phontho will be willing to bear the shame of letting one of the Capitol's great works be destroyed under their watch. That's the sort of shame that gets even those of status exiled or executed."

"With Makao drawing near, our forces are split. We're badly outnumbered on both sides, yet still they hesitate." Thera wished that she had the wisdom of an experienced tactician, like her father, or someone gifted for such things, like Jagdish. The best strategist she had currently was occupied riding around the cold desert, and as usual the god in her head was no help at all. "They can't know how fast we intend to destroy the aqueduct, but they have to know the longer they wait, the more damage we inflict against it. Yet they've only sent harassers while their main body does nothing."

"Hopefully it won't matter. The instant that bomb goes off, we're moving out." Murugan emphatically gestured toward where their horses were tied to a stunted desert tree nearby. "No debate, Prophet. We should already be leaving. Your risalders know to retreat as soon as they hear the explosion or see the smoke. After that, getting you back to the Cove safe becomes our only priority, and that'll still take a miracle because they're sure to hound us the whole way home."

"You're a faithful bodyguard, Murugan Thao," Javed said. "That is a difficult obligation to fill when your charge worries about others more than herself and feels no fear."

Thera laughed. "I'm not Ashok. I'm terrified right now. I'm just good at hiding it."

There was a noise behind them, and Murugan spun about, hand flying to his sword. Except it was just the wind blowing through the sage. Their horses were stomping nervously, tugging at the branches they were tied to. They'd sensed something. Probably the smell of blood from the clashing skirmishers.

"You feel responsible for every one of them, don't you?" Javed asked, so quietly that it was difficult to hear him over the wind. "Every man who fights for you, you're as loyal to them as they are to you."

"Of course I am." She gave him a curious look, but Javed kept his mood inscrutable. "Only I'm also responsible for every casteless the Capitol would murder if we stood aside and did nothing. We might lose today, we might all die today, we might spend the rest of our lives running, but it'll be because we tried to do the right thing, and that has to be worth it."

"You are not at all what I expected, Thera Vane."

That just made Thera shake her head. She'd never wanted any of this. The bolt from the heavens had sent her on a path of woe and the Voice was a curse. It had taken everyone she'd loved and left her nothing but the barest survival. Now, after years of only worrying about herself, somehow, here she was, trying to save an entire people.

"Oceans, priest, I'm not what I expected either!" She turned her nervous attention back to the enemy army, and muttered, "What are they waiting for?"

After a long moment, Javed said, "A decapitation strike."

"What?"

"They'll infiltrate, seize the commander, secure any objectives, and then give a sign for the obligated warriors to begin their assault during the confusion. It is a standard witch hunter tactic."

"How do you know that?" Except there was movement to her side, barely caught in the corner of her eye, and by the time she turned, she was face-to-face with a tiger.

Its fur was already covered in blood.

"Assassins!" Murugan drew his sword and flung himself at the beast in front of Thera, but another tiger had slunk up from behind, and it leapt upon his back, carrying him face-first into the ground. Its jaws clamped around Murugan's shoulder and teeth bit deep into meat.

Thera reacted without thought, tugging the small throwing blade that was strapped to her wrist free, and hurling it at the cat atop Murugan. Despite her crippled hands, despite hours of failure in practice since she'd been burned, the instincts of Vane were still in her and the little blade hit true, slicing into the tiger's cheek. It reared back, and Murugan rolled over, swinging his Thao broadsword.

That tiger let out a terrible scream—almost a woman's scream— as the blade was planted deep into its neck.

Except the first beast crashed into her, a paw upon each shoulder, and Thera was driven against the ground so hard with the weight of the cat atop her that the air burst from her lungs.

For a moment she was helpless. The beast's claws could have sliced her wide open, but didn't. *They were trying to take her alive.* One of her arms was pinned, but with the other she went for a knife on her belt. A swiping paw effortlessly caught her, and a single claw extended, piercing deep into the muscle of her forearm.

Thera cried out, but then she went to thrashing and kicking, trying to free herself. Another paw landed on her, crushing her cheek hard into the sand, as if it meant to suffocate her, but she bit one toe as hard as she could. The tiger looked down at her and snarled.

Murugan slammed into the distracted tiger's side, driving his sword straight through its belly. "Die, beast!" With shoulder flayed wide, and blood droplets flying in every direction, Murugan somehow shoved the tiger off her. "Run, Thera! *Run!*"

As soon as the weight was gone from her chest, Thera sprang up. The chunk of fur in her mouth turned back into human skin and she spit it out, still tasting demon magic and blood.

Yet a third tiger came seemingly out of nowhere and hit her from behind, and this one swiped her with its claws. Pain like fire rushed down her back as she was hurled violently into the brush. Before she could even understand what was going on, teeth locked around her boot heel, and she was being dragged away on her face. Desperate, she grabbed for anything she could, but branches broke off in her hands, and her fingernails tore off against rocks.

Despite the blood gushing down his armor, Murugan got up again and bellowed, "Let her go and fight me, wizards!"

The one dragging Thera released its jaws from her boot—and left her there gasping—to go after Murugan. The two wounded tigers were back up and circling, still alive despite the terrible wounds Murugan had given them only because of the incredibly powerful magic upon them.

In the swamps of Bahdjangal, Murugan Thao had been overcome by fear and run from a demon, abandoning his brothers. That had been a shame he had worn ever since. But on this day, he stood defiant between three magic tigers and his prophet, brave as any mortal warrior there had ever been.

The one with the neck injury leapt first. Murugan sidestepped and slashed, but the tiger he'd run through was right behind the first, and it bit him on the sword arm, mercilessly tearing it to the bone. Except Murugan had no quit in him, and rather than let the witch hunter take him down, he dragged the thrashing monster to the edge of the cliff even as it savaged him, and wrapped his remaining arm around its head.

The bodyguard looked right at Thera, as if to say he'd done his best, and then he took them both over the edge.

"Murugan!"

Her bodyguard was gone. There was nothing to do but run. Her back and arm were in agony as she got back up and tried to get away.

This time it was human hands that grabbed her. She drew another knife, but her strike was easily blocked, and then her wrist was trapped in a crushing grip. Another hand grabbed her by the collar and swung her around so that she could see her attacker.

"Javed?"

"I'm sorry that I'm not what you expected either."

Enraged, she tried to hit him, kick him, but it was no use. The traitorous priest was too strong, and far more martially skilled than any of them had expected. He struck her once, a hammer blow to the side of the head, and Thera went down, stunned.

As the desert spun around her, the remaining two tigers turned into a man and a woman, who had one hand pressed hard against her bleeding neck.

"The rebels are about to destroy the aqueduct." Javed flipped Thera over and expertly bound her hands behind her back with a length of cord.

"We know. Orders are to let them," the man said.

"Way to help out, Javed," the woman said through a pained grimace.

"I had to hide my magic." As soon as Javed said that, the man threw a chunk of demon toward him, which Javed caught and stashed in a pocket. Then Javed dragged Thera to her feet by her bloody arm. "They've got a sensitive among them."

"Yeah, as soon as we got close a wizard girl sensed us and sent a runner to warn this one. We killed him on the way in. Let's go."

Over the ringing in her ears, Thera could hear the roar of charging armies. This was what the enemy had been waiting for. The battle was joined. Nobody was coming to save her now.

"You're a traitor, Javed."

"Can't betray something I never believed in."

"You believed. I saw it."

Javed just kept dragging her away. "Shut your mouth."

"You saw the Forgotten. You know it's real."

"Their wizard's making the fire pattern in the canyon," the male witch hunter warned.

Javed spun Thera around, so the aqueduct was in view in the distance. "Might as well let you see the fruits of your effort, though if Omand is letting this happen, it must benefit him somehow."

"You're a liar."

"And you are a flea riding on the back of a monster beyond your comprehension. All your work was for naught."

She spit in his face.

Javed wiped it away, and for just a moment, she thought she saw regret there, but then it was gone.

Laxmi's magic worked true. The packed Fortress powder went off with a *boom* that echoed through the canyons. The mighty structure shuddered. Water splashed from the top.

Yet it stood.

Had Eklavya and Gupta been wrong?

Except then the aqueduct began to crumble, as cracks spread across the upper stones of first one pillar, and then the other. They began coming apart, slowly at first, but then rapidly in a cascade of increasing destruction. Water sprayed from the seams. The upper conduit buckled and the entire span across the canyon collapsed. Tons of stone crashed down and shook the entire desert. A great cloud of dust rose but slicing through the middle of it was a river of water, falling, to be wasted upon the sand.

# Chapter 36

~~~~~~~~~~

After weeks walking beneath the ocean, Ashok enjoyed the feeling of sun and wind upon his face once again.

He was never given to displays of emotion, but for the first time he understood why warriors often made a big show of kissing the ground of their homeland after returning from a long campaign. This was Lok beneath his feet. Fortress was long behind him. As much as this land had done him wrong, it was his country, and the home to the only thing left in the world that he loved.

The underworld's exit was well hidden in the plains northwest of MaDharvo. Moyo hadn't known the place names, but from the collector's secondhand description of the area, Ashok had assumed as much. To the west was Garo, and it was tempting to go there first to teach them a lesson for betraying him to Devedas, but he only considered that for a moment, for in the distance to the north he could make out the hazy outlines of the Akershani mountain range where the Cove was hidden.

"I have returned," he told the empty countryside, and then began his long walk across the plains.

Ashok ran whenever there was sufficient light. He drank from streams and the occasional puddle, as his Protector gifts would prevent him from becoming ill. There was no time to forage, but every day he found the opportunity to kill something. If there was fuel available, he'd cook it. If there wasn't, he simply ate the meat raw.

He possessed almost nothing beyond the ragged clothes upon his back. Even his stolen sword had been too badly damaged in the fight against the Dvarapala to be of much use, so he'd left it behind. The lantern, rope, pick, and remaining oil from his journey had been left at the last cache in the down below, as future collectors would certainly put those tools to good use. The less he carried, the faster he could move, and the less time it would take time to get back to Thera. All he had was a collector's folding knife, Moyo's fire starter, and a great deal of guilt for being away from his obligation for so very long.

The plains were too deserted. It was if all the people were hunkered down, hiding before a storm. There were no patrols to avoid. He spied a number of casteless villages along the way, but each of those had been deserted or burned. Their state left a taste in his mouth worse than the rancid water he'd been surviving on. He passed towns but didn't bother to stop. Stealing some horses might have sped up his journey—it would certainly have made it an easier one—except he no longer had the authority to take whatever he needed, had nothing to trade, and was too proud to steal. He may be the most feared criminal in the world, but he was no thief.

It was growing cold, but his body was entirely healed from his ordeal in the sea and dungeon, so he felt strong. Enough of his hair and beard had grown back he no longer looked like a shorn monk, and the strange Fortress clothing he still wore was so dirty and damaged from his journey through the underworld that if a patrol did see him, they'd probably assume he was wearing casteless rags and react accordingly, which meant Ashok would have to murder them all, so it was best to remain unseen.

Each morning, the mountains were a bit closer.

After many days he came across a single lonely tree, and, oddly enough, standing beneath it was a horse.

The gelding wore an Akershani saddle. It was there, contentedly munching the yellow grass, as its rider sat in the shade, back against the narrow trunk. Ashok approached cautiously, but this didn't feel like a trap. As he got closer, he saw that the fallen rider had been terribly beaten, and every visible bit of skin was covered in cuts and bruises. His hands had been smashed into gnarled, malformed claws.

Remarkably, the man was still alive, and his bleary eyes opened a crack when he heard Ashok's footsteps.

"I started going home, trying to forget what I'd done," he managed to croak through a bloody mouth of broken teeth. "How could I? Their deaths are on my head."

The wounded man turned his palms up, revealing that he had somehow managed to cut his own wrists. Then Ashok saw that a jagged, broken deer femur was still lying at his side, bloody. That must have been quite the feat of determination to saw through his veins since his fingers looked as if they'd been methodically beaten with hammers.

"Why have you killed yourself?" Ashok asked.

"No choice. They made me talk." He wheezed, then stared through Ashok, as if unsure if this was real, or the phantom of an expiring mind. "I see Ashok Vadal."

"I am here."

"The Forgotten's warrior lives."

Ashok knelt next to the dying fool. "What happened?"

"The Cove...Bharatas is attacking the Cove." The man let out a long wheeze. "He carries an ancestor blade."

Ashok was incapable of feeling fear, but a cold dread came upon him, for he knew all too well what a bearer of a black steel blade could do against rebels, because he had done it himself, a great many times. "What of Thera? Is she there?" Except there was no response. Ashok took hold of the man's shoulders and shook him, but his head rolled forward, lifeless.

He rose and had to take a deep breath to steady himself. The plains were too vast. The odds of him coming upon this man just as he took his last breaths were no coincidence. Keta's spiteful gods had wanted him to hear those words, either to taunt him for not being there to protect their Voice, or to warn him to hurry.

# Chapter 37

~~~~~~~~~~~~~

Keta had never felt such desperation before.

Each day the reservoir had been a bit lower as the invaders dug more trenches to the lake, draining their precious defense to flood the valley below. Keta had prayed for rain to refill their reserve, but none had come.

The giant gate that the ancients had constructed took hours to open and close, otherwise they could have simply let the invaders walk up a dry tunnel, and then suddenly opened it and washed them all away. So instead Keta had ordered the building of a second dam, right at the entrance, with the hopes of luring the warriors in, and then bursting it. That had worked, but not as well as he had hoped, as whoever was leading the force below had been clever enough to only send a token force to test them. All their hard labor had drowned maybe ten poor fools at best and wasted a great deal of their remaining water.

As the reservoir ran dry, Keta had tasked every able-bodied man in the Cove to collecting and piling stones in front of the tunnel. By that point, he would have collapsed the entire thing if he could, but the ancients who built the Cove had made their tunnel from a form of cement that was far too durable. If they had used all the Fortress powder left in the Cove, it would have only broken a small bit of it.

323

The warriors below had been relentless, methodical. As the faithful piled up rocks, the warriors tore them down. They must have brought in workers or slaves from somewhere else because they were able to form a chain of bodies, from top to bottom, and stones were thrown out the bottom as quickly as Keta's people added more.

There was an oil seep in the very bottom of the crater, so Keta directed men to bring up as much of the stuff as they could. They would pour it through the cracks until they were sure it was soaking the feet of the invaders on the other side, and then light it on fire.

That caused them to retreat, but once the smoke cleared, they came again.

Day after day they did this, until their oil was as depleted as their water. It took time for the seep to refill, which was sufficient for the Cove's regular use, but not for this.

From the lookouts, it seemed that more warriors kept arriving as the siege went on, until it was as if the entire warrior caste of Akershan was assembled below, waiting to kill them.

The great house must have dispatched its wizards as well, as great black birds, far too large to be natural, began to circle far above the Cove, constantly watching.

Keta had wizards, and a fortune in demon hide, but their brains were still recovering from the spell that had only recently been broken. Laxmi had been the most coherent of them, but she'd gone with Thera. Whether they'd be of use or not, he told the freed slaves of the Cove's situation, gave them all the demon they could carry, and asked that when the Akershani attacked, to do the best they could with it. To their credit, each of them had vowed to fight on behalf of the rebellion that had saved them from the House of Assassins and provided them with a home.

At night Keta slept next to the empty reservoir, with a meat cleaver next to his head, so he could be there to lead his people when the inevitable breakthrough happened. It was hard to sleep through the continual banging of picks and shovels on the other side. By day he directed their defenses, and he prayed constantly, begging the gods to send them a miracle. The rest of the time he wondered how he had failed the gods, that they would forsake their chosen people so.

He saw no way out. The Sons of the Black Sword were fearsome, but even if they returned now, they were too few to defeat such a mighty army. He had very few trained fighters. He had a handful of old Fortress rods; the Sons had taken all the fine ones procured by Ratul with them. There was no other escape. He couldn't even name another Keeper and pass the sacred Book of Names on, so he had hidden the sacred tome in a hole, wondering as he buried it if a thousand years of secret history would die with him.

The one resource Keta had was laborers, so they cut down trees and piled up logs. Once every loose stone had been found, they broke more with hammers. They carried buckets of dirt from the farming terraces and dumped them atop the barrier.

Then one day a wizard set thirty of his laborers on fire.

The fire had come right through their shoddy wall, searing flesh and burning hair. The faithful caught on the edge of that conflagration had run screaming, clothing ablaze.

The aftermath was horrifying.

Keta cursed himself for not predicting such an attack. He'd known they had wizards. He should have expected such trickery. Worse than the injuries and deaths was that it slowed the work. Once the faithful were afraid to approach their makeshift wall, they began losing ground, and the barrier between them and warriors weakened.

The freed slaves tried to explain what wizards could and could not do. Such a fiery trick required a great deal of demon, and the farther it was sent, the more it needed. So Keta had ordered the faithful back. They still had the narrow spillway channel where the tunnel ended. Here, out of range of the magical fire, they would stand. They could hold the lakebed above it, firing their Fortress rods, throwing spears, launching arrows, and hurling stones down at any warriors who came through the chokepoint. They would put up more defenses, sharpened stakes, and stone walls.

Except they'd not had time to accomplish all of that, for the Akershani had grown tired of this siege and decided to finish it, once and for all.

That night, Keta had been trying to comfort some of the loved ones of those who had been burned earlier, when the screaming had started. His head snapped up reflexively, and without thought, he ran back toward the tunnel.

A Fortress rod discharged with a crack of thunder. Voices cried out in terror and agony. Keta recognized the sound of men dying.

There was chaos at the spillway. At first he thought that the last of their wall had crumbled, but then he saw it was still standing, though the rocks were shaking from the renewed onslaught against the other side.

Somehow, there was a single Akershani warrior standing there as if he'd materialized from thin air, and already splayed out around his feet were many of the faithful men of the Cove, their limbs severed and arteries spraying.

*How?*

And then Keta saw the great black birds blocking the stars as they passed by overhead. Wizards had dropped this killer into their midst.

Except it was only one man.

"Attack!" Keta roared as he pulled the meat cleaver from his belt.

The Akershani was dressed in armor and furs, with a horse's mane flowing from the back of his helm. He heard Keta's command, then lifted his sword in a mock salute, only it was no sword at all. It was destruction given form. It ate the torchlight. It was blacker than the night. Blacker than the endless nothing the Law declared was all that lay beyond death.

All the faithful guarding the causeway rushed him. The warrior was there, then he was gone, moving between their bodies and leaving them in pieces. An axe was thrown, but with a flick of his wrist the handle ruptured into splinters and the head went spinning away. Arrows were launched, but it was if he knew they were coming and simply moved out of the way. Another bullet struck the ground where he'd been standing—

And then the real slaughter began.

The rebels fought hard, but that was because they didn't realize the terror that they were facing. Keta did. He grabbed the nearest man by the shirt and dragged him close to shout in his ear. "Run back to the Cove! Tell them I said to hide! All the women and children, go into the deepest corners, the bottom of the crater, among the terraces. They must run and hide and not make a sound and pray the warriors pass them by. Go! *Go!*" Keta shoved him away, waited to confirm that he would deliver the message, and then turned back to witness the murder of his beloved faithful.

The killer acted with inhuman swiftness, intercepting every attack with ease, even the ones that came from directions he couldn't possibly see, and each time that black sword moved, another man received a horrifying wound. The black steel went through flesh as if there was no more resistance than air. When it pierced bodies, it didn't just cut them, it tore them asunder. It shattered their spears. It broke their clumsy wooden shields. Only steel seemed to slow the thing. Bones exploded into splinters.

Four more men died before Keta could blink, and by the time he opened his eyes it was six.

For a moment, he was back in Great House Uttara, in that awful moment he had seen his first attempt at rebellion die, as Devedas killed all his friends and broke the spirit of the remainder. Ratul had given him the book and ordered him to run, to become the only survivor. This was that all over again, but so much worse.

Only this time Keta did not run. There was nowhere left for his kind to run to.

"For the Forgotten!" Keta lifted his cleaver and charged.

The warrior slipped out of the path of the Keta's blade, then backhanded him to the ground with one gauntlet.

He'd not even seen that coming. With head ringing and lips bleeding, Keta lay there, knowing he should have died, but somehow hadn't.

His foe had already moved on, with black steel singing. Within the span of a few heartbeats most of the Cove's defenders died horribly. The rest of the rebels turned and ran, but the warrior followed, slicing through spines and cutting off legs. Dizzy, Keta got up and went after him. He slipped in a puddle of blood, fell, but staggered back to his feet.

The warrior sensed his approach and turned.

"In the name of the Forgotten, I command you to stop!"

Surprisingly, the warrior paused, but not out of fear, rather out of curiosity. He reached up and unfastened the mask of his helmet to let it hang, revealing a surprisingly young face. "I see you give orders here, but who are you to command me?"

"I am Keta, the Keeper of Names, high priest of the Forgotten. Cease this violence and leave my people be!"

"A priest?" Incredulous, the bearer sneered at the meat clever. "Put that silly thing down. Does 'priest' mean you rule these fools?"

Keta kept the cleaver raised. "I am their guide. It is my purpose. It is what I have been called to do."

One of the fleeing rebels turned long enough to loose an arrow, but the bearer struck it from the air without taking his gaze from Keta. "My uncle wanted me to be a Historian. Look how *that* turned out."

"This is sacred ground, bearer. The gods will curse you if you harm their chosen in this place."

"Brave words, but I'll risk it." He nodded toward the barricade as rocks tumbled from it and picks burst through. "I didn't kill you because it's clear you were some kind of leader. Surrender to my men for questioning and be spared." Then he began walking after the retreating rebels to continue his bloody mission.

"*No!* I will not surrender." If all Keta could buy with his life was a bit more time for his people to hide, then it was well spent. "I know your sword requires you to accept all challenges."

The blood-soaked warrior turned back and laughed at him. "It does require that, you brave, strange little man."

"Then I challenge you." Keta was terrified. Shaking. "Offense has been taken!"

The warrior's smile died. "More offense than you can imagine was given when your kind took Chakma."

Had the duel been accepted? Keta did not know these things.

The two of them stood ten feet apart, surrounded by severed limbs and lacerated bodies. As a casteless, Keta had been a butcher. He had seen thousands of living things rendered into their component bits, but never as roughly as this. The top of the spillway had turned into a slaughterhouse beyond imagining. Keta could hear the moans of the dying, the crackle of torches, the crumbling of their barricade, and the distant sounds of his terrified people, desperately trying to hide.

"What now?"

"Ask your illegal gods for help and hope that makes some difference, I suppose."

Keta did. *Forgotten, please protect your children. Conceal them from the warriors' eyes. Accept this humble servant's sacrifice.*

Then he rushed forward and swung the cleaver with all his might.

The bearer moved so quickly that Keta didn't even understand what happened. His hand simply came apart.

His momentum carried him past his foe, but then he stumbled, stunned by the ruin left at the end of his arm. The cleaver was on the ground. Some of his fingers were atop it, still twitching. What remained of his hand had been split in half, and his pinky dangled by a thread of tendon. Keta could see white bones through the red mess.

Then the pain arrived and put him on his knees.

A large rock was rolled aside, and warriors clad in gold-painted armor began rushing through the hole.

"Secure this prisoner," the bearer said, gesturing at Keta. "He'll know the rest of the rebellion's secrets. Send up ten more paltans. I want a thorough search of every inch of this place. It's time to clean out this nest of rats."

Keta was in such pain he could barely think, yet he could still pray. *Please, Forgotten. Lend me some of your strength.*

Before the warriors could reach him, Keta struggled to his feet once more, reached down with his left hand, knocked the severed fingers aside, and took up his cleaver again. The pain was so unbearable that all he could do was tuck his crippled limb tight against his chest.

"They are not rats. They are free men and our duel is not over!"

The bearer seemed surprised to see Keta standing. "It was over before it began."

"This is our home. I built it." Keta was wobbling, knees quivering, as the blood from his hand soaked his shirt and ran down his chest. "We just wanted to be left alone. We only wanted to be free! I do not yield! *The faithful will never yield!*"

The warriors paused, looking between defiant Keta and their master, unsure what to do.

The bearer gave the Keeper of Names a slow nod. "Respect."

And then he rammed the black steel blade through Keta's guts.

# Chapter 38

~~~~~~

Ashok had entered the valley and immediately begun killing.

He didn't announce himself this time. Instead he moved silently in the shadows between the trees. Alternating the Heart of the Mountain between aiding his hearing and his vision to pick out all the sentries, and then to give power to his limbs to strike them with incredible speed, ending their lives before they could make a sound. Each life taken brought him a few yards closer to home.

Snapping a lookout's neck got him a sword. He drove that sword through the back of the next guard's head and that gained him a spear. A spear thrust earned him a crossbow.

As he crouched in the bushes between the corpses he saw that there had to be thousands encamped in the valley ahead of him. It didn't matter. Every warrior in Lok could be in his way and that still wouldn't have kept him from his obligation.

Except Ashok couldn't fight them all. He needed to get as close to the tunnel as possible before they raised the alarm.

The Akershani had dug several big ditches to steal the rebels' water. Of course their defenses had let them down. Ashok had warned the rebels to never count on water. It was the home of hell and even in its purest form remained deceitful and fickle by nature.

The drainage ditches were mostly empty now, and deep enough that they would be shadowed from torch light, so Ashok jumped down into one and began crawling through the mud.

The closer he got to the lake, the more warriors he could hear. They were all around him, standing on the banks above, but their attention was elsewhere, and he kept crawling through the shadowed muck. Every warrior he managed to pass was one less he'd have to fight his way through to get home.

There was a great deal of noise ahead. The army was excited. Ashok risked lifting his mud-covered head over the edge long to see the source of their joy. A pair of birds, dark and unnatural as demon hide, descended from the sky and returned to their human forms as they touched the ground. The wizards were wearing the green and gold of Great House Akershan, and the air around them crackled with dissipating energy cast off by their transformation.

Ashok didn't even need to call upon the Heart to hear the wizard's words, since they were delivered with such boisterous pride.

"We have delivered Bharatas to our enemies. The bearer of Akerselem is inside, killing them all!"

As the wizard's words were repeated across the valley, a thousand warriors cheered.

Ashok was out of time.

The entrance was a mere fifty yards away, across the now empty lake bed. From the look of it, a great many casteless had been pressed into service to clear the path. They looked haggard, worked near to death. Rather than exterminate the casteless as ordered by the Capitol, these warriors would use them up first, and then kill them. There had to be a great many casteless laboring inside the tunnel to create such a gigantic pile of debris outside.

"The way is partly clear. We can see the other side," an officer at the mouth of the tunnel declared as he received the message that had been passed down the line. "First paltan is squeezing through now! Everyone else form up. You've got your marching orders. Let's go."

The eager soldiers began pressing toward the entrance.

Between Ashok and his goal were at least two paltans of warriors, excited to be sent up the tunnel to finally put Akershan's troublesome rebellion to the sword. Despite being surrounded

by swordsmen, the two wizards remained the most immediate
threat. The rest of them he would count on darkness, confusion,
and speed to carry him through.

"Bharatas drowns their crater in blood!" one of the two wizards
boldly declared, right before Ashok's crossbow bolt pierced his
belly. Ashok had been aiming for his heart, but the mud upon
the string must have slowed its velocity.

The other wizard saw the bolt hit his companion and reflexively
grabbed for the demon bones dangling from his sash, only Ashok
had hurled the spear as soon as he dropped the crossbow. The
spear went all the way through the wizard and burst out his back.

Ashok was out of the ditch and running before even the sharpest
warrior realized what was happening. The nearest turned just in
time to see a flash of steel, and then Ashok was crashing through
them, colliding with armored bodies. There was no time to fight
them. This was pure desperation, and Ashok called upon the Heart
to grant him all the strength it could. He snatched a sword from an
unsuspecting man's scabbard, and then laid about him on both sides.

All the closest soldiers saw was a being made of mud rushing
between them, and then their comrades falling and squirting blood.
Those farther away just heard clanking and cries of surprise and
pain. Ashok specifically targeted the ones carrying lanterns or
torches, because with each one of those to fall, the darker and
more chaotic it became.

These men were merely obstacles between Ashok and his
duty. They reacted, but too late. He dodged a thrust and ran his
sword across that one's wrist. He rolled beneath a sword, slashing
a warrior's legs as he came back up. He shouldered another one
aside, and then kicked another in the chest. The instant after
that one hit the rocks Ashok leapt over him to slam into the
final rank. A man grabbed his arm, but the hand could find no
purchase on slippery mud-coated skin. The final man met him,
steel to steel. It was a risalder who had been ready to lead from
the front, but Ashok knocked his blade aside with one sword,
and slashed his throat with the other.

Angruvadal was angry within his chest.

He'd gone through that paltan like a worker's plow through
soil, without getting so much as a scratch upon him. Sprinting
toward the entrance, he spun one blade behind him to block a
thrown spear he hadn't even seen.

*Just like the old days.*

The warriors at the entrance met him bravely, but Ashók hit them like a sea demon. Swords flashing faster than they could even hope to track. He turned aside a spear thrust and cut the back of that warrior's hand, crashed into another to hurl him back against the stone, and dropped the last one with a vicious slash across the thigh.

Casteless who had been forced into servitude screamed and got out of his way as he ran up the tunnel with all the might of Akershan chasing right after him. Ashok sprinted as fast as he could, leaving his pursuers behind, practically flying between the unfortunate casteless.

"It is Fall!" shouted one of the casteless at the entrance who had seen Ashok cut down the guards. "The Forgotten's warrior is here!"

There were many warriors scattered throughout the tunnel to oversee the casteless. They were holding lanterns aloft, trying to figure out what the source of the noise was below them. They probably assumed that it was their brethren, roaring for the fight, until Ashok barreled straight through them. They were fortunate he was going too fast to pause long enough to take their lives.

"Fall!" That casteless cry was echoed up the tunnel, words traveling faster than Ashok could run. "Fall has come to save us!"

"They're going to kill you all when this work is done!" Ashok bellowed. "Fight them! Rise up and fight!"

His own words surprised him, for the final chains of the Law had snapped.

"If you are to die, die as whole men! *Fight!*"

The casteless looked down at the stones they'd been passing down the line, and with nothing left to lose, they began attacking the warriors. The tunnel behind him exploded into desperate violence.

The end was just ahead, where the Akershani elite would be serving as their army's spearhead. They would be their house's best, in armor, training, and ferocity, marching in after the bearer to systematically annihilate all resistance. Ashok knew the routine, for he'd led such charges many times himself in service of the Law.

From how few torches were burning ahead, most of the elite paltan was already through, which meant the rebellion's defenses had shattered. Knowing Thera, she would refuse to hide behind the Sons. To defend their home, she would insist on being at the front.

Ashok ran faster than he ever had before in his life.

The exit had been blocked by piled stones, but a hole had been created, the width of a narrow door. The soldiers' attention was forward, on their prey, hungry for battle. They didn't even hear him coming. He drove both blades into two different spines. He crushed another against the wall, smashing the soldier's helmet against the concrete hard enough to crack the skull within. The final warrior who was passing through the cut, Ashok crashed into his back, and rode him to the ground, stabbing.

Then Ashok was back in the Cove.

The spillway was filled with bodies. Akershani warriors were all around him, with many more climbing up the embankment toward the terraces, eager to slaughter rebels.

Lying before him, with belly split open and bowels spilled upon the ground, was the Keeper of Names.

*"Keta!"*

Ashok slammed a pommel into the nearest warrior's throat. As his victim collapsed, choking, in an armor-clanking heap, the rest turned to face him. The defenders were dead or gone. The spillway was shoulder to shoulder with fighters, and there were more on the embankment above. Two dozen spears were pointed his way, and behind those were even more swords. There was no darkness to hide in. Surprise was gone. Even Ashok couldn't defeat this many ready and skilled foes, armed only with weapons of normal steel.

Sudden whips of fire cracked through the ranks. Warriors roared in pain as flesh seared and furs ignited. One of the warriors was snatched from atop the embankment and lifted into the air, screaming, in the talons of a massive black bird. Fifty feet up, it let go. Figures appeared from seemingly out of nowhere, striking at the warriors, and then vanishing back into nothing. A warrior was engulfed in a cloud of stinging insects and thrashed about as they crawled inside his armor to tear at his flesh.

"The rebels have got wizards!" their risalder warned. "Watch for—"

Ashok crossed the spillway and split the officer's jaw from the rest of his face.

A man in casteless rags appeared at Ashok's side, wielding an entire demon femur like it was a club. He swept his other hand down in a hard motion; the air seemed to bend, and five soldiers were pulled from feet and sent flying back, as if yanked by invisible ropes.

It was the slaves they'd freed from the House of Assassins.

As the wizards mercilessly ripped the elite paltan to pieces, Ashok rushed to Keta, and fell to his knees in the spreading pool of blood. "Keeper, I have returned."

Keta was alive, but barely. His eyes were unfocused. His breath was a rapid, shallow, panting. Dropping his swords, Ashok pressed his hand to Keta's abdomen, but saw that he was done for. A normal man couldn't survive such a terrible black steel wound.

Ashok pulled him close. "Keta, can you hear me?"

"Ash...Ashok?" Despite the pain and fear, there was hope in his voice. "Ashok? You're alive?"

"It's me."

"I prayed for a miracle. The gods always provide." All the color was gone from Keta's face. "Save our people."

"I will. You rest."

"I see...I see..." Keta stared past Ashok, up at the stars, out past the stars. "It is not a great nothing. It is...glorious. I'm not afraid."

"You never were."

Then Keta, the Keeper of Names, died in his arms.

They had met with mad whisperings through the window of a prison cell. This man had tried to become his guide and had instead become his friend.

Ashok would not fail him.

The world came rushing back. As wizards slaughtered warriors, Ashok lowered Keta's body, gathered his stolen swords, and rose. He thumped the nearest wizard on the shoulder, and she spun around, scared out of her wits and ready to whip him with beams of fire, but luckily she froze when she recognized him. The fire that was curling around her arms disappeared with a puff of smoke.

"It's the one who freed us!"

"I am."

"Hurry." She pointed toward the terraces. "The assassin has gone up the road to kill everyone."

*Assassin*. Of course, the bearer would seem as terrifying to them as their old harsh masters. It appeared the slaves were simpletons no more. Whatever curse Sikasso had put upon them had somehow been broken. They would have to do.

"I will deal with him. More soldiers are coming up the tunnel. Can you stop them?"

"We are awake, but weak, and only starting to remember who we are." The woman reached into her pockets and pulled out *fistfuls* of demon. "Will this be enough?"

Ashok hoped so and raised his voice so all the wizards could hear. "Children of the Lost House, you will let no warriors past this point! Thera saved you from Sikasso. Keta's people took you in and gave you a home when you could neither think nor speak. Hold this ground or they will all die!"

The wizard woman gave him a grim nod, then engulfed the end of the tunnel in fire.

# Chapter 39

~~~~~~~~~~

Ashok sprinted across dark terraces, chasing the bobbing torches ahead.

Passing the mangled corpses of those who had tried to stop the bearer, he could tell that Thera wasn't among them, nor did he recognize any of the bodies as belonging to the Sons of the Black Sword. Had they already fallen back to the terraces?

The small group of warriors had reached the ancient buildings around the upper edge of the crater. While he was in Xhonura a palisade of sharpened logs had been constructed around the Sons' terrace. It was chaos as the fleeing rebels tried to get inside. There were warriors right behind them, and more fanning out toward the other terraces.

The Cove's ancient buildings were carved from solid rock, but whatever could burn, be it supplies, wagons, or beds, the Akershani were putting it to the torch. The fire quickly spread to large piles of cut hay, creating a terrible inferno.

The bearer was easy to pick out from the others, as he was the one ranging ahead, picking off threats with near impunity, driven by forty generations of instinct, and armed with a sword that obliterated flesh. Ashok went straight at him.

Of course, the bearer sensed him coming, and turned to see Ashok running into the firelight. Somehow the bearer recognized his new foe and shouted, "We meet again, Black-Hearted Ashok! I am Bharatas, son of Arun, bearer of mighty Akerselem!"

Ashok didn't even slow down. This was not a challenge. This was no duel. This was vengeance. Pure and simple.

"Offense has been—" But then Bharatas had to parry Ashok's vicious attack.

Ashok's rage burned cold. Even furious, his strikes were disciplined, perfectly timed cuts. Armed with a pair of Akershani sabers, he fought like a westerner, leading with one, trying to kill with the other.

Yet each time Akerselem intercepted those killing blows, for its prior bearers had fought the swordsmen of Harban before and knew their tricks. With every impact, terrible nicks were put into the stolen swords. With perfect footwork, Bharatas kept moving back. The two of them covered twenty feet that way, until Bharatas brought Akerselem around in an arc that would take Ashok's arm off. He intercepted it, but the unforgiving black steel snapped the last few inches off the mundane saber. Ashok launched his elbow at the bearer's head, but they hit forearm against forearm.

Bharatas was armored. Ashok was not, and he felt that hit down to the bone.

They parted and circled.

"You should not have killed my friend," Ashok said.

"You killed my entire family!"

"Which ones were they?"

Bharatas roared and lunged for him. Ashok danced aside, but despite the bearer's anger that had merely been a feint, and Akerselem narrowly missed his flesh. Bharatas pressed on, with a fearsome onslaught that took everything Ashok had to stay ahead of the hungry blade. Even the best steel had no chance against an ancestor blade, and the damaged saber shattered. Without hesitation, Ashok flung the hilt at Bharatas' eyes, then slashed at his hip with the other sword. The first was ducked, the second blocked, then Bharatas countered with a slash from below that Ashok had known was coming only because Angruvadal warned him to move aside.

The bearer wasn't the only one with black steel ghosts whispering to him.

The other warriors must not have realized this fight was not for them, because they foolishly rushed to the aid of their house's hero. Both combatants sensed their charge at the same time.

"Stay back!" Bharatas warned, but Ashok went straight into the warriors who had blundered into a battle beyond their comprehension. They were dangerous men, the finest their house had to offer, but in this battle they were merely obstacles to put between his body and a black sword.

Ashok moved through them, dodging, reacting, spinning and crashing. Warriors fell. Bharatas followed, but before he could make it through the tangle of limbs, Ashok struck with a mighty downward blow. Instinct saved Bharatas life, but it cost one of the warrior's his.

"Damn you!" the bearer shouted as he lunged past his dying man.

Effortlessly, Ashok switched to the Gujaran sword style, spinning the blade in an arc from the wrist, hoping to catch Bharatas by surprise, but the ancestors of Akershan must have been well traveled, because Bharatas slipped around the rhythm of the blade, dipped low, then nearly took Ashok's head.

Another brave warrior used that opportunity to drive a spear at Ashok's back, but Angruvadal saw that coming, and Ashok rolled around the attack, caught it, and used the leverage to hurl the warrior head-first into a pile of burning hay. Spinning the spear around his shoulders, Ashok thrust it at Bharatas, but one stroke of Akerselem split the blade from the shaft.

"Can't you see this is Ashok Vadal?" Bharatas shouted to be heard over the screaming. The warrior got out of the hay, aflame and thrashing, and stumbled away, blindly falling over the edge into the dry pasture of the terrace below. "Concentrate on the rebels and leave the Black Heart to me!"

Only the Akershani warriors weren't the only brave fools here tonight, and a group of rebels rushed into the fray as well. They were armed with hay forks, mattocks, and wood axes; one was even swinging a chain. They also outnumbered these cut-off warriors six to one and fell upon them with a savagery born of desperation.

While the lesser men clashed, Bharatas undid his mask, showed his face, and demanded, "Do you know who I am now?"

"A dead man." But the bearer seemed content to speak, and that would allow Ashok to catch his breath. "Tell me why I should care."

"Outside Dhakhantar, we fought on horseback. You were on

a great white stallion. You split my head open and left me to die on the plains."

"The decrepit phontho's bodyguard." The boy had fought well, even before being chosen by an ancestor blade. "You were the best among them."

The two of them circled, while the killing continued around them. "While I wandered, delirious, you took Chakma, and my family died at the hands of a fanatic who named himself god king."

Ashok would make no excuses for what he had done. Thera could not sit idly by while the casteless were slaughtered. They'd not wanted this war, but Ashok knew he was responsible for the mad reign of Pankaj, for that fanatical fool would never have been able to conquer that city without his help. The evil that had befallen those people was upon Ashok's head.

"I am guilty of this crime."

"And you will pay. This sword allowed me to take it up only after I promised I'd use it to kill you."

Bharatas came at him with a horizontal cut. Ashok moved aside, but the black sword was already waiting for him, and nearly spilled his guts. It took a chunk from the saber's guard instead. They parted, but only for an instant, because then Bharatas was upon him with renewed fury, striking over and over, the ancestor blade moving with blinding speed. Ashok was forced back, colliding with brawling warriors and rebels.

The second saber snapped as Ashok used it to intercept a brutal overhand blow. The barest touch of black steel split his shirt and left a burning cut from sternum to belly, but then Ashok rammed his shoulder into Bharatas and forced him away.

The bearer immediately moved to strike again, but then he saw that Ashok's sword was broken and took a step back. "This will not do. Somebody give this man a sword!" Only then Bharatas looked around and realized all his men were busy dying, so he bent down, picked up a dropped rebel blade, and tossed it over.

Ashok caught it by the hilt. It shouldn't have been surprising to see such a gesture from a bearer, but Bharatas had just shown himself to possess more honor than Devedas.

"I know who you are now." Ashok raised the narrow blade to his forehead in salute.

"Good. I needed you to understand before you die."

The new sword was in the sirohi style of Sarnobat, with a light, curved blade for speed, but with a heavy guard to bind the opponent's blade, so Ashok shifted into the eastern style, as taught to him by swordmaster Ratul. Either Bharatas or his sword recognized what Ashok was doing, and he shifted his stance to counter.

The two met between the flames.

Bharatas was an excellent swordsman and Akerselem made him far better. Only Ashok was possibly the greatest fighter in the world, and what the shard of Angruvadal added was a mystery. With lightning speed, they clashed, broke apart, then clashed again, scattering the warriors and rebels around them.

Their blades locked, and Ashok twisted the guard hard into Akerselem, trying to lever Bharatas' wrists down. Immediately the black steel began to chew through the normal metal, but Ashok had something that even a bearer did not, and in that moment he called upon the Heart of the Mountain to grant him overpowering strength.

The sudden change threw Bharatas off, and Ashok flipped him hard over his hip onto the ground.

Bharatas hit with a clang of armor, and rolled away, spinning Akerselem defensively to keep Ashok away long enough to regain his feet.

Ashok used that moment to scoop up a six-foot length of chain from the hands of a dead casteless. As Bharatas rose, Ashok whipped it at his foe. He'd been hoping the bearer would reflexively use his sword to block it, and perhaps momentarily trap the deadly thing, but Bharatas lowered his head and let his helmet take the blow, then launched himself directly at Ashok.

Angruvadal warned him what was coming, but every response was a bad one. Ashok chose the best of those and braced for impact. Their blades struck and locked together, Bharatas hit Ashok, drove him back, and the two of them fell over the edge of the terrace into the grass fire below.

They landed hard, both of them immediately attacking each other from the ground, sword trapping sword, as free arms collided, then knees and elbows. Ashok spun the chain, letting it wrap around his fist, and then he punched Bharatas in the helmet with it repeatedly, using the Heart to hit so hard it left dents. Bharatas slammed one gauntlet against Ashok's jaw, but then Ashok rolled backward and sprang to his feet. Armored, it took Bharatas a bit longer to get up, but it was hard to rush a man who was keeping a sword that could split a man in two between them.

Their battlefield was aflame, but the grass here was grazed short by the rebels' flocks, and Ashok kicked his sandals into the dirt to stir up a cloud of dust to keep from burning his feet too badly. Bharatas' sash of office had caught fire, but he ripped it off and snapped it at Ashok's face, much as Ashok had just whipped him with a chain. Bits of flaming silk flew as Ashok cut it from the air.

His skin had been seared. How badly he didn't have time to check. His opponent was wearing metal, leather, and padding. Ashok was wearing scraps of Xhonuran rags. Instinct had told Bharatas to take their fight into the flames. Ashok did his best to steer his opponent toward what had already turned to ash, but a black steel razor forced him back toward the burning grass.

Except he knew wherever he went, duty would require Bharatas to follow.

Ashok turned and ran, calling upon the Heart to leap over the biggest part of the blaze. Bharatas gave chase, crashing right through. Ashok went over the edge, landing on the next terrace down, but barely slowed as he ran to the next ledge, down, and then toward the next.

Sure enough, Bharatas was right behind him.

The deeper they went down the crater, the darker it became. Four terraces down, once the firelight was a distant flicker, Ashok threw himself to the side, crouched, and waited. This level was a rocky boulder field, with plenty of places to hide.

Bharatas jumped down, landed, and sure enough, Akerselem had been expecting Ashok's ambush. The thrust was parried. This wasn't the first time one of its bearers had been forced to fight in the shadows.

But how much had those prior bearers done so? The two of them were equals in instinct. His foe was well trained and better armed, but Ashok could make himself stronger, or faster . . . *or able to see in the dark.*

Blades crossed. Sparks flew as Akerselem devoured steel. With the chain still wrapped around his hand, Ashok let himself go blind in order to give terrible might to his arm and he drove his fist into Bharatas' helm, hard enough to break an ox's skull. The strap broke as the helmet was turned away. Akerselem paid him back with a wicked slice across Ashok's left bicep.

Not only did black steel kill better, it hurt more too.

Bharatas was breathing hard. The blow to the head had shaken him. Ashok knew a hit like that would have left his ears ringing, and in the dark, once unable to hear, fear would set in. Except there was no stopping this warrior, and Bharatas kept swinging at where instinct told him Ashok would be.

Only in forty generations, Akerselem had never faced a foe like this, because there had never been a foe like unto Ashok before.

Bharatas slashed. Ashok came in behind it, and his cut laid the bearer's face open from lip to ear.

Ashok should have died then, running right into Akerselem's responding thrust, but faster than any Protector, faster than any bearer, one with Angruvadal, he moved aside, and the black steel blade was driven deep into a boulder rather than Ashok's body. Immediately Ashok slashed Bharatas' extended arm, right through the unarmored inside of his elbow, cutting tendon and joint.

The bearer stumbled, sword hand falling dead and useless, while Akerselem remained embedded in the stone. Bharatas reflexively reached for it with his other hand, until the tip of the Sarnobat sword split his glove and sliced deep into his wrist.

The two of them stood there in the dark, breathing hard, as Bharatas' lifeblood ran down his arms.

"I have lost?" he managed to ask through his torn-open face.

"I am sorry for both you, and your people."

"I failed my family." Bharatas slowly sank to his knees as the strength bled out of him. "I failed the sword."

Ashok looked at the deadly thing, stuck there. It reminded him of Angruvadal in nature, only curved to suit the fighting style of the plains horsemen. "You did not fail it. I know what it means to fail an ancestor blade. You fought as a bearer should, while trying to fulfill your obligation to your house. See? It is unbroken."

"Good." In his dying moments, the young warrior didn't curse Ashok. He didn't need to. Circumstances had cursed Ashok far more than could be mustered by the hatred of one man. Would Keta have hated this warrior who had killed him? Probably, but more, Keta would have pitied him, for never knowing what it meant to be free.

"I must return to the battle. Do you have any final words, bearer?"

346          *Larry Correia*

"To the ocean with you, Black Heart...I just hope someone takes good care of my horse."

Ashok made it as quick and painless as possible, driving the sword beneath Bharatas' ear and straight into the base of his brain.

Akerselem remained buried in the boulder, and for a moment Ashok wondered what would happen if he tried to take it for himself. Would it find him worthy, as Angruvadal had? Or would it take offense, and end his life? The will of black steel was unknowable. Did it truly pick Bharatas because he had vowed to kill him? Or had it offered up Bharatas as a sacrifice, to deliver another ancestor blade into Ashok's bloody hands?

# Chapter 40

The Sons of the Black Sword had been on the run for days, relentlessly pursued by the Devakulan army through the high desert canyons. They'd clashed several times, always giving worse than they received, but when outnumbered this badly, what did it matter? Eklavya knew they could kill ten each and Devakula would still have enough men to defeat them.

Their mission had succeeded, the aqueduct had fallen, but at what cost?

They'd taken many casualties. It was unknown who was dead and who had simply been cut off during one of their battles in the dark and scattered. Hopefully those would be able to regroup and make their way back to the Cove without being caught. They'd lost half their horses to fatigue or injuries, so most of the Sons were on foot now. Their gunners were out of powder. The men had barely slept for days.

They'd lost track of their prophet and their priest during the battle at the aqueduct. Their only hope was that Thera was among one of the smaller groups that had been split off in the chaotic retreat, and that they had shaken their hounds. She'd thrived as a criminal. If anyone could escape the Law, it was her.

The main body of the Sons, meanwhile, was too easy to track. And from what their advance scouts said, they'd taken a bad turn during the night, and there appeared to be no good way to climb out of the narrow canyon they'd been marching down. They'd reached a dead end. A thousand vengeful warriors were only a mile behind them, and the weather was getting colder.

"Yeah, I know, Kharsawan. You've said all that before," Shekar told him after Eklavya had outlined their dire situation to the other officers once again.

"If you aren't thinking of the future, you aren't thinking at all, Somsak," Toramana admonished him.

"Any of you come up with any bright ideas?"

Eklavya shrugged. "Not a one."

"That's what we officers are for," Gupta said. "Recognizing real problems and then proposing terrible solutions."

They knew they were going to die today, but that drew a laugh from all of them anyway.

"The plan stays the same, then," Ongud declared. "The Sons of the Black Sword will make our last stand here."

A few hours later, the army of Devakula marched into sight, then stopped, just out of what they probably assumed to be gun range. This garrison was local, so this was familiar terrain for them. They must have known the Sons had no way past these high canyon walls, except straight through a force that greatly outnumbered them. The warriors were taking their time, because their leader was probably hoping the Sons would despair once they realized they were trapped.

Only the Sons were as fearless as the man who had named them. They were prepared to meet their fate, and then go to meet their gods.

Eklavya paced back and forth in front of his infantry, shouting encouragement, checking their equipment, and giving last-minute instructions. In a head-to-head battle like this, the brunt of the engagement would be theirs, spear to spear. Behind them were the archers of Toramana and crossbowmen of Shekar. Ongud's cavalry would use their bows until they saw a good opportunity to strike. Gupta's gunners would serve as their reserve, though their fearsome Fortress rods were merely awkward staves now without their precious powder. It was fortunate that the enemy had not yet realized that fact, or they probably would have charged already.

He saw Laxmi waiting to the side and went to speak to her. "Good morning, wizard."

"Hello, warrior," she said. "Are you ready?"

Eklavya suspected she meant if he was ready to die. "Oddly enough, yeah. I suppose I am."

The tiny, quiet, unassuming girl had been a potent force against the army of Devakula during their retreat, launching their ambushes by setting their most dangerous enemies on fire, and a few times turning into a tiger to terrorize the warriors during the night.

"I have a little bit of demon still."

"You should use what you've got left to turn back into a tiger, then when they attack you can escape past them in the confusion."

"I've thought about doing that." Except then she shook her head. "But I think I'll stay and help."

"That's brave of you, but you don't need to waste your life for us. The Forgotten brought us together. We asked for this fight. You didn't. Go. Please. Something good needs to come of this retreat. You're too pretty to die here." And then Eklavya regretted those foolish words as soon as they left his mouth.

Except the wizard girl blushed. "I'll be behind your spears. Whenever your arms get tired and need to rest, call my name and I'll set some of the enemy on fire. I should be able to do that a few times before I run out of magic."

It was too bad they were about to die, because otherwise Eklavya would have to check with the Keeper of Names to see what the Forgotten's rules were about proposing marriage to a wizard.

"They're on the move!" Ongud shouted. "Get ready!"

Eklavya turned to see the enemy had begun marching toward them, shoulder to shoulder, rank upon rank, filling the entire canyon. They had even brought a drummer to set the cadence. "Go," he told Laxmi, then ran back to his place among his men, at the center of the line. He donned his helm and took up his long spear. One nice thing about the Cove was that it grew strong, straight trees.

"This is it, Sons of the Black Sword! Fight for your prophet! Fight for your freedom! Fight for your gods!" The infantry roared in response.

The warriors closed slowly at first, probably worried about the legendary Fortress rods that had laid waste to the Akershani army at Garo, except when there was no flash of thunder and death, the drumbeat quickened, and they started marching faster.

It was cold in the shadows of the canyon walls. The Sons were one small cluster of troops, far from home, low on numbers, food, water, and sleep. The enemy was made up of fresh troops, motivated because they were fighting a criminal invader inside the borders of their homeland, and these criminals had just destroyed one of their proudest landmarks.

Against such numbers Eklavya knew the Sons would be lucky to survive ten minutes, but oh, what a fight that would be.

"They're above us too!" someone cried.

He looked up and around, and sure enough, there were figures appearing atop the canyon wall behind them, dozens of them. They'd be able to launch arrows and drop rocks on the Sons with impunity. *Oceans.* How'd they find a way up there? That was the danger of fighting the enemy on their ground.

"They've got us surrounded!"

Thinking quickly, Ongud shouted, "We have to advance! Get off this wall! Punch through the enemy!"

"You heard him!" Eklavya bellowed, knowing that his spearmen would have to lead the way. "Infantry, on me. Forward. *Forward!*"

Their small group started toward the massive army before them.

Except then the strangest thing happened. The Devakulans stopped.

Banners dipped. The drumbeat changed. Their officers had called a halt. They were staring up at the canyon walls as well.

Those were *not* their men above.

Fortress rods fired. Smoke billowed across the top of the canyon. The opening volley tore through the Devakulan lines, bullets punching straight through shields and armor plates to tumble through flesh. Warriors collapsed, some dead right there. Others screamed and clutched at their ruined limbs.

More figures were appearing at the top of the canyon along the right wall, directly over the Devakulan flank. Eklavya squinted to see against the bright sunlight if they were friend or foe, but then he got his answer when the jugs of Fortress powder they hurled down detonated, blowing Devakulan warriors into bloody pieces.

"Who are they?"

"It doesn't matter. Now's our chance!" Ongud shouted. "Break them!"

"*Infantry, double march!*" Eklavya roared, and that was heard and repeated by his havildars, and now their row of spears was moving at the equivalent to an easy run.

The mysterious gunners kept firing, not in volleys as Gupta taught, but individually, each man going as fast as he could. Only since they were shooting downward into tightly packed ranks, there was hardly any way they could miss, so every bullet sowed pandemonium. An officer in the back was swept off his horse. Archers collapsed. White and black banners dropped as their carriers were gunned down. Even their drum was cut off by a bullet.

Once the Somsak's powerful crossbows were in range, bolts flew over the infantry's heads. More of the enemy fell.

His men had learned well, and they remained shoulder to shoulder as they moved as one. With only fifty yards between them before the two sides collided, Eklavya prayed their wizard could hear him, and bellowed, "Laxmi, now!"

The center of the enemy's front rank was consumed by a rolling ball of flame.

They were headed right for that spot, where burning warriors were crashing against their brothers and disturbing their line. "Ready spears!" All of his men dropped their weapons to chest level, aimed at the enemy.

It was in that moment that Eklavya realized that the enemy's front rank wasn't made up of their best. They were their worst. Many of them turned and fled, crashing back into the other ranks. Some even threw their spears on the ground. *Of course.* Their phontho had assumed the Sons still had powder for their guns, so he'd kept his better troops back, hoping their bullets would be spent against their least valuable soldiers. It was callous, but it made sense, especially if their commander had heard about the route at Garo.

Only now their more experienced troops were farther back being randomly pierced by bullets or shredded by falling bombs, while their inexperienced and expendable men faced the brutal and blooded Sons of the Black Sword.

The line struck, spears thrusting. Eklavya's first attack bounced off a shield. His second slid over the top and pierced a Devakulan's throat. Looking back and forth, Eklavya saw the resistance was crumbling before them and roared, *"Step!"* He'd drilled them thousands of time. The line took one stride forward and kept on stabbing. More of the enemy fell. "Step!" Again. Bodies toppled. Warriors broke.

Except now better combatants were rushing forward to take their place. The enemy had multiple ranks. To span the canyon and keep from being flanked, Eklavya had *one.*

Arrows flew back and forth. The enemy archers' attention was split, as some of them were aiming at Eklavya's infantry, but most were futilely trying to hit the gunners looking over the cliffs. Meanwhile, Toramana's swamp men *never* seemed to miss. An arrow killed the man at his side, and their single line became thinner.

From where he was standing, Eklavya could only see carnage and the combatants immediately around him. From the saddle, Ongud must have seen an opportunity, because suddenly the Sons' cavalry was galloping to one side. "Infantry, part on the left!"

His havildar on that flank began shouting, "Make a hole! Make a hole!"

The line split, but only for a moment, because then Ongud's cavalry rushed through and Eklavya saw just enough to realize they were riding down the fleeing lead paltans and heading straight for the enemy archers.

The men fought as Eklavya had taught them, as Jagdish had taught him. Many of them hadn't even been born in the warrior caste, but they all fought like they had. Each man did his part, but that didn't stop them from dying. Gaps appeared in the line. Another rolling ball of fire bought them time to breathe. Then he realized that the gaps were being plugged, as Gupta's gunners were running forward to take up every spear that got dropped. They lacked the skill and cohesion, but by the gods he could appreciate the fight in them!

His spear got lodged in a man's pelvis, and when he couldn't wrench it out, he went to his sword. Exhaustion, fear, and desperate rage caused order to crumble. It was no longer a line, it was simply a mob of very angry men doing their best to kill one another. And the warriors of Devakula were very angry indeed.

At one point Eklavya killed a man, only to get bashed over the helmet by his friend. He found himself lying facedown in the sand as boots stomped all around him. He'd never fought in the sand before. It was remarkably absorbent and soaked up blood as fast as they could spill it.

Laxmi must have seen him go down, because all the Devakulans ahead of him suddenly burst into flames. Eklavya got back up and hacked his way through the ash. Spear points struck his armor. Swords rebounded off Kharsawan plate. But between the help of the gods, his brothers, and a wizard, he wouldn't die that day.

Battles could turn on the smallest bit of chance, and though he couldn't see it at the time, afterward Ongud would tell all the Sons of how in the midst of slaughtering their archers, he had looked over just in time to see the enemy phontho standing in his stirrups, screaming orders and directing troops, when a Fortress bomb landed close enough to roll beneath the phontho's horse.

All Eklavya knew was that a horn blew, and suddenly he was fighting fewer warriors. Then none at all. And he was standing there, arms burning, struggling for breath, as the Devakulans retreated from the canyon, still under heavy fire.

Hours later, ragged and exhausted, the Sons of the Black Sword met their rescuers.

Eklavya couldn't believe his eyes, for at the head of a group of workers—each of whom was carrying an astounding two, three, or even four Fortress rods—was a familiar figure. A man of tremendous girth and stature, with a booming voice that had become well known to all the Sons who had wintered in the swamp of Bahdjangal.

"Well, well, it's fortunate that you found yourselves in trouble so near to one of my many illegal gun factories! Lucky for you lot I'm being exceedingly well paid to come and save you!" the jovial magic smuggler boasted. "It appears that once again the fearsome Sons of the Black Sword have found themselves deeply indebted to their humble servant, Gutch!"

# Chapter 41

~~~~~~~~~~

It was a long journey, the road north to the Capitol. The desert gave a man too much time to think about all the things he had done.

The witch hunter rode upon a black Zarger steed, roaming far ahead of the convoy of Inquisitors and obligated warriors. They would guard their magical prisoner all the way back to the Inquisitor's Dome—or Tower of Silence, as his brothers had told Javed was the new name of their Order's home.

Thera Vane had been bound, gagged, and placed into a wagon, kept under watch at all times. Javed left the guarding of her to the other Inquisitors, as it enabled him to avoid her accusing glares. Her hate shouldn't have mattered to him, yet it did.

The high desert was behind them. Before them were the endless white sands of the low desert. The convoy was led by two senior witch hunters, himself and Nikunja. The bodyguard, Murugan Thao, had proven quite the hero, managing to kill Senior Witch Hunter Madhavadas, and he had injured Witch Hunter Lekhani so badly that they had been forced to leave her in Akara to recover. Even if her wounds didn't turn septic and kill her, she'd certainly have to retire from the Order. That had been a very fine showing for a warrior the other Sons had once dismissed as a coward.

Thinking of the Sons of the Black Sword put Javed into a dark mood. Normally after completing such a difficult assignment he was left with a feeling of deep accomplishment. There was great satisfaction in doing something most would consider impossible. This time there was only that nagging feeling that lesser men called shame.

Javed had demanded that a hundred warriors of Makao escort them all the way back to the Capitol. The other Inquisitors were doubtful such an escort would be needed, as the Sons of the Black Sword had been forced to flee south, scattering into the canyon lands, trying to evade pursuit, and they would be lucky to survive. There was no way the Sons would be a further danger. They had no way of knowing which way their prophet had been taken, and even if they had, they'd never be able to avoid the armies of two great houses and catch up.

Only Javed knew the Sons far too well, and he had insisted the warriors accompany them. The Sons were not to be underestimated. Some of those men had subjected themselves to traveling by river, to fight demons and wizards in order to get their prophet back once before, and at that time they hadn't even met her yet. Thera Vane was a woman who inspired loyalty, whether she was really the old gods' mouthpiece or not.

Javed shook his head and dismissed that thought. There was no such thing as gods. It was a trick. She was a liar, just like him. She inspired loyalty in fools and fanatics, nothing more, just like all other false prophets who had come before her. Thera was a criminal, and capturing her was one more stepping-stone on Javed's path toward greater status. The Grand Inquisitor rewarded loyalty, and would repay him for this accomplishment. The last time he had been in the Capitol he had bedded an arbiter from a Zarger vassal house, Artya, who was a fierce and calculating beauty, and one of Omand's conspirators in his plot to overthrow the judges. After this assignment Javed would have the status to take her as a wife if he felt like it. She was exceedingly rich.

Kings need men. Important men. Wealthy men. Great would be his reward. He'd have title and an estate. There would be no more pretending to be a humble rice merchant, living in tents in the desert, or lowering himself to consort with madmen and the foulest criminals. He'd murdered enough. He'd deceived enough. The emptiness he felt even after fulfilling this difficult an assignment proved that the thrill was gone. It was time to take the Grand Inquisitor's favor and move on to a better life.

Yet when Javed closed his eyes he kept seeing two naïve children from a swamp, who had died simply because his mission had required their silence.

The desert was so vast it lulled men into melancholy thoughts. Javed realized his scouting had taken him too far ahead of the convoy. The wagons were distant shapes twinkling in the mirage. There was nothing around him but sand and cacti. The day had grown hot, and he paused to wipe the sweat from his brow.

There was a woman standing ahead of him on the road.

The desert here was flat. He should have seen her from a mile away. There was no place to hide, and she was dressed in voluminous black Zarger robes, a stark contrast against the pale sand. It was as if she had suddenly formed from nothing.

A wizard, then, stepping from the space between worlds. Javed pulled up the silk Inquisitor's mask that Nikunja had supplied him with. Since he was wearing the badge of his office, it would not do to let some outsider see his face. Then he dismounted his tired horse, and with a demon tooth in one hand and his other hand upon the hilt of his sword, he walked toward the stranger as she continued walking toward him. They both stopped, twenty feet apart.

"I am on official Inquisition business. Identify yourself, wizard."

Her face was veiled. Not even her eyes could be seen in the shadows beneath her hood. Her voice was neither old nor young. "You know who I am."

"I assure you, I do not."

"Except you bear my name."

Javed cocked his head to the side. "I do not cross the desert to listen to riddles."

"You are Witch Hunter Javed?"

He scowled behind his mask. "I am."

"Then you bear my name." She put one gloved hand over her heart. "For I am *the witch*."

That was impossible. That was a legend as old as the Inquisition. "The sun has driven you mad, Law breaker."

"I am far older than your Law. It does not apply to me."

"Don't toy with me, wizard. Who are you really?"

"I am Unassailable. I am the Mother of Dawn, She of Many

Forms. Created in the image of one of the old gods from the world before, I watched from the sky as the first men set foot on this world. It was my duty to be their advocate. I was already ancient when the demons fell. I gave counsel to Ramrowan, and the generations that followed, until their pride became too great for them to listen, and this land was consumed by sin. Forsaken, I could do nothing as the rivers ran red as the royal line was cast down. Your Order exists because of me, out of fear of me, your entire life has been a vain attempt to stop *me*."

Javed took a step back as he drew his sword, but then he steadied himself. "The great witch was defeated by the Inquisition long ago."

"They tried. Only they did not succeed."

Surely this was no ancient creature of legend or Inquisitors' secret history lesson come to life. "Trouble me with no more lies, woman. This is your final chance to identify yourself. You act like an illegal wizard and you talk like a religious fanatic. The penalty for either of those is death."

"Don't hide behind the Law, Javed. We both know the Law means nothing to you. It is an excuse, made by a man hungry for destruction, because he was hollow and knew no other way to fill it. Did you provide such a stern warning to all those you murdered in Shabdakosh, Karoon, Lahkshan, or Ambara?"

His missions had been of the utmost secrecy, known only to a handful in the entire Inquisition. "How do you know of those?"

"Most of the people you killed were not even believers. For their persecution you at least had the excuse of *duty*." She positively spit the word. "For the rest, they were simply in your way. Tell me, Witch Hunter, did you warn Parth and Rawal of this penalty before you took their lives, and left their bodies stuffed in a hole?"

Javed lunged forward, thrusting his sword at her heart.

The blade was torn from his hand and hurled into the distance.

The robed woman was gone, and in her place stood a thing beyond comprehension. It was a goddess, ten feet tall and made of glowing silver. Her many-armed form swept Javed from his feet as the desert was consumed by blinding light.

Her words hit like thunder.

"*I should end you for your evil. I should make you pay for what you have done to my children. You should suffer for your deceit. You should feel the pain of every drop of innocent blood you have ever shed and be crushed to dust beneath the weight of what you have done."*

Javed cowered on his knees before the beautiful and terrible thing, not just because she could kill him on a whim, but because he knew that *she was right.*

Within the Cove, he had seen a different way, building rather than tearing down, helping rather than hurting, creating instead of destroying, and he had still betrayed them for it.

*"You saw the Forgotten and denied it. It is one thing to lie before men, but it is impossible to lie before a god."*

"What do you want from me?"

*"Repair the damage you have done."* The giant was gone, and Javed was lying in the road at the feet of the woman in black. Instead of six arms, she had but two, and she squatted down next to him. "A new age is here, Javed. For good or ill, every role must be filled. Three and three, they must be in balance. The mask and king are set upon their path. The demons are coming. It is my responsibility to provide a general, a voice, and a priest. I am in need of a priest. You will have to do."

He could barely see, barely hear, barely understand. "I can't. I am stained. What of Keta? He is a righteous man."

"Alas, the noble Keeper of Names has been killed."

That wrecked him even more. In Javed's corrupted way, Keta had probably been the nearest thing he had to a friend. Had that death been his doing as well? It likely was, somehow.

"Ratul, Keta, and now it must be you; there will not be time to prepare another. You must take up the book and finish his work. You must become the Keeper of Names."

With tears in his eyes, Javed told the Mother of Dawn, "I swear I will make this right."

"You had better... You can begin by saving our Voice."

Then she was gone.

# Chapter 42

Thera was tied up, miserable and plotting her escape, when she heard the rapid approach of hoofbeats. Through the open canvas of the back of the wagon, she saw that an Inquisitor had a body draped over the back of his saddle. When she saw the body was Javed, it made her smile. Hopefully that traitorous scum had been struck dead because his rotten heart had burst.

"Help! I found the witch hunter fallen upon the road. He is delirious from the sun."

*Damn. The bastard's still alive,* Thera thought. That would teach her to get her hopes up.

The convoy came to a halt as the Inquisitors tried to revive their fallen man. The other witch hunter rushed to where they had laid Javed in the shade of another wagon. "Fetch him some water, quickly."

She would laugh and laugh if Javed died of heat stroke, as that was the most humiliating way for a Zarger desert dweller to perish—assuming he actually was from there and hadn't been lying about that like everything else. In the meantime, while her regular guards were distracted by the fallen witch hunter, she would work the fraying cords around her wrists against the rough edge of a pried-up board as long as she could. The fresh stitches in her arm and back indicated the Inquisitors wanted to deliver her to the Capitol alive rather than dead, but those injuries made the repetitive sawing motion an agony.

Only Thera wasn't the type to give in to despair. She'd been captured before, and had survived far worse situations than this... or so she told herself. All she needed to do was get free, find a knife, slit some throats, sneak past some Inquisitors and a whole bunch of warriors, steal some supplies and a horse, and escape across the desert. That wasn't easy—far from it—but that certainly wasn't impossible.

When one of the guards shouted a warning that a large group of riders was approaching from the southwest, Thera felt another spark of hope that maybe it was the Sons, and they'd somehow eluded their pursuers and found her.

Except a moment later that happy idea was dashed, when one of the Makao soldiers shouted that he recognized the banner of their phontho. This wasn't a rescue. It was just more reinforcements for her captors.

Thera realized Javed had woken up, and was staring right at her, almost through her, so she quit sawing and tried to act as if she'd been doing nothing at all. Only he hadn't seemed to notice her furtive actions, as his eyes were wide and wild. He seemed confused and afraid, as he lay there in the shade of a wagon, panting like a wounded animal.

Thera found that odd, but if she was lucky that was what two-faced traitors looked like before dying from excessive heat.

The other witch hunter, Nikunja, held a cup of water to Javed's mouth so that he could drink, and before the warriors got there, he pulled up Javed's Inquisitor's mask to grant him some dignity. The entire time Javed just kept staring at Thera. If the annoying gods who had drafted her had any sense of justice at all they'd at least allow her to get her hands free long enough to plunge something sharp into the false priest's throat.

The newly arrived Makao warriors rode alongside the wagons, their horses lathered and breathing hard, indicating that they'd set a brutal pace to reach the convoy. That was a stupid and dangerous thing to do in the arid desert unless it was absolutely necessary, even in the cooler seasons. In typical Makao fashion, their armor was too pretty, too ornamented and colorful, and it brought back the long-neglected disgust she felt toward the house that had conquered Vane and made it a vassal.

Witch Hunter Nikunja addressed the still unseen leader of the riders. "Good to see you again, Phontho, but we have no further need of assistance...unless you bring word of the demise of the Sons of the Black Sword."

There was a brusque answer, but Thera couldn't make out the words...except there was something about that tone...

"That is impossible," the witch hunter said. "There's no time for diversions. We are to take our prisoner directly to the Tower of Silence."

The phontho said something else, and since he had gotten closer, she could actually hear him a bit better. There was something familiar about that voice...

Nikunja laughed nervously, looking to his fellow witch hunter for aid, but Javed still appeared incoherent. "You speak foolishness, Phontho! This so-called prophet falls under Inquisition jurisdiction. You agreed to that yourself!"

The phontho was close enough now that his voice was unmistakable. "That was before I learned her name. If your prisoner is in fact Thera Vane, we're taking her to Kanok for trial. In the unlikely event she's not executed, you can have her when we're done."

It was *him*. A cold, sick knot formed in Thera's stomach. She'd rather go with the Inquisition. Better to die on the dome than go back to Makao.

"I cannot allow this. There's no way for us to reach Kanok and be back across the mountains before winter."

"Too bad, Witch Hunter. It appears you have a handful of Inquisitors, one of whom appears deathly ill, while I have two hundred men and a whole lot of desert to bury bodies no one will ever find." There was a creak of leather as the phontho dismounted. "That is the only diplomacy I will offer you today."

"This is outrageous. You would risk angering the Grand Inquisitor?"

"To get first crack at this particular rebel I'd provoke the Grand Inquisitor, all the judges, and every demon in hell. From the way your masks are pointed, she's inside there."

Boots crunched through sand as a shadow approached on the other side of the canvas. Thera steeled herself, and once again wished her hands were free. As much as she'd fancy stabbing Javed, killing this man would be far more satisfying.

The fabric was swept aside, revealing a warrior with an eye patch and a jagged scar that crossed both sockets.

*So I missed an eye. Unfortunate.*

Dhaval Makao sneered. "It's been a long time, wife."

# Chapter 43

~~~~~~~~~~~~~~

In most of Lok, when winter arrived, battle stopped. Summer was for fighting. Winter was for surviving. But not in the north. Their temperate weather was considered a blessing, but Jagdish found himself wishing for the break of snow, because he was *tired*. His men had been victorious, over and over again, but it took more than the people's adoration to sustain them. There came a point where even the fiercest warrior just wanted to sit on his balcony and drink beer without having to worry about another battle tomorrow.

In a proper house war, Vadal should have been able to defeat Sarnobat easily. Except a third of the army of Great House Vadal was now distracted dealing with Vokkan aggression in the west, and Harta had ordered away the other third to fortify Vadal City so it would not appear an easy target to this strange force that was coming from the Capitol offering *help* ... which was an offer no one in Vadal believed to be real. That peculiar army was made up of paltans from all the other great houses and Capitol Orders, and was led by Devedas, formerly Lord Protector, who now bore the odd new title of Raja.

It was to discuss the threat of this Capitol army that Jagdish and many other phonthos had been temporarily called back to Vadal City. He hated leaving his men to fight the house of the wolf without him—and if Sarnobat's bearer finally came out to fight while Jagdish was away that would be just his luck—but orders were orders, and Jagdish's time in the east had earned him a reputation as a master strategist. He'd spent several days in staff meetings, as phonthos argued and arbiters asked them foolish questions, and they made plans and contingencies within plans . . . the usefulness of which would depend entirely upon what Raja Devedas' true intentions were, and if he was coming to Vadal to be a savior or an invader.

The meetings gave him headaches, but there was one good thing about being back in the city for a time, and that was being able to see his daughter again. As long as they were at war, the younger children of the officers would be granted quarters in a lavish estate in the warrior district, where they would be well guarded and cared for. There was wisdom in his caste offering this, as leaders don't lead as well if they're distracted with worry for their families.

Jagdish walked up the stairs, calling out, "Pari, Baba is home." From the other side of the curtains his daughter made a gleeful noise as she heard his voice. That giggle would always make him smile. "What a day it's been," he said as he entered, expecting it to be Raveena tending to Pari, but instead it was a different woman, who he had not met before.

"Greetings, Phontho Jagdish."

An unfamiliar woman was seated on pillows, as Pari played with her dolls on the floor. She was perhaps a bit younger than Jagdish was, with some paint decorating her face, jewels in her hair, and wearing a fine dress cut to accentuate her—rather noteworthy—figure. The stranger was extremely beautiful, so much so that Jagdish was temporarily speechless, as that wasn't the sort of thing one expected to find in his private quarters without putting in a request.

"I didn't send for a pleasure woman. What are you doing with my child?" He looked around, saw no one else was there, then shouted, "Raveena!"

She seemed momentarily taken aback by his reaction, tilted her head to the side, as if confused, and said, "Your maid is in the kitchen helping your cook. She left little Pari in my care for a moment and I was happy to help. You have a very gleeful and energetic child, Phontho Jagdish. It is nice to meet you."

Pleasure women were a common sight in any warriors' district in Lok, but apparently those obligated to serve the highest rank and status in Vadal City were far lovelier than any he he'd seen before. "I apologize that you have wasted your time, miss. There's been a mistake."

"Oh, has there?"

"I've not asked for any female company."

"Really? Do you not like females?"

"What?" Jagdish laughed rather than take offense. "I like females just fine, thank you."

"Because for a man of your rank, a district of this quality wouldn't discriminate in the services it is happy to provide with no questions asked... If it is not that, am I not pretty enough to suit you?"

"Oh no, you are exceedingly attractive." In fact, he had only known one more beautiful in his entire life, but even the thought of Pakpa made Jagdish feel guilty for talking to another woman. He tried to think of how to put this gently, because he wasn't the sort to insult anyone who was simply trying to do their job. "I am loyal to another."

"I was told you were a widower."

"Yes, I am." And Jagdish left it at that. "Please give your masters my apologies, and my army will still pay for your time."

"That's kind of you." The exceedingly charming pleasure woman nodded thoughtfully. "Clearly mistakes happen."

Raveena swept into the room, drying her hands upon a towel. "Oh, Master Jagdish, I didn't hear you get home. Dinner will be ready soon. I have prepared an extra place for Lady Shakti."

"*Lady* Shakti?"

Their guest shrugged. "I never said otherwise."

Jagdish grimaced. Clearly, mistakes did happen.

She rose to greet him with a proper bow. "I am Shakti, daughter of Phontho Gotama of the Mukesh Garrison, and I am currently obligated as a warrior caste envoy to the Vadal City court."

Jagdish returned the bow, and went extra low to show apology. "Phontho Jagdish, Eastern Border Guard."

"Pardon, I thought you two had met already," Raveena said. "Sorry, Phontho. Lady Shakti also has quarters within this estate. She asked if she could join us and—"

"Raveena, would you take Pari into the kitchen for a moment?"

"Of course." Sensing the sudden awkwardness, she immediately swept Pari into her arms and carried her away, even as the poor girl squealed in protest because she'd clearly been enjoying playing with Lady Shakti.

Once the worker was away, Jagdish sucked the air through his teeth, before saying, "Ah . . . My sincere apologies about the mistaken identity. I was not expecting a guest."

Surprisingly, rather than take offense, she laughed at his discomfort. "I've been called worse things than a pleasure woman."

"So you're Gotama's youngest?"

"That's me."

Which meant she was an unmarried woman of high status, visiting a widower without any sort of proper introduction or chaperone. He'd almost gotten into a duel with Gotama once, and he rather liked the old man now, so he'd hate to do it again over something stupid. "Where is your father?"

"Back on the border as far as I know. Stuck between the wolf and all the refugees from the fires in the Goda. Somebody who actually knows what they're doing has to mind the line while you're away getting raked over the coals by panicking first casters with no concept of how to fight a war."

"And your escort?" A woman of her status was bound to have a bodyguard or two.

"They're somewhere. They're used to me escaping their clutches by now. May I sit down?"

"I don't know if that would be appropriate—" Except she had already done so. "Or not." Jagdish adjusted his sword belt so that he could sit as well. "What can I do for you, Shakti?"

"Well, I wanted to meet the legendary Jagdish Wizard Slayer, without all of that pomp and carrying on that surrounds official proposals. People are never themselves at such things. They're very stuffy. A woman has to do her research. You can't just take anyone else's word about someone's character. You have to see for yourself."

"I don't know what proposal you're talking about."

"Arbiter business. Mere formalities." She waved that away as if that was nothing.

Gotama hadn't spoken much about his family, but he had described this one as *precocious*. Thus far that seemed an understatement.

"I've been looking into you, Jagdish. You're a very interesting man. Father said you fought with great courage and skill on the Night of Ten Thousand Demons."

"Is that what they're calling it now?"

"They are. The first songs that went around the warrior district called it the Night of a Thousand Demons, but that lacked gravitas, so they multiplied the demons by ten."

"It was daytime, and there were still probably more demons than that."

"Of course, but Father said they were very small demons, and 'night of a hundred thousand demons' is too much a mouthful for a proper chorus. Have you not heard the songs?"

"I've not. I've been busy."

"It's rare a warrior gets songs written about him for more than one event. I could sing you one of the new ones. I have an excellent singing voice."

*What a curious woman...* "I don't doubt that at all."

"Let the men have their drinking songs, I say. The pillar of fire terrified everyone. In the aftermath of something so inconceivable, they need something to rally around, and who better than a man who was already a legend? More importantly, though, Father told me you're a good leader. You always do what is best for your men, and they love you for it. There are plenty of strong warriors. There are very few who have good hearts."

Jagdish was baffled where she was going with this. "I try."

"No, I don't think you do. From everything I've heard you don't have to try because being honorable comes naturally to you. You are loyal to a fault, and your weakness is that sometimes that loyalty is even extended to criminals and fanatics."

He couldn't take offense at someone stating the obvious. "The Sons of the Black Sword were what they were. Those fanatics were some of the finest men I've ever led into battle."

"See what I mean? That attitude is why they keep writing all those songs about you. My father tried to marry me off to strong—but uninteresting—men before. So I thwarted those attempts. There are as many ways to sabotage an arbiter's marriage arrangement as there are to raid a town."

"Hold on now." Gotama had only mentioned that idea in passing, and he had done so while Jagdish had a great many other worries on his mind. "Lady Shakti, I'm sure your father has your best interests at heart, and I don't know what plans he has set into motion, but trust me, I'm not a good candidate for marriage right now."

"On the contrary, I know the politics involved far better than Father does. What do you think I've been dealing with every day to pass the time while trapped in this dreadfully boring city? Harta Vadal praises you in public, but seethes against you in private. You've made yourself too valuable to him to ruin. Obviously, allying my family with yours would still be a gamble, but I think your legend will outlast our Thakoor's animosity. The lower ranks of our caste look to you as everything it means to be a warrior, and they aspire to live in your image. You have replaced Ashok in their hearts."

"No one can do that."

"You underestimate the sting of betrayal. However, I neither met nor traveled across the continent with the Black Heart while fighting all manners of evil. So I suppose if I let Father go through with his plans, I would just have to settle for a legendary war leader who has won our people's highest award for valor, and who has a potentially bright—or disastrous—future. You're no bearer-Protector, but some girls would still think you're quite the prize."

Jagdish couldn't help but laugh.

"What's so funny about my scheming? I've put thought into this."

"I feel like I'm a prize horse being evaluated before an auction."

"Don't you realize? You very much are." Shakti just stared at him for a moment, and Jagdish realized there was great cleverness in those eyes. "I speak of your future as a gamble, as you're clearly headed toward greatness or utter failure. There is no in-between. You are of such status and potential that some family will inevitably take that bet, but if they recognize your vulnerabilities, they'll only offer up one of their dumber, expendable daughters, so that way if you do fall, they're not out much."

At first, Jagdish had been confused by all this, but now he was intrigued. "You are rather analytical."

"I enjoy this sort of thing."

"I can tell."

"Our caste is very good at making gains on the battlefield, and then losing those gains in the courts. There is a certain cunning required in the courts that most of our caste lack. I believe your greatest vulnerability is a lack of political savvy. That's what I would bring to our alliance. The two strongest garrisons in the east would be united by marriage, and you would gain a guide in the area in which you are most vulnerable."

This was all very sudden, and Jagdish leaned forward, suspicious. "And what benefit would you get out of this deal?"

"Spoken like a man whose first arranged marriage was to seal a contract for the delivery of bread."

"It did, and being married to Pakpa turned out to be the most fortunate thing that ever happened to me. I'll tolerate no unkind words about my family."

"I would never." Shakti seemed sincere on that. "You truly loved her, didn't you?"

"Very much."

"I am glad for you. I'd hope for such fortune myself, but happy marriages are rare for those of our status. We get what we are given, and *that* I can't abide."

"*There is no freedom. Everyone has their place,*" Jagdish quoted the familiar saying. "Does the Law not apply to you too?"

"Asks the one man in Vadal who seems to violate the Law whenever his honor requires it, and yet somehow survives."

Shakti had him there.

"I would rather choose my place than take the one that's forced on me, Jagdish. That's why I keep ruining Father's carefully laid plans to marry me off. If I'm ever to love a man, I suspect I would have to pick him myself."

"That's the one advantage of having no status. Nobody cares who you wed." Jagdish chuckled, as his marriage to someone of the worker caste had been meant as a punishment, and oh, how wrong they'd been. "It's the nature of high birth that you be used for leverage to bring prosperity to your family."

"Your duty to your house will require you to wed someone eventually. Why settle for a dreary dullard? Even someone politically astute can yearn for happiness."

That was true...Jagdish knew his caste would order a marriage eventually, but he had kept pushing that thought aside. He had a war to fight. A daughter to raise. When his house needed a warm body of sufficient status to seal some trade deal or peace agreement, he would do as he was told. Thinking about another marriage as anything other than fulfilling his obligation made him feel like he was being unfaithful to Pakpa.

"You ask what do I get out this potential arrangement, Jagdish? For the last year I've heard tales of this humble soldier who did his duty only to be dishonored for events beyond his control, who then did the impossible to regain his name. A hero who has seen the incredible and lived to tell the tale, yet also a man who loved his wife no matter her status, a father who is noted for how much he adores his daughter, a master who has never raised an angry hand against a servant, and a commander whose men would follow him across the sea to fight the host of hell... How could I *not* be intrigued?"

Jagdish blushed at such flattery. "You're good at painting pictures with words, Shakti. But those are just things people say about me. I'm merely a soldier, same as many others. Don't mistake those tavern songs for reality. For all you know I'm an angry drunk who kicks dogs for amusement."

She had a *very* pretty smile. "And you underestimate how thorough I am. I study politics like you've studied war. Intelligence is valuable in both. When you mistook me for a pleasure woman, you were surprised, because despite your newfound wealth you've not requested the company of a single one since your wife passed. I know of your arrangement with the smuggler Gutch, how you were willing to shelter a wanted librarian from our own Thakoor, and how you were smart enough to tell stories to warriors across Vadal to pressure Harta to spare such a heroic life. Over and over you demonstrate loyalty, pragmatism, and wisdom. Marry me, and in ten years you'll be head of the warrior caste."

"Oceans, woman..." Jagdish didn't know if he should be offended or impressed. "How many of Gotama's marriage contracts have you ruined?"

"I've lost track. At least five or six. I'm a practically ancient twenty-five years old now, so the poor man has nearly given up hope of ever being rid of me."

"No wonder his hair's gone white."

"Notably, you're the first candidate Father actually respects. Which is an impressive endorsement. At least enough of one to inspire me to look into you more." Shakti smoothly rose. "Well, I must be going now."

"You won't stay for dinner?" Jagdish stood as well.

"No. I think I hear my bodyguards frantically calling my

name as they search the compound, thinking I've been kidnapped. Clearly this scandalous meeting never occurred."

"Of course..." Jagdish considered his next words carefully. "I will await your family's proposal."

"While you wait for the official letter to arrive, you will surely ask around about my character, as I did with yours. No need to be embarrassed, it's what I would advise you to do."

Jagdish opened the door for her. "Good evening, Lady Shakti."

"Farewell, Phontho." She brushed past him on the way out, and that soft touch was the closest he'd been to a woman in a very long time. She even smelled nice. "Now that I've spoken with you in person and you've met my expectations, I shall refrain from setting the arbiter's correspondence on fire."

After Jagdish closed the door behind her, he stood there feeling a little flushed.

"Dinner is ready." Raveena returned to the sitting room. "Did Lady Shakti leave? She seems so nice."

"Nice yet frightening." That union would be like picking up an ancestor blade. It would either end in glory or a terrible demise. "I believe I might be getting married again."

# Chapter 44

~~~~~~~~~

The sword was still embedded in the stone.

Ashok had come to this terrace to think, and to be tempted.

The Creator's Cove was safe for now. With the rebels' great store of magic, the slaves turned wizards had held the tunnel. Afterward, Ashok had delivered the dead bearer's body back to his army. Once he declared who he was, and that he had defeated Bharatas, the Akershani warriors had fallen back. They had probably reasoned that if they continued to attack, Ashok would destroy their sacred sword. He would never make such a dishonorable threat, but why would the warriors assume otherwise? By now they must have heard that he had shattered an ancestor blade before. He was the Black Heart, Ashok Sword Breaker, the most feared and hated criminal in the world.

It was an odd feeling, to be despised by so many.

The fires had been put out. Their dead gathered, the injured tended. Over the ensuing days many of the wounded had succumbed to their wounds and gone on to the great nothing beyond. Despite their losses, the faithful were happy to have survived. Yet they were still afraid, and Ashok knew not what to do about that. Their hiding place was found. Their priest was dead. Their Voice had gone to some unknown destination. Ashok had saved their lives, but he didn't understand how to lift their spirits.

The first snow clouds were in the air. Wherever Thera and the Sons had gone, it was unlikely they would be able to make it back before these mountains were cut off from the rest of the world for a season. Ashok had to decide what to do, and quickly. Would he leave these people defenseless to be slaughtered in the spring, or leave and try to find the woman he was obligated to protect?

It was difficult being a free man. When he followed the Law, all the difficult decisions had been made for him. Freedom required conscience. That was a dangerous thing.

Far down the terraces, deep in the crater, Ashok sat in front of a boulder with a sword in it, pondering, and not finding any good answers.

Someone was walking down the lane, which curled like a screw down the interior of the Cove. Even though they were barefoot, Ashok heard the footsteps while they were still very far away. A motherly casteless woman approached, nervous and hesitant. "General Ashok, sir? I've a message for you."

He didn't recognize her, but that was not unusual as there had been a great multitude that had joined the faithful while he had been in Fortress. From her necklace hung a carved wooden hook, a symbol of Ashok's returning to life upon Sikasso's meat hook. He didn't care for the constant reminder of that agony, but it meant something to the faithful, and many of them had taken to wearing that symbol.

"A message from who?"

"Keta, the Keeper of Names."

Ashok had cremated Keta's body upon a funeral pyre so recently that his clothing still smelled of smoke. Only the caste-less was not speaking of ghosts, as she held out a piece of paper, folded, with a wax seal.

"We found it in his things. Your name is on it. I think he wrote it when he figured we were 'bout to die."

Ashok took the letter, broke the seal, and read.

*Ashok,*

*If you are reading this I am gone. This ink may be wasted, for many believe you have already preceded me to the other side, but I have faith you still live and will find your way back to us. When last we spoke I begged you not to duel*

*Devedas, but you always do what you must. I know that is
why the gods picked you.*

*I have hidden the Book of Names in a place you will
suspect to look. Javed must take it now and carry on that
vital work.*

*With me gone, Thera will need you more than ever before.
Protect her and the gods will protect us all. Nothing else
matters. Accept the blessings they offer you, and they will
provide a way for you to fulfill your obligation. When you
are done we will meet again in the paradise the gods have
prepared for their faithful servants.*

*Your friend always,*
*Keta*

The casteless woman was walking away, but Ashok asked,
"Why do you try to deceive me?"

She flinched, seemingly afraid. "What? What do you mean,
General Ashok? Have I given offense?"

Too tired to be angry, Ashok held up the letter. "Keta did
not write this."

"I don't know. I just found it with your name on it and—"

"It is a rare casteless who could even read my name. You
are literate?"

She put her hands together, bowing and begging, as a real
casteless would instinctively do. "Some of us get taught to read.
Keta could. Some learn in secret, like me."

"This letter is not Keta's words. It reads like the man's sermons,
but not the man himself. His handwriting would be known to
any who have seen the genealogy, and easily forged."

"Apologies. I don't know what to tell you."

"Accept the blessings they offer me? Timely counsel, as I visit
this place every day, deciding if I should try to take up a second
ancestor blade." Ashok gestured toward where Akerselem waited.
"Wondering if it will find me worthy, or be insulted, and leave
me maimed or dead. Am I still a bearer? Did the black steel
itself send Bharatas to test me?"

"That's all beyond me. I'm a simple—"

Ashok cut her off. "Why do you wish for me to draw the
sword, Mother Dawn?"

Her demeanor changed immediately as the act was dropped.

This was no mere groveling casteless, but rather someone with secret knowledge beyond them all, and the pride to match. "I am caught. How did you know?"

"The mysterious woman who arranges the way, who sets many on converging paths. You come and go as you please, and distance is no matter. To some you appear a warrior, others a worker, young, old, it matters not. Always somehow knowing the unknowable and guiding the faithful to where they need to be. When we met the first time, you wore the face of a crone, and offered advice I needed to hear."

She returned and sat on the grass across from him, seeming to enjoy the opportunity to talk freely. "That's not the first time we met, merely the first time I introduced myself. I have been there your entire life, in one form or another, for you are the most important of them all, the pinnacle of generations."

"You are not the Forgotten."

"No. But I knew him once."

"What are you really, then?"

"I am whatever I need to be for whoever I am trying to guide at the time. I prefer to steer with a gentle hand. Some do not listen. For them I must be stern. However, I am limited in how much I can meddle. The more I tamper with the pattern, the more things can go astray, which is why our conversation must be brief. My kind cannot lead, we merely predict, and suggest. I am the last."

"That does not answer my question."

"You're not ready for that answer. None of you are...yet. Perhaps you never will be. Not even I can see that far. I will answer your other question, though. Why do I want you to take up this sword? Because it is your destiny, Fall."

"Angruvadal was my destiny."

She chuckled, as if Ashok had said something childlike. "Oh, Fall, *all* black steel is Angruvadal."

His brow furrowed in confusion. "That cannot be."

"Or an aspect at least. They wear different names, but every piece in the world, whether it be the Heart of the Mountain, any of the ancestor blades, or even the shard that pierced your heart and altered your body, comes from the same source, and that source is in very great danger." She got up and dusted off her skirts. "Now I must be going."

Ashok was still trying to comprehend her words. "Wait."

"That wouldn't be wise. I have interfered with you too much as it is. This must be the final time we ever speak."

He had many questions, but Ashok understood what it meant to live by a code. "Farewell, then."

Mother Dawn began walking away, but paused, and looked back over her shoulder. "One last thing, Fall. These people will be fine. You are a weapon, not a shepherd. Thera is on her way to Kanok and she will need you there."

Then she was simply gone.

Ashok couldn't even attribute the exchange to a hallucination because she'd left an imprint in the grass and a forgery in his hands. He crumpled the lie and threw it away. Keta probably would have found the whole thing a faith-building experience somehow or found the situation amusing and then turned it into an object lesson to use in his preaching.

He stood and went to the black sword.

Should he take the word of some trickster creature? For if Akerselem found him as unworthy as he felt right then, he'd end up cutting his own throat. And what did he really know of the ways of black steel? The shard in his chest hadn't just changed him, so that he could not drown, freeze, or starve—it had taken over his body and spoken to the Dvarapala with a voice that wasn't his own.

Except she had said Thera needed him, and though he would doubt and question every other word from her mouth, that much he believed. And with the entire might of the Law stacked against them, they would require every advantage he could take. In Jharlang, Angruvadal had fulfilled one of the Voice's prophecies, destroying itself to save the rest of them. It had done as expected of it, regardless of the cost. Ashok could do no less.

He reached out, but then hesitated. The last time he had done this, he had been but a child—a tiny casteless blood scrubber—and in the days before he had inadvertently touched Angruvadal, he had seen it dismember all who tried to pick it up.

"I am Ashok Vadal. Your last bearer fought with honor for his house. I am not like him. I am a rebel without house or caste. I am no longer a Law-abiding man. I offer no apologies for this. Criminals call me general, or even Ramrowan reborn, but I do not seek those titles. I am just a man who creates my own law, and all I can vow is that I will use you to dispense it as righteously as I can. If you take offense at this attempt, do as you will."

Ashok drew the sword from the stone.

Dressed in mismatched armor from several houses left behind by the Sons, and atop the same magnificent white stallion he had seized in Dhakhantar, Ashok Vadal rode out of the darkened tunnel and onto the dry lake bed.

A thousand Akershani warriors readied their weapons.

His horse reared back, front legs kicking, as Ashok lifted the curved black steel blade high, so all could see it devouring the sun.

"Behold the new bearer of Akerselem!" he roared and an entire army recoiled in shock and fear. "This place is under my protection. Withdraw from it or die! Then go and tell your Thakoor that if he wants his family's sword back after I am dead, he will leave this empty land alone. Let these mountains be a safe haven for the casteless. It will be open to all who wish to join them, and you will not harm any who attempt to come here, or I will take this sword to a place none of you dare follow and it will be lost to you forever. I am Ashok Vadal, and I have spoken!"

Ashok kneed his mount and the stallion was eager to run, straight toward the army of Akershan.

They got out of his way.

With sword held aloft so there could be no doubt, Ashok made his way between the spears as the warriors made a path for him.

The challengers would come, an endless stream as before. Arrogance and jealousy made that inevitable. And though Ashok had forsaken their Law, he would still accept their duels. The sword deserved nothing less.

Except there would be no challengers today, for these warriors were still struggling to understand their sudden defeat. They would do as they were told or else.

Once past the warriors, Ashok said, "Go, Horse." For that was what he called every steed he had ever cared for enough to name.

Horse snorted, disappointed to not fight an entire army, as was his spiteful nature, but then he ran like the wind from the valley, leaping effortlessly over the recently dug trenches. The faithful had told Ashok that the Sons had brought Horse back from Garo, but he had been too surly and violent to let anyone else ride him. Ashok respected that.

It wasn't until they were far past the stunned army and galloping across the plains that Ashok lowered the sword. The black steel felt surprisingly natural in the hand, and when he looked upon it he was surprised to see that it was no longer curved like an Akershani saber but had somehow taken on the more familiar form of a Vadal longsword.

"Hello, old friend."

With ancient black steel in hand and heart, Ashok rode after the woman he loved.

# Chapter 45

⚡

The Grand Inquisitor had not talked to the prisoner in the months since its trickery had been revealed. It was best to let it believe that Omand remained angry. Of course, he didn't like being bested at the great game, especially by a demon, but he never let petty emotion distract him from his ultimate goals.

On the contrary, from every setback came new opportunities, and this had been no different. Though initially furious at the demon's treachery, in the end the judges had granted Devedas more power than the Law had ever entrusted to one man. At this very moment Omand's agents were busy ensuring that Devadas would be forced to wage war against the only great house with the resources sufficient to threaten Omand's plans.

Far more importantly, in its gloating hubris the demon had inadvertently revealed something that Omand might be able to use against it. Using that new knowledge, he had immediately begun planting seeds, and today he would find out if there would be a harvest.

Sure enough, the prisoner had been expecting him. Its near-featureless head was watching him through the thick glass as he approached the tank. Even close, it was barely visible through the filthy, murky water. The thing had no expression, but today

383

it seemed almost eager to him. Today was different, and they both knew it.

Preparing the complex magical pattern, Omand placed his palm against the glass.

"It is done. The casteless have been utterly destroyed. There are millions dead across the land." Then Omand opened his mind just enough for it to see the images of slaughter, burning buildings, and fields strewn with bodies and soaked with blood. Those images were real. "I have received word from Inquisitors in every great house. The Great Extermination has been successful."

Demon glee was a much different sensation from demon rage, but just as jarring.

*Ramrowan death death death*

"Yes. The work is done. So very much death."

*Known truth known*

His ploy had worked. Omand took a deep breath, and the muggy room tasted of stagnant saltwater and mold. "Now for our agreement, once you give me what is owed, I will have you returned to the sea. As you have said, remainder upon kill. The killing is done. Now show me what remains."

Never before had he seen the demon like this: excited, its vestigial, regrowing limbs twitching.

*Remainder*

Then it showed Omand the true path of the source after it had been struck from the sky. It burned its way through the clouds, plummeting toward the northwestern part of Lok, streaking across the Gujaran peninsula, to crash through the canopy of jungle, burying itself deep in the ground. Unlike when the prisoner had led him to the ancient demonic weapon that had failed to erupt during their first attack against Lok, this time Omand saw the source itself, and it was clearly not of demonic construction. From above he could see the gigantic thing lying in the crater dug by its impact, which quickly began to fill with river water that hissed into steam as it hit the scalding-hot object.

The demon sent him a message at the end, one far too complicated for the handful of human words he had taught it before. It was difficult to understand, but it was a promise, and even... *a thank-you?* Through the torturous screeching that threatened to burst the blood vessels in his head, the demon assured him this was the real location, and to enjoy this reward... while he could.

*What did that mean?*

Omand would worry about that in a moment. Pattern broken, Omand removed his hand from the glass, shaken, and had to pull down his golden mask long enough to wipe the bloody tears from his eyes. The demon remained on the other side of the glass, and its head split open, showing its tiny new teeth, almost as if it were proud of itself.

"Taraba, bring me the map of the northwest continent." His assistant rushed to the tank, unrolling one of the many detailed maps he had brought with him to the dungeons. Omand had to work quickly while the images were still fresh. Besides the regular guards there were several other Inquisitors present as well, each of them something of an expert on Lok's ancient archaeological sites. "And whichever one of you is the most familiar with the Gujaran jungle, come here."

Taraba spread the map across a nearby table as a guard held up a lantern so they could see better. Omand eyed the eastern coast of the peninsula until he recognized the shape of a bay and river it had gone past, then he worked his way up the line. The terrain would have changed since the demon's fall, but the old texts spoke of the ancients building a temple atop the site. "Here." When he tapped the spot with his fingertip, it left a drop a blood. "I do not know this place. What is there?"

The Gujaran Inquisitor studied it for a moment. "That's deep wilderness, Grand Inquisitor. There are many ancient ruins in that area, but nothing of importance that I know of."

"Excellent. Fewer witnesses to trouble us." Then Omand looked back toward the tank to find that the demon was no longer in the window. The bubbles indicated that it had just swum away. *No matter.*

"There are witch hunters stationed in Rangsiman. Have them obligate an expedition, warriors and workers armed with digging tools, and dispatch them to secure all the ruins in this general location immediately. Someone fetch me a better map of that specific area. I will narrow it down to a more precise location and send them word."

Even loyal Taraba didn't know what this was about, but he could sense his master's excitement. "The Capitol Library has detailed survey maps. I will send for one."

"This is a great day, Taraba. A truly great day."

"What's there, sir?"

"Power beyond imagination." Then Omand twitched as he felt a strange sensation in the air. A pattern had been formed nearby, consuming so much energy that it was unmistakable even to those who were not sensitive, as every Inquisitor instinctively turned toward the tank at once.

Omand immediately ran back to the tank and peered through the glass.

Through the gloom, the demon was nothing but a shadow at the bottom, but it was doing *something*.

The creature was working magic.

In all the years it had been in Inquisition custody, the prisoner had never done anything like this before. Omand hadn't even known that demons could use magic.

"Empty the tank. Do it now!"

The guards sprang into action, two of them turning the creaking metal wheel at the base. The pipe opened and fetid water shot out, rushing toward the drains, but not fast enough. The spell was still building. Omand stepped away from the tank, took some of the black steel from his belt, visualized a pattern to direct the energy to a pinpoint of incredible force, and directed that against what had to be the thickest glass in Lok.

It shattered.

Thousands of gallons of water exploded outward, knocking Inquisitors off their feet and throwing them across the room. Omand avoided the rushing wall by rapidly switching his focus to the pattern, which enabled him to step into the dark space just outside reality. He waited for most of the force to subside, then walked back into the real world. Knee deep in rapidly moving filth, he shouted, "Harpoon the demon! Drag it forth immediately."

The stench was so bad that Omand had to resist the urge to vomit inside his mask, but explosively draining the tank had interrupted the demon's spell. The pattern had been broken.

The Inquisitors along the open top of the tank began hurling their harpoons into the whirlpool. Even with only vestigial, regrowing limbs, the demon was still incredibly dangerous, but the men obligated to this room were well practiced. Each time they missed or failed to penetrate the demon's hide, they'd use the ropes to haul their harpoons back up and try again. It still took dozens of hits before one of the barbed shafts found an exposed patch of white flesh to pierce. One Inquisitor screamed as he realized the rope had wrapped around his foot. The demon spun, rolling the rope around its body, and jerked that man over the side. Immediately after the splash it tore into him. The baby teeth within its fearsome jaws were still razor sharp and the remaining water turned red.

The water level had fallen below the broken window now, so the Inquisitors who were at ground level were able to get back to their feet, except for the Gujaran who had managed to get himself slammed against a wall in such a way that the impact had broken his neck.

As more and more shafts were sunk into the thrashing demon's flesh and the ropes pulled tight, it was slowly immobilized, and lifted from the tank. When it reached one edge, the demon keepers hooked it with specially designed pole arms and dragged it into its special harvesting enclosure. Heavy steel bars were thrown down, locking it inside.

Omand waded back to the tank and looked through the broken window. Hidden in the filth was what appeared to be a heap of demon bits, tiny chunks of bone, and milky flesh, wrapped together with strips of skin. The prisoner had built some manner of magical device out of its own discarded parts. "Do not disturb that until I have a chance to examine it."

While Omand climbed up the water to the top of the tank, the demon renewed its thrashing, violently throwing its body against the bars. Never before had any of them seen such fury from the crippled thing.

The guards tried to stop him from walking across the upper grate to the captive. "It's not safe, sir."

"Do not place your hands on me," Omand snarled, and they quickly moved aside.

The demon stopped its violent movement long enough to hiss at him through the steel bars.

"What have you done?" he demanded with the aid of black steel.

The demon sent him a message of anger and joy, of triumph, and a long wait worth it. It was a barrage of images and sensations. Omand could have the source. It meant nothing to the demons now. All that mattered was their revenge. As long as the blood of Ramrowan continued, the land was safe. With them gone, the land was doomed. The prisoner had seen that the line of Ramrowan was ended. Thus the time of man was at an end.

*Revenge blood death all*

Omand stumbled and had to hold onto the rail to withstand the mental onslaught. *The source was real.* The demons could freely offer him godhood, for to their kind what would it matter if Omand became an immortal? It would just give him more time to contemplate the total annihilation of his species. Omand could be a god, alone.

"Oh, you foolish beast. The casteless are not all gone. They're still being slaughtered as we speak, but many remain scattered across the land."

*Known truth seen*

"You saw the lie I constructed for you to see. Once I knew you could spy on the messages we sent between your bones, I had my men send endless reports of massacres that never happened, and tables counting all the imaginary dead. The process has begun, and now that the bloodletting has started can probably never be stopped, but the work is far from done. I tricked you."

The demon hissed and slammed its head against the bars. Steel bent. Hinges cracked. And Omand prepared another pattern, the most lethal one he knew.

"That's right. You showed me the way to the source for *nothing.*"

Furious, it threw itself against the gate over and over, until it burst open, and the demon spilled onto the walkway, slithering toward him, dragging half a dozen harpoons and ropes.

Omand raised the black steel clutched in his fist and willed it into the devouring pattern. The black steel disintegrated into dust, but rather than blowing away, it moved with purpose across the catwalk, and when it struck the nearly impenetrable demon, its flesh began to disintegrate. The prisoner's skull burst, spraying milky blood across the catwalk.

Thirty years they had known each other. Yet it had filled its purpose.

"Harvest it all," Omand ordered the stunned Inquisitors as he wiped the black steel ash from his hands.

Taking up one of the hooked polearms, he used that to carefully lift the demonic device from the now empty tank.

It must have taken a very long time for the demon to accumulate so many loose parts of itself, probably left dangling after a multitude of harvestings, to slowly construct this thing in the murky shadows of its tank where the guards would not see. Omand examined the device, and immediately recognized it for what it was, for the shape was very similar to the pattern used for long-distance communication. Just as his Inquisitors used pieces of this demon to send messages between them, the demon had made this to send a message to...he knew not where.

Omand had to find out, so he rested his hand upon the damp device and dwelled upon the familiar pattern.

It was more of the mind-splitting silent shriek that was demon tongue that had been sent into the distant ocean depths, and it was only from Omand's long exposure that he was able to decipher the message's meaning at all.

*It is time.*

# Epilogue

~~~~~~~~~~~~~~

Two farmers stood by a well.

The day was warm. They were thirsty from their labors.

Except that when the first drank from the freshly pulled bucket, he recoiled in disgust. "The well's gone bad!"

"No way. Let me see that."

The workers' fields depended on this well. It had been dug exceedingly deep a long time ago and had provided good water for generations untold.

The second took the bucket, sniffed it, then gagged when the smell hit his nostrils. "It smells like it came out of the ocean."

"Don't be foolish. Somebody must have thrown a dead cat down there or something."

"Trust me. I grew up near the seashore. I'll never forget that stink." He cupped one calloused hand into the bucket and lifted the water to his lips, only to promptly spit it out. "Saltwater!"

Why did their well suddenly taste like the ocean?

They were far inland, hundreds of miles from the sea.